WING COMMANDER™
THE PRICE OF FREEDOM

W9-BCD-745

WILLIAM R. FORSTCHEN
BEN OHLANDER

BAEN

THE PRICE OF FREEDOM

This is a work of fiction. All the characters and events portrayed in this book are fictional, and any resemblance to real people or incidents is purely coincidental.

A Baen Books Original

Baen Publishing Enterprises
P.O. Box 1403
Riverdale, NY 10471

ISBN: 0-671-87751-8

First printing, November 1996

Distributed by Simon & Schuster
1230 Avenue of the Americas
New York, NY 10020

Printed in the United States of America

DEDICATED TO

Jennifer and John,
Rhonda, and Liz,
Friends, and more than friends

and to C.S. Forester.

• PROLOGUE

Major Tom Vale toggled his navigation plot to the
Nephele system and smiled as the system diagram appeared
on his heads-up display. The convoy, made up of three
small freighters and his escort of four lightweight Arrows,
would arrive at the jump point late, but well within
acceptable parameters. Unless, of course, one of the old
transports blew another engine. That kind of delay would
kick his entire schedule into a cocked hat.

He traced his finger along the patrol route. His Arrows
had to escort the convoy to the jump point, but the patrol
legs through the system could be trimmed if he needed
to make up time. He leaned back in his seat, glad he'd
solved the toughest problem he was likely to face all day.

The circuit was a typical Nephele milk run—long and
boring. He had survived twelve years of fighter combat
against the Kilrathi, and two more of rough-and-tumble
peace on the frontiers. The command of a patrol squadron
on a third-rate system was the perfect assignment for him
to coast out his career and retire.

He grinned happily. He was entitled to be bored, he
even enjoyed it. He made it a point to complain regularly
to the personnel office, however. The rear echelon bastards
at Central Casting would have collective apoplexy if they
thought an officer was happy in an assignment.

The section's leading element, made up of Tiger and
her wingman, Sparrow, pushed ahead of the convoy's main
body. One fighter remained above each flank of the leading
transport, ready to intercept targets closing on the convoy
from the front. He glanced back at his own wingman.
Scarman kept loose station on his port side, behind and
below the civilian ships.

1

He opened the squadron's common channel and cleared his throat. "Fuel check," he said.

"Eighty-three percent," replied Tiger.

"Seventy-two," from Sparrow.

"Eighty-six," answered Scar.

Vale nodded, satisfied. Wingmen usually used more fuel than their primaries, and Tiger had been keeping Sparrow busy. He remained cynically amused that his ability to bring fuel home found such high praise in his Officer's Efficiency Reports. His superiors, all combat veterans whom he felt should have known better, wrote more on his OERs about his ability to husband scarce resources than they did on how well he trained his squadron or led it in combat. Ah, the peacetime fleet, back to polishing brass, kissing butts, and fighting against nothing more dangerous than boredom.

The Kilrathi War was less than two years over, and it seemed to him that the navy was already busy forgetting everything it had learned in three decades of conflict.

He knew he really shouldn't have been surprised at how quickly the emphasis had changed after the war. Fleet construction provided jobs, and could be justified to a Senate intent upon rebuilding the Confederation's shattered economy. Military supply, combat readiness budgets, and training funds didn't contribute as visibly to local employment and could be easily, and often, pared. The result was that an officer who could save money was more competitive for promotion than one who could save lives. It was a truism that hadn't changed in centuries. Unfortunately.

Tiger's voice crackled across his radio as she instructed their resident rookie on the finer points of leg patrols, the "burn-and-turns" that were the daily bread for a system defense squadron. Marlena had done wonders in bringing the squadron's newest member up to speed in such a short time. He was glad he'd gone out on the limb for her. Her mouth had hopelessly damaged her prospects for promotion, even during the war.

He listened to her issue brief instructions to Sparrow,

then make gentle corrections as the rookie attempted to execute them. Her usual sarcasm vanished as she worked with the younger pilot. He grinned. He hadn't expected her to be such a strong trainer. He made a mental note to add a line of praise to the "Comments" section of Tiger's OER. A kind word from him in the "plays well with others" section might be enough to convince a board that she was ready to put on captain's pips. Otherwise, she would be dismissed at year's end for "excessive time in grade."

Sparrow, the rookie, had a fine hand, good instincts, and a reasonably good eye for deflection shooting. He would be a fine asset to the squadron once his training was complete. His attitude needed work, however. The kid had visions of daring missions from strike carriers dancing in his head. The reality of duty on a backwater like Nephele was hard for him to bear, especially as a lone "newbie" in an outfit full of jaded veterans.

Vale knew the kid chafed at not having been born early enough to "do his bit" in the war against the Kilrathi. He reminded Vale of all the young hotshots whose dreams of glory all too often ended in an empty casket shot into space. Their "glory" usually turned out to be a name engraved on a beer glass in a pilots' bar, and a medal mailed home in lieu of a casket.

His tactical plot chirped, drawing him away from his mental meanderings. The *Ashiri Maru* was drifting. Again. He selected the *Maru*'s channel from the comm menu.

"Aces leader to *Ashiri Maru*," he said, hoping his voice didn't betray his irritation.

His comm-screen flickered, the channel menu replaced by the *Maru*'s master, a hatchet-faced woman he knew only as Frost. "Now what d'ya want?" she asked in a sullen, exasperated voice. Her expression made it quite plain that he'd interrupted her in the middle of a critical ship's operation. He guessed from the filth he saw on the bulkhead behind her that cleaning wasn't a high priority on her ship.

"Adjust course to conform to the convoy's movements,"

he said. He thought he sounded a bit imperious, even to his own ears. He tried to soften his tone. "You're drifting again. I told you before that we can't protect you if you wander too far."

"An' as I've told you, General," she replied, scratching her armpit, "what you going to protect us *from*? There ain't nothing here in Neph', 'ceptin' you an' us. I dunno why you war-boys keep harassin' honest folks. The fighting's over, right?"

Vale sighed. The *A. Maru's* master stared defiantly back at him. It was times like this that he actually missed the war. Then he could have invoked the Emergency Decrees for failing to comply with military authorities and blown the smirking bitch into next week if she so much as looked at him cross-eyed. Martial law, he mused, had its good points.

He was still trying to frame a civil answer to her when Sparrow cut into the channel. "Sparrow to Knave." Vale smiled indulgently at the kid's excited voice. "I got something on my scanner. One red pipper . . . Wait, it's gone now."

Vale frowned at his tactical display. A free comet or garbage sack shouldn't have vanished like that. Vale guessed the boy was jumping at shadows.

"Roger, Sparrow," he replied, "maintain surveillance. Call me if you get a repeat." He tapped his control yoke in thought. Sparrow was ahead of the transports and on the port side, with Tiger to starboard. It was barely possible that Sparrow might read a scanner signal that was just out of Tiger's range.

He switched channels to Marlena's frequency, "Knave to Tiger."

Tiger's face appeared in his screen, her head moving back and forth as she scanned the area around her. "I know what you're going to ask, boss," she said. "No, I didn't see it." She paused a moment. "Do you want him to intercept? It'd be good practice."

Vale considered it. "No, we'd best not. Fuel allocation's

been cut once this quarter already. We need the gas more than he needs the practice."

Tiger's face clouded. "Parsimonious bastards. The ink wasn't even dry on the treaty before they cut the budget."

Vale said nothing. He agreed with her, but wasn't about to let himself get caught criticizing his bosses on an open channel. There were far too many unemployed majors flying bar stools for him to have any illusions about his indispensability. "Keep an eye on it," he said. "It was probably a sensor artifact or a spurious contact, but you never know."

"Roger," Tiger replied.

He tried to ignore the sense that something was wrong. Sparrow's contact troubled him. The kid's scanners were new, in good shape, and decently maintained. Anomalies weren't unusual, of course, and there was a lot of junk floating around to give a momentary reflection, but something just didn't seem right. Nephele was as predictable and as boring as mess-hall eggs. Odd events just didn't happen there.

Vale shook his head. The kid had gotten worked up over nothing, and was now making the whole flight jittery. It was probably nothing.

The pilot waited patiently while the convoy appeared on his long-range scanner. He counted seven craft, just as he had been told to expect. They were late, a fact that disturbed his sense of order, but which had no relevance on the outcome.

He checked his Kilrathi-style cloaking device. It was working, rendering him invisible to both their scanners and the naked eye.

He waited for the ships to wander into visual range. Four early-model Arrows hovered in a sloppy formation about their three charges. He frowned slightly. He had expected better escorting tactics from Confederation pilots. The Fleet had let things slide since the peace.

He smoothed his facial features, mastering his expression

and his feelings. Emotion impaired judgement and efficiency. He struggled to purge himself of all feeling—the better to do what was needed. When he cued his wingman's frequency, his voice was as cold and still as a winter morning.

"Seether to Drakes," he said. "The old man was right. Targets sighted. Let's do it." He checked the raiders' coded transponders to ensure all four ships were in their correct positions. Two hung off of each bow of the convoy, for now matching their course and speed with the freighters like sharks after a school of fish. He sent his wingman the preset code to attack, then goosed his throttle and aimed for the convoy. "Remember," he said, "no survivors."

He checked his ship's status, then switched his ready ordnance to an IFF missile. It was a "fire-and-forget" weapon, one that required no further attention from the pilot once it was launched. The missile would lock on a target's electronic signature, then would follow it until it ran out of fuel or was hit.

Drake Two dropped out of cloak to his right, firing a dumb-fire missile as he bored in on the first transport. The dumb-fire was a powerful, unguided rocket that probably wouldn't get a kill on the freighter, but would certainly shake it up.

He followed Two's lead, dropping his own cloak as an Arrow grew in his sights. The Confederation fighters exploded into action, scattering like startled quail as the lead element of Drake flight appeared literally out of nowhere and ripped through the center of the formation. Drake Two broke hard to the right and opened up on the leading pair with his tachyon cannon, rifling shots around the Confed fighters. The Arrow on the convoy's starboard bow heeled sharply over, accelerating away in a complicated corkscrew maneuver.

Seether smiled grimly to himself, his mask of indifference slipping. The Arrow pilots were better than their formation flying had suggested. He licked his dry, thin lips. Good, he thought, his people could use some live-target practice.

✦ ✦ ✦

Vale was just about to order Sparrow back to the convoy when he caught a glimpse of movement out of the corner of his eye.

He was just turning his head towards it when a single red dot appeared on his tactical display, flickering into existence on the convoy's starboard bow. A second red pipper appeared, this one to port. It took him a moment to realize the significance of the red dots as . . . enemy.

"Tallyho!" he yelled, cuing the squadron's general circuit. "Bandits! Vector one-zero-one degrees and three-three-zero, Z plus forty. Tiger section, break and attack!"

"I copy, Knave," Tiger replied, "we'll take the bandit on the left." Vale saw her accelerate towards her target. Sparrow followed a second later, angling back towards his wing slot from his advanced position in front of the convoy.

He caught quick acknowledgments from Scarman and Tiger, then a beat later from Sparrow as each reported weapons readiness. He knew that doctrine called for aggressive intercept as far from the vulnerable transports as possible. He just wished he'd had more time to intercept.

Vale hauled his own control yoke to the right, nearly standing the nimble fighter on its tail as he hit his afterburners and turned to attack. Scarman turned smoothly with him, the plume of his afterburner glowing white as he matched his burn to Vale's.

"Tallyho, boss. I designate Target One," Tiger said, her voice calm. "Range, six thousand kilometers to target. Accelerating to eight hundred KPS." The raider, at first glance a heavy fighter, opened up with twin columns of fire. Tiger spiked her craft into evasive maneuvers that took her past the raider and out of its gunline. She pirouetted neatly and arced in on the raider's flank, her guns blazing.

Vale turned his own attention towards the bandit who'd angled towards the rear of the convoy. The enemy's red pipper glowed and swelled as he turned towards it. He goosed his afterburner, inhaling as the increased thrust pressed him back into his chair. He was glad his inertial dampers appeared to be functioning well—he'd have been thrown around the inside of the cockpit without them. His lasers and ion cannon weren't nearly as heavy as the raiders'; he could only hope that he had a speed and maneuver advantage that would balance the scales.

He had a quick glimpse of Tiger trading fire with the first bandit, while Sparrow now maneuvered to the flank.

The missile alarm chimed in his ear, its Dopplered pitch warning him of a lock-on. A yellow dot appeared on his scanner and quickly accelerated towards him. "Damn," he said, then cued his radio. "Scar, evasive. Then break and attack."

He rammed the throttle forward as Scarman broke away, leaving behind him a string of missile decoys. Vale kicked in his afterburner and hauled his control yoke down and left as he fought to open as much room between himself and his wingman as he could. The missile ignored the chaff and Scar to lock onto him. He cursed under his breath.

The two trailing transports loomed in front of him, their drive plumes brightening as they accelerated to the best of their ability. He flashed between them, hoping their mass would throw off the missile. He craned his head around and saw it closing rapidly, its lock-on intact. He banked and cut back, using the lefthand transport as the pivot for his tight parabolic turn. He snapped out of the turn, his course reversed. He dropped chaff pod after chaff pod, hoping the signal simulators would lure the missile away from him. The warhead yawed after the first and detonated.

Vale looked frantically around. The leading freighter bloomed fire along one flank, the result, he thought, of a missile or rocket attack. A torpedo would have reduced the little ship to free atoms. He checked his tactical display and saw one intruder arcing in towards the hindmost transport. Scar whipped and saw-bucked in the distance, apparently locked in his own dance with a missile. This guy is good, Vale thought, he's taken us both out of play long enough to get in close to the freighters.

Tiger and Sparrow were tied up with the second bandit and were in no position to help, leaving him with no option except to go one-on-one. He hoped to stay out of the raider's front arc and its big guns. He angled his Arrow towards the raider and hit his throttle. His fighter jumped forward, the acceleration pressing him back in his seat in spite of the inertial dampers.

The intruder turned slightly as Vale closed, affording him his first good, long look. The thing was sleek and completely black, except for a pair of glowing, top-mounted Bussard intakes, suggesting a jump capability. It looked ultra-state-of-the-art to him, utterly lethal and unlike any design he had seen. It sure as hell didn't look Kilrathi.

He pushed his throttle back, cutting out his afterburner and slowing his headlong charge to better target his weapons. He fired his ion cannon at range, more for his own morale than from any real hope of inflicting damage.

The enemy ignored his pinpricks to fire quad energy weapons at the transport. The bolts punched through its flimsy screens and hulled it deeply. The freighter's single defensive turret opened up, a pathetic single stream of laser beams to answer its mortal wound. He sent the transport a quick interrogative.

The ship's master answered at once, his face appearing on a jumping, static-filled screen. Vale saw drifting smoke behind him. "We're here," the *Elgin Dailey*'s master said, "Y'all just keep it that way. Drives are intact. We'll hold station." His face faded as Vale saw a secondary explosion mushroom out of the transport's side. He suspected the *Dailey* was in more trouble than it let on.

The raider turned on him, snake-quick, and fired. Four beams of lambent energy crossed close in front of his prow, brightening the inside of the cockpit with reflected energy. A single bolt plowed into his forward phase shield, wiping it out and chewing up his frontal armor. His damage board showed a stabilizer hit. He punched his throttle to the stops and hauled back on his stick as he scrambled to get away from the enemy fighter. He poured on the coal, trying to escape as bolt after bolt passed close by. His rear shields weakened but held as the near misses ripped past.

He brought his Arrow around, trying to cut across the heavier fighter's vector and accelerate away before the black ship could follow. The raider tumbled in space, its nose turning to track Vale's Arrow. He saw a bright red flare and closed his eyes. He opened them to see Sparrow arcing in from his upper right, his lasers and ion cannon slashing at the raider.

The black ship continued to rotate in space, turning now to follow Sparrow. Vale kicked his own ship into an autoslide and pivoted back to fire on the raider. He kept the deflection shots going, turning his own Arrow to keep the black ship under fire. The deflection angles were changing too quickly for either his AI to predict or him to track. He missed with most of his shots.

Sparrow's shots slowed, the quad fire having drained his capacitors. "I'm outta here," the kid shouted into his mike. Vale picked up the gist of the message through the feedback as Sparrow poured fuel into his afterburners. The black ship rolled, then fired into Sparrow's rear quarter, slewing the little ship around.

"Damage?" he asked as Sparrow cleared the raider's guns.

"Transmitting," the kid replied, sounding very subdued. The schematic of Sparrow's fighter solidified on his screen. He saw that the kid's afterburner, rear armor, and stabilization systems had been hit. One more solid hit and Sparrow would be history.

Vale looked across the convoy in time to see a raider pinion Tiger's fighter, catching her in its bright beams like a pushpin through a butterfly. Vale watched her ship stagger under twinned hammer blows as the cannon stripped the Arrow of its phase shields, armor, and skin. Pieces began to spall and burn.

Vale heard her scream, a long, drawn-out wail of fear

and agony that abruptly ceased as the black ship fired again, this time with all its weaponry.

The black ship did a victory roll as it flashed past the expanding debris cloud that marked the remains of Tiger's ship, then began to close in on the convoy. Vale glanced around, realizing too late that he'd lost track of the second raider.

"Keep your eyes open," he said to Sparrow, "the other one's still out there."

Scar cut his drives, autoslid, then boosted after the black ship that had killed Tiger. The Confederation pilot pulled his Arrow into a tight inside loop, trying to flip up and descend on the larger ship's vulnerable back. The raider was ready. It shifted, linking the two ships with multiple columns of firepower. Scar's Arrow, immolated on the beams, detonated.

Vale realized as he looked in vain for a life pod from Scar's ship that resistance was futile. The convoy was lost. It was time to salvage what he could, in this case a young pilot who didn't deserve to die. "Sparrow," he said harshly, "disengage. Get home and make a full report. Intelligence'll need to know what we saw here."

The other Arrow slowly turned away. Vale felt ice in his guts as he saw the two black ships slashing in towards the transports. He rammed his throttles to the stops, punching the little ship towards the convoy. A tiny voice inside his head screamed at him to disengage, to run for home, to live. He gritted his teeth and bored in to attack.

His target fired its missiles, volleying them all off in a single salvo against the *Elgin Dailey*. The weapons bloomed in explosion after explosion as they punched into the *Dailey*'s guts. Vale watched the stricken ship slew out of formation and angle away. A massive explosion rocked the transport, blowing off the front section containing the bridge and the life bubble. It tumbled alongside the remainder of the ship, still spewing gas and debris.

Vale checked his scanner and saw Sparrow running flat out for home. Vale's chest tightened as he saw one of the black ships flicker into existence behind the rookie. The raider accelerated and fired a missile. Sparrow dodged and weaved, trying to avoid the warhead. His maneuvering cost him enough forward speed for the fighter behind him to close. The black ship fired.

"Hail, Mary, full of grace . . ." Vale heard Sparrow whisper as the bloom engulfed the back half of the light ship. The multiple impacts spun Sparrow to his right, killing his drives and snapping him end over end. The Confederation pilot's prayer turned into a long scream that ended only when the ship exploded. . . . The rookie never had a chance to eject.

He turned his attention back to the two raiders closing in on the transports. He fired on the closest, switching to lasers and plinking at the heavier ship from long range. The raider ignored the fire while it poured shots into the third transport, the *Red's Gamble*. The raider walked hits up the freighter's defenseless spine.

The *Gamble* burned brightly, its cargo outgassing and oxidizing through the holes punched in its hull by the raiders' cannon. Vale saw flames licking out into open space, an indicator of the intensity of the inferno within.

The second raider bored in on the *Gamble* and fired, hitting the stricken transport with both tachyon beams and a heavier weapon that ate whole sections of the freighter. The transport detonated a moment later, one moment coasting in open space with bright jewels of flame winking along its sides and the next vanishing in an actinic flare. The detached, clinical part of Vale's mind noted that the ship's reactor core must have detonated.

A fourth black ship dropped out of cloak on his right flank, firing as it closed the range. His Arrow rocked under the black fighter's hits. Vale slashed his control yoke back and forth, frantically trying to dodge the converging weapons' streams. He felt his drives fail.

He glanced down at his display. System after system glowed red. The eject warning flashed. He reached down between his legs, groping for the yellow-painted eject bar.

The ship heeled to one side, hit by another salvo. He glanced up. The raider loomed close, its weapons pointed at his cockpit. It fired from point-blank range, twin bolts of violent energy that blanked out the ship behind. Vale didn't even have time to register pain. . . .

Seether felt the adrenaline drain away as he squeezed his trigger and saw the last Arrow disintegrate into atoms. The pilot, with squadron leader's markings on his fighter's tail assembly, had been passably good. He would have felt a more enduring respect for his opponent, except the Confed pilot was dead. He had no respect for the dead. Death was the ultimate failure, and he could not abide failure.

Drake Three's face appeared on his comm-screen. "Target area sterile," she said, "no signals and no pods. The last transport is attempting Mayday." She glanced downward a moment. "Jamming successful."

Seether nodded and cut her off. "Drake One to Drake flight—stand by for test procedure." He brought his ship around in a tight arc and began his attack run on the sole remaining transport. The pigboat wallowed from side to side, trying to evade his ship. He narrowed his eyes as he closed on the ship. "I'm lighting the 'flash-pak.' " He flipped the safety cover off a special firing button and poised his thumb over it.

The transport filled his forward view, growing larger and larger until he could see the rusted surface details. The transport's single gun sputtered at him ineffectually.

He held his attack run to the last possible instant, then mashed the firing key. He immediately felt the difference in the ship as the thin, convex disc was ejected from his bay. Small thrusters located along its edge gave it ballistic stabilization as it spun and latched onto the transport's hull.

Seether pulled the control yoke back, kicking in his maneuvering thrusters as he swept in a tight turn around the waist of the transport. He emerged above the disc just as it began to vibrate and shimmer. The whole transport visibly shook as surface components ruptured and detached under the strain imposed by the disc. He held his position as the *Ashiri Maru* shook and rumbled. A violent flash of oxygen and explosive fuels burst out of the hole in the ship's hull and exploded. A second fireball, then a third emerged as the ship's interior spaces detonated in sequence. The final blast loomed over the stricken ship's side like a malevolent flower. When it faded, only the *Ashiri Maru*'s outer hull remained, a charred and scorched husk.

Seether recorded the ship's death on his gun camera. He chuckled, the sound like dice rolling in a cup as he cued Drake Two's channel. "I'd call that a successful 'test,' wouldn't you?" He didn't wait for a response. He reoriented his ship towards the hulk and launched a conventional grappling mine. He watched the weapon tumbling towards the wreck a moment, then hit his "All Call" as he ghosted in after the falling mine.

"Seether to Drakes. Come about to course three-one-zero, Z minus twenty and stand by."

The mine hit the hulk and detonated. Seether whipped his ship around in time to catch the blast on his rear shields, just as he hit his afterburners. He let the blast propel him forward, accelerating him towards his waiting wingmates. The adrenaline faded, leaving him cold. He used the mine-drop and afterburner trick to test himself, probing himself for fear the way he might test a loose tooth with his tongue. He prodded himself, satisfied with the results. No fear.

"Cloak on my command," he ordered. "Now."

The four unmarked, black fighters vanished, leaving behind only the hulks and the dead.

• CHAPTER ONE

James Taggart, Assembly Master of the Confederation Senate, retired brigadier, and ex-spy, looked up at the vaulted ceiling of the Hall of the Great Assembly. The Great Hall's acoustics had been designed to allow a speaker to address the highest galleries without electronic amplification. The acoustics also concentrated all the sound in the room down on the dais.

The Senate was in full cry. Eminent men and women from across the Confederation shouted and gestured at each other, each trying to be heard above the din. News services from a half dozen affiliated worlds aimed pin-mikes at their representatives. Lobbyists and flesh pressers of a dozen stripes worked the aisles, hobnobbing with the legislators who allocated power and, more importantly, money. Taggart found the whole show cynically amusing, very pathetic, and utterly fascinating.

It occurred to him that he had come a long way since the war. Then, as "Paladin," he had plugged along in silent obscurity, spying and doing one classified operation after another for king and country. He would have vanished into obscurity had it not been for Admiral Tolwyn and his spectacular failure with Operation Behemoth.

Taggart had put his own scheme together. Colonel Blair had gotten lucky over Kilrah, dropping the Temblor bomb and knocking Kilrah out of the war and Taggart into the limelight. Taggart had come away as "the man who saved humanity," especially as Blair had fled the public's adoration.

He laughed as he recalled how little time it had taken before the deal makers and the image shapers came snooping after him. They'd helped him ride the rising tide of his fame to the Senate, then to the Master's Chair. It was an almost unprecedented honor for a freshman Senator, especially as he'd refused to open his black bag of tricks to engineer his promotion. His election had been done openly and honestly, and it was one of his proudest moments.

Taggart glanced at his watch. The time for unstructured debate had finally ended. He took the heavy wooden gavel and began to tap the handle against the clapper. The sound, electronically enhanced, thumped out across the floor, warning the Senators that it was time to bring their remarks to a close. He kept politely tapping for several minutes, then reversed the hammer in his hand. The second sweep crossed the hour. Now he could get serious. He raised the gavel to shoulder level and brought it down hard.

Boom! Boom! Boom! The heavy wood struck the clapper, resonating throughout the chamber. The nearest Senators actually winced as the thrumming washed over them. Taggart continued to pound the gavel until the sound diminished enough for him to be heard.

"Order," he demanded, "order."

The Senate quieted, the last diehards sitting only as Taggart threatened to whack the gavel again.

"You will all have the opportunity to voice your opinions on the occurrence on our Border Worlds frontier," he said soothingly. Damn, Paladin, he thought to himself, you really are becoming a politician. When did dead pilots and ambushed ships become an "occurrence"? He gritted his teeth, projecting a false smile before he continued. "But we will first hear from the Commander of the Strategic Readiness Agency. Admiral Tolwyn has graciously agreed to appear before us and provide us with his preliminary assessment of the raids." He half-turned towards his guest. "Admiral Tolwyn."

Admiral Geoffrey Tolwyn stepped up to the podium, resplendent in his dress uniform. Taggart noted that the admiral had worn all of his decorations, gilding his chest in gold, silver, and bronze. It was an impressive show, at least to the rubes in the cheap seats.

Taggart suspected that Tolwyn's star had fallen enough

after his pet project had failed for the admiral to feel he had to resort to such theatrics to make his point. In Taggart's assessment, he believed that Tolwyn had rebounded nicely, and was again ascendant, but apparently the admiral was taking no chances.

Taggart watched the admiral step up to the podium and look out onto the ranks of assembled notables. Tolwyn's gaze seemed coolly appraising, as though taking the Senators' measure. His expression grew grave as he pulled a thin sheaf of papers out of his tunic and spread them out on the lectern.

It occurred to Taggart, as he watched Tolwyn, that the admiral was the best politician of all of them. How else could the man—who'd nearly been cashiered after the Behemoth debacle—bounce back to run the Strategic Readiness Agency as his personal fiefdom? The man was a survivor, with more lives than a cat.

Admiral Tolwyn cleared his throat and began. "Ladies and gentlemen of the Assembly: as the Commander of the SRA, I am charged with many duties. Foremost among these is the protection of the frontiers of our galaxy."

He looked down briefly. Taggart noticed that while Tolwyn had notes, he hardly referred to them. It was also clear that Tolwyn had mastered political speech-making, using the slightly stiff, overblown rhetoric that was all the rage with the log-rolling set. The Tolwyn of old would neither have been so polite to those he considered mealy-mouthed civilians, nor would he have stooped to talk to them in their own language.

"Unfortunately," the admiral continued, "I don't have any answers. The attacks have left no survivors and precious little evidence. Confed Intel has given it their best shot, and to date has come up empty."

Taggart knew the last to be a subtle dig at himself. His own service was Intel, and semi-independent of the Fleet. Paladin had kept it that way, in spite of Tolwyn's attempts to absorb the uniformed element of the intelligence community.

"We have," Tolwyn continued, spreading his palms humbly, "absolutely no proof of who is doing this."

The Senate erupted in chaos. Many senators had constituents who were affected, owned ship lines, or wanted to put in a plug for "law and order" on general principles. Some blamed pirates while others accused the Border Worlds militia of treachery. Other, darker theories, of conspiracies and secret Kilrathi attacks, were bandied about. Taggart banged his gavel.

Tolwyn raised his hand—and the room quieted, much to Taggart's concealed irritation. He wished he commanded as much respect from the legislators. He recalled, to his sour amusement, that he had until he became one of them.

Tolwyn gave Taggart a wintery sidelong look. "Well, I'm sure we all have our theories. . . ." He rolled his eyes slightly, allowing Taggart to see that his contempt for civilians was intact. "But let me tell you," he said, raising one index finger for emphasis, "that while it is a mystery now, it will not be one for long." Taggart wondered if Tolwyn was going to give some inkling of his plan.

The admiral instead humbly lowered his eyes, a gesture Taggart knew to be pure artifice. "As most of you know, I've spent a lot of time on the frontier, both fighting the Kilrathi, and in building the peace. The Border Worlds are a wild lot—full of rogues, privateers, and the Border Worlders themselves." His voice took on disapproving tones. "Their loose society encourages irresponsibility and indiscriminate growth rather than cooperative and controlled development of resources for the benefit of *all* humans."

Taggart looked at Tolwyn, contemplating the admiral with hooded eyes. Tolwyn had just disclaimed knowing who the culprits were, and now was steering the senators towards the Border Worlds. He wondered what agenda the admiral had tucked up his gold-braided sleeve.

One senator leapt to his feet, interrupting both Tolwyn's speech and Taggart's line of thought. Taggart glanced at the man, whom he really thought should be old enough to know better. "Scoundrels!" the senator thundered, pounding his hand on his desk for effect. "That's what they are! They should be punished for what they've done!"

Another backbencher, unwilling to be outdone, also stood. "They're hoodlums! Rebels who're preying on innocent ships!" Taggart saw they were playing to the cameras and dismissed them.

Tolwyn didn't. He shook his head sadly. "Let me remind you, senators, that during the long war with the Kilrathi, the Border Worlds were a strong ally."

Another senator jumped up to interrupt. "And now they're attacking us!"

Taggart sighed. It must be the full moon, he thought. They seemed, after just the tiniest bit of nudging from Tolwyn, to be ready to blame the Border Worlders on general principles, much less on hard evidence. He looked up into the galleries, relieved to see that while many faces were hard with anger, many others looked contemplative and skeptical.

Tolwyn, again the voice of reason, continued. "Do not allow lust for revenge to cloud your thinking . . ." He gave Taggart another sidelong glance and a tiny, wintery smile. "We mustn't forget who our friends are."

Many of the senators present nodded assent, agreeing with the admiral's sentiments and missing the byplay on the dais.

Taggart had no doubt whatsoever that the admiral had just put a shot across his bows. Counterintelligence had actually been Admiral Richard's bailiwick and not his, but the hard truth remained the same. Counter Intel had failed to catch the Kilrathi renegade, Hobbes, before he'd betrayed his human allies and returned to his own kind. That lapse had cost Tolwyn his precious Behemoth and his shot at ending the war. Tolwyn had made no secret of the fact he thought Paladin might have sabotaged his pet project.

"However," Tolwyn said, his voice hardening as he delivered what Taggart thought would be his real pitch, "we must also keep in mind that during the war, certain social and political changes were taking place along the frontiers." He paused. "We don't know what is going on inside the Border Worlds themselves. We don't know if these raids may reflect a change within the Border Worlds governments, the rise of criminal elements on the frontier itself, or if these are just random terrorism events or even common piracy." He paused. "Until we get hard evidence, however, we must assume that the Border Worlds are as they have always been . . ." He paused, showing the slightest hint of skepticism, "our friends."

Terrorism, Taggart thought, is many things, but it is never "random." And it was common knowledge that the Border Worlds had refused to release the carriers acquired from Earth until long after the Kilrathi had begun their assault. The frowns he saw in the gallery suggested that he wasn't the only senator to make that connection. He smiled slightly, amused at Tolwyn's ability to play both sides of the aisle.

Tolwyn grasped the podium with both hands, taking physical control of it as he thrust his head aggressively forward. "I don't know who is doing this," he said, slowly and distinctly, letting the moment build, "but I shall find out. And then . . . I will see to it that it stops."

The senators clapped and cheered. Taggart banged his gavel repeatedly, trying to restore order. He waited until the clamor had been reduced to a buzz, then looked down at Tolwyn. Tolwyn had played the body masterfully, gathering the senators in and building his case. Any legislator challenging Tolwyn's position would be seen as coddling the Border Worlds or condoning the attacks. No one wanted to be put in that position with so many cameras about.

Taggart saw he had two choices: he could tack with Tolwyn's gale, or be blown by it. The decision wasn't especially difficult. He put on what he called his "political face," the bland, friendly expression everyone in the Hall wore most of the time.

"Admiral," he began, trying to match Tolwyn's sense of

presence. His own style was more folksy, and didn't lend itself well to this type of occasion. ". . . our relations with the Border Worlders have been damaged by these, um, incidents. They've claimed to suffer from attacks similar to ours, and share similar concerns. Tensions between our government and the Border Worlds are high and we want this situation defused as quickly as possible. Time is of the essence."

Tolwyn nodded gravely. "I shall assume personal control of the investigation." He raised his voice. "And I shall use all of the forces at my disposal to find the perpetrators . . . and defuse them." He grinned then, a shark's smile.

Taggart swallowed at the thought of Tolwyn's fleet carriers deploying to the frontier, and how the Border Worlds were likely to respond to that. He tried to think of a way to put some back-pressure on what was happening, to slow the tides of the moment. He opened his mouth to suggest a more low-key response, then glanced up, uncomfortably aware that all of the vid-cams in the Hall were pointed at him. "The Assembly looks forward to the results of your investigation," he said lamely. He tried to change the spin of Tolwyn's victory, to make his commission investigative, rather than active. "We shall decide a course of action within, ah . . . a fortnight of your completed report."

Tolwyn made a show of gracious acceptance. Taggart knew Tolwyn had gotten what he wanted, and now could afford to be gracious. Tolwyn turned slightly. Taggart was certain he did it to be better seen by the cameras. He raised his voice slightly, enunciating clearly for the journalists. "Thank you, Paladin. When you served under my command I knew I could always count on you," the admiral said. "I accept your vote of confidence on behalf of the Strategic Readiness Agency, and we shall endeavor to match your timetable for action."

"Two weeks," Taggart said, convinced Tolwyn was playing him, annoyed at Tolwyn's pointed reference to his once having been subservient to him. He searched for some sign of smugness or victory in the admiral's eyes, and saw nothing. Tolwyn's expression remained cool and still.

The admiral gave him another small smile. "Two weeks."

Taggart shook his head fractionally as Tolwyn turned back to the lectern. He had just been backed into agreeing to a fortnight's unspecified operations with unspecified forces along a potentially explosive frontier. He just hoped that Tolwyn knew what the hell he was doing. For all their sakes.

Christopher Blair picked up his wrench and counted to ten. His knuckles still throbbed from where he'd bashed them while trying to open the aerator pump's access cover. Sweat rolled down his face, soaking his shirt and dripping into the pump's guts. He rubbed the back of his hand across his forehead, then pinched his fingers together on the bridge of his nose to try and wipe away the stinging stuff.

He looked up at the thin blue sky and Nephele Prime. Prime was an insignificant main sequence yellow G-type star on the edge of nowhere. Nephele Two was tucked just on the inside of the "green band," the range of distances that a planet could occupy that would support human life. Two barely fit the criteria, resulting in a biosphere only marginally adaptable for human beings. The planet's principle exports were sand and rare earths, with just enough agriculture to provide the locals with some vegetables.

Blair had picked the place for its isolation, as had most of the other emigrants. His nearest neighbors were a monastic group of Zen Buddhists, whose hobbies appeared to be meditating and leaving him alone.

The long lines of sight had been the hardest thing for him to get used to on Two. The ability to see all the way to the horizon was something that just wasn't possible on a carrier deck. It had taken him a long time to decide he liked having room to stretch his elbows.

Nephele also offered air that hadn't been through a 'fresher, water that didn't have a chemical aftertaste, and

unrecycled food. It was paradise, compared to the Fleet.
Or so he told himself. Daily.

He looked down at his salt-crusted watch. It was only
nine A.M., local time, but the temperature was already up
over 42 degrees centigrade. He suspected that it would
top 45 before noon. That conclusion took very little
deductive reasoning. Two topped 45 degrees every day.

The blazing heat drew his attention back to the task at
hand. The broken pump was supposed to draw water from
the aquifer deep below the farmstead and up into porous
pipes below ground. The water would then be forced into
the soil around the plants, giving them the precious liquid
they needed to survive in Two's desert regions. Losing
either the pump or suction in the well shaft would require
repriming the system, a costly and difficult prospect.
Meanwhile, his plants would broil in the brutal sun.

He applied the spanner to a broken solenoid, removing
it in only twice the time the manual said it should take.
He replaced it, dropping the new part in the sand and
bashing his hand. He finally got the access panel closed.
The pump hummed and clicked to itself as it ran its internal
diagnostics program, then flashed SYSTEM READY on a tiny
screen.

Blair crossed his fingers and hit the starter button. The
machine began to shake and rattle as the old solar-powered
engine tried to turn over. "Come on, you old piece of . . ."
he said, then stopped as the pump rumbled to life. He
exhaled in relief, then dropped his head in frustration as
it died.

He checked the diagnostics. The display read SYSTEM
FAULT.

"No kidding," he grumbled. He took the wrench and
attacked the solenoid again, tightening and loosening it
in its socket to try and get a better contact. He hit the
starter again. The machine flared to life, sputtered, and
died.

Blair sighed in frustration and looked across the hectare
or so of crops that surrounded him. The plants would be

wilted by nightfall if he couldn't get water to them, and surface irrigation was out of the question. Water pumped onto the plants during the day would either evaporate at once or would act as a lens, concentrating the sunlight and searing the vegetation even more. He needed to get the pump operational, and soon, or his crop was finished.

He thought he'd done well to eke as much life out of the desert as he had, and with virtually no experience. It had seemed like such a good idea at the time . . . to spend his days creating life rather than destroying it. The process, though, had proven to be full of heartache and physical pain. He couldn't decide if he was proud of his meager accomplishment or sorry he'd ever begun it.

He knelt beside the aerator again and began to work the wrench into the solenoid's socket. He thought that perhaps the new part was bad. He hadn't thought to bench test it before he tried to install it. He cursed. It wouldn't have been the first time the Farm Bureau had sent him a new part that arrived broken.

He gave the engine a third try. It sputtered and died. This time a sound like a gulp came from the inside of the machine as it failed. Blair swore sulphurously as the display flashed SYSTEM INTEGRITY LOST—PIPE PRESSURE FAILURE. He had no choice now but to have the pump reprimed. He'd lose a significant portion of his crops before that happened.

He threw the wrench down with an oath and stalked off towards the run-down-looking house, noticing for the dozenth time that the place needed a new coat of paint. He wasn't especially disposed to do much more than recognize that the need existed. His domestic urges didn't include painting, especially in Neph's blistering heat. The notion of contracting a job like that locally was laughable. Not that he could afford it, even if he could cozen someone into doing it.

He stepped around the clutter on the steps and went inside to make the repair call. The house's main room was cluttered rather than dirty, with memorabilia covering every horizontal surface. The walls had no decoration other than old two-dees of comrades (many long dead), his framed citations and promotions, and curios picked up during twenty years of war. The room looked, he mused tiredly, like a display from a military museum. Which, in a way, it was.

He stepped over to the fridge plugged in next to his easy chair, reached in, and grabbed a beer can. He pressed the icy-cold plastic against his sweaty forehead, sighing in relief at the feel of the container against his heated skin. He glanced around, looking for his holo-comm controller. It was, for the moment, lost. He decided he wasn't particularly in the mood to look for it. The Farm Bureau could wait. God knows, he thought, they're going to make me wait, once I call.

He plopped into his chair, surrounded by a litter of magazines, books, and a trash bin half full of dead beer cans and food cartons.

The remote control for the holo-box was still sitting on the chair's arm. He picked it up and idly turned on the box. The news channel appeared to be carrying a feed from Earth. He checked the caption on the bottom of the screen. It was a delayed telecast from the Assembly Hall on Earth, and only two days old. He raised his eyebrows in surprise. The short delay suggested that the news must be really hot. Nephele was so far from Earth that what tapes they got were usually ten days old at the earliest. He settled back in his chair and opened his beer, interested in what the government had to say.

He cued the sound. The announcer's voice came from multiple speakers that were supposed to have been set into the walls but were instead scattered around the floor. ". . . and we've been told," her earnest, young voice said from off-camera, "that Admiral Tolwyn himself will be addressing this session of the Assembly on behalf of the Strategic Readiness Agency. Assembly Master Taggart's office has informed us that the nature of Admiral Tolwyn's remarks is not yet ready for release. We've heard from 'highly-placed sources' that the admiral's address will deal with the raids on Confederation shipping, likely by Border Worlds forces. Back to you, Miguel."

Blair took a slug of beer and belched as the pundits took over, trying to predict what Tolwyn would say. The camera zoomed back in on Taggart, who looked faintly bored. Paladin's done well for himself, Blair thought. Taggart's moustache and hair were still more blond than gray and the smile lines around his eyes had grown a little deeper. Blair decided that life as a politician agreed with him.

Taggart glanced at his watch and started banging his gavel, trying to bring the floor to order. Blair noticed that he wasn't having much luck at first. The room finally quieted, and Blair listened as Taggart introduced Tolwyn. Blair laughed again. Paladin appeared to have lost his accent. He'd always suspected Taggart's thick, Scottish brogue had been a put-on. A spy with a burr just didn't fit Blair's image of a secret agent.

Blair's laughter died as the admiral stepped up to the podium, his dress uniform aglitter with awards and decorations. The sight of Tolwyn stirred mixed emotions in Blair. The admiral had at one time thought Blair to be a turncoat, or, worse yet—incompetent, as a result of the loss of the *Tiger's Claw*. Blair had since proven otherwise, mostly by accomplishing more than his fair share of Tolwyn's suicidal missions.

Blair considered Tolwyn's reputation for risk taking with other people's lives to understate the facts. The admiral's willingness to sacrifice anyone or anything to achieve his objectives had long been lauded in the popular press. He was "the man who got things done."

Blair had often been placed in the position of being one of those sacrificed, a singular honor he had rarely appreciated. He'd always managed to come back. Many of his friends, also flying on Tolwyn's orders, hadn't been so lucky. Tolwyn had won more than he'd lost, the butcher's bills notwithstanding. Tolwyn, so far as Blair knew, had never expressed remorse for those who'd died pursuing his schemes.

He listened, unimpressed, as Tolwyn laid out his case for mounting a major expedition to the frontier. There hadn't been much going on since the Kilrathi War, and Tolwyn was doubtless looking for some action. He laughed. The old war-horse was trying to find an excuse to get out and ride his carriers.

The news reports had indicated that the raids hadn't been more than a pinprick. Tolwyn's reaction seemed to him to be more akin to smashing grasshoppers with a sledgehammer than a military operation, unless the press was downplaying the real situation. He shrugged. He laughed out loud as Tolwyn maneuvered the Senate into anointing him with a strike force. If Tolwyn wanted to chase pirates with a battle fleet, then that was fine with Blair.

The only part of the situation that disturbed him was Paladin's surrender. Taggart appeared to be Tolwyn's loudest cheerleader, helping to write the admiral a blank check for his private little war. Blair wondered how that boded for the future. The military, through the admiralty courts and martial law, had usurped much civilian authority in the name of protecting humanity from the Kilrathi. Blair had watched the government use one pretext after another to slow the transition back to complete civilian rule. Blair had been skeptical that Paladin, as a former military man, would do his part to restore the civilian government's prerogatives. This abdication seemed to confirm his assessment.

A chiming sounded from the depths of the room's clutter, drawing him from his ruminations. He stood, drained off his brew, and began sorting through the piles in the main room, in search of the comm-unit's remote control. He regretted the passing effort he'd made at tidying up the clutter. He'd only managed to move the piles around enough to lose track of everything.

He rooted through end-table drawers and among the seat cushions, through piles of dirty clothes, stacks of books and magazines, and piles of printouts. The comm-unit buzzed again, giving him a vector to zero in on. He found the holo-comm box hidden under an article discussing more efficient planting strategies, and a thick pile of newsfaxes.

He checked the unit, his eyebrows climbing in surprise at the flashing light. He read the display. "Incoming—planet." He turned the unit over, trying to refamiliarize himself with the device. He couldn't remember if this was the second or third message he'd received since he'd bought the place, but he hadn't had enough mail for him to bother learning how the unit worked. He pressed one button on the side of the box. The room darkened while a section of wall slid back to reveal a holo-tank.

Rachel Corialis' face appeared, blurred and scratchy from a hundred playbacks. "Chris," her sad voice said, "I can't do this anymore. I can't spend my life on a backwater, and I can't stand the way you've crawled into that bottle." She took a deep breath, on the edge of tears. "You won't let me help you, and I can't live this way." She looked down. The playback fuzzed her voice into a scratchy whisper. "Chris . . . I love you but . . . goodbye. . . ." Her image faded as the old chip lost resolution.

"Damn," Blair said, under his breath, "I thought I erased that." He squinted at the controller again, then hit another button.

The signal jumped and flickered, then settled down to reveal Todd Marshall grinning at him from the tank. Blair groaned.

"Same to you, old buddy," Marshall said sarcastically, glancing around the part of the room he could see through Blair's pickup. "Nice place you got there. I like the style—early bachelor." He looked at Blair again. "I hope you put the goats outside before you go to bed."

Blair kept his expression still. "Hello, Maniac." He glanced at Marshall's shoulder pips, pleased that he was still a major. "Sorry about your promotion." He didn't try very hard to hide the insincerity in his voice.

The fleet had apparently decided that it was a bad idea

to give a colonelcy to a pilot whose callsign described his state of mind. Blair, for once, agreed wholeheartedly with the armchair warriors. Maniac had abandoned far too many wingmen for Blair to want to entrust a squadron to him.

Marshall's face twisted in a sardonic expression that Blair had come to loathe. "Yeah, well, now that the amateurs have taken over, it's getting harder for us professionals to get ahead. I was supposed to get a squadron."

Blair kept his face still, unwilling to give Marshall an opening. He checked the source code of the call, confirming it as on-planet. "What brings you this far out?"

"I was just passing through," Maniac said, his voice thick with sarcasm, "and I smelled pigs. So I said to myself, 'I wonder what the Scourge of Kilrah is doing these days?' So I dropped by." His smile turned unfriendly. "You know, chief, most washed-up fighter jocks take on honorable occupations, like drinking or whoring." He paused. "But, farming, that's disgraceful." He chuckled.

Blair, unamused, placed his thumb over the disconnect button and held it up where Marshall could see it. "If this is a social call, Maniac," he said, "then I'm through being sociable."

Maniac raised one hand, his expression turning serious. "Listen, hotshot, you gotta meet me at the starport. I'll be in the canteen. We have to talk."

"We're talking now," Blair answered.

Maniac shook his head. "Not good enough. The channel could be monitored. This is important, too important to leak." He paused. "Look, a lot of lives are on the line here. It's vital I see you." He grinned. "So, see if you can fit me into your busy schedule, okay?"

Blair thought a moment, then nodded. "All, right. I'll hear you out." He paused. "This had better not be a game."

The holo faded in a burst of static, leaving Blair in the darkened, slightly musty room. He sat long into the morning, thinking. He eventually stood and walked out onto the porch where he looked out onto his crops a long moment. He turned his back on them and went inside to pack.

Blair stepped down the shuttle's ramp, pleased that he had been able to book a last-minute hop on the intercontinental. A gust of brutally hot air seeped around the mating collar that connected the walkway to the atmospheric shuttle's side. He walked down the walkway and into an icy blast of air conditioning. He shivered in the sudden heat change, gratified that while Two's starport lacked for virtually every amenity, it did have a landing dock and collar for smaller ships. He was certain that otherwise he would have melted crossing the starport's concrete ramp. He decided that he was going to have to get a cold drink inside him before he suffered heatstroke.

The starport was located on Two's equator, where ships could take advantage of the planet's rotational velocity to boost into space. Blair's home was in the much more reasonable southern latitudes, where asphalt didn't slag and run. He made it a point of going to the port as little as possible, to avoid the heat.

He rapidly concluded that the starport hadn't improved much since the last time he had been there. He walked up the grime-covered access ramp from the shuttle and passed a small, dust-caked window that faced the small field. He paused a moment to look out the thick plexiglass.

Small freighters lined one side of the field, their structures wavering in the rising thermals. Three landing circles, their concrete basins lashed and battered by the drive streams of dozens of ships, marked the area where the outbound ships staged for departure. A pair of closed lift-trucks loaded cargo onto a dirty and smoke-streaked short-haul atmospheric transport that squatted near the port's sole runway. The hulks of a half-dozen abandoned spacecraft lay cluttered on the far side of the field.

The shuttle lifted up to ground level behind him, raised by the small elevator that served the passenger area. It rolled slowly towards the departure area. He gave some thought as to how he planned to get back home, once he'd heard Maniac's pitch, then realized he didn't really care. He was here, and that was enough. He turned away from the window, threw his flight bag over his shoulder, and walked towards the concourse.

The inside of Two's starport had been built around a commercial area, with several offices for local freight lines, a broker, a few tired-looking shops, and several restaurants and bars. The whole place was done in lively pastels that both lightened the gloomy surroundings and showed every speck of dirt. The floor was carpeted in some kind of tough, age-spotted commercial fiber that had worn through in spots.

He angled for the canteen, certain it hadn't been moved. Pilots hung out in spacer bars, usually located within spitting distance of the starport's front gate, if not on the premises. Two made it easier by packing most of its facilities in close together, to reduce the amount of air they would have to chill.

The canteen was a dive located along the far wall of a tiny plaza built off the main drag. It appeared to share space with a pawnshop and what he guessed was either a brothel or a hotel, if not both. He slung his bag more tightly over his shoulder, crossed to the canteen, and entered.

He entered the outer alcove and was immediately struck by the din of the noisy crowd within. He glanced up and saw a clock displaying the local time. Eleven-thirty, and the place was already packed. He checked his bag in a rented locker and pocketed the key before he entered the main bar. His rough plan was to do a quick recon and find a good table before Maniac entered. A sign saying NO WEAPONS ALLOWED flashed on and off over the door.

He stepped though the inner batwing doors and glanced around. The place had been a pilots' hangout during the war, catering to the long-haul patrols and transit jockeys ferrying fighters out to the frontier. The walls were decorated with two-dee renderings of warcraft throughout the ages, from primitive prop-driven aircraft to state-of-the-art fighters and bombers. Bric-a-brac and pilot memorabilia were scattered about on shelves. Models hung from the low ceiling, scattered between the ceiling fans, dancing lights and holos of yet more machines.

The place had always seemed contrived to Blair. Two had never had enough of a military presence to support a pilots' bar on its own, so it had to depend on transients.

Blair glanced around the main bar, looking for Maniac. The bar was filled to overflowing with the flotsam of a half-dozen races and a hundred planets. Pimps and whores of every possible color and gender plied their trades next to homeless vets begging for a handout or a drink. Several spacers in the shiny boots and creased flight suits of one of the inter-system liners swapped lies and swilled drinks with a pair of Confed pilots in rumpled flight suits. The next table had a woman with a tattooed face and green hair who fed cherries from the bar to a spider monkey perched on her shoulder. Blair watched the animal a moment, uncertain if its bright blue hair was a mutation or a dye job.

Men and women, many in remnants of Confederation uniforms—mostly identifiable as Kilrathi War veterans by their decorations and badges—littered the small round tables that surrounded the central area. Many drank or were drunk, while others played cards or dominoes. They shared the bored, listless expressions that Blair had come to associate with people who had no place to be and nothing much to do. Drug dealers worked the corners of the bar, plying the drunk or stoned with their wares, and occasionally discreetly rolling the comatose. Money changers and cardsharps sized up the rubes and each other.

Terrans stood cheek by jowl with aliens, Border Worlders, and mixed races, all talking at once—jabbering, negotiating, arguing, fighting, and drinking. The noise, the activity, and the odors—sweat, and oil, and vomit—clogged Blair's senses.

He recovered some of his poise and worked his way a little deeper into the closely-packed mass, enough that he could pick up snippets of the conversations around him. Everyone was looking to score, whether it was money, stolen property, sex, power, or off-planet. They all had some need they wanted met, and were willing, often frantic, to trade.

He moved into the center of the room, shifting his ID plate and credit chips into his front pockets. He looked around the room, searching for Maniac.

He shook his head, tiring of the game. Too much had changed since he'd retired to his farm for him to be comfortable with the situation. He made for the bar, seeking a safe haven while he pondered his next move. The bartender, seeing him place his elbows on the cheap, wood-grained plastic bar top, placed a glass in front of him and poured him a stiff drink.

Blair looked up, puzzled. "I didn't ask for this."

The bartender shrugged. "I only serve one kind here. I figured that's what you came in for."

Blair looked at the amber-colored liquid. He took a careful sniff, then wrinkled his nose at the smell of raw alcohol. He lifted the glass and took a sip, his first whiskey since Rachel had left. He coughed slightly as it burned a track down his throat. The stuff may have been rotgut, but it was better than the hooch produced by many ships' stills and far superior to the stuff he'd brought with him.

He cleared his throat. "How much?" he asked, indicating the glass.

"One point two," the bartender replied. "Standard credits only. None of that Border Worlds trash." He looked at Blair examining the glass. "It's cheap at the price."

"It'd be cheap at any price," Blair replied sourly. He handed his credit chip to the bartender. The bartender ran the charge, then looked up at Blair hopefully. "A tip?"

Blair thought a moment. "Don't go outside without a coat."

The bartender returned his credit chip and walked away, a sour expression on his face.

Blair was just turning around to scan the bar again, when someone bumped into him, spilling part of his drink on his hand. He quickly held the glass away from his clothing while he turned his head to curse at his jostler. The profanity died on his lips. A grizzled veteran, wearing the scraps of what had once been Confederation crew coveralls, looked up at him with rheumy eyes. He reeked of cheap whiskey and other, less savory odors.

The veteran wiped the back of one dirty hand across his mouth and tried to focus on Blair. "Hey, kid," the man said, "can you spare a vet a drink?"

Blair glanced over the old man's coveralls. The man's patches had been removed at some point, leaving dark shapes where they had protected the material beneath from fading. Blair thought he recognized some of the shapes. "Were you a flyer?"

The veteran drew himself up in pride and met Blair's eye. "Yep," he said, "started out as a turret gunner on a Broadsword. Got m'self a field commission as a pilot and flew em'."

"What happened?" Blair asked.

The man sighed, exhaling a stench into Blair's face, "I din't have no college, so I lost m' commission in the 'reduction in forces' when the war ended." He shrugged, his face a mix of pain and humiliation. "I flew off the ole *Liberty* for nineteen years. I was a plank-owner, been on her since her commissionin'. That shoulda' counted for sometin', ya know?" He glanced away and his shoulders slumped. "Poor girl—the *Liberty*, I mean. She fought hard an' did her part, ya' know, then got broken up for scrap. It was like she was nothing."

Blair nodded sympathetically. "Yeah, it's hell." The vet gave Blair a hard look. "I was on the *Concordia*," Blair supplied, "so I know all about losing a ship."

The vet dipped his head in agreement, accepting Blair as a member of the club. "Say, you don't know of any spacers takin' on crew, do ya?"

Blair shook his head. "Sorry. Why don't you go down to the hiring hall?"

The vet shrugged. "There's nothing there. The Cats got awful good at going after our transport in the tail end of the war, and with the loss of the shipyards on Earth and the scale-down after, there ain't been a whole lot of constructing. What slots there are got captains and majors scrambling for third mate's jobs." He looked morose. "It's bad, especially for a RIF"ed lieutenant like me."

"Yeah," Blair agreed.

"Ya know," the vet continued, "we fought awful hard and awful long to win the war, an' for what? There's still Cats out there, making trouble, an' pirates, an' whatnot. Nothing's going like it should. It's like we lost the war, too." He looked down meaningfully at Blair's drink. "You can't get a decent glass of whiskey." He pointed at the amber liquid. "Just bilge waste."

Blair opened his mouth to speak, only to have the vet run over him. "Prices of everything been going up. It's like everthing's fallin' apart."

That's because it is, Blair thought. The war had gone on so long it had achieved a life of its own. He hadn't realized until after he had retired and had to live on the civilian economy just how much of it had become geared to support the war effort. That, coupled with the devastation of the Kilrathi attack on the home worlds, the sheer expense of the war, and the loss of the cream of human generations, had drained off what few resources were available to maintain the economic infrastructure.

The vet was looking at Blair intently. "Look, buddy, if I'm bothering you . . ."

"No," Blair replied, "sorry. I was thinking of . . . old friends. Comrades, you know?" It was the safest answer that came to mind.

The vet nodded, drawing his sleeve across his mouth again. "I didn't mean to ramble on," he said, "it's just— you spend your whole life workin' for something, working for victory, you know. Then we got it—an' then what? They throw us all out, tell us we gotta find jobs—like there was any to be found. An' they tells that *now* we gotta contribute, ya know." His face turned bitter. "Like we haven't been."

"Well," Blair replied, shrugging his shoulders, "I don't think anyone ever planned on what would happen if we won. I think we were so focused on just surviving that we never stopped to think about what would happen the day after peace broke out." He ground his teeth. Maybe we should have realized, he thought, we got a little taste of this during the truce before the Kilrathi surprise attack on Earth. But then we had Earth's industry and the Inner Colonies to carry some of the weight . . . and they were now ashes.

The vet cleared his throat. "Um," he said, "about that drink . . . ?"

"Sure," Blair said. He reached into his pocket for some folding money and saw Maniac through the crowd. The major looked as he always did, intense, and never more so than when he was putting the moves on a woman.

Blair thought a moment, then peeled off a five-credit note. It was little enough, but would get the vet a decent meal and a shower, if not a room. He pressed the money into the startled man's hands.

The veteran tried to refuse it. "No," Blair said, "take it. As one survivor to another."

The veteran frowned and reluctantly accepted the largesse. "Thanks, buddy," he said. He looked at Blair a long moment. "Sorry, I din't catch your name."

Blair smiled grimly. "Smith," he said, lying. His own name carried too much fame for him to use it casually. He stepped quickly away from the bar, looking for where Maniac had disappeared through the crowd with the girl. It took only a few steps to see where Maniac had drawn her. He could tell from her expression that she didn't seem overly impressed with his line of approach. He laughed to himself. If I get there in time, he thought as he walked towards the pilot, I may be able to do my civic duty and keep him from crashing and burning.

Blair was just about to tap Marshall on the shoulder

when the pilot leaned forward towards the woman. "So, baby, whaddya say? I got us a room."

The woman pursed her lips as though she'd bitten a lemon. Blair whistled in sympathetic pain as she slapped him hard across the face and stormed away. Blair stood there, a knowing smile on his face, as Maniac turned towards him. Todd Marshall rubbed his cheek ruefully.

"It's amazing how unpatriotic women get as soon as a war stops," Manic said cheerfully. "All I did was offer to let her keep my morale up for me."

"As I recall," Blair replied dryly, "that line didn't work any better *during* the war."

Maniac gave Blair his trademark smug grin. "You never know till you try." He shrugged and tipped his chin towards the bar. "Who was the bum?"

Blair made a sour face. "Bomber pilot. Got caught in the RIF. No real prospects, so he hangs out here, cadging drinks."

Maniac nodded. "The RIF took out more good folks than the Cats did." He shrugged. "Things're tough, especially for the bastards who put it all on the line and now have nothing."

Blair looked back at the bar, his mood introspective. "You know, Maniac, when I was a kid, space was the place to be. It meant opportunity. The colonies were growing exponentially, the economy was good, and even the war was an exciting thing—fighting aliens for humanity. Now, it's like we've lost something. Space is like everyplace else, just another junkyard."

Maniac stared at him, as startled as if Blair had begun spouting Kilrathi mating poetry. "Colonel," he said, placing enough stress on Blair's rank to be borderline insubordinate, "are you sure you ain't been on that farm too long?"

Blair wasn't in the mood to banter. "The farm's a peaceful life, Major. Quiet. Serene. Stable. Zen Buddhists next door. You wouldn't like it."

Maniac laughed, harsh and mean. "I've always said you'd go soft. I just didn't expect your head to go first."

A loud crash spared Blair the need to answer. He turned in his seat to see the source of the commotion. He saw a man in a dark flight suit with sandy hair standing, his chair knocked over behind him. He grabbed the veteran Blair had spoken with by the collar. Blair didn't hear the exchange between the two men, but he did see the dark man give the vet a deliberate backhand across the face. The vet tumbled backward, spilling across the table. The younger man stepped up to the groaning vet and kicked him first in the hip with the point of his boot, then again in the gut as he collapsed.

Blair looked quickly around for a bouncer. No one seemed particularly interested in helping the older man. He had stood up and was rushing over to help before he considered the implications of what he was doing. The dark man cocked his foot back and kicked the man in the kidney as Blair approached. Blair grabbed the man by the shoulder and whirled him around.

"Enough," Blair started to say. He froze as the man whipped his flight jacket open. He caught a quick glimpse of the man's name tag as he whipped a short black handle from its pouch on his belt. The man flicked a switch. A red, disembodied point appeared about four inches above the tip of the weapon.

"Laser knife!" someone yelled to Blair's right.

Blair felt his guts tense. He had little experience with blades of any sort, much less any as nasty as this. All he knew was that laser knives were plunging weapons that could also inflict severe surface burns depending on whether the attack was a pierce or a slash. He glanced up, meeting the dark man's cold blue eyes.

His opponent held the knife low, with the point towards Blair's gut. He played the blade back and forth, whirling the tip in precise figure eights. Blair had no doubt the man knew exactly how to use the weapon.

He tried to remember his own hand-to-hand training. The only piece that came to mind was to watch his opponent's waist, the center of gravity. The man chuckled, causing Blair to look up again. The sandy-haired man smiled, a wintery splitting of his lips.

"Bad move, friend," he said, "I don't like being touched." He whipped the laser knife up, stabbing for Blair's midsection. Blair went to block, crossing his wrists, palms down, in front of his stomach. He realized too late that the dark man's slash was merely a feint. He had just begun to dodge back when the man hit him with a roundhouse punch to the temple. Blair staggered back, his vision exploding into a mass of stars. He staggered to the right, trying to dodge a second punch.

His attacker feinted again, this time snap-kicking him in the head. Blair managed to interpose his arm in time to keep the kick from connecting, but the shock numbed his arm. The blow staggered him, knocking him off balance and slamming him face first into a plastic laminated concrete wall. He saw, through crossed eyes, a smear of blood.

The man stepped up behind him and kicked him in the back of the knees. Blair folded up like an accordion and started to slide to the floor, turning as he fell. The man caught him by the throat and slammed him back up against the wall. Blair winced at the impact and tried to grab his arm. The noises in the bar faded as the man started to squeeze Blair's throat, choking off his air.

Blair felt his face swelling as blood, trapped by the man's grip, pooled under his skin. He scrabbled his hands ineffectually as his air supply was cut off. Blair, his eyes feeling as though they were going to burst, looked frantically around the bar. The patrons, distracted from their own concerns by the action, watched silently. Their expressions ran the gamut from boredom to active interest in the blood. The bartender stopped polishing a glass, but made no effort to help.

The sandy-haired man leaned in close. "I don't like to be touched," he repeated in a low, soft voice. He loosened his grip enough for Blair to take a single, sobbing breath. "And I don't like people meddling in my private affairs."

He raised the laser knife, letting Blair see the red dot as he drew it closer to his throat. "It's going to cost you."

He smiled, his thin lips skinning back from white teeth. The grin looked feral to Blair. He began to tighten his grip once again on Blair's throat. Blair fought desperately to free himself. He felt his tongue bulge out of his mouth and a line of spittle run down his cheek. His face grew hot and his heels drummed against the wall.

The dark man had just placed the laser knife under Blair's chin when his head suddenly jerked to the left. Maniac came into Blair's blurred line of sight, a high-output laser pistol stuck in the man's ear. Maniac ground the weapon in cruelly, smiling as he leaned close. Blair saw the dark man's associates rise from their own seats and close on Maniac.

"Tut, tut," Maniac said, screwing the pistol more deeply into the man's ear canal. He pulled the man's jacket back, revealing his name tag. "I haven't killed anybody in a week, Mr., uh, Seether, and I'm due." He gave the sidekicks a glance, then said. "If you lowlifes don't back off we're gonna find out if your boss's scalded brains'll match the decor." Blair noticed that the dark man seemed utterly unfazed by the situation. The wintery blue eyes flicked back and forth a moment, as though considering his options.

"Alright, friend," the man said to Blair, "call off your dog."

"Nope," Maniac interjected, "this is my play. You talk to me." He punctuated his sentence by forcing the pistol harder against the man's head, tilting it to the side until the muscles in the man's neck stood out in sharp relief. Blair saw the first reaction from the pilot, a gritting of the teeth as the hard metal and front sight blade dug into his ear. A thin rill of blood ran down his ear and into his collar.

The knife disappeared from Blair's sight. The dark man slowly released Blair and raised his hands to shoulder height. Blair stumbled out of the way behind Maniac and fell to his knees, choking and retching as he sucked air through his tortured windpipe. He tried to get his trembling hands under control, and failed.

Maniac stepped back, opening a kick's distance from the dark man. Blair, still rubbing his abused throat, saw the man tense and shift his weight slightly as he had before snap-kicking Blair. He was about to warn Maniac when the major whipped his gun up, extending it at arm's length and pointing it between the man's eyes. "Give me an excuse," Maniac said, "please."

The man appeared to ponder the situation a moment, then backed slowly away. He gathered his associates with tiny gestures as he retreated. "We'll meet again," he said, looking past Maniac to Blair, "that I can promise you." He backed to the door, then left, followed by his associates.

"Well," Maniac said, his voice a mix of amusement and disgust "if that don't beat all. Here I am with my gun stuck in his ear, and I can't even get the time of day from him." He looked at Blair. "Is he a friend of yours?" His eyes widened. "Colonel," he said, "you're pale as a ghost. If I didn't know better, I'd say you're scared." He paused. "Hell, you *are* scared."

Blair tried to control his racing heart. He swallowed several times. "I don't know," he said weakly. "He was fast, faster then me. He had me cold, Todd, and there wasn't anything I could do about it. That's never happened to me before." He dabbed his hand to his lip. It came away bloody. He realized he must have cut it when the sandy-haired man had slammed him into the wall.

Blair interpreted Marshall's expression as a mix of concern and contempt. That, if anything, made him feel worse. Maniac opened his mouth to say something, then gestured for Blair to precede him. He looked worried.

"Um, Colonel," he said diffidently, "maybe we should call this off. Maybe you should just go back to your farm and feed your pigs."

"Call what off?" Blair asked.

Maniac shrugged. "Look, I was looking for Colonel Blair,

the war hero who blew away Kilrah—Mister Heart of the Tiger. I'll just tell 'em I couldn't find him."

Blair felt himself getting angry. "Maniac, you called me up here. What the hell do you want?"

Maniac shrugged. "I guess it really ain't my problem if you're not up to speed." His face gave lie to his words as he indicated a place for Blair to sit.

Blair took his chair and leaned back, trying to relax his tense body. His hands still trembled slightly in what he told himself was an adrenaline reaction. He hunched his shoulders, trying to ease the throbbing in his neck and throat. "So," he said, trying to lighten Maniac's glum mood, "what's this important matter you wanted to discuss?"

Marshall frowned. He glanced back at the area where the brawl had happened. He shrugged again, as though making an internal decision.

"Colonel Christopher Blair," he said. He tried to sound official, but his heart wasn't in it. "In the name of the Confederation Space Force Reserves and by the authority of Emergency Decree 394A, it is my duty to inform you that you have been recalled to active service in grade of full colonel, with all the pay and benefits accruing and blah, blah, blah." He punctuated his announcement with a malicious grin and a flash of his usual humor. "Have a nice day."

Blair sat stunned, his jaw open. "Haven't you heard, Maniac? The war's over. We won. I'm out of it. Retired."

Maniac shrugged. "Not anymore."

Blair rolled his drink between his hands. "Why me?"

Maniac raised his palms upward. "I dunno. All I know is that somebody thinks they need you."

Blair leaned in towards him. "Who is 'they?' "

Maniac looked offended. "You'll find out." He rolled his own glass between his hands a moment, his brow furrowed in thought. When he spoke, he wouldn't look Blair in the eyes. "Look," he said, "lemme do you a favor. Go home."

"Let me get this straight," Blair snapped, "first you drag me into this . . . then you want me out?" His eyes followed Maniac's back to the scene of the fight. "I see," he said, understanding Marshall's reluctance, "you don't think I can handle it."

Maniac shrugged. "I've seen you hurt, I've seen you angry, I've seen you every way possible, or so I'd thought. I never saw you scared before. I kept waitin' for you to kick his ass, but you didn't. You froze." He sighed, his expression that of a man facing a difficult truth. "I think you lost whatever you had, Colonel, and involving you is a mistake."

Blair sat in silence, thinking through his options. He'd wanted nothing more than to get out of fighters, to free himself of the military and the memories when the war ended. Two years on the farm, however, had softened the hard edges and put a gloss of time over the hurt. His hands, of their own accord, began to clench, as though gripping a control yoke. He realized how much he ached to get back into a cockpit—how much he'd wanted this since he'd walked away from the farm.

He looked up at Maniac. "When do we leave?"

Maniac scratched his nose. "Well," he said, "I'm not sure *we* do."

Blair let his expression grow cold. "That decision, Major, is not yours to make."

Maniac studied him a moment, his expression unreadable. "Uh, well," he said at last, "I've made arrangements to have a pair of fighters staged. They're up at the port, fueled and ready."

Blair set his drink down and stood. "Let's go."

Maniac made a rude noise. "Don't we have to go to your house or something?"

"Just give me a minute," Blair answered. He fetched his phone out of his flight bag, punched in a number and waited. Maniac listened, shaking his head as Blair hurriedly said something in an unintelligible language and then clicked off.

"What was that all about?"

"I just told my Buddhist neighbors the farm's theirs. A donation to the church."

Blair forced a smile.

"Let's get the hell out of this hole."

• CHAPTER TWO

Blair stood in the anteroom leading to the *Orion's* observation deck, cooling his heels and savoring a cup of real coffee with real cream. He could not recall the last time he had sipped the genuine article, certainly not since his emigration to Neph Two. The beans didn't grow there naturally, and the imported stuff was far too expensive for a colonel on retirement half-pay.

He inhaled the rich aroma as he wondered why Tolwyn had recalled him. It certainly wasn't because he was one of the admiral's favorites. His relationship with Tolwyn had generally been polite, though cool. He smiled. Tolwyn rarely did anything without reason, though his having reasons and his communicating them were two different things entirely.

He teased his swollen lip with his tongue as he pondered why Tolwyn had selected the *Orion* for their meeting. The admiral would have to travel out from Earth to L5, an unusual expense of both time and money for him to commit to a mere colonel. He wondered what made such effort necessary, unless the admiral had other reasons for being on the station.

The presence of the battle station at the Lagrange point surprised him. He knew that the *Orion* had been in low earth orbit as part of Terra's last line of defense and that the Kilrathi had severely damaged it in their attack. He tapped the cup against his teeth as he tried without success to recall a newsfax or tape-delay broadcast reporting the move. He doubted that it had been reported, a lapse he found curious given the station's size and the tremendous expense of boosting it up Earth's gravity well.

Why the sudden interest in L5? he wondered. A body

placed there would remain indefinitely, courtesy of the offsetting tugs of gravity of Earth, Luna and the sun. He knew that in Earth's ancient history there had been an attempt to use L5 and the other Lagrange points as construction sites for huge metal colonies, but the discovery of the jump-drive and the plethora of main sequence stars with Earthlike planets had nixed that. Now, it seemed someone was taking a step back in history.

An aide de camp entered through the thin door that separated the anteroom from the upper observation deck. "The admiral will see you now."

Blair regretfully surrendered his coffee cup to her. She opened the door and stepped back, gesturing for him to enter.

Tolwyn stood on the opposite side of the room, hands clasped behind his ramrod straight back as he looked out the large observation windows. Blair saw two huge silvery, lattice-covered shapes in the middle distance. He suspected that his shuttle's circuitous inbound route had been designed to avoid giving him a view of them.

Blair crossed the room to him, letting the sounds of his heels on the metal floor announce his presence. He stepped to within six feet of the admiral's back and brought his heels together with a soft click as he came to attention. "Colonel Christopher Blair of the Space Forces Reserves, reporting as ordered, sir."

Tolwyn didn't turn. "That was a bit formal for you, wasn't it, Colonel?"

"I'm not used to being drafted, sir," Blair replied dryly, "I'm a little vague on the protocols."

Tolwyn tipped his head slightly. "I had my reasons." He paused. "At ease, Colonel. Will you join me by the window?"

Blair broke from his brace and moved to stand at Tolwyn's right, where he could see both the ships and Tolwyn's face. He stood silently a moment, taking in the panoramic view.

Blair glanced at the admiral. Tolwyn's uniform (shipboard, officers' greens, flame retardant) was creased and impeccably tailored, as always. His own uniform had been in a box in the quartermaster's stores until twelve hours before. It fit, but not well. He'd always been casual about his uniforms, preferring to let his reputation do his talking for him. This time, however, he felt rumpled and shabby.

Tolwyn turned towards him, his blue eyes unreadable in his seamed face. Tolwyn looked as he always did, neither old nor young, his close-cropped white hair notwithstanding. Blair chose to remain at ease, rather than coming to attention as regulations and custom dictated. The two men shared a long look.

Tolwyn was the first to look away. "I see you've put on weight," he said, patting his own flat stomach. "Civilian life must agree with you."

"I get along," Blair replied noncommittally.

Tolwyn nodded agreeably, the first thaw in his cool demeanor. "You took up sheepherding, didn't you?"

"Farming," Blair corrected dryly.

Tolwyn shrugged, his casual dismissal suggesting the two were one and the same. "I envy you."

"How's that?" Blair asked warily.

"On the farm, issues are simple," the admiral replied, "out here, things get tougher."

"How's that?" Blair repeated, his attention fully on the admiral.

Tolwyn pointed down towards the blackened frames that jutted from the *Orion's* side. "That," he said, "is all that remains of launch bay number three. A single Darket flew into it and exploded. The bay was full of fighters, fully fueled and armed, and all spotted for launch. The explosions destroyed the bay and spread fires through the ventilation system before the computer closed them down. Havoc spread throughout the station. A quarter of the crew died." He looked at Blair. "All from a single Darket."

"I don't understand," Blair replied.

"Sometimes, Colonel," Tolwyn said, "a tiny flame can start a great big fire." He pursed his lips. "My job is to put the flames out, before they become fires." The admiral shifted his gaze. "They're beauties, aren't they?"

It took Blair a moment to realize that Tolwyn had changed the subject and was referring to the twin super carriers hanging in space. "Yes, sir," he replied, choosing a safe answer.

Tolwyn smiled. "These are the future of power projection—our newest fleet carriers, the *Vesuvius* and the *Mount St. Helens*. They'll be CVs 70 and 71 when they're commissioned." He smiled. "They're the best, most modern expression of tactical design and thought."

Blair turned his attention to the huge ships. He had seen news-vid reports of their construction, but the holo-tapes hadn't given him any idea of their sheer size.

The carriers looked to be about twice the length of the *Concordia*, which had been one of the largest CVs in the Fleet before it had been destroyed over Earth.

The nearer ship appeared to be largely complete. It had two cigar-shaped external bays that ran parallel to its center mass and were connected by short, squarish pylons. The bays were well-proportioned, their lines flowing into the main hull and giving the massive ship a sleek, lethal look. Blair, accustomed to the boxy, utilitarian appearance of Terran construction, whistled in surprised appreciation.

The second ship, floating somewhat further away, was still under primary construction. Blair could see the shiny exposed ribs of the unfinished launch bays and the exposed skeleton around the nose. Hundreds of lights glittered like fireflies along the ship's flanks. It took him a moment to realize the winking stars were welders.

"They look Kilrathi," he said.

"We *have* incorporated the latest Kilrathi technology," Tolwyn admitted grudgingly, "which might account for the superficially Cat appearance. We borrowed some ideas from the super carriers they launched against Earth."

Blair said nothing, seeing a flicker of emotion on Tolwyn's face. It had, indeed, been Tolwyn's finest hour, Blair realized. A bomb carried by a Kilrathi agent had wiped out the Joint Chiefs and Tolwyn was named commander of all Earth defenses in the crisis. It had been Tolwyn who had warned against the Kilrathi truce, which had granted the Cats time to bring their new carriers on-line. It was Tolwyn who led the masterful fighting withdrawal all the way from the frontier to Earth orbit . . . it was Tolwyn who had saved humanity when all seemed lost. Blair felt a moment of sympathy for the admiral. If, at that moment of victory, Tolwyn had been lost he would have been remembered forever as the greatest hero of the war.

Blair remembered how, in spite of all their differences, he had looked upon him with awe during that campaign; calm, unflappable, inspiring those around him to give their all, for they knew the man at the top was the best combat commander in the fleet. If only he had retired then, or been kicked upstairs to head of Joint Chiefs, the humiliations that came afterwards would have been avoided. Blair guessed that it was there that this change in the admiral had really started. Joint Chiefs should have been his next command, but political insiders, many of whom had fallen for the Kilrathi truce, were quickly back in the saddle and pronounced that the admiral was "too valuable a field commander" to be pulled from action by the promotion. Tolwyn was the goose who had laid the golden egg of a victory undreamed of, but when called upon to do it again, he had failed. That failure must now be eating at his soul.

"The design of these new ships, in spite of the borrowing, are entirely human, Colonel. I was head of the advisory board that laid out the specifications."

Blair sensed that Tolwyn had somehow picked up on his thoughts; he looked away from the penetrating gaze.

"Each will mass a quarter million gross tons, carry a crew of seventy-eight hundred, and will maintain a complement of over four-hundred fighters and utility craft."

Blair whistled again. A fleet carrier generally carried a single wing with about a hundred fighters and bombers. "I thought they were propaganda," he said.

"Oh?" Tolwyn's eyebrows arched in surprise. "How so?"

Blair shrugged. "I didn't think we had the ability to build something this big." He glanced at Tolwyn. The admiral nodded his head fractionally, signalling him to continue.

Blair took a deep breath. "The Kilrathi bombs wiped out most of Earth's northern industrial cities. They also pasted the lunar shipyards." He tipped his head towards the ships. "It just doesn't seem possible to build these without a shipyard or local industry, especially with a depressed economy. We've even heard rumors of starvation and food riots."

Tolwyn frowned. "You ought to pay closer attention to the real news. We've made considerable progress in rebuilding infrastructure." He tapped his chin with one forefinger. "Still, you may have a point." He nodded his head decisively. "We'll get some media up here, let them see the construction firsthand. That'll answer the propaganda question. It might boost morale as well."

Blair wanted to comment that he suspected the sight of such extravagance might, in fact, have the opposite effect with a lot of civilians.

"Admiral," Blair asked, gesturing towards the *Vesuvius*, "how *are* you doing this?"

Tolwyn pointed toward a small cluster of ships hovering near the carriers. "Those are foundry ships," he said, "mobile factories designed to travel from system to system, building the tools that planets needed to fix and upgrade their industries. I saw that they could also serve as a stopgap until we were able to restore our shipbuilding capability. So, I borrowed them." He smiled proudly. "Their output is a fraction of what Earth's was, but beggars can't be choosers."

"What about the Inner Worlds?" Blair asked. "Don't they need them?"

Tolwyn shrugged. "They're enterprising people. They'll figure something out." He looked slyly at Blair. "They might even build more for themselves."

Blair let his sarcasm show. "Wouldn't you just take those, too?"

"Probably," Tolwyn replied, taking him at face value. "I could use a few more." He tipped his chin towards the foundry ships. "They really are marvels. With them, we can produce everything we need right here on site, right down to smelting our own ore. We get some raw ore sent up from Luna, mostly specialty stuff for alloys. They boost it up using railguns. Most of the iron ore we get, though, comes from the asteroid belt out beyond Mars.

"All our mining ships have to do," Tolwyn elaborated, "is apply enough energy to knock the asteroids out of their orbits and aim them at L5. I'm told the vector mechanics are tricky and it takes the ore a couple of years to get here, but we get most of the iron we need for durasteel for a few centi-credits per ton."

He laughed. "That's why we're building here." He patted the observation port. "Occasionally, the catchers miss a piece and we have to dust it, but this old girl still has enough juice in her to do that."

Tolwyn tipped his head towards the grapefruit-sized moon. "We've also begun a reclamation project for the ships we lost at Luna. We do import a lot from out-system, but it's less than you might think." He smiled as he looked out on the ships. "I've seen to it that these two have a pretty high priority. Getting transport hulls to haul what we need isn't a problem."

Isn't a problem? Blair repeated silently. He thought of his troubles getting spare parts on Nephele. The colony world's problems seemed emblematic of the Confederation as a whole; a deteriorating economy, a worn-down infrastructure, and an exhausted population compounded the lack of trade, jobs, and confidence in the government. Taken together, they added up to a serious crisis.

It appalled him that the factory ships and the transports were being used to build warships and haul military freight rather than being used to rebuild the economy.

Blair frowned, surprised at his own internal shift. He

had no adult experience in the civilian world before his retirement, and hadn't really understood what the populace was going through to support the war. Two years grubbing in the dirt in Nephele to bring in a crop and fighting with the Farm Bureau had broadened his horizons in ways he'd never expected.

Tolwyn didn't miss the shift in his expression. "I take it you don't approve of my little project?"

Blair shook his head. "Admiral, we just finished a war—a war we were losing. We got lucky with one sucker punch, but otherwise we were on our way out." He glanced over at Tolwyn. "For what's being committed here," he paused, trying to organize his thoughts, "in terms of resources, wouldn't it have been better to build two or three new fleet carriers, or better yet—a couple of dozen jeep carriers, which you thought up in the first place?"

He saw the flicker of a smile at the intended compliment and his own response was one of feeling angry with himself for sucking up in such a manner. The problem was the jeep carrier concept had a hell of a lot of merit; they were cheap to build, and could put assets into a dozen systems for the price of one standard carrier. An old buddy of his, Bonderavsky, had risen to rear admiral at the close of the war commanding a jeep carrier task force.

"We need transports as well, sir. They could serve a dual purpose of replacing the fleet transports lost in the war while helping rebuild the economy, and a bunch of these factory ships . . . you know, to help rebuild the economy . . ." He faltered under Tolwyn's bemused glance.

"When did you become a bleeding heart, Colonel?" Tolwyn asked, his voice light. "Please remember that even with these two on-line we'll still have only two-thirds of the fighter strength we had before the attack on Earth."

"I thought the war was over," Blair said dryly.

"Don't fool yourself," Tolwyn said quietly. "We're still at war." He paused. "We're at war to save ourselves." Blair kept his expression neutral as Tolwyn continued. "We're mired in a depression, Colonel. The unity that held us together through three decades is fraying now that the Kilrathi have faded. Law and order are concepts that are crumbling throughout the Confederation. We're drifting, losing our sense of purpose."

He looked away from Blair and out the observation port. Blair saw his face reflected in the glass, framed by the two carriers. "These ships are symbols that we are, in spite of our current troubles, undiminished. They'll unite us now that we have no enemy to face."

"Are they symbols?" Blair asked, alarmed by the direction and tone of Tolwyn's words. "Or threats?"

"Colonel," Tolwyn said coldly, "you're on the edge of being insubordinate. The second you put that uniform on, you were subject to Fleet discipline."

His voice softened. "In the Kilrathi, we had a common enemy, something we could face together. Now that's gone, and we're losing touch with our common heritage." He looked at Blair. "We have to work together to restore our common faith, our unity."

Blair took the olive branch. "So, what does that have to do with me?"

"I'm sure you've heard of the crises in the Border Worlds," Tolwyn said.

"Bits and pieces," Blair answered. Then unable to resist the gibe at the continuing censorship, added, "The news services aren't as informative as they once were, however."

Tolwyn nodded, again taking Blair's comment at face value. "In the last several months, Colonel, we've suffered a series of escalating attacks. It started with pirate raids, terrorism, sabotage—all conducted by persons unknown and on a fairly small scale. It's since grown to include attacks on convoys, guerrilla raids on Confed bases, and direct attacks on isolated Confed military units. It's gotten serious enough to merit a Fleet reaction."

He looked at Blair and began ticking points off on his fingers. "Our mission is twofold. The first and most immediate mission is to protect Confederation lives and property by putting a stop to these activities. Our second task is to determine if these are random acts perpetrated by opportunists or if this is part of a larger campaign to undermine Confed authority."

Blair looked at him, his voice tinged with incredulity. "You called me back for this? A police mission? Don't you have any other pilots?"

Tolwyn clasped his hands behind his back again. "I'm sending the *Lexington* to patrol the sector adjacent to the Border Worlds and investigate the situation. I need your fame, your presence, to take some of the starch out of the raiders until we get organized. Hopefully, you'll help keep the situation under control until we can get it resolved."

"What if I decline?" Blair asked.

"I believe, Colonel," Tolwyn said without emotion, "that the Border Worlds are, at the least, turning a blind eye towards the raiders. They may actually be providing them aid and comfort, if not actively participating. I think your reputation, and by extension the implicit threat of what you did to Kilrah, will help scare them back into sanity."

He shrugged. "I won't stop you if you turn us down. You can go back to your farm and grub your rutabagas while we do the grand things. Or," he said simply, "you can join us—and maybe avert a war."

He abruptly pivoted and walked towards the door. Blair turned towards him. Tolwyn stopped at the door and looked back. "I've booked you in the Arrow simulator at 1900 hours—to get your certification up to date." He smiled thinly. "The raiders are using our equipment, so you'd better factor for that, too."

Blair turned back to the portal as Tolwyn left, studying the twin super carriers. They made him uncomfortable, though he couldn't say precisely why. He turned away from the twin ships. Tolwyn was his only route back into a cockpit, and the only life he'd ever really known. He hadn't realized how badly he'd missed it until Tolwyn had offered it to him. The decision, in the end, was easy.

He turned his back on the twin ships and started for the

combat simulators. He could, if he hurried, book extra time. A tiny voice inside told him he was going to need it.

Blair felt the familiar thump as the *Lexington*'s utility shuttle's gear hit the landing bay floor. He'd had to restrain himself from criticizing every aspect of the kid's flying ability. Face it, Chris, he said to himself, you're a lousy passenger. You'd rather fly the crates than be hauled around like freight.

The shuttle cleared the landing markers, more commonly known as the "bull's-eyes," and powered towards the embarkation area. Blair leaned forward in his spartan sling seat and watched the tell-tales over the side hatch. They flickered from red to green, indicating that the *Lexington* had restored artificial gravity and atmosphere to the landing bay.

The shuttle's internal PA, plugged into the *Lexington*'s operations frequency, scratched out "All hands, secure from recovery operations. Flight deck pressure positive. Gravity positive. Landing bay secure for normal operations." Blair listened for the real instruction that everything was fine. He smiled as it came. "The smoking lamp is lit." He was back.

The shuttle hissed to a halt just inside the embark point. He stood and swept the technical manual for the Hellcat V into his flight bag, then went forward to collect his dunnage. He turned to the side portal, spun the manual lock and keyed the opening sequence. It lifted up, leaving him flabbergasted.

A dozen Marines in dress grays formed a double row leading from the base of the shuttle's ramp. The ship's captain, a black man of average height with a receding gray hairline, stood at the end of the human corridor. A small formation of officers came to attention behind the captain while a Marine corporal, carrying the ship's commissioning pennant, grounded the oak staff with enough force for the ferrule to strike sparks on the deck. An untidy knot of thirty or forty other crew members in work uniforms stood behind the official delegation, rubbernecking.

Blair walked down the shuttle's angled ramp, stepping carefully to avoid taking an embarrassing spill. The instant his feet touched the deck a bosun raised her hand to her lips and piped him aboard. He sighed, seeing no choice but to play out the charade. He dropped his bags, came to attention, and waited for the twittering to end. He then marched smartly between the double file of Marines and halted in front of the captain. "Permission to come aboard, sir?" he asked formally.

"Granted," Captain William Eisen replied loudly, his eyes dancing with amusement. He stepped forward, his hand extended. Blair took it, exchanging a warm handshake.

Blair recalled that it had been Eisen who had met him upon his arrival on board the TCS *Victory*. "This seems like *déjà vu*," he said, "except this ship is much nicer."

"Home, sweet home," Eisen replied. "Welcome aboard, Chris." He grinned again, a fierce warrior's grimace that showed Blair what Eisen's Zulu ancestors must have looked like while they were slaughtering Englishmen. "We sure as hell need you."

Blair gave him a concerned look. "Is it as bad as all that? Tolwyn gave me the impression we'd just be showing the flag."

Eisen made a noncommittal gesture. "We'll talk."

Blair glanced at the cluster of waiting officers and crew. Their stares were making him uncomfortable. "Why are you doing this to me?" he asked, *sotto voce*.

"It's more for them than you," Eisen said softly, clapping Blair on the shoulder with his free hand. "Most have never seen a real war hero before. Knowing that you're aboard'll be good for morale." He smiled. "So play along, Colonel. That's an order."

Blair surrendered. "Okay, sir. Now what?"

"Allow me to introduce you to my senior officers," Eisen said, speaking again in a normal tone. "I'm having you meet the wing officers later." Blair shot him a look. Eisen's face was unreadable.

Eisen steered him through the formation, meeting the ship's officers, the Marine detachment commander, and a select group of the *Lexington*'s complement. He knew several officers and crew from shared tours of duty during the Kilrathi war. He was, as always, better with faces than names, but their grace in helping him remember the associations made the situation easier for everyone.

He endured the reception better than he'd expected, accepting the crew's good wishes with some aplomb, and murmuring platitudes about doing one's duty and leaving the rest up to fate and the news-vids. Eventually, they made it through the last of the handshakes and introductions. Eisen wasted no time in dismissing the crew, leaving him alone with a relieved Blair.

Eisen looked at him, his eyes glinting with mischief. "Do you remember our little bet, Colonel?"

"Which bet would that be?" Blair answered.

"The one I made you at your retirement dinner," Eisen said, grinning, "when I said you hadn't flown your last mission."

Blair rolled his eyes. "Oh, yeah, that bet. I was hoping you'd forgotten." He looked around the flight deck, noting the fresh paint and the new equipment. "The *Lexington* sure puts the old *Victory* to shame."

"Yeah," Eisen said, "you should have seen her after the Battle of Earth. The defenders kicked her out of lunar dry dock as a decoy. The Kilrathi savaged her, internal explosions gutted her, and the crew got wiped out. Normally, the hulk would have been left to drift or given an honorable end with scuttling charges, but the Fleet decided that a dead hull was better than no hull at all." He grinned. "It turned out that it would have been cheaper just to scrap what was left and start over."

He looked up at the overhead fondly, "She's the *Lady Lex*, the Grey Ghost, resurrected from the dead, the eleventh ship to bear the honorable name. Treat her right and she'll always bring you home."

"Speaking of treating you right," Blair said, "it looks like the Confed's been taking good care of you."

Eisen's expression went flat. "Yeah," he said, after a pause, "they've been taking good care of me." Eisen's non-answer piqued his curiosity.

Eisen smiled thinly. "Allow me to give you the Cook's tour of the ship. My orderly'll see your bags get to your quarters."

"All right, sir," Blair answered, still a little unsettled by Eisen's quick mood changes.

Eisen led Blair out of the embark area and towards the maintenance area. "How're your certifications?"

"I got about six hours in an Arrow simulator yesterday, enough for a provisional rating," Blair answered. "Everything else has lapsed."

Eisen chewed his lip a moment. "Well, our simulators here are on the fritz. Bad software. We'll get you checked out on our inventory tomorrow." He paused. "I want all your check-rides done as soon as possible."

He showed Blair through an open blast door and into the fighters' recovery area. There, they watched flight crews scrambling to attach and detach blue-painted dummy ordnance to Hellcats' weapons bays and underwing stores. Each crew vied with the others to finish a practice loadout while being observed by their crew chiefs. A master chief, his back to Eisen and Blair, timed the competitors and made notes on a clipboard.

Blair looked around the bay, again surprised at how clean and new it looked. "You keep a tidy ship."

Eisen glanced around, as though noticing the state of the bay for the first time. "We had a partial refit just after the armistice," he said. "We had our drives tuned and our air exchanged. The refit crews spruced the living quarters up a bit, too." He grinned, the pride in his ship shining through. "The rest is homegrown, a lot of hard work done by good people."

Eisen raised his voice. "How's the drill going, Master Chief?"

"Good," the chief said simply, "but it could be better." He turned, his seamed face breaking into a broad smile as he saw Blair. "Well, I'll be damned."

Eisen gestured towards Chris. "You two know each other?"

Blair laughed. "You might say that. Thad and I go way back."

Blair smiled at Eisen's puzzled expression. "Chief Gunderson was my crew chief during my stint with the system defense forces after the *Tiger's Claw* incident. I'd been exonerated by the court-martial but my career seemed to be pretty much over. Thad held my hand and kept me from blowing my brains out until I could get back in the game."

The old master's mate took Blair's offered hand. "That would be Master Chief Thad to you, sir."

"Congrats," Blair said, pleased at his friend's success. "What's your billet?"

"I'm the wing's chief of maintenance," Thad replied. His expression turned slightly disapproving. "On this side of the ship, anyway. It'll be good to have someone of your caliber on board."

Blair stared at him a moment, uncertain how to respond. Eisen stepped into the growing silence. "Excuse us please, Chief," he said while steering Blair away.

"What was *that* all about?" Blair said. "What did he mean by 'on this side of the ship'?"

"This ship, like every other, has its divisions," Eisen said cryptically. "But we'll get into that in a bit."

He led Blair to the small service lift that lowered them down a level to the main fighter deck. Blair felt his spirits lift as he saw the ranks of Arrows, Hellcats, Thunderbolts, and in the distance, Longbow bombers. Flight crews swarmed over the warbirds as they performed the thousands of routine maintenance tasks necessary to keep the craft operational.

"What's the wing complement?" Blair asked.

"Four squadrons," Eisen answered. "One each of light, medium, and heavy fighters, and attack bombers. We're rigged out for scout, escort, point defense, and attack."

The numbers surprised Blair. "Four squadrons? That's it? The usual complement's nine or ten."

"That, my friend, was during the war," Eisen said, smiling. "And before one of Tolwyn's sleights of hand. The Assembly went on a budget-cutting spree. They mandated the Space Force cut a third of its squadrons."

Blair winced. "Ouch."

Eisen gave him a conspiratorial wink. "Not really. The wartime strength of most squadrons was ten birds. Tolwyn reverted to the old pre-war Table of Organization, which called for sixteen fighters per squadron. He cut one third of the squadrons, all right, by transferring their birds to other squadrons. He met the Assembly's goal without sacrificing end-strength." He laughed softly. "You have to hand it to the old bastard."

"I wonder what Taggart had to say about that?" Blair asked.

"Paladin?" Eisen said, "I don't know. I do know the Assembly's Readiness Committee wasn't amused that Tolwyn stole a march on them. They told him he could keep his wings, if he cut Fleet strength. He agreed. We sent the 40 series CVs to mothballs and another eleven thousand highly trained people to the breadlines."

He scratched his cheek. "What a Pyrrhic victory. I think the Assembly wanted to make him eat crow for making them look like fools. I don't think they expected him to give in." He paused and shook his head. "I sure as hell didn't."

Blair counted on his fingers. "Four squadrons times sixteen equals sixty-four birds. You're still thirty-odd short."

"We have sixty active, actually," Eisen said, "plus spares. Our Longbow squadron is one flight short and we've detached our second Hellcat and Arrow squadrons."

Blair glanced at Eisen. "Why?"

The captain looked troubled. "We're operating all of our regular operations out of the portside bay. The starboard has been taken over by researchers, doing god-knows-what." He smiled at Blair's concerned look. "Actually, they're supposed to be evaluating pieces of Kilrathi technology for adaptation. They have fifteen or so Kilrathi fighters in various states of disassembly and a squadron or so of Thunderbolts and Hellcats that they use as test beds. It's all 'black budget' stuff. No one, not even me, is allowed over there."

Blair thought Eisen's misgivings about the situation were written all over his face. Eisen cut him off with a tiny shake of his head before he could ask any more questions. Blair shrugged, silently agreeing to let the subject drop.

He allowed Eisen to distract him by taking him over to the nearest Arrow. He liked the rakish, aggressive look of the little birds. They were nimble and responsive, fighters a pilot strapped on, rather than climbed into.

The fighter's crew chief stood and watched possessively as Blair ran his hands over the angular prow, feeling the armor's spongy surface. The ablative, conductive armor looked smooth and unpatched, an indicator the ship had never been in combat, at least not since its last refit. He inspected the twin ion cannon mounted in the Arrow's chin. Discoloration covered only the tips of the cannons' barrel shrouds, indicating that the weapons had been barely fired.

"Is the whole wing this new?"

"Yeah," Eisen replied, "pretty much. Most of our wartime birds were in pretty bad shape, so BuWeaps authorized batch replacements for all four squadrons."

"How's the wing organized?" Blair asked.

"Let's hold off a bit before we get into that," Eisen said.

Blair's internal warning sounded. He turned to face Eisen. "That's the second routine question you've brushed aside, Captain. There's something you're not telling me."

Eisen acknowledged the hit. "Let's go up to my day cabin. We need to talk."

Blair followed him towards the lift. He caught a glimpse of an odd-looking piece of equipment bolted to a portable test rack. He walked over to inspect it more closely. "Unless I miss my guess, this is a wing root from a Dralthi. What's it doing here?"

Eisen's eyes grew guarded again. He reached his hand out to pat the assembly mounted on a metal cradle. "This little jewel mounts a device that seems to channel energy directly from the main drives to the weapons. The people in the other bay have been using our diagnostic equipment on it, trying to nail down why it works."

Blair looked skeptical. Guns were generally too temperamental to handle spiking power flows that came from trying to draw directly from the engines. Capacitors acted as intermediaries on most fighters, smoothing out and delivering precisely controlled energy flows. They kept the weapons from eating a power surge that disabled them. Their major drawback was that they almost always ran out of power before the pilot ran out of targets. Blair knew the quest for a capacitor-smooth, direct-engine feed had long been a BuWeap priority.

"Do the eggheads think this gizmo is the Holy Grail, then?" he asked sarcastically.

"Well," Eisen replied uncertainly, "Tolwyn's trained monkeys seem to think so."

"Tolwyn's . . . ?" Blair asked, "The researchers aren't from BuWeaps or BuShips?"

"No," Eisen answered, "neither bureau is on board. This is one of Tolwyn's pet projects, it reports directly to him." Eisen's expression grew still. "But that's really not important."

They lapsed into silence as Eisen led him to his day cabin. He took a seat in one of Eisen's comfortable chairs, content to let Eisen guide the conversation. The captain, for his part, puttered around the wet bar.

"Do you take your whiskey neat or on the rocks?" Eisen said. He laughed at Blair's pained expression. "It's the real stuff," he said. "We pulled a shore leave at Gonwyn's Glory about three months back. The Glory is one of the largest distilleries in the Colonies. They had mountains of prime liquor stacked up and no way to move it off planet." He laughed. "The stuff was dirt cheap. I had ratings sneaking it on board in case lots." He poured a generous measure into two stone-cut glasses, then dropped a couple of ice cubes into each. "It got so bad," he continued, "that my division officers stopped doing locker inspections. They couldn't open a cupboard without finding a bottle in it."

"What did you do about the booze?" Blair asked.

Eisen shrugged. "I ignored it. Fleet regs stipulate that all ships remain dry, except during designated celebrations, or, at the captain's discretion, the lounges. I put the word out that I'd let the stashes slide as long as the crew kept the liquor discreet and all readiness reports came back double A. One failed report and I swore I'd tear the ship down from top to bottom and space every bottle on board. It's worked out pretty well."

Blair took the glass Eisen offered him, uncertain as to how to refuse. He was thoroughly sick of the petroleum waste that most people tried to pass off as scotch. Eisen raised his glass. "To the fossils who keep the Fleet running." Blair lifted his own glass, returning the toast. "And to the fossils who keep running the Fleet." Eisen laughed as he sipped his drink.

Blair sniffed the amber liquid. He received no immediate indicator the stuff was lethal. He risked a cautious sip. The whiskey flowed across his tongue like warm, liquid velvet, then washed down his throat to warm his gut. "That's good!"

"Yeah," Eisen said. He seemed to be having trouble framing his words. Blair leaned forward and took another sip while Eisen organized his thoughts.

When he spoke, it was without preamble or warning. "Chris, I want you to take over the wing."

"What!?" Blair blurted. The whiskey went down the wrong pipe, sending him into a coughing spasm. He used the respite to cover his surprise and confusion. "Tolwyn didn't say anything about that," he said finally, once he'd gotten himself under control.

"What *did* he say?" Eisen said, his expression unreadable.

"Precious little," Blair replied between coughs. "I was under the impression I'd be a supernumerary of sorts. I thought he wanted me for my looks. You know, fly a mission, show off my medals, scare the locals into behaving, and stay out of trouble. That sort of thing." He looked up at Eisen. The captain appeared unimpressed. "You want me to command your wing?" he said at last.

"Is that a problem?" Eisen asked coolly.

Blair took another sip of his whiskey. "No, not at all." He paused, uncertain as to how to proceed. "But don't you have a wing commander?"

Eisen topped off his own drink, then held the square bottle out to Blair, who consented to another generous measure. "Do you know Jesse Dunlevy?"

Blair leaned back in his seat. "Short woman. Red hair?" He waited for Eisen's nod before he continued. "We did Hellcat transition training together. She graduated first in the class."

Eisen nodded. "Well, she had a 'good' war. She ended up in cruisers—commanding a half-squadron on the *Bainbridge* as a major. Eighteen confirmed Kilrathi kills and several commendations. She made lieutenant colonel just before the Great Hate ended." He took a deep slug from his glass. "Chris, she got her second pass-over for colonel."

Blair closed his eyes, sensing what was coming next and hating it. "So, she's out?"

"Yeah," Eisen replied, "they're sending her out to traffic control on Luna on the same shuttle that brought you in." He paused and looked into his glass. "She's one of the best, Chris. I'm going to be sorry to lose her."

"So," Blair asked, "how do I fit in?"

Eisen rolled his glass in his hands. "Tolwyn's reorganization resulted in the wing commander's slot being re-rated for a full colonel." He laughed sourly at

Blair's look of disbelief. "Seriously. It was easy to consolidate the junior officers. We just cut up the affected squadrons and transferred the pilots. No one on this ship even had to trade bunks. It wasn't so easy for the command grades. I went to bed with thirty-four major and light colonel billets and woke up with sixteen. It was the worst casualty rate I'd seen since the Regnard disaster."

He shrugged as he took another drink. "Chris, a lot of majors and colonels ended up without chairs when the music stopped." He picked up a folder that had been out of Blair's sight and handed it to him. "See for yourself. I've got lieutenant colonels commanding squadrons and majors commanding flights. When I found out you were joining us, I held the wing slot open."

Blair took the folder and set it on the table, unopened. "How did Jesse react to the news I'd be her replacement?"

"About like you'd expect," Eisen said. "She took it like a pro. In a way, it was better that it was you who replaced her rather than someone else."

"How's that?" Blair asked.

"She got bumped by the 'Heart of the Tiger' himself," Eisen said bluntly. "Nobody in the Confederation can compare résumés with you. She won't lose face by being relieved by *the* preeminent hero of the Confederation. No one else could be expected to do better. Understand?"

Blair looked away, uncomfortable with Eisen's conclusions. He tried hard not to think about the woman whose career he might have accidentally ended by turning up. Eisen unknowingly twisted the knife.

"She killed the rumors about the transition before they could start," he said. "She passed the word to the pilots at a formal briefing. She made the whole thing sound like it was her idea." He tipped his glass in silent salute. Blair joined him, still uneasy about the situation. "You should have a smooth road," Eisen said, "thanks to her. The wing is trained, they have excellent morale, and they're combat ready."

He suddenly seemed to notice Blair's discomfiture.

"Chris," he said bluntly, "she was passed over twice. She was history—Standard Operating Procedure. Two strikes and you're out." Blair looked up, startled by the harshness in Eisen's voice.

He felt the alcohol seeping into his system. "Okay. When do I meet the wing?"

The captain looked at his watch. "In about ten minutes. You'd better drink up."

Blair felt overwhelmed. The whiskey in his system didn't help. "You don't screw around, do you, Captain?"

"No," Eisen replied. His voice grew a touch warmer, "And when we're here, just us fossils, you can call me Bill."

"All right," Blair answered, then after a heavy pause, "Bill."

"You'd better run along to the pilots' lounge, Chris."

Blair stood and handed his glass back to Eisen. "Aren't you going to join me . . . us?"

"No," Eisen said, "this is a wing show. I'm Fleet. I'd be out of place. This is your first chance to meet your people, and you don't need me underfoot."

"Yessir, umm, Bill," Blair replied. It occurred to him as he navigated to the door that the whiskey had gone down far too smoothly. Not an auspicious way of starting your tour, Chris, he said to himself.

The door opened on command, sparing him the embarrassment of fumbling for the manual control.

"Colonel," Eisen said from over his shoulder, "don't stay out too late. We're jumping out for the Hellespont system as soon as the task force is assembled. The operations briefing'll be at 0600 hours. I'll expect you to be there with your recommendations and any changes you want made to the flight roster."

Blair turned in the open doorway. "Will there be anything else?"

"Yes, you'll need to recalibrate your watch for our eighteen-hour ship's day." Eisen dropped the glasses into the bartop's automatic 'fresher. "I'll expect all my department heads to remain on the Alpha shift until further notice."

Blair dipped his head in acknowledgement.

Eisen met his eye. "You'd better hit the gym, Chris, the first chance you get." His expression warmed. "We like our heroes trim on the *Lexington*."

"Yes, sir," Blair said. He kept his voice light, the better to hide his embarrassment. Drunk and fat, he thought, what a stellar beginning.

The *Lexington* was the same class as the TCS *Concordia*, allowing him to find his way to the pilots' lounge without difficulty. He entered and was gratified to see that only a handful of the wing's sixty-odd fliers were present, rather than the whole wing at once. He glanced quickly around the room. Everyone present was junior, either a captain or lieutenant, except for Maniac Marshall. The major stood, a glass in one hand, holding forth to a small group of young pilots.

Marshall's voice rose above the crowd. "I'm not sure I agree with that, Lieutenant. The Holy Writ says that it's Border Worlds radicals who're causin' all this trouble. You ain't gonna challenge the Holy Writ, now are ya?"

Blair stood back against the door, watching the tableau. A fresh-faced young officer, glass in hand, shook his head. "No, sir," he replied, "my older sis served with the Border Worlds during the war, over in the Landreich sector. She used to tell me stories about how scratch-built their fighters were. The stuff we've been hitting is brand new—top of the line. It doesn't sound like the same troops."

Maniac shrugged. "Has it occurred to you, Lieutenant, that maybe they've upgraded their inventory? It sure ain't pirates carrying around that kind of firepower."

"Sir," the pilot pressed, "if it is the Border Worlds, then why take on the Confederation? We'll wipe the floor with 'em."

"I flew with them," Maniac said. "They're gutsy—sometimes suicidal."

"But why?" the lieutenant asked.

. "Maybe they just want to go their own way," a third officer offered.

Blair watched the conversation with growing alarm. Talk amongst seniors and veterans was one thing, but Maniac was doing the rookies no favors in letting them wag their tongues.

Marshall seemed to realize the same thing. "That'll be enough of that," he said. "Just obey your orders and you'll be fine. Leave policy to the politicos." He looked up, as though seeing Blair in the room for the first time. "Speaking of the devil . . ." he said.

The younger pilots turned and came to attention.

"At ease," Blair said.

He was about to walk over to the small group when he saw another familiar face in the crowd. A young lieutenant rose as he approached, a huge smile plastered over his oriental features. "Vagabond!" Blair said. "Damn, it's good to see you."

Winston Chang came around the table to shake hands with him. "Look what the solar winds blew in," Vagabond said, smiling broadly. "It'll be good to serve with you again, sir."

Blair saw the inevitable deck of cards on the table. "Still trying to clean out the universe, Lieutenant?"

Chang grinned sheepishly. "I'm working on it, sir." He paused to pick up his deck of cards. "Wanna cut cards? Loser buys the winner a drink."

Blair looked up from the cards and noted that most of the pilots who'd surrounded Maniac had gravitated towards the table. Maniac, for his part, looked irritated. Blair watched him angle towards a drink caddy and slam pieces of ice into his glass. He made a mental note to have what Tolwyn called a "come to Jesus" meeting with the major.

He put aside his concerns with Todd Marshall as Vagabond did host's duty, introducing Blair to the wing. Chang revelled in the notoriety of having flown with one of the few Confed pilots to earn a Kilrathi Hero Name. He played it up, much to Blair's amusement. Kid-vids of the war had portrayed Blair as young and lantern-jawed, diving onto Kilrah with a steely look and an urbane witticism. Chang played to that image. The younger pilots ate it up.

Blair saw a mixture of awe and reverence on their faces that made him distinctly uncomfortable. He made pleasant conversation with each in turn as Chang introduced them, exchanging bits about his past and learning their faces. The names would come later. He felt himself slipping back into comfortable old roles, evaluating strengths and weaknesses and making estimations of pilots' capabilities based on personality traits he observed. The pilots trickled in and out of the reception, some in duty uniforms, others in flight suits and utility coveralls. It was a casual mix, the sort Blair usually preferred.

He eventually broke free from the main group and angled for the bar. The barkeep, one of the pilots on relief duty, poured him a generous libation. He glanced around, feeling very much out of place. He was a fighter jock and over forty, an old man playing a young man's game. It didn't help his mood that most of the pilots were half his age, many among the first post-war classes to finish the academy and flight school.

He was pleased to see, however, that the pilots were a tight-knit group. Colonel Dunlevy had taken them well in hand, helping them cement the crucial bonds that welded them into a team. He knew he was lucky that she'd left him with so few problems. He also knew, however, that it was her team, one he would only command. He would never *be* a part of it. He felt a jolt of sadness, a quick recollection of the easy camaraderie and the feeling of truly belonging to the wing.

He realized that the situation would have been different if he'd been able to build his own wing, trained it his way. Then he'd have felt less alien, less a spectator, and more a participant.

Angel Devereaux's face floated in his memory. "You can never go back," she whispered in his mind. He winced.

She'd said that to him as he'd grown maudlin over the vagaries of the Fleet that had first brought them together, then separated them. Angel had been his lover, his friend, and his salvation on the old *Concordia*, back when Tolwyn had wanted his head on a stake. The memories of her—her smile, the warmth in her eyes, the way she looked in certain lights—hit him hard.

He recalled his last sight of her—writhing in agony in a growing pool of her own blood on the floor after being disemboweled in a public Kilrathi execution. His eyes clouded. Her death reminded him of the deaths of dozens of others—all his comrades and peers who had been killed.

Eventually, the reception ended. The senior officers waited until their juniors were done before they made their presence known. The juniors in turn knew when to make themselves scarce. The wing's leaders, the lieutenant colonels and majors who'd make or break his command, filtered in, tanked up at the bar, and joined the informal circle.

Blair learned from the command group that Colonel Dunlevy had arranged the pilots' work schedules so that they'd arrive in a trickle to the reception, rather than *en masse*. She'd also made it plain that she didn't want the troops' seniors around, thereby stealing Blair's thunder. It didn't surprise him the least little bit that Marshall had disregarded that instruction.

The wing's officers struck Blair as cool and competent. Most seemed young for their ranks, until he recalled his own time in grade. He made small talk with them, letting them feel him out. He made it quite plain that while he had definite ideas about how the wing should be run, he had no plans to make arbitrary changes just to show he was in charge.

That assertion stood him in good stead, with only a few of the squadron officers looking skeptical. Most took him at his word and began to thaw a bit, once they were confident that he wasn't going to make extra work for them.

The talks, chats, and cross-chatter began to unnerve

him after a while. The command group had been together since the *Lexington* had begun her current cruise. They'd suffered through the post-war reduction in forces, then the wing's reorganization. They were a tightly-knit group, and very fond of Colonel Dunlevy. They accepted the rules of the game, the same rules that forced her out and brought him off the bench to command them, but they didn't have to like it.

Blair realized he would have to work hard to earn their trust, harder than he would with the younger pilots. The senior officers had been in the war themselves, and so weren't overawed by his awards. They'd also been in the peace and had been carrying a lot of water for the Confederation while he'd been farming and drinking.

He found himself recharging his glass quite often as he listened to their war stories, their loose laughter. Most of the tales dealt with events that had happened after the war. Blair noted with alarm that the jargon had changed, even in the short time since he'd retired. Pilots, like all military people, evolved their own cryptic lingo—a mishmash of flight terms, service acronyms, and communications chatter. Blair was able to follow most of the new terms, but it was another reminder that he was out of touch.

He eventually made good his escape, claiming the need to prepare the next morning's brief. He snagged a bottle of Gonwyn's Glory on his way out, then navigated the half-familiar halls to his cabin.

The wing commander's quarters were enough like Jeannette Devereaux's on the *Concordia* to make him halt in the doorway in confusion. Of course, he chided himself, the *Concordia* and the *Lexington* were the same class, built from the same plans.

Nonetheless, the similarities haunted him. He collapsed in a chair very much like one Angel had in her quarters, broke the seal on the bottle, and took a deep pull. Alone, in the semi-dark, in *her* room, the ghosts came swarming back. Old faces drifted across his sight as he recalled things they'd said. Most of the faces belonged to the dead, many of the rest had been RIF'ed. He drank directly from the bottle, letting the whiskey wash over him like a tide.

Later, quite drunk, he raised his calloused hand and stared at it. It appeared to be steady. He wondered if he still had what it took to survive in combat. Or had the years away from the flight line conspired with his age and the hooch to rob him of the edge he'd always had? Was he a ghost with a service record, surviving on past glories?

He'd always counted on his reflexes being a touch faster, his instincts a little better than his opponents. He'd never met anyone faster . . . until the icy-eyed man had jacked him up against the wall. He had been too slow, for the first time in his life.

The man would have killed him if Maniac hadn't intervened. He'd never doubted his abilities before, and the realization he could be beaten hit him hard. He sat, worrying that he would fail and wind up dead. Or, worse yet, that he'd get other pilots killed because he couldn't handle the situation.

He sat long into the night, brooding. He knew his worries were a cancer that sapped his confidence and made him vulnerable. Was he becoming afraid?

His sleep, when he finally collapsed into his bed, gave him no rest.

• CHAPTER THREE

Blair walked onto the flight deck, trying to juggle his helmet, callsign list, tactical book, and flight recorder. His head still ached from his binge, in spite of the antihangover pills a sympathetic hospital corpsman had given him. Now you know why you shouldn't drink whiskey, he said to himself.

He had been fortunate that his squadron commanders were all prepared to brief him on their squadrons' readiness, saving him the need to do more than nod sagely from time to time. He just hoped his hangover cleared up before launch. Trying to fly with one was a stone bitch.

He didn't see the pilot waiting by the access door to the maintenance bay until he stepped into Blair's path.

"Sir?" the man said, startling him. Blair jumped, almost dropping his helmet. He looked the young man over, desperately trying to remember his name. The kid was one of the dozens of pilots he'd met with shiny new wings. He had trouble keeping them sorted out.

"Yes, umm, Lieutenant . . ." Blair faltered.

"Carter, sir," the lieutenant supplied helpfully, "Troy Carter. Callsign Catscratch."

"Yes, Lieutenant," Blair said as he tried to recover his composure, "what can I do for you?"

"Well, sir," Carter said enthusiastically, "I just wanted you to know how much of an honor it is for me that you picked me as your wingman." Blair didn't have the heart to tell the kid that he'd simply been at the top of the flight rotation, and that Blair hadn't given it a moment's consideration. The rookie cut him off before he could answer. "I just wanted to let you know, sir, that I won't let you down."

Blair looked at him a moment before he realized the kid expected some kind of response. "I'm sure you won't." He started to walk towards the maintenance area where crews were completing the final preflights on the ready group. Carter fell in step beside him. Blair ignored him as he tried to get the pile in his arms under control. He finally managed to dump the entire mess into his helmet. He stepped into the main bay and angled for his own bird.

Blair nodded in satisfaction. His orders to have one flight each of Arrows, Hellcats, Thunderbolts, and Longbows prepared for immediate launch had been carried out, in spite of numerous raised eyebrows from the senior squadron officers. The flight crews had worked quickly and professionally to get the fighters ready on short notice. Blair couldn't recall seeing a wartime carrier operate any more efficiently. He reminded himself that the peacetime fleet literally had the cream of the war's veterans to choose from. The *Lexington* had no excuse for inefficiency.

"Sir," Catscratch asked, interrupting his thoughts, "if you have a couple of minutes, I'd like to discuss the mission."

"It's a simple jump recon, Lieutenant," Blair replied. "What else do you want to know?"

"Well," Carter answered, "I know having a strike force in the chute is doctrine when a carrier comes out of jump. They taught us that at the Academy. Most wings just put one squadron on alert. Why'd you decide on a mixed force?"

Blair looked at him a moment, trying to decide through his thumping head whether or not to be sarcastic. He chose a straight answer. Sarcasm took too much work. "Task forces are terribly vulnerable during jump," he replied. "They can only go through the gate one at a time, and peacetime rules stipulate a five-minute interval. Most wings use a defensive philosophy, preparing their point-defense squadron to cover the task force while it gets organized." He stepped towards his own Arrow. Carter, his face intent, followed. "That'll surrender the area of space around the carrier to an enemy. You invite a strike."

He twisted his head around, trying to decide if he felt better. "The other option is to prep for a magnum launch, getting everything ready. That puts one hell of a strain on the ground crews and will eat into your sortie rate."

He shrugged. "I prefer the middle ground, enough ships for defense and a modest strike." He stopped and looked at Catscratch. "We'll launch a reconnaissance as soon as we're out of jump. In the event we find a target, then we'll launch the Hellcats and Longbows. That way we're not passive. We're lashing out, even if there's a strike inbound. In the event we do get hit, the Thunderbolts and Arrows will pull point-defense duty. Understand?"

Carter dipped his head twice, nodding quickly. "Thank you, sir," he said. Blair saw the kid's expression was one of almost reverence, as though he'd been given the secrets of the universe. Blair wanted no part of that hero worship. "These're based on wartime procedures that Captain Eisen worked out a long time ago. It's his plan, not mine."

He turned away to inspect his Arrow. Catscratch, his sense of importance touched, went towards his own fighter. Blair watched the kid through sidelong glances as Catscratch checked intakes, tugged and pulled at the slung ordnance, and inspected the safety tags that locked the weapons out while they were in the maintenance bays. The kid, Blair decided, was conscientious and diligent. Yeah, he grumped to himself, and probably also cheerful, thrifty, brave, and clean.

He climbed up the short ladder and into his cockpit, taking extra care not to bang his head on the raised canopy. That would have been an embarrassment he wasn't prepared to endure, and he wasn't entirely certain his head wouldn't fall off.

The crew chief helped him strap in, then handed him his helmet. He put it on, then plugged the interior cables into the intercom box. The helmet came alive, crackling and scratching as the headset purged the static electricity from the system. He raised one thumb, indicating he had communications. The crew chief pulled the ladder away, then moved to finish the preflight.

Blair watched her plug into the fighter's starboard diagnostics panel as he pulled out his own checklist.

"I show engines, weapons, and shields green," Blair said, checking each system in turn.

"I confirm," the crew chief replied. "I'm still getting an intermittent flutter in your portside control array, but nothing outside normal specifications."

Blair thought he detected a touch of hesitancy in the chief's voice. "Trouble?"

"No," the chief said, "it isn't enough to rate a down-check. I'll make a note in the maintenance log to run a full diagnostic as soon as the mission is over."

They ran the rest of the checklist without incident, verifying the fighter was combat ready.

"All systems green, Colonel," she intoned.

"Okay," he said, "setting guns to preheat and arming missiles." She quickly ducked under the right wing and pulled the arming clips from the missiles. Blair watched his diagnostics as the seekerheads on the infrared and IFF missiles uncaged and ran their warmup cycles. The chief stepped out from under the left wing and into his line of sight. She held her hands up, her fingers splayed for him to count the ribbons dangling from the arming pins looped around her fingers.

"I count six," she said, "two IFF, two infrared, decoy dispenser, and ejection system." He switched to his internal graphic and checked his stores load. "Correct," he replied, "all systems green."

"Okay, sir," she said, "the bird is yours." She smiled. "Try not to make too much work for me."

He allowed the ghost of a smile to cross his face. "I'll try," he answered.

She stepped back as he sealed his canopy and radioed the flight control officer. "Arrow Seven-Three-Seven, callsign Alpha Six, reports ready." Lieutenant Naismith gave him a terse acknowledgement. Blair shook his head, remembering that the Arrow's telemetry information would give the communications officer a precise readout on his status at any time he was within range. He sighed. He hoped Naismith chalked the *faux pas* to his being rusty, rather than nagging. Then again, he'd heard the comm officer had a reputation for going by the book. He might like the redundant checks.

He glanced around the maintenance bay. Cockpit canopies closed and engines began cycling as the strike group members warmed up their drives.

He looked at his chronometer, checking the time to jump. The task group would proceed through the jump point singly, with each ship running up to flank speed and entering the nexus at a slightly different angle. Fleet doctrine called for evasive maneuvers upon completing transition. The carrier's inertial dampers would mask almost all of the stresses. Blair knew he'd still feel sick and nauseated before the jump was halfway over.

He tried to distract himself by monitoring the flight wing's command and control circuits. Naismith chose that moment to run systems checks with each of Blair's strike elements.

"*Lexington* to Group Six," the comm officer said in his dry, businesslike voice. "Status?"

"Scout Six, standing by," Blair said.

He listened as Strike Six, Escort Six, and Raid Six all reported readiness. He looked around one final time, pleased by what he saw. His own four Arrow fighters were spotted first on the launch deck, ready to begin their recon of the Hellespont system as soon as the *Lexington* completed the jump. Behind them were the four Longbows of Strike Six, together with their escorting Hellcats. The four Thunderbolts of Raid Six, two armed with ship-killing torpedoes, stood off to one side. They were the ready group's reserve, capable either of launching their own smaller raid or of reinforcing the strike group.

Four other Thunderbolts, designated "Thor," stood by

as the fleet's point-defense element. That element would
remain under the control of the *Lex*'s flight officer.

Blair glanced at his watch again and saw they were less
than two minutes from the jump. He took a deep breath.
"Alpha Six to Six elements," he said, "stand by for
transition." He watched the maintenance crews flee the
bay for their quarters. Jump transition was something no
one wanted to do standing up.

The jump klaxon sounded, warning the ship's crew that
the carrier had begun its final run. Blair closed his eyes
and gritted his teeth as the *Lexington* entered the jump
point.

He felt as though he were being stretched, his molecules
spread over a dozen cubic parsecs. The feeling lasted only
a second, but seemed to go on forever. It was a frightening,
disorienting feeling. His world snapped back in place an
instant later as the *Lexington* exited the nexus, presumably
in the Hellespont system. Blair's already delicate stomach
fluttered as the *Lex* began her preprogrammed evasive
maneuvers.

"Flight control to Group Six leader," Naismith said, his
voice cool and detached, even after jump. "We're getting
a distress call. Stand by to launch and intercept."

"Roger," Blair replied, trying not to sound as frayed as
he felt. He heard the quick click as the flight boss assumed
control of the frequency.

"Arrow Seven-Three-Seven. You are first in queue. Stand
by for scramble."

Blair felt the launch cradle begin to inch forward as
it moved to the on-deck position beneath the launch rails.
He heard the rumble and roar as the launch bay's
atmosphere was evacuated. He felt the familiar anxiety
begin to grip his guts as the cradle bumped again and
began to rise. The launch elevator quickly lifted the cradle
to the staging area behind the launch bays and deposited
it on the rails. The cradle passed through the primary
force curtain and into the zero-gee, zero-atmosphere
launch bay. The deck crews, wearing pressure suits and

magnetic boots, loaded him into the tube with wartime alacrity.

"Launch Deck to Flight Control," Blair heard the duty officer report, "Seven-Three-Seven spotted on 'Cat Two. Ready for launch."

Blair braced his shoulders against the seat back and gripped the control yoke firmly. He looked up at the launch control officer in her lighted socket. She waited for his raised thumb, indicating that he was ready. She gave him a salute, then glanced down at her board. He turned his head back to the front, trying to ignore his pounding heart and dry throat. Carrier launchings were the second most dangerous non-combat operations a pilot could perform, after carrier landings. He'd almost rather face a pack of Darket light fighters than the launch bay.

"Flight control to Scout Six. Scramble."

The moment of launch took him by surprise, as always. The roar of his engines on full afterburner merged with the roar of the catapult as the Arrow leapt forward. His weight doubled and doubled again as the G forces built. He tried to inhale against the crushing weight on his chest, desperately sucking in air through tightly clenched teeth. He felt the bladders in his flight suit's legs inflate to force pooled blood back into his body. He saw stars appear ahead, at first dimly through the bay's forward force curtain, then sharply and brilliantly as Arrow 737 burst out of the bay.

The fighter's inertial dampers, freed of the *Lexington*'s floor field, snapped on. The sensation of acceleration and the extra mass vanished as the dampers compensated for the acceleration. He breathed a quick sigh of relief. He'd survived another launch.

He pulled the Arrow into a steep left-hand turn, in order to clear the *Lexington*'s bulk if his main drive failed. He recalled one hotshot on the *Tiger's Claw* who'd ignored the clearing turn, then lost his engines. The sixty-thousand-ton strike carrier hadn't left enough of the fighter to bury, much less the pilot.

The Arrow, freed of the *Lexington*'s bulk, picked up

the distress call. ". . . day. Mayday," a scratchy voice said, "this is the packet *Velden Jones*. We are a convoy under attack. Our escort has been disabled. We are under attack. May . . ." Heavy static built as jamming cut off the rest of the message. Blair switched to his own navigation plot as Naismith updated his map. The convoy's location appeared, as did an asteroid field several thousand klicks beyond.

Catscratch rocketed out of the starboard launch tube a moment later. Blair kept his lazy left-hand turn as Carter punched his afterburners to take up his station to Blair's wing. Blair kept his turn long enough for the last two fighters of Scout Six to complete launch and form up.

"We're here," one of the other Arrow pilots announced.

"Radio silence!" Blair snapped. "Form on me." He turned his fighter toward the distant fight and hit his afterburner. The loose diamond behind him followed smoothly, boosting towards the beleaguered convoy.

The formation took only a few minutes to cross open space to the stricken ships. Blair watched with a sickening feeling as convoy ship after ship faded from his tactical screen. He knew, even as he boosted his fighter to its maximum velocity, that they would be too late to save the transports. The last of them vanished from his tactical plot just as he came into extreme visual range. There was no sign of the attackers.

He led his small force into the middle of what had been the convoy. One ship detonated as they passed through, vanishing from the pilots' sight in a flare of blue-white. Blair saw several hulks, the remains of the Confed transports, drifting in macabre formation. Their blackened remains and hollowed appearances made them look like giant insect husks. One ship tumbled end over end, its drives still glowing with residual heat. Blair detected no signs of life or active energy signals from any of the ships.

The senselessness of the attack mystified and angered him. He could understand destruction as an act of war, or even comprehend raiding for booty, but this annihilation without apparent cause infuriated him. He cut his drives, easing up between a pair of blackened and destroyed ships. He then activated his gun cameras to record the remains. He wanted people to see the carnage that had been wrought.

"All right," Blair said, trying to master his emotions as he completed his recording, "the bastards can't have gone far. We'll run some fish-hook search patterns and see if we can't pick them up. If you find them, stay off the radio. One of you stays put and trails the target while the other hightails it back to the *Lady Lex* for the strike force. Questions?" He waited a moment, then called the flight's second element leader. "Varmint, assume course 040. Use your own discretion on your outbound legs, but don't wander out of the *Lex*'s range. Remember, radio silence."

He tapped his thumb on his control yoke, then aimed the Arrow away from the destroyed convoy. Catscratch followed smoothly, staying perched just off his left wing as Blair brought them onto their own search course. They boosted together, accelerating to maximum standard velocity. Blair kept one eye on his readouts, balancing his thrust and fuel consumption as the readout hovered around 520 kilometers per second. He ran out along his base course, checking his tactical scanner for any signs of the raiders.

He held course and speed for several minutes, alternately checking his scanner readouts and looking out of the cockpit for visual clues. They saw nothing on the outbound leg. He had just reached the decision to bend the search pattern back to the left and pick up another pie-wedged slice of space when he caught a momentary blip on his scanner. It flickered blue and red, as though the Arrow's computer was uncertain of the blip's identity as friend or foe. It flickered again, turned red, and vanished. Under other circumstances Blair would have ignored it as a sensor artifact. The contact had been too fleeting and uncertain for a good lock-on.

He switched to a low-powered tight-beam laser link and called Catscratch. "Did you see that?" he asked.

"See what?" Catscratch replied.

Blair would have been a lot happier if his wingman had also seen the trace. He considered a moment, then made his decision.

"I think I saw something, maybe a radio signal," he said. "It's worth checking out." He checked his nav plot, letting his voice harden. "Assume course 330 Z plus five. Kill your IFF and data telemetry systems."

"Our side won't know it's us without the IFF!" Catscratch protested.

"It'll reduce our own electronic signatures," Blair said. "Do it. And stay off the radio."

"Aye, aye, sir," Catscratch said, a touch petulantly. So much for the hero worship, Blair thought sourly.

He touched his throttle, kicking in his afterburners and boosting his speed to try and close on the ghost contact before it moved too far out of range. He also tried to keep his approach somewhat oblique, the better to stalk his quarry.

They quickly closed on the location where Blair had caught the signal. He ran several crisscrosses, hoping to pick up another trace. Nothing. The longer he ran search patterns, the more he felt he'd been chasing gremlins.

He was just beginning to feel a little silly about the whole thing when he caught another momentary blip on his scanner, again at extreme range. This time it remained steady, though on the very edge of his detection range. He brought his fighter around to center it in his scanner's inner ring.

It remained reassuringly solid, enough for him to switch to his target tracker. The red cross glowed brighter, indicating that his AI had achieved lock-on. He smiled. So much for gremlins. The target began to post a diminishing range in small numbers below the graphic. He waited for the AI to give him a target identity on the tactical scanner, then frowned as the screen remained blank. Either the fighter had no match in its inventory of ship types, or more likely, it couldn't secure enough targeting data to run a match. He was torn between trying to close the distance to get a solid identification and risking detection.

The desire for stealth won out. He switched his throttles back, to maintain their relative distances. The range to target stopped dropping. The enemy craft was still well out of visual range, but close enough to provide the targeting system with a passive signal. He smiled. He wondered what Lieutenant Carter was thinking now that his hunch had paid off.

Blair was careful to keep his distance from his target. The Arrow was a narrow, wedge-shaped ship with a small cross section and few vertical surfaces. It had the smallest scanner signature in the fleet. Blair hoped to use that to his advantage. If he was lucky he could keep his opponent just within scanner range, while depending on his smaller signature to remain invisible. That way he could remain undetected long enough for the target to lead them back to its base.

He knew he was working with a good theory, but it was one talked about more than practiced. He wondered who he was outsmarting, his enemy or himself.

He checked his speed. Four hundred kilometers per second. He frowned at the odd velocity, then checked his range. It held steady at a little over 12,000 meters. He opened his tactical book and flipped through the technical data. Neither the Longbow bomber nor its Kilrathi equivalent, the Paktahn, could sustain 400 KPS without hitting afterburners. He checked the Thunderbolt's configuration as well. The T-bolt could carry a torpedo, but couldn't maintain the speed without burners.

He tried to put himself in the enemy pilot's seat. He'd just finished his mission. It'd be time to relax and go home. If he didn't need to use afterburners to make base, then why bother? And if he did, then why use so little? The enemy (a fighter?) was moving only a few KPS faster than it should have been. The contradiction puzzled him.

He flipped through his book again. A Hellcat modified

to carry a torpedo? Or perhaps a Draltha? Either would explain the speed, but the configuration would test the frame's limits. He recalled how his experimental Excalibur had handled when he'd carried the Temblor Bomb. The weapon had reduced the nimble fighter to a space-going pig. He rubbed the Hellcat's page between two fingers. A torpedo-carrying Hellcat was possible, but it just didn't *feel* right.

He almost crowed with glee when he saw the profile of a larger ship appear on his scanner, lurking on the edge of the asteroid field. The capital ship's size suggested that it was either a fast transport or a small warship, possibly a frigate or light Kilrathi destroyer. The enemy craft bored in towards the ship, then vanished as it landed. That confirmed the ship as the enemy's base.

Bingo, he thought exultantly. He backed off his speed, enough to let the enemy mothership open up some distance. He cued his laser link. "Scratch," he said, "hit your burners and scoot back to the *Lex*. Bring the strike force here."

"How'll I find you again?" Catscratch asked.

Blair thought a moment. "I don't think we're going to wander too far. I'll keep an eye out for you." He paused. "Don't forget to turn your IFF back on, unless you want to tangle with a T-bolt."

"Roger," the rookie replied.

Blair watched Catscratch's fighter heel sharply over, then vanish as he blasted away under full afterburners. He smiled at the youngster's enthusiasm, then looked back at the target. It would be a while before Catscratch brought the strike force back. He could best use the time to do a quick recon and prepare targeting data for Dagger, Strike Six's leader.

His first step was to obtain a computer identification. He switched to targeting mode and selected the ship. He then began a long, slow loop, designed to bring him around behind it. He, like most pilots, believed that a capital ship's scanners were less efficient directly astern. Once behind it, he crept up on the target until he saw its drive plume, winking and flaring like a star in the distance. It accelerated, turning away from the asteroid field, its mission apparently complete.

Blair yawed wide to the right, far enough to get a decent profile view of the ship. The targeting computer flashed a graphic over the ship, then listed a likely class identification in the targeting box. Blair sucked air in through his teeth as it selected Caernaven frigate. The Caernavens were an older, but still serviceable class.

He flipped to the tactical book again, this time to the Caernaven's page. He wasn't surprised to learn that the Confederation had stricken the ships from active service. Many were held in reserve status or had been mothballed. Others had been sold to the Border Worlds, or, stripped of their guns and weapon systems, to private concerns. The Kilrathi had even captured a few as trophy ships. Blair ground his teeth in frustration. The Caernavens were, without a doubt, as common as dirt.

He boosted his speed a bit, to confirm the computer's ident with his own visual inspection. It looked to him like a Caernaven, except for a lozenge-shaped blister along its belly. Blair guessed the blister marked the profile of a landing bay, perhaps one large enough to handle a half-dozen strike craft. The shape of the bay nagged at him, but he couldn't dredge up the recollection.

The frigate killed the notion that the attack had been a botched raid for booty. No warship that small had enough cargo space to make a pirate raid profitable. Blair was willing to bet that whatever hold space the frigate did have was tied up in servicing the fighters. No, the objective had definitely been to kill ships.

He dropped back to extreme visual range of the frigate. He thought he caught a glimmer of motion at the front end of the frigate's launch bay. His target tracker flickered a moment, showing enemy ships for an instant. They vanished. He looked down, puzzled. Was it a sensor artifact? Some special weapon launched by the frigate?

He was drawn from the question by distant signals he guessed were from the incoming attack force. He prepared a tight-beam burst transmission reporting his findings, then squirted it in the strike force's direction.

"Tallyho," he heard in his headset, "one bogey bearing 330."

He quickly moved to turn his IFF on. "Disregard," the voice said, "it's friendly." Blair smiled at the man's disappointed tones.

He shook his head in wonder as the strike force fell into position around him. Catscratch had brought the entire group, with enough firepower for a fleet action, much less a single lousy escort ship. He paused, then realized the fault was his. He hadn't actually told the younger pilot not to bring the entire ready group. It was a less-than-auspicious beginning for his tenure as wing commander.

The rookie, oblivious to Blair's ruminations, resumed his customary wing slot.

He heard a crackling in his headphones. "Dagger to Alpha Six, that's it? One frigate?" Blair heard the disbelief in her voice. "This is going to be like hunting bunny rabbits with a fusion cannon." Her voice turned serious. "The target's a Confed class ship. Is it a confirmed?"

"Yes," Blair answered, thinking of the landing the enemy fighter had made.

"All right," Dagger said, "we're still under peacetime rules of engagement. I'll have to get firing authority from the *Lex*."

"Roger," Blair replied, "I'll give them a chance to surrender while you get clearance." He boosted ahead of the formation before he switched to a high gain radio circuit. He selected a common commercial channel to transmit.

"Unidentified frigate," he said, "this is TCS *Lexington* Strike Group Six leader, callsign Heart of the Tiger, ordering you to heave to and prepare to be boarded." He disliked using his Kilrathi hero-name but reasoned that if the raiders were Cats, it might carry more weight. No such luck. The frigate's drive plumes brightened. The ship accelerated to flank speed. Well, Blair thought sourly, so much for impressing 'em.

He cued his radio again. "Frigate, this is your final warning. I am authorized by the admiralty courts to destroy you if you do not comply with my instruction to heave to." The last was, to Blair's knowledge, a lie, but the frigate was unlikely to know that.

The ship's only response was to engage with its defensive batteries. Blair cut his speed to open up more range as three streams of red-orange lasers began to flash past.

"Well," Dagger said, "that tears it." Blair nodded in agreement, then looked down at his comm board. It registered an incoming tight-beam burst signal. Dagger was a step ahead of him in decrypting it. "Alpha Six," she said, "I have authority."

"Roger," Blair replied. "The strike is yours."

Her voice cooled as she assumed control. "Dagger to Tazman. Set up for an anvil attack on her port bow. I'll take the starboard. If she turns to evade one of us, she'll give the other a clear shot." She paused. "Let your wingmate take the first shot. As long as we've got overkill, we might as well get some practice in."

"Strike Six to Raid Six," she said, switching to the Thunderbolt leader.

"This is Troubador," the T-Bolt leader replied. "What can we do for you?"

"Skin him," Dagger said.

"No problem," Troubador replied.

Blair watched the four heavy fighters blaze ahead, their afterburners almost blinding him as they leapt to attack. The frigate immediately engaged them, firing its defensive batteries as the T-Bolts closed like a pack of lions after a gazelle. The Longbows split into two sections, each covered by a pair of Hellcats, and began to work their way around to the frigate's bows. Blair kept Catscratch close to him and flew high cover. Life was bad enough without having his strike force get jumped by another force.

Blair watched Raid Six engage the frigate. He saw the

multicolored beams arc from the noses of two Thunderbolts as they chewed into the frigate's defensive shields. The first pair peeled off, their capacitors exhausted from the high energy demands of firing all six forward weapons at once. The second pair engaged. Blair watched the shields flare as the combined fire of plasma and photon guns ripped the frigate. Blair watched the first Thunderbolts swinging around to reengage the frigate's defensive batteries. Each of the frigate's three laser turrets fell silent, battered into submission by the heavy fire.

The Thunderbolts continued to harass the ship, even after its weapons were destroyed. They swept in close, making faked passes at her and firing across its bows. The Longbows settled, two on each bow of the frigate, and came to a dead stop.

"Begin target acquisition cycle," Dagger said.

"Roger," her wingman replied.

Blair knew the process would take a half minute or so as the torpedo's tracking system defeated the frigate's electronic defenses, jamming, and phase shields.

He used the time to make a final appeal. "Heart of the Tiger to unidentified frigate. Your weapons are gone, you are defenseless. Heave to and surrender now, or you will be destroyed."

He waited. "I have signal lock-on, phase counter lock-on, warhead armed, bearings set and matched," the Longbow pilot called, forgetting his callsign in the rush of the moment.

"Engage," Dagger said.

The Longbow accelerated towards the frigate, shortening the range before firing the deadly torpedo.

"This is your last warning," Blair said.

He heard a single voice, weak and scratchy, from his earphones. "Go to hell," it said.

The Longbow suddenly swerved away from the frigate. "Torpedo away," the pilot yelled, his voice high-pitched and excited, "running hot and true. Range twenty-six hundred."

The warshot struck home a moment later, detonating

its multimegaton fusion warhead in a blue-white flash. The weapon ate into the frigate, causing an even brighter secondary explosion. When the flare cleared, Blair saw nothing of the frigate.

He tried to feel something positive, jubilation at accomplishing the mission, satisfaction at avenging the convoy, anything. Instead, he felt empty. Senseless waste compounding senseless waste. He waited a moment to let the younger pilots chatter, to allow them their moment of exultation.

"Time to go home," he said tiredly.

Blair looked over his notes as Dagger finished her portion of the after-action report. He hadn't met Major Wu Fan before he'd joined the mission, but he'd already discovered her to be a formidable woman. Her grandmotherly features and tiny frame belied the whip-sprung steel within. She was known to the squadron she served in as executive officer as "Mother." Blair thought it likely the nickname had been bestowed with as much fear as affection.

Major Fan concluded her remarks crisply, smacking the pointer in her palm for emphasis. "Longbow one-zero-one-four, commanded by Lieutenant Grigsby, fired a single Mark IV antiship torpedo. It struck the target vessel just aft of the bow strakes, destroying it. There were no survivors." She paused, concluding her remarks. "What are your questions?" She glanced at Captain Eisen, the *Lexington*'s division officers, and the wing's senior pilots. "None?" She turned towards Colonel Blair. "Sir?"

Blair stood and took the pointer. "What follows," he said to the assembled officers, "is my assessment of the attack on the convoy. I do not assert that this *is* what happened, only that this is what *might* have happened." He turned towards the wall projector behind him. "Lieutenant Carter, if you please."

Catscratch grinned from his control console. The room darkened to reveal a single dead transport floating in space. "You will note," Blair said, pointing the light at the enhanced still image of the hulk, "that whatever hit this ship blew portions of it from the inside out. You can see in this enhancement where portholes have been blown out, and have slagged back against the hull. That suggests some very high temperatures, rather than a garden variety explosion."

He switched to a second still. "The astro-navigation section did a wonderful job editing the gun camera footage, and Lieutenant Commander Garcia's intel people did the technical work." He used the pointer to indicate several holes with outward puckered metal and ejecta. "Their conclusions," Blair said, "are that the transports were hit by some kind of missile that pierced the hulls. The weapon, through some process we don't yet understand, superheated the ships' atmospheres until they ignited. The ships literally burned from the inside out, giving these transports' hulls this distinctive gutted look."

He took a deep breath, aware he was about to leap from fact to supposition. "The actual damage requirement, as compared to a Mark IV ship-killer, is very low. They only need to cook the atmosphere, not disrupt structural integrity. That may allow the weapon itself to be fairly small, certainly smaller than a ten-meter-long Mark IV torpedo."

Carter switched the still to a graphic of the action while Blair took a sip of water. "The ship I followed back from the freighters to the frigate was moving too fast to be a bomber or a torpedo-armed heavy fighter. The weapon that killed these transports might be small enough to fit on a standard missile hardpoint. That would permit medium, perhaps even light fighters, to have a ship-killing capability. That fits with the speed characteristics I witnessed."

He waited for the murmurs of disbelief to subside before he continued. "There were rumors that the Kilrathi were working on such a project for their Strakha-class stealth fighters before the war ended. This might be an outgrowth of that effort."

Eisen spoke up. "Colonel, do you believe the Kilrathi are responsible for this outrage?"

Blair shrugged his shoulders. "I don't know, sir, but it doesn't seem quite their style." He turned back to the still of the freighter, hanging dead in space. "The Cats generally ignored transports as being beneath their notice, beneath contempt. When they did hit our convoys, they usually went after the escorts. Once they'd killed those, they would usually at least make an attempt to capture or board ships. Hobbes told me it was an expression of their predatory past, the glory of taking prey back to the lair."

Blair felt a jolt of pain at the mention of his friend and ally. It still hurt to think that Hobbes had been a mere persona, a false personality overlaid on a Kilrathi agent to infiltrate the human ranks.

Eisen smiled thinly, drawing Blair back from his memories. Blair realized the *Lexington*'s captain was softballing him questions, making the briefing easier on him.

"How about pirates, then?" Eisen asked.

Blair looked at his notes. "Again, sir, the lack of any apparent attempt to board and loot seems to argue against freebooters or privateers. They plunder for resources. Destroying ships gains them nothing." He paused. "The wantonness of the destruction suggests an act of terror, or war, rather than piracy." Blair stepped away from the podium, leaving his last words hanging in the air.

Eisen stood up. "Thank you, Colonel," he said. "We'll be beginning the briefings for tomorrow's move to the Tyr system in about twenty minutes. Why doesn't everyone get a cup of coffee while we get the podium ready?"

He gestured for Blair to join him. They walked together to the coffee urn staged in the corner of the room. "You don't do things by halves, do you?" Eisen asked, chuckling. He didn't wait for Blair to answer. "The Tyr system is right on the edge of the Border Worlds. Tolwyn's made no secret that he thinks they're the culprits." He gave Blair a long look. "So let's just hope your war supposition is wrong. Otherwise, we'll be right in the thick of it, and in a nice, provocative fleet carrier."

• CHAPTER FOUR

Blair sat in the heavily padded briefing room chair, trying not to doze while the *Lexington*'s pilots assembled. He was gaining some insight into just how report-driven the peacetime Fleet had become. Training schedules, flight rotation rosters, fuel consumption reports, officer evaluations, maintenance schedules, and duty officer assignments all vied for his immediate attention. He felt that his head had barely touched his pillow before an orderly had awakened him to attend yet another briefing.

Maniac plopped down into the seat beside him, his flight suit open to the waist and a sardonic grin on his face. "Hey, Colonel, sir, I hear you had good hunting. There aren't many commanders who'd use half a wing to bag a frigate."

"One of these days, Major," Blair retorted, "that mouth of yours is going to get you in trouble."

Maniac started to answer, but was cut off by a loud "Attention on deck!" They stood as Captain Eisen entered the briefing room, flanked by a small coterie of the carrier's senior staff members. The captain walked purposefully to the lectern.

Blair guessed from his grim-faced expression that they had entered the Tyr system to do more than "show the flag."

"At ease," Eisen said. He wasted no time in waiting for the pilots to get settled before he began. "This briefing is classified Top Secret, with violations for disclosure subject to penalty under Section 12 of the Security Act." He looked up at the pilots. "Now that we're past that, I can tell you that we have been reassigned to the Tyr sector for the purpose of handling a very ticklish mission." He turned towards the wall screen as the first graphics began to flow across it.

"The TCS *Louis B. Puller*, an assault transport of the

Pelileu class, has been assigned to extract a hostage currently being held by Border Worlds forces on Tyr Seven. The hostage carries diplomatic credentials and has been seized in violation of interstellar law. Our mission is to provide top cover, ground suppression, and tactical air support to the Marine contingent assigned to pull her out."

"Her?" Maniac said softly, sniffing the air.

"Hush," Blair whispered.

Eisen ignored the byplay. "The locals have accused her of spying and intend to move her out-system to stand trial for planning acts of espionage and sabotage. Confed Psychological Operations believes they'll try to milk the situation for propaganda purposes." He looked around the room. "Questions?"

A young captain sitting in front of Blair raised her hand. "Sir, does this mean we'll be operating directly against Border Worlds forces?"

Eisen took a deep breath. Blair heard the scratching of pens on knee boards cease. The room grew deadly silent as every pilot waited for an answer. Eisen placed his hands on the lectern. "The locals are not going to appreciate us launching a raid into their territory. They may move to interdict us in their space, or they may try to stop us from taking the hostage out." He paused. "It could get hot."

Blair frowned, unhappy with Eisen's answer. "What, then, are the rules of engagement?"

Eisen looked grim. "In the event Border Worlds forces react to your presence, then you may assume they will mount an aggressive defense. Under those circumstances, the commander, Third Fleet, authorizes you to initiate fire." He looked around at the sober-faced pilots. "No hazard passes and no shots across the bow. You will fire first, and you will shoot to kill. That goes for fighters as well as ground defenses. That, people, comes directly from Admiral Petranova."

Blair saw several of the veterans exchange glum looks. Many had flown with Colonial pilots during the war, shared beers and beds with a quite a few, and had often made fast friendships. The thought of exchanging laser bolts with former comrades gave them no joy.

Blair shared their reluctance. The "shoot to kill" order troubled him more than a restrictive "defensive fire only" would have. The presence of nervous, jumpy, or glory-hungry pilots on both sides, flying in close proximity during a crisis situation, was an explosive combination by itself. The free-fire instruction could be just the spark needed to touch off a pitched battle, or just possibly, a war.

He shook his head. Great, Chris, he thought sourly, there's nothing like being an optimist.

"Well," Eisen said, unbending a little, "with that bit of cheery news, let's get down to business." He turned towards the display screen, while the pilots adjusted knee boards and notepads. The wall behind him lit up with a navigation map and a graphic of Tyr Seven. "The *Puller*," he said, using his pointer, "will use a company of Marines for the drop. They will be making a direct assault on this three-building complex, which has been code-named Orange in your briefing books. Our intelligence sources assure us that this is where the hostage is being held."

Maniac snorted and rolled his eyes in disbelief. Blair, who'd suffered through many similar assurances that turned out to be dead wrong, made no comment.

Eisen gestured towards the seated pilots. "The *Lexington* will be covering the *Puller*'s assault lander." He used his pointer to trace the path on the map. "Colonel Blair will lead a section of eight Hellcats that'll pound the ground defenses. Major Marshall will command the top cover with four Hellcats and four Arrows. The mission'll be supported by two flights of Arrows on launch stand-by. A flight of Thunderbolts'll act as the *Lexington*'s ready group."

Eisen tapped the pointer against the screen. "Our job is to buy time for the grunts, both on the bounce and after the extraction." He smiled wryly. "It figures that the Marines aren't certain which of these three buildings the hostage is in, so you'll have to give them time to work."

Blair's sense of unease grew as he considered the implications of a live suppression mission.

Eisen glanced down at him. "You look troubled, Colonel. Do you have a question?"

"Yes, sir," Blair said, feeling compelled for his pilots' sake, to ask for clarification. "All this," he asked, pitching his voice to carry, "for one diplomat? Why the rush? I mean, we could end up in a pitched battle if we, and they, aren't careful." He paused to gather his thoughts. "I mean, have the implications of this been thought through?" Blair felt the eyes of the other officers on him.

Eisen looked down at his notes. "I'd like to try and make this a clean operation, Colonel. I'm more interested in getting our diplomat out than I am in kills." He looked up at Blair. "However," he said uncomfortably, "Third Fleet seems to want this to be as much a 'chastisement' for the Colonials as a snatch-and-grab operation. They want to show they won't tolerate confining or maltreating our diplomats."

Blair traded skeptical glances with Maniac. The Confederation had hundreds of diplomatic personnel on dozens of planets in the Border Worlds sector, most of which were well out of carrier range from the frontier. He wondered if the raid would trigger reprisals against diplomatic personnel on other planets. He considered pushing the matter further, then realized that Eisen wasn't happy with the situation either.

He surrendered the point by turning his attention back to his briefing book. It included maps and diagrams of known defensive sites, the locations and types of assigned Colonial fighter craft, recommended weapon load-out configurations, building floor plans. The wealth of information available on the target far exceeded what pilots usually received, indicating an extraordinary intelligence preparation. This was no ordinary mission. He paid *very* close attention during the rest of the briefing, troubled by the possibility that this time he was not flying on the side of the angels.

The launch sequence, form-up, and the approach to the target planet went without incident, in spite of his worries. His ruminations about the mission came to a head when they entered Tyr Seven's territorial space. Four obsolete Border Worlds fighters, likely performing leg patrols, scrambled to intercept the approaching task force.

"Lynx flight to inbound craft," said the Colonial leader, "you are crowding our reserved navigation area. Back off." Blair considered himself lucky he didn't recognize the voice.

"Tallyho," Maniac replied cheerfully, "four Ferrets in two-by-two diamond formation. Alpha flight—break and attack. Beta flight—stay behind the transport with me. Alpha, execute attack plan White."

The four Arrows peeled off, blasting their afterburners to close on the four startled Ferrets. One Ferret died at once, cut apart by an Arrow's twinned ion cannon and lasers. The rest of the obsolete light fighters tried to scatter, but were out-performed by the newer, more heavily armed Arrows.

The last Ferret exploded less than a minute later. "Scratch four bogies," Maniac reported, his voice flat and professional. "Standing by to assume top cover. It's all yours, Green Leader."

Blair paused, looking at the spinning debris that marked the dead fighters. "Green Leader to Greens," he said, trying to ignore the feeling that what they were doing was wrong, "initiate target suppression."

He felt curiously detached as he watched the two flights of his section heel over on their left wings, each diving in sequence into Tyr Seven's upper atmosphere. The fighters' phase shields flared as they reacted to the thin upper reaches of the ionosphere.

He glanced to his right and saw the Marine landing craft's maneuvering thrusters glow briefly. The assault craft slowed below orbital velocity, tipped forward onto its nose, and plunged downward. Blair smiled grimly. He'd heard that riding a drop ship into combat was one of the roughest rides in the galaxy. The grunts were in for a rough trip.

He boosted his own thrust and corkscrewed his fighter into Tyr Seven's outer atmosphere. Telltales on his console began to wink as the fighter's skin heated. The Hellcat plunged downward, screaming through the thin ionosphere towards the security of the lower atmosphere. The sky above him shifted from black to blue-red and the horizon lost its rounded look. Vapor trails appeared behind the other seven ships as they bored in on the defensive sites indicated in their briefing packets.

The leading Hellcats began reeling off targeting data as they closed on their objectives. Their calm voices grew excited as they began to track inbound surface-to-air/surface-to-space Sprint missiles. Flares, chaff, and missile decoys blossomed around the diving ships. The first Sprint salvo missed cleanly, bursting amongst the trailing decoys. Blair hoped to be under the SSM's umbrella before the crews reloaded the launch rails.

He touched his throttles again, accelerating towards the ground. A blue-gray flare appeared from the woody terrain below, warning him of another missile launch. His cockpit warning chimed, alerting him to the warhead's lock-on. He wrenched the Hellcat over on its side and hit his maneuvering thrusters, accelerating his side-slip while he popped a pair of missile decoys into the space where he had been. He tumbled away from the Sprint, then increased his dive angle to recover control. The missile flashed by, looking like a white, metal-vaned pole as it passed.

He steepened his dive, watching his relative distance counter spin off numbers as it served as an altimeter. The flare cloud of the missile's launching site resolved itself into a full-fledged SSM battery, with a number of missile tractor-erector-launchers ringing a central fire control station. Blair thought the configuration looked suspiciously like a bull's-eye. He aimed his Hellcat at the center of the cluster, then switched his targeting reticule to lasers. The SSM site fired thermal and electronic missile decoys as he bored in. The self-propelled missile caisson stationed behind each TEL spat laser fire at him from their cab-

mounted automated turrets. Work crews scrambled to load
fresh missiles onto the TELs' rails. Blair found the airspace
around him growing hotter as the lasers' fire grew
increasingly accurate.

His reticule centered on the rightmost TEL. He placed
his thumb on the firing button, then withdrew it as he
remembered one of Maniac's old tricks that might allow
him to disable the site without killing anyone. He grinned
maliciously and punched his afterburners, accelerating into
a powerdive onto the Sprint site. He pulled out at the
last second, blasting over the TELs at treetop level at
something better than Mach Two.

The rolling shockwave from his sonic booms and roaring
engines scattered the Sprint crews like ninepins, shattering
windows and knocking equipment askew. Several
crewpeople lay still, while others rolled and writhed, their
hands covering their ears. One launch rail rotated and
elevated in his direction, then fired a single missile, too
far off azimuth for a lock-on.

The Hellcat raced into a narrow valley that served as
an escape route from the Sprint site. Blair glanced back
and saw small trees flying as the overpressure from the
sonic booms tore them out of the ground and scattered
them through the air. The valley slashed left and right,
narrowing quickly as he blazed down its length.

He quickly hit his braking thrusters, slowing to tactical
speeds as he pulled up slightly from the valley floor. A
second Sprint wobbled into the sky behind him, indicating
the site was still active.

He shook his head. So much for non-lethal. He pulled
his stick back, pulling the Hellcat up out of the valley and
into a half loop. A quick rightward flick on the yoke pointed
the fighter back towards the site. The Sprint crews fled
their equipment as he aligned his sights on the nearest
TEL.

Blair centered the first launcher in his sights and fired.
His lasers chopped up dirt and terrain around the exposed
hog, then plowed into the TEL and caisson. The Sprint

on the rail detonated in a blue flash as its fuel cells exploded. The blast carried away the top of the TEL's armored cab. A massive secondary explosion engulfed the vehicle a second later, shredding it. He saw the circular compression haze from the explosion's overpressure topple the unprotected caisson and rip through the adjacent TELs.

Blair used another quick Immelman to reverse course and duck back into the valley shelter. Burning rockets tumbled out of the caisson, detonating in turn and spewing burning fuel onto a second launcher. It burst into flames a moment later, its own missiles chain-detonating and expanding the inferno. High explosives added their punch, momentarily snuffing the flames and casting fuel and explosives over a broader area to reignite. The trees surrounding the site caught fire, ignited either by sprayed fuel or from the intense heat as plastics and flammable metals caught fire.

Blair took a long look at the site as he brought his Hellcat up out of valley and slowly orbited. Bodies lay strewn across the woods. The wounded, some on fire, lay writhing in the open. Many of the other crewpeople, seemingly unhurt, wandered aimlessly around the periphery of the flames or fled the inferno.

He looked at the dead, troubled by the sight of human bodies. He'd spent too long considering humans as allies for him to be easy seeing them dead by his hand, regardless of the reason.

His radio came alive with the chatter of pilots engaging targets. He listened a moment, following the course of the action. His suppression section appeared to be doing a good job of eradicating the Border Worlds defenses. Two other Sprint sites' graves were marked by plumes of ugly black smoke. Road networks, the local runway, and even the nearby town's power grid were all under attack. The assault transport paced back and forth, covered by two of Maniac's fighters, waiting for Blair's all clear to begin their attack run.

He pulled his Hellcat out of its orbit and aimed it back towards the main complex.

"Gamble to all Colors," Naismith said, his voice scratching in Blair's ears as the atmosphere weakened the *Lexington*'s signal. "Telemetry indicates all primary targets destroyed. Proceed to Phase Two."

Blair waited for the Marines and Maniac, Red and White respectively, to respond. "Green Leader," he said, "proceeding with Phase Two."

Blair switched channels to the Marines' main tactical frequency. "Green Leader to Blue Transport Five-Three-Five," he said, "defenses suppressed. Beginning landing zone prep on Objective Blue."

The transport's pilot clicked her mike twice, indicating she'd heard the transmission. The assault ship veered towards the compound. Maniac's two Hellcats hit their afterburners and blasted skyward, rising vertically on columns of thrust.

Blair's communications scanner locked on Maniac's tactical channel. "Colonel," Marshall said, "I got trouble. I got lots of Border reinforcements inbound. It looks like older stuff, Ferrets and some Rapiers. We can hold 'em, but don't waste any time. Okay?"

Blair watched as one flight of Hellcats continued their low orbits over the complex, patrolling the air against low level aggressors or ground targets. He picked up his own flight over the assault transport and led them in towards the landing zone.

The designated LZ proved to be a landing pad set between the three buildings made of reinforced thermocrete. The complex didn't look overtly military to him, but it had the universal gray, dismal look of government construction done on the cheap.

Hellcats dropped out of formation to attack the ground targets, blasting anything of even marginal military value with lasers and missiles. Blair hit two unoccupied ground-based lasers in quick succession, destroying both, then killed an unarmed atmospheric shuttle parked unobtrusively by one building. His laser bursts smacked into the shuttle and the building beyond, collapsing one corner of the structure. A giant explosion bloomed to his left front and a quick whoop of victory followed from Green Three. Flames from the burning woodline joined the dozen-odd fires and greasy-black columns that smudged the sky.

The assault transport swept through the rising smoke, banking hard towards the landing zone in the plaza between the complex's buildings. Laser fire licked out from its upper and lower turrets at likely looking hulks, clumps of vegetation, or whatever seemed the slightest bit threatening to the gunners.

Long plumes of sparks sprayed out from underneath the landing skids as the transport's pilot made a fast-in combat landing. The transport's rear ramp dropped while side doors dilated open. Door gunners sprang into operation, joining the turret gunners in hosing the walls of the surrounding buildings with heavy fire.

Blair smiled as he heard the Marines' recorded bugle call sounding the charge. He watched the first squads sprint down the ramps and take up circular positions around the ship. The grunts quickly opened fire, their laser rifles and heavy weapons joining the lander's turrets in raking the buildings' walls. Teams carrying rocket-propelled grenades deployed from the transport and fired their ordnance against the weakened structures. The heavy fire tapered off as the RPGs blew gaping holes in each of the three buildings.

Heavily-armed assault parties then streamed down the ramp and entered the damaged structures, firing their miniguns and fléchette launchers as they went. Blair's scanner locked on the Marines' frequency. He was appalled at the heavy volume of fire he heard crackling in the background as the non-coms directed their forces. The noise gave every indication that the grunts were racking up a serious body count. He hoped they didn't kill the diplomat, or the mission would fail.

"Objective Blue secured," a female voice said after what seemed like an eternity, "We're bringin' her out. She's in good shape."

Blair grinned. All they had to do was to get the hostage back on the assault transport and go home. Then it would be over.

A second Marine's voice crackled in his headset. "Objective Red secured and sterilized." Blair felt his heart flip-flop. Objective Red? What the hell's Objective Red? He flipped through his briefing book and saw no reference to an Objective Red. "Objective Gold secured," snapped a third trooper a second later, "preparing charges."

Blair tried to suppress his anger. The mission specified a single objective—freeing the diplomat. Obviously, the Marines had more in mind than a simple rescue. Eisen, he thought furiously, is going to hear about this.

He monitored the ground force's tactical channel as the Marines began to retreat towards the transport. Blair saw one cluster of grunts in haze-gray camouflage surrounding a woman in bright blue. They quickly led her on board the transport while the balance of the force pulled back to a tight perimeter.

"This is Landing Craft Five-Three-Five to Blue Leader. We got the package. Get us out of here, Colonel." Blair looked down at the landing zone as the rear guard ran up the ramp. The shuttle's hatches closed. Its idling drives spooled up, throwing clouds of concrete dust and debris across the landing area.

"Five-Three-Five to *Puller*. All present and accounted for. Casualties light. No friendly KIAs."

"Roger, Three-Five," Blair heard the *Puller* respond, "initiate mission closure." The pilot responded with two clicks on her radio. She lifted the shuttle vertically, turning it as it rose to orient onto its new course. One building slowly folded in on itself, its outer walls falling inward like a collapsed house of cards. He realized after a moment that the collapse had been caused by a demolition charge, rather than battle damage.

The assault transport flared upward, using small expendable rockets to help it achieve escape velocity. Blair assembled his four fighters tightly around it as protection from any Sprint sites that might have escaped detection.

The second flight of Hellcats formed behind them, making a dense double diamond around the transport. He switched channels to Maniac's frequency and nearly cursed as the welter of excited voices filled his ears. Marshall's forces were mired in a pitched battle just outside the planet's atmosphere. A second group of signals indicated that the *Lexington*'s ready group had already been committed to the fray and that Eisen was preparing to commit more reinforcements.

Blair's arrival with the transport redoubled the battle's intensity. The Border Worlds fighters fought bitterly, hurling themselves with reckless abandon against the Confed strike force as they attempted to pierce the defensive wall to attack the shuttle. Blair felt heartsick as his pilots burned down the obsolete fighters.

Eventually, even ferocity had to give way to firepower. The arrival of the Thunderbolts and their heavy forward armament finished the Border Worlders' attack. Most of the Colonial fighters could outrun the heavy T-bolts, but with the shuttle as their target, they had to run a crushing gauntlet. Six fighters tried and six died. The Border Worlds forces sullenly withdrew from the T-bolts' range. They continued to harass the trailing Confed ships until the *Lexington* fired a few warning shots from her defensive batteries.

Blair toted up his losses while he waited to enter the landing cycle. The wing appeared to have lost only five ships: a Thunderbolt, a Hellcat, and three Arrows. He guessed the Colonial losses at about two dozen, not counting those who would limp home but never fly again.

The *Lexington*'s search-and-rescue shuttle had launched at once to begin pilot recovery operations. Blair was gratified to see the SAR ship tractoring in both Confed and Border pilots.

The Marine transport raced towards the *Puller*, closely shadowed by Maniac's half-squadron. It landed on the *Puller's* oversize recovery deck, then was quickly tractored inside. The *Agamemnon*, a Confed heavy cruiser detailed to guard the transport, closed up quickly. The two ships, in close formation, immediately boosted away from the task force and towards the out-system jump point.

"Hellcat One-One-Three-Seven," Blair said, "request landing instructions."

"Copy, Three-Seven," flight control responded. "We show all systems green. You are first in the chute."

Blair exited his holding pattern and lined up with the rear of the portside fighter bay. He saw the distant blinking lights that marked both the runway and the edge of the bay itself.

"Three-Seven on final," Blair announced as he touched the landing configuration toggle. He checked the telltale to ensure the gear was down and locked. "Gear green."

He twitched his control yoke to the right, nudging the fighter onto the correct glide path and lining up with the landing bay. He felt the sweat bead on his forehead as he over-controlled and drifted towards the ship's drive exhaust. He nudged the throttle back to the left, slowing his velocity and pulling back onto the correct glidepath. He held his breath as the landing patch centered itself directly ahead.

"Call the beam," the flight officer said.

Blair nodded in satisfaction as the crossing network of tractor beams caught the Hellcat, causing it to buck and rock. "Roger beam," he replied. He relaxed his grip on the control yoke and cut his main drive. "Thrust zero, controls zero." He kept his hand poised over his throttle control. Tractor beams were temperamental creatures. A pilot caught short when one failed would end up embarrassed, if not dead.

"Three-Seven," the flight officer intoned, "I copy zero-zero. Your vector is good, velocity 125 KPS relative. Happy landings."

"Three-Seven to Control," Blair answered, completing the ritual, "thank you."

The computer-controlled landing system held the fighter within the beam until it was correctly positioned relative to the flight deck, then released it. Newton's Second Law took over, gliding the fighter onto the deck. The front of Blair's ship flared briefly as the static discharge from his phase shield reacted with the landing bay's force curtain.

He touched his reverse thrust as his rear landing gear made contact, slamming the front wheel onto the deck. The bay's magnetic repulsion fields snapped up, slamming him into his restraints as the Hellcat's inertial dampers were overwhelmed by the *Lexington*'s magnetic field. The interlocking internal network of tractors caught him a second later, jerking the fighter to a stop. Blair tasted blood inside his mouth, then realized he'd bitten his lip.

All in all, he was satisfied. It was his first serious combat mission and live carrier trap in two years, and both he and the ship had survived the experience intact. He licked the blood off of his lip and waited for the magnetics to disarm. They snapped off, freeing the ship to taxi to the recovery elevators.

He felt the ship's gravity a moment later, and heard the whoosh-hiss sound as air flooded the bay. He boosted his throttles slightly, just enough to give him steerage way to the elevator. He was surprised at how loud his engines sounded in the confined space.

Lieutenant Naismith's voice rang through the bay. "Secure from recovery operations. Crash crews to stand down. Captain passes to all hands a Bravo Zulu—good job, folks."

Blair waited until the fighter was safely in the recovery elevator and descending to the maintenance bay before he popped his canopy and shut off his engines. He took a deep breath of the *Lexington*'s air, tasting its dominant scents of oil, smoke, and lubricating fluids. The air, redolent of ship's odors, was somehow reassuring to him.

Maniac waited for him as the lift opened onto the

maintenance bay. He stood casually, hip-shot, with his helmet and pressure vest slung over his shoulder. "A little out of practice, aren't we?" He touched his finger to his lip, then mimed pulling away blood.

Blair held himself in check, unwilling to rise to Maniac's bait. He dabbed at his lip, wincing a little at the pain. "A little," he admitted, "but I'm sure that'll pass." Major Marshall, Blair noted wryly, might be a few chips shy of a logic board, but there was nothing wrong with his ability to land either a fighter or a cheap shot.

"Colonel," Maniac said, abruptly changing the subject, "I need to show you something." He laid his finger alongside his nose, indicating the need for secrecy, and beckoned Blair to follow him.

Blair, torn between annoyance and curiosity, removed his flight helmet and climbed out of the cockpit. He tossed his helmet to his crew chief, whose name he still hadn't learned, and walked after Maniac.

Marshall led him to his own Hellcat, then climbed the roll-away platform and into his cockpit. Blair leaned over the canopy and watched him place his helmet between his knees. Blair looked questioningly at Maniac, who responded by reaching under his console and popping the small black flight recorder out of its slot. He fished a short wire bridge out of his pocket and used the alligator clips to secure the bridge to the recorder. He plugged the assembly into his helmet speaker.

"Listen to this," Maniac said, "I picked this up while you were comin' up the gravity well. It's low band stuff, on a civilian radio. I could only hear one side of it."

Blair leaned close to listen as the tiny helmet speakers crackled and popped. ". . . no," the soft voice said, "it was definitely Confed forces . . . Hellcats. They took out all of our SSMs, SAMs and fighters . . . death toll is about sixty, so far, but we haven't started recovering casualties." Blair squeezed his eyes shut, jolted by the sudden pain. The Border Worlds had been their allies, once, and many Colonials had been his friends.

"It gets better," Maniac said. Blair leaned closer as the recording grew scratchier. "They went for the infirmary, the data core, and the holding area . . ." Static blotted out what followed ". . . they killed the medical staff, lined 'em up and shot 'em. They also got their agent out. . . . No, they blew up the records area. I don't think we're going to recover either the data files or any of the bio-weapon samples we captured. At least we got her before she could spread the stuff."

"Bio-weapons?" Blair asked. "Did he say, 'bio-weaps'?"

Marshall shrugged noncommittally and pulled a tiny spanner out of his pocket. He removed the alligator clips, then laid the spanner across the recorder's poles. Blair heard a soft "crack," and caught a whiff of ozone.

"Damn cheap black boxes," Maniac said, "they're always shorting out." He grinned slightly as he reached back under his console to replace the recorder.

"Why'd you show me this?" Blair asked.

"Just thought you ought to know," Maniac replied. Blair stood back as he made to exit the cockpit. Maniac's crew chief approached, her expression curious as she looked from one senior officer to the other. "Check the cockpit," Marshall said, his voice as smooth as glass. "I caught a whiff of burning circuits as I landed." She dipped her head as Maniac led Blair towards the pilots' debriefing area.

Blair looked at Maniac. The man was a cipher to him. They had spent nearly their entire careers together, soundly disliked each other, and yet somehow managed to work together when the need arose. Maniac had survived in combat through his sheer unpredictability, a characteristic he carried with him into the wardroom, as well as the cockpit. Blair stared at him, trying to divine the man's motivations.

Maniac stopped him just outside the debrief area. "Rumor says we're jumping into the Masa system to join the Third Fleet."

Blair felt his eyebrows arch up. "The *whole* Third Fleet? That's a lot of ships."

"Don't forget that's Tolwyn's old force." Maniac scratched his nose. "An' Petranova's a Tolwyn wanna-be. She'd kill her own mother to get a third star."

Blair looked at him a long moment, then made the decision to gamble. "This whole operation has an odd feeling about it," he said, watching Maniac for a response.

Marshall looked around, seemingly unconcerned. "Oh, how so?"

Blair pressed on. "The captain's been acting strange. I don't recall seeing him this nervous before, and his behavior at the briefing was definitely odd. I can't help but wonder what he's keeping bottled up."

"I wouldn't worry about it," Marshall said, dismissing Blair's concerns. Blair started to say more, but held his tongue when Maniac opened the door to the debriefing area.

"Shall we, Colonel?" Marshall said, effectively ending the conversation.

Blair rubbed his still damp hair as he slid in next to Maniac and the squadron commanders on the *Lexington*'s embarkation area. He glanced around, noting that all of the carrier's division and squadron officers were present. "What's up with the dog-and-pony show?" he whispered. "I was in the shower when I got the all-call."

"We got us a visitor," Maniac whispered, "a VIP shuttle inbound from the flagship." He paused. "I'm betting it's some kind of official greeting now that we've joined the Fleet. Eisen's not saying a word, but he did call for a formation." Blair swivelled his head to see the captain step from the lift and walk towards the formation. Blair thought he looked worn and drawn. *I wonder when he last slept?* Blair thought.

Eisen took his position in front of the ship's officers and faced towards the empty landing bay. He dipped his head fractionally towards Lieutenant Naismith, who stood to one side. The flight officer spoke softly into his headset. Blair watched as a single shuttle angled in towards the flight deck and made a glass-smooth landing on the furthest magnetic trap plate. He shifted his weight slightly to take the pressure off his ankles. He was loath to admit he'd fallen out of the habit of standing in formation.

The shuttle taxied towards the embarkation area.

"Atten—," Eisen said, turning his head to issue the command over his shoulder.

"Atten—," Blair echoed, along with the division officers.

"—Tion," Eisen completed. The officers and crew representatives came to attention in a rather scattershot fashion. Eisen, Blair knew, wasn't one for spit and polish when there was work to be done. He just hoped the VIP coming on board understood that, too. The *Lex*'s crew may have been one of the best in space, but their formations looked like hell.

The shuttle completed its taxi roll and stopped. The side portal opened and a solitary officer stepped out. The bosun, standing closest to the shuttle, began to pipe him aboard. Blair, his shoulders and ankles stiffening under his brace, looked sidelong at the man. The visitor was tall and athletic-looking, with Fleet captain's pips on his glove-tight dress blues. He looked to Blair to be in his mid-forties, with a stern, no-nonsense expression on his handsome face. Blair thought he looked like a holo-vid director's version of the dashing carrier skipper.

A dozen hard-eyed men and women wearing Marine powder-gray battle fatigues filed off the shuttle behind him and fanned out in a loose circle. Blair noticed that all carried wicked looking machine pistols with sound- and flash-suppressing barrel shrouds. They were the sort of weapons intended for close shipboard work— old fashioned low-velocity, heavy-caliber, bullet-firing guns.

The officer stepped up to Eisen, came to ramrod stiff attention, and snapped off a crisp salute. "Captain Hugh Paulson requesting permission to come aboard, sir," he said, his voice crisp and melodic.

"Granted, sir," Eisen replied, his own casual salute

looking sloppy by comparison, "and welcome aboard." He paused. "To what do we owe this honor?"

"I'm carrying orders from Regional Command and Commander, Third Fleet," Paulson said self-importantly.

Blair could just see the corner of Eisen's mouth twitch upward in a smile. "Those must be important orders for you to have personally carried them so far."

Captain Paulson reached into his tunic and pulled out an official-looking envelope. "All orders are important, Captain," he replied.

Eisen assumed a neutral expression. "Ahh . . . of course."

Paulson used one hand to deftly break the envelope's seal and remove the documents. He snapped the pages open and began to read in a loud, carrying voice.

"Captain William Eisen," he said, "by authority of the Commander, Third Fleet, you are hereby relieved of command of the TCS *Lexington*. By the authority of Rear Admiral Elsa Harnett of the Admiralty Court, you will consider yourself confined to quarters pending transfer to Jupiter Station. There you will undergo investigation pertaining alleged violations of the Security Acts and Section 212 of the Admiralty Court Directives."

Paulson folded the papers and extended them towards Eisen, who slowly raised his hand and took the documents. "Sir," Paulson said formally, "I relieve you."

Eisen unfolded the papers and looked down, reading the orders for himself. He raised his head, his expression unreadable. "Sir," he said softly, "I stand relieved."

Blair stood, appalled, as Paulson took a sidestep, allowing Eisen to step forward. The *Lexington*'s former captain vacated his place of command, exchanging places with Paulson. The ritual was over in a moment, yet Blair felt his whole world turn upside down. He could tell, from the quiet susurrus of whispers and the shifting behind him, that the news took the officers by unpleasant surprise as well.

Paulson turned, his cool gaze surveying the assembled officers. "I wish the circumstances of my command were different. However, I have every confidence that Captain Eisen will be cleared of the allegations and that he will return to duty soon." Paulson smiled warmly, a politician's smile. Blair noticed that his eyes remained cool and detached. "The *Lexington* is a proud ship, with a proud reputation, and I have every confidence that together we will continue to enhance that reputation."

Blair's knees were beginning to ache. He flexed them slightly, trying to restore the circulation. Eisen, he thought grimly, would have put the ship's company at ease before beginning a speech. Paulson might have missed that small piece of diplomacy, but he was mercifully brief.

"I will be hosting a reception for the division chiefs and senior officers this evening in my quarters. I trust you will all attend." He nodded for the bosun to release the formation, then walked toward the lift. The Marines formed up around him, their eyes flicking over the angry crewpeople as they passed.

Officers broke ranks and clustered around Eisen as soon as the lift doors closed. The captain seemed at once gratified and embarrassed by the support. Blair joined the queue, pressing close to extend his regrets.

Eisen looked at him. "See me later, Chris," he said, "we have to talk."

"Aye, sir," he said, and turned away from the crowd. He almost blundered into his crew chief. He tried for the dozenth time to remember her name, and failed.

"Sir," the woman said, "I finished locking down that problem on your Arrow's portside stabilizer. I'm having the bird brought up here to the landing bay so you can do a systems run before you sign off on the repairs."

Blair nodded. "Thank you . . ." he waited, hoping the woman would fill in her name for him. She didn't take the bait. "You're welcome, sir," she replied, and walked away. Blair turned away and saw Maniac looking at him.

Marshall glanced after the departing tech. "What is it with you and female crew chiefs, Colonel?" He laughed unpleasantly. "As I recall, you were hot-bunking with that grease monkey on the *Victory*, as well as that lieutenant. You seem to take the notion of women serving under you literally."

Blair made no effort to contain his anger. "That, Major," he snapped, "will be *quite* enough of that."

"I suppose," Maniac said, "but it would be nice if you'd stop playing with women who're young enough to be your daughters."

Blair felt his temper slip a notch. "You're one to talk."

Maniac gave him a lazy grin. "Well, Colonel," he said, "*I* never made a pretense of virtue." He laughed again. He glanced towards the still-open shuttle. "Paulson looks like a real stickler for the rules." He looked at Blair. "Eisen may have made allowances for your fraternizing with the troops, but I don't think Paulson will." He tapped his skull. "So, try to do your thinking up here."

He turned and walked away before Blair could mount a counterattack. Blair gritted his teeth, angry at himself for letting Maniac get under his skin. He wished spacing was still a legal punishment. Maniac, he thought acidly, was long past due for a whiff of hard vacuum.

He turned back towards the cluster around Eisen. The *Lexington*'s captain was not acting like a man who had just been relieved in disgrace. The captain laughed and joked with the assembled officers, seemingly unaffected by his ouster. Blair watched as he worked his way through the cluster of well-wishers and walked towards the personnel lift, his head held high and with a surprising spring in his step.

Blair waited a few moments for the captain to get a good head start, then followed him back to his day cabin. He paused a moment outside the door, then thumbed the door chime. Eisen, in his shirt sleeves and with a glass in his hand, opened the door to Blair's second ring.

"Come in, Chris," he said, his voice warm and casual.

Blair followed him into the main room. He hemmed and hawed, uncertain which of the dozen-odd questions he wanted to ask first. He tried a joke. "I heard you were under arrest. I umm . . . thought you'd have a guard outside."

Eisen smiled. "Actually, I did. The Marine detachment's commander rather reluctantly sent one up, a *very* unhappy corporal. I sent him down to the chow hall to get something to eat." He laughed. "The boy kept trying to apologize to me."

Blair made a polite noise, then abandoned his forced good humor. "Hell, Bill," he said angrily, "this is nonsense. You're one of the best captains in the fleet—you even wrote the Academy text on carrier ops. Now, out of the blue—you get relieved. What the hell's going on?"

Eisen shrugged, his face impassive. "Between us fossils," he said, "this wasn't a complete surprise." He turned away from Blair to examine the half-dozen holo-stills of the *Lexington* hanging on the wall. "In its own way, it's actually rather a relief."

He looked at Blair and laughed. "Sit down and close your mouth, Chris, you look like a fish." He paused to swirl the dark amber liquid in the glass. "The Confederation's changing . . . and so's the Fleet. It's not like during the war, when all you had to do was run your ship and win battles that were real battles and not headquarters maneuvering games." He drained his glass, ice cubes clinking together. "It's different now, more ambiguous." He grinned at Blair. "I like things straightforward."

Blair nodded. "I know the crew is behind you, sir. They aren't happy about the situation."

Eisen smiled. "I appreciate their concern, Chris. Tell them that the old man's going to be fine."

Blair rubbed his hands together. "So, what happens next?"

Eisen looked at his empty glass, then fished a cube of ice out of it. He crunched it, chewing it into water as he spoke. "I'll be shipping out soon. I'd like to make sure it's kept quiet. No send-offs, no teary good-byes."

Blair nodded in understanding. "Understood, sir. Will there be anything else?"

"Yes," Eisen said. He looked uncomfortable. "Captain Paulson was saved from being terribly embarrassed today," he said, "because of the tendency of combat officers *not* to wear their decorations." He waved at Blair's chest. "We've both got enough junk to cover our undershirts, as well as our tunics."

Blair nodded. He had a sinking feeling that he knew where Eisen was headed. He closed his eyes as Eisen continued. "Captain Paulson doesn't have that problem."

Blair shook his head in disbelief. "Are you telling me he has no line experience?"

"None," Eisen replied. "Nada. Zip. Zero." He rolled his glass in his hands. "Paulson's made a career out of polishing desk chairs. He was a program manager down at BuWeaps. Apparently he shepherded the Mark V torpedo and the third generation mass drivers through their development, for which he's received promotions and commendations aplenty." He smiled. "An old friend in BuPers heard some rumors Paulson was coming to relieve me. He's sending me Paulson's service record. Apparently, the guy last saw action on the *Potemkin* as a junior lieutenant."

Blair blew out his breath in surprised exasperation. "How'd he pull off staying out of the war?"

"Paulson's well connected," Eisen answered. "His family was part of the Reming-Krug weapons consortium. He kept his cushy job through looks, connections, and his willingness to play slightly dirtier politics than those around him." Eisen laughed. "He may look the part of the dashing, honorable Fleet captain, but don't let that fool you. The man is a snake."

Eisen picked up his glass. "Most of the R-Krug facilities got wiped out when the Kilrathi pasted Earth. Paulson landed on his feet. He's been doing R&D liaison work since the war."

"An armchair pilot's been given *this* ship? In this touchy situation?"

Eisen took a sip of his own drink. "Well, Chris, that

armchair pilot is now your skipper." He shrugged. "And it isn't as though we're at war right now. Paulson's got to get his ticket punched to get promoted. He needs a combat command, preferably one with an enemy body count. This little fracas isn't much," Eisen concluded, sounding a little sad, "but it's the only war we've got right now."

Blair snarled an oath.

Eisen looked up at him, his expression unreadable. "I take it you don't approve."

Blair gave him a long look, then elected for complete candor. "No, sir, I don't like it. Not one damn bit. This whole mission stinks."

Eisen stepped over to the wet bar and poured Blair a generous drink. He poised the bottle over his own empty glass, paused, then refilled it halfway. "Go on."

Blair set his glass on the end table by his chair and rubbed his hands together. "Everything I've seen since I got involved in this is supposed to point towards the Border Worlds." He took a deep breath, uncertain as to how to make his case. "It doesn't wash. I mean, the Colonies were our allies during the war. They were loyal. Many of the best people in the Fleet were Border Worlders. Remember it was Kruger and the Landreich Sector Fleet that pulled the flanking action which helped save Earth. Gutsy fliers. Hell, I'd fly with them any day."

Blair noticed Eisen's eyebrow arc up. "Past performance is no guarantee of future performance. You should know that."

"Speaking of past performance," Blair continued, "none of the Border Worlds ever signed the Articles of Confederation. Technically, they're sovereign nations— free to do as they please."

Eisen smiled. "Well, the fact that they accepted regular commissions in our Fleet and permitted themselves to be fully integrated into our supply network argues otherwise. They acted as though they were members of the Confederation, and that was enough. The fact that they never signed the Articles of Confederation becomes a moot point." He paused to take a sip of whiskey. "Consider it to be the diplomatic equivalent of the common-law marriage."

He looked at Blair. "When viewed from that standpoint, the Articles become a minor technicality, one of those little details that got overlooked during the war."

Blair shook his head. "Since when did the constitutional issues become a 'detail'? As I understand it, they didn't sign the Articles, so they aren't bound by them."

"The Confederation can play it either way," Eisen answered, "it can count the Border Worlds as renegade provinces, and move to put down the rebellion, or it can agree that the Colonies are free and independent, and therefore responsible for the raids. They can then claim Colonial aggression and go to war. Either way, the Border Worlds get screwed."

"All I know," Blair said stubbornly, "is that this whole thing seems fundamentally wrong. The frigate we hit at Hellespont could have been Border Worlds, or maybe not. Caernavens're as common as dirt. The Tyr raid was . . ." He paused, uncertain about what to say about Maniac's recording. He couldn't prove the conversation had happened, and had no desire to discuss what he'd heard about biological weapons without hard evidence. ". . . full of hidden agendas. The operation those Marines ran was *not* in my briefing book." He stopped, surprised at how angry he sounded. He took another sip as he tried to calm himself.

Eisen looked at him thoughtfully, then smiled. "Everybody has an agenda, Chris. We all have to decide which ones we can live with." He stretched his shoulders. "Pretty soon we'll all have to choose."

Blair, troubled and upset, looked at Eisen.

"You'd better go," Eisen said, "you don't want to be late to Paulson's little party."

Blair laughed. "Ha!" he replied dryly, "I'm underwhelmed. I'm going to inspect some repairs to my Arrow."

Eisen escorted him to the door. "I don't know how long

I'll be on board, Chris," he said, "but as long as I am, my door is open." They shook hands warmly. "Colonel, it's been a privilege to command you."

Blair released his hand. "I'll drop by later, sir."

This good man was a prisoner on the ship he had commanded less than an hour ago. That thought continued to nag at Chris as he departed Eisen's day cabin for the landing bay.

Seether angled the long-range shuttle towards the *Lexington*. The copilot, who was actually the shuttle's regular pilot, watched him work the controls with the attentiveness of a jealous lover. Seether couldn't fault him for his attitude. He, like most pilots, hated to sit and watch someone else fly. That was doubly true when the observer was the one who'd actually signed for the bird.

He made a few lazy loops while waiting for permission from the flight officer to enter the landing cycle. The brief delay gave him the opportunity to mull over just how they'd gotten themselves into their current mess with Captain Eisen.

The *Lexington's* former commander should have been easy to recruit. His personality was a perfect match with PsyOps' profile. He was a decorated combat veteran with a reputation for doing what was needed, no matter how grim. The process of coaxing him into the project should have been, in Seether's opinion, a straightforward affair— just show him the imperative and leave him alone to draw his own conclusions.

Seether wasn't the only one who had thought Eisen would be a sure thing. The old man had been so certain he would join "The Project" that he'd arranged for Eisen to take command of the *Lexington* before securing his allegiance. In hindsight, that had been a grave mistake, one of the very few the old man had made.

Seether didn't know what had gone wrong, but suspected that the recruitment had been botched from the outset. He guessed that the so-called experts had tried some kind of complicated mind game when all that was called for was some soldierly common sense. Their initial approaches had either been rebuffed or ignored and Eisen's closely monitored communications had quickly shown that he would not, could not, support their cause.

Eisen's rejection had come as a nasty surprise, and had left them scrambling to cover for his sudden liability. The *Lexington* was simply too critical to The Project's success to be commanded by a non-believer. Her captain had to be one of them, body and soul. Eisen wasn't, and therefore had to be replaced as quickly as possible.

Paulson's only advantages were that he had the nominal command rank needed for the *Lexington*, that he had been a member of The Project from the time the Kilrathi had reduced the majority of his family's factories to smoking, irradiated glass, and that he was available. Paulson had lobbied incessantly for a command that would secure his promotion to rear admiral. Seether shook his head. The pimple had simply been at the right place at the right time when Eisen's head had gone on the chopping block.

He was less than amused that the higher-ups had chosen to overlook the fact that Paulson wasn't fit to command the ship. He had neither the temperament nor the experience. Seether's loud complaints against his assignment had produced one unexpected and unpleasant outcome. He'd been assigned to baby-sit the bastard— never mind that his own tasks had to be put on hold and his schedule disrupted. Still, orders were orders.

Seether wondered if the higher-ups realized that the decision to cashier a commander as famous and popular as Eisen was bound to be problematic. Harnett's Admiralty Court could be counted upon to provide a convincing trial and an appropriate verdict. Unfortunately, convicting Eisen couldn't be done quietly unless he was willing to permit it. Seether doubted they'd be lucky enough for Eisen to agree to throw himself on his sword for the greater good.

Eisen had friends in high places who wouldn't be pleased to see him cashiered. They were bound to make trouble, and would certainly mount a vigorous defense on his behalf. They would doubtless bring attention to the circumstances of his relief and perhaps provide him with a venue to tell his side of the story. The Project couldn't risk that kind of exposure.

Seether rubbed his hand across his chin. The best way to ensure Eisen kept his mouth shut was to close it permanently, a prospect as unsavory as it was necessary. It would be unfortunate for a man of Eisen's tremendous talents to die, but it would tie up several loose ends at once. The trick would be to make the man's death look like an accident.

He glanced at his watch. Paulson would have to approve Eisen's use of a *Lexington* shuttle to take him to the *Euralius* for transport back to Jupiter and Judge Harnett. Seether would need to know which shuttle Paulson was going to approve in order to arrange the "accident." The timing would likely be dicey, but at least he didn't need approval from on high. His orders would bend that far.

The thought of having to depend on Paulson for even the smallest thing galled him. The captain had doubtless received his summons to report to the landing bay, but there was no way he would know he was being assigned a keeper. Seether grinned tightly. Paulson, who apparently thought he was actually going to command the vessel, was about to have what the old man called a "come to Jesus" meeting with Seether. Paulson, he thought maliciously, wasn't going to like it.

He received the "landing approved" signal from Naismith, lined the ship up with the flight deck, and brought the shuttle smoothly into the *Lexington*'s bay. He wasted no motions, using precise finger pressures on the control yoke to flare the ugly little ship into a crisp three-point landing. The magnetic floor plates grabbed the shuttle, bringing it into contact with the center of the bull's-eye with a sharp clang.

He smiled, permitting himself a small indulgence. The *Lexington* was one of his favorite warships. She was the last of a long line of proud vessels to bear the hallowed name, a veteran who'd given her life and her crew to defend Earth. He had been pleased to be at her recommissioning and watch her rising, phoenixlike, from her ashes to resume her rightful place at the forefront of Earth's thinned defenses.

He looked up at the awards painted on the shuttle bay's crash bulkhead and smiled. The battle honors went all the way back to when she was sailing the blue seas of Earth rather than the blackness of space. The *Lex*, truly a lady, bore her honorable scars well. He silently asked forgiveness for inflicting Paulson on her.

The landing tell-tales winked green, advising him that the flight deck officer had released his ship from the powerful magnetics. He steered for the embarkation ramp to await Paulson's arrival.

He saw one of the Third Fleet's posh VIP craft standing ready on the far side of the recovery maintenance bay. He shook his head fractionally, the only evidence of his disapproval. He suspected that the Fleet would have had an easier time maintaining its fighting edge if the brass hats were forced to fly in standard shuttles, with their uncomfortable sling seats and exposed conduits, rather than the winged sofas they preferred. It would figure that Paulson would have one of *those*.

A contingent of Marines entered the landing bay and spread out, each clearing a section of the landing deck and herding the last of the crew out the doors. He laughed, deep in his throat. Paulson had obeyed his instructions to the letter. Perhaps he can be taught, he thought sarcastically.

He slipped out of the pilot's seat and into the spartan passenger compartment. The six newest members of the *Lexington*'s detachment waited, sitting erect and unmoving in the shuttle's uncomfortable sling seats. Six sets of cool brown eyes turned to regard him. "Stand by," Seether said as he crossed to the shuttle's side hatch. The pilots, their expressions neutral and dispassionate, nodded as one.

He unsealed the hatch and stepped into the open door, yawning to equalize the pressure in his ears with the ship's atmosphere. Paulson stood waiting on the deck with two guards at his back. Seether was willing to bet they were armed.

"T-t-to what do we owe this pleasure?" Paulson said, trying and failing to act casual. Seether smiled to himself. The captain's being nervous was a very good thing. It kept him honest.

He crooked a finger at Paulson, summoning him into the shuttle. The *Lexington*'s putative commander followed, blinking in the sudden gloom as he entered the shuttle. Seether turned towards him and reached into his tunic. Paulson tensed until he saw the data holo-cube in Seether's hand. Seether, pleased at his ability to instill fear into the man, handed him the cube. "You'll find this contains mission details and instructions from the old man." He paused, making certain he had Paulson's undivided attention. "I have been assigned to command the *Lexington*'s detachment, for the time being. You will obey my orders from now on, completely and without question. Do you understand?"

His blunt words startled Paulson out of his nervousness. "Now, wait a second," the captain protested, "*I* command the *Lexington*!"

Seether found himself tiring of the situation. Paulson was nothing more than a parasite who had used his access to "black funds" to buy influence. The vague accounting within the super-secret funding process let him funnel huge amounts of resources, personnel, and money to The Project, sidestepping Fleet comptrollers and government auditors. His ability to be devious had served The Project well. However, he was no longer in a position to tap that river of money. That made him expendable.

The rumor mill said that the old man himself had gone to Paulson, hat in hand, when he needed discreet funding. Paulson had doubtless called in those markers, setting a rear admiralcy as his payoff. It galled him to watch Paulson using the *Lexington* to punch a ticket. The *Lex* deserved better.

He looked up at the captain. Any tiny inclination towards tact vanished. "You may command this ship," he said coldly, "but I command *you*. As though I were the old man himself. Do you understand?"

Paulson nodded silently, then looked away. He seemed to notice the six men in their black flight suits for the first time. "Who're they?" he asked.

Seether tipped his head to one side. "*They*," he said quietly, "are none of your business. You will list them on your crew roster as part of the technology assessment team." He let his voice grow condescending, trying to coax Paulson into a reaction. "All you need to know is that they will work for me, and me alone. You will not put them on your duty roster. You will forget you saw them."

Paulson looked as though he was going to make an issue of being lectured. He looked defiant a moment, then seemed to collapse in on himself. He licked his lips and dipped his head. "All right," he said simply.

Seether felt his contempt for Paulson increase a notch. The man hadn't even the juice to stand up for himself. "You may leave now," he said, making no effort to hide his disgust. Paulson set his jaw, then turned away. "Remember," Seether said as he stepped out of the shuttle, "you take your orders from me."

Seether glanced at the six. They might have been made of stone for all the reaction they showed. "Let's go, people," he said, "we have work to do."

Blair closed the Arrow's canopy and checked the repair printout. The crew had replaced the entire starboard attitude modulation sensor and control unit. He clicked his tongue against his teeth. Replacing a modulation assembly was a second echelon maintenance task and usually done in a repair facility. He wished he knew more about his crew chief. Then he wouldn't have to second-guess her abilities.

His instincts told him to deadline the bird until he could get a second opinion on the repairs. He knew the crew chief would correctly interpret that as a lack of confidence in her abilities, thereby killing any chance of establishing the kind of rapport they would need to have to work together.

He'd originally planned to run a quick diagnostic before signing off on the repairs. Now, his best interests were to run the full inspection program and hope that gave him enough information to decide on whether to down-check the bird.

He looked at his watch. A full diagnostic would take almost half an hour, long enough to make him late for the reception. Paulson appeared to be a stickler for trivia. He would doubtless be unimpressed with a wing commander who showed up late to his party. He sighed. Why couldn't anything be simple?

He flipped a mental coin. Paulson lost. He brought the fighter's command system up, borrowing power from the auxiliary power unit. The cockpit readouts flickered and stabilized as the APU came on-line. He cued the system into its diagnostic mode, ordered a full internal inspection, and settled back to wait while the ship's computer poked and prodded every on-board circuit, system, and connection.

He closed his eyes to rest while the Arrow clicked and hummed to itself. He'd been short on sleep, and was finding himself falling back into the pilots' habit of catnapping whenever the opportunity presented itself.

The flight deck's alarm klaxon sounded, the tones pitched to cut through massed fighter engines and the clamor of the recovery deck. He sat bolt-upright, his heart pounding in his chest. The evacuation strobes began to flash and the deck's "Zero-atmosphere" warning lights winked amber. "Warning!" a computer voice announced, "Zero-gee operations to commence in two minutes. All non-essential personnel evacuate the recovery deck. Warning! Two minutes to zero-gee."

Blair watched the work crews streaming for the exits. He knew that zero-air, zero-gee operations were the norm when recovering fighters, but to the best of his recollection all of the *Lexington's* birds were on board. He looked down at his console. Regulations called for him to evacuate the bay during zero-air. That would require him to abort the test cycle and start over. He had no desire to do that.

He glanced around and saw the last of the recovery deck crews passing through the access hatches. No one remained in sight. He checked his canopy, making certain it was airtight, then hunkered down to hide from the safety team. Their job would be to sweep the recovery deck and ensure no one lingered without a pressure suit.

The personnel lift door opened. Blair expected to see crash crews in pressure suits emerge. Instead, Paulson stepped out from the personnel lift with two armed Marines at his back. Blair's mouth went dry as he realized the grunts were from the dozen that Paulson had brought on board, rather than from the *Lexington's* own contingent.

Paulson's pet Marines swept the bay. He caught a quick glimpse of one of the team members as she skirted the edge of the ordnance-stripping area. The woman wore Marine gray instead of the safety crews' bright orange. She shifted to one side, peering down into the wells that housed the missile defusers. Blair saw she wore a sidearm, a nasty looking M-42 machine pistol. Whatever the hell was going on in the landing bay didn't involve recovering fighters.

The guard commander signalled the all clear. The grunts jogged towards the personnel hatches and rammed gauging spikes into the handwheels, blocking them. Blair blinked, surprised at the flagrant violation of standing orders. Sealing fire doors was a court-martial offense and a damned stupid thing to do.

The automatic strobes marking the center of the approach lanes began to flash. A shuttle, one of the new jump-capable, long-range jobs, passed through the curtain and landed crisply in the center of the middle bull's-eye.

Blair whistled silently. Landing a pigboat that smoothly required a lot of skill. The pilot was good.

Paulson walked towards the shuttle. The ship's side hatch opened and a compact man in a black flight suit leaned out. Blair felt the hairs prickle on the back of his neck as he recognized the pilot who had almost killed him in the bar. He racked his brains a moment before he could match a name to the face. He focused on the remembered image of the man's name tag. Seether.

"What the hell?" Blair whispered. His sense of alarm grew stronger as he watched Seether crook his finger at the visibly nervous Paulson. The *Lexington's* captain meekly obeyed, following the black-suited pilot back into the shuttle. They emerged a few minutes later, followed by a group of a half-dozen pilots wearing black flight suits and carrying flight bags. Blair noticed that all of the pilots were about Seether's height, and nearly identical in appearance and build.

The pilots trooped into the personnel lift. The jump shuttle pivoted on the landing circle and took off, passing through the force curtain as it launched off the recovery deck's rearward facing ramp. Paulson's Marines waited for the shuttle to clear the bay before they removed their gauging spikes from the hatches, permitting the dogging wheels to spin freely. They withdrew, surrendering the deck to the perplexed and angry-looking deck crews that began to wander in the open doors.

Blair waited a few more minutes for the grunts to clear out, and the flight deck to return to something like normal before he popped the Arrow's canopy and climbed out.

He stepped down onto the ground, using the Arrow's retractable ladder. A single guard in powder gray stepped out from behind the Arrow next to Blair's. Blair wasn't certain which of them looked more surprised. He met her eye as his feet hit the metal decking, exchanged a quick nod, and brushed past her towards the exit.

He cleared the flight deck, expecting at any moment to hear the guard shout or an alarm sound. He took the lift to the senior officers quarters with the intention of making a beeline for Eisen's quarters. He paused, reconsidering. Eisen was a prisoner. His wings were clipped and he was being monitored. There was little he could do.

Maniac, he thought glumly, was the only officer on board with sufficient rank to be useful and whom he knew well enough to take into his confidence. He walked to Marshall's quarters and entered without knocking. It wasn't until a second after he stepped through the door that he recalled that Maniac slept with an armed hand laser under his pillow.

Marshall looked up from his computer terminal. Over his uniform trousers, he wore a loud Hawaiian-style shirt that looked like the precise color of a hangover.

"To what do I owe the pleasure, Colonel?" he asked in a voice that sounded like a mix of amusement and annoyance.

Blair saw no choice but to plunge ahead. He described his experiences on the flight deck. Marshall swore loudly when Blair told him that Seether was on board the *Lexington*.

"You're absolutely certain it's the same man?" Maniac asked.

"Yes," Blair answered. "Why?"

Marshall smiled contentedly. "What a coincidence. Do you remember Corinne?"

Blair thought a moment. "Cute redhead," he asked, "used to work in the comptroller's office?"

"The same," Marshall replied with a tomcat's grin. "She's in charge of the *Euralius'* personnel section." He leaned back in his chair. "I was chatting her up earlier and mentioned your little fracas back on Nephele. She remembered Seether's name from somewhere. She said she'd use her access to look into it."

"And?" Blair asked impatiently.

"She passed me some tidbits about Mr. Seether," Maniac said.

"Such as?"

"Nothing much," Maniac replied with shrug, "just some training records and pilot certification updates for Seether and eight others. Their check-rides were all done while they belonged to a unit titled only '212.' Corinne remembered that '212' was some kind of classified special operations team formed at the end of the war for reasons unknown. She said that the program has retained its funding, even though the war's over. She said she'd try and find out what it was supposed to do."

"And?" Blair asked.

"I'm supposed to call her back." He raised one eyebrow. "You want to listen in while I find out what she's learned?"

Blair settled into a chair and made a "go ahead" motion with his hand.

Maniac activated his holo-tank, then keyed in the access number. The screen fuzzed and cleared to reveal a hatchet-faced woman in a security uniform and a buzz cut.

"Umm," Maniac asked, "where is Lieutenant Commander Hartely?"

The woman looked hard at him, as though memorizing every feature. "Major Marshall, is it?" she asked harshly, "Hartely's been relieved of duty, pending investigation. Can I help you?"

"No," Maniac said, "I was just calling on an old friend . . ."

The screen went blank. Maniac spun in his chair. "She cut me off! What's going on here?"

"I wish I knew," Blair replied.

"Well," Maniac said, still angry, "at the rate things are going, I'd say that pretty soon we're all going to have to figure out whether we're going to stand for this kind of nonsense."

Blair opened his mouth to answer when the ship's alarm klaxon sounded. Lieutenant Naismith's voice boomed over the loudhailer. "All hands to general quarters! Ready group to launch tubes! This is not a drill!"

"What the hell?" Blair demanded.

Maniac looked at him. "Would you care to join me, Colonel?" he asked, "I've got the ready group this week and I know you need the flight hours." He grinned, his earlier troubled expression slipping away. "Besides, I know how rusty you are."

"Thanks," Blair answered drily, "I'd be delighted."

• CHAPTER FIVE

Blair settled in the Hellcat's cockpit and snapped his helmet on. Maniac kissed the side of his fighter before climbing the short ladder and leaping inside. Blair rolled his eyes. Marshall's rituals were known throughout the Fleet.

He laughed to himself as he plugged his helmet into the console and cued his comm-panel to Lieutenant Naismith's flight control center. "What's the mission?" he heard Maniac ask, his voice all business. Blair had to remind himself that he was merely an observer and that the ready group was Marshall's to command. He had often used the observer loophole on board the *Victory* to fly in the wing slot so he could rate his subordinates' combat abilities. It served here to preserve Maniac as the commander of record for promotion purposes.

He was surprised when Paulson cut into Naismith's frequency. "Major," Paulson said, "we've got a critical situation on our hands. Captain Eisen has stolen a shuttle and fled the *Lexington*."

"*What?*" Marshall snapped, forgetting all discipline. "Would you repeat that?" Maniac said, after a moment.

"Eisen has jumped ship," Paulson repeated. "You are to bring him back."

"What if he won't come back?" Maniac asked.

"Then you are to destroy the shuttle," Paulson said simply, "by any means necessary."

Blair looked at Maniac. Marshall's expression of disbelief matched his. "You can't be serious," Maniac snapped.

"I'm very serious, Major," Paulson replied, his voice growing angry. "You have your orders. You are to terminate him with extreme prejudice if he doesn't return at once."

Blair shook his head. Terminate with extreme prejudice? That was the kind of language normally reserved for the holo-vids, not for real life. What the hell was Paulson playing at?

"Execute your orders, Major," Paulson said. "Now."

"Aye, aye, sir," Maniac said skeptically. "Ready Group Four prep for launch."

Naismith came on the net, his voice carefully neutral. "Roger, Cobra Leader. Stand by for ready group scramble on base course two-twelve Z plus ten. Your target is *Lexington* shuttle Oh-One-Four. Commence launch operations in three-zero seconds."

"I copy target as Zero-One-Four," Maniac repeated. "Ready for launch." Blair heard him mutter under his breath. "I wouldn't want to blow up the wrong shuttle."

Blair was fifth in the chute of eight ships, giving him plenty of time to brood. He knew Eisen faced charges in the Admiralty Court, but hadn't taken them seriously. Judge Harnett's court job during the war was keeping civilian shipping in line. Blair considered it a joke—a home for wayward admirals who were kept busy by issuing fines and stern lectures to ship owners. Its authority had rarely been extended to serving officers.

The captain had been the darling of the press after the attack on Kilrah. Blair was certain Harnett would never actually put him through a trial for fear of the political repercussions.

Besides, Blair told himself, Judge Harnett and Eisen were both Fleet. The Fleet looked after its own. Nothing would happen, even if Eisen was guilty. The Fleet hated the embarrassment of showing its dirty laundry, and as a consequence often covered for the stupid and the incompetent. Eisen had to know the political factors swung too strongly in his direction for him to be seriously worried.

So why jump ship? That thought nagged at Blair as his launch cradle hurtled him down the tube and out into space. He formed on Maniac's wing as the squadron commander's voice crackled in his headset. "Cobra Leader to Cobra Four, form on me. Assume course two-one-two, speed 700 KPS on afterburners."

The fighters locked into formation and boosted towards the fleeing shuttle. Blair chewed his lip, wondering what Maniac would do once they got to the scene. He could, in theory, override any order Marshall gave. Such an action would leave him subject to professional protest. He was, after all, supposed to be an observer.

He saw a blue dot appear at extreme range. Blair switched to his targeting system and locked onto the shuttle. He watched the range steadily diminish as they overtook the slower ship.

"Cobra Leader to Eisen, please respond."

"I'm here, Maniac," Eisen answered at once. He sounded jaunty to Blair, as though he hadn't a care in the universe. "Maniac, remember that old drink you introduced me to? What was it called? Blue Two, wasn't it?"

Blair frowned. Eisen was telling them to switch to an old scrambler channel they had used on the *Victory*. Eisen's request to use a non-standard frequency would land Maniac and himself in hot water once they got back on the *Lexington* if Paulson figured out what they were doing. Maniac paused, apparently also torn over whether to comply.

"Great drink," Blair said, taking the bull by the horns. "Wish we had one now." He had to manually key in the frequency, then lock in a non-standard scrambler pattern. Maniac followed a second later, his voice sounding hollow as it ran through the scrambler.

"What th' hell are you doin', Cap'n?" Maniac demanded.

"Well," Eisen replied, "it's pretty obvious that I'm not out here for my health. Not with you yahoos gunning for me."

Blair scratched his forehead in disbelief. Eisen sounded far too relaxed considering the seriousness of the situation. "Then, why are you out here, sir?" Blair asked.

"I'd have thought that was pretty obvious, Colonel," Eisen

answered, "I'm defecting." He paused. "Chris, Todd, it's something you should give serious thought to as well."

"This is insane," Blair answered, "why are you doing this?"

"I don't have any choice," Eisen answered, "but I have my reasons—good ones, I assure you."

"What reasons?" Blair pressed.

"Sorry, Chris," Eisen answered, "I can't go into that now. I can't be certain how secure this channel is."

"What do you care?" Maniac injected. "You've already gone over the wall."

"What I know is too damned explosive to transmit where anyone with a recorder and a decrypter can hear it."

Blair tried to suppress his confusion and outrage. "Cap," he said, "you can't expect us to take all this on faith."

"Actually, Chris," Eisen replied, "that's exactly what I'm expecting. We've known each other a long time. Do you really believe I'd ask you to turn your coat without having good reason?"

Blair felt ill. "I've served the Confederation for twenty years," he said, "regardless of what it's cost me." He thought of Jeannette Devereaux and felt the old grief well up. He shook his head, trying to force down the welter of emotions within him. "Captain . . . Bill," he cajoled, "come on back. Let's get this sorted out."

"Sorry, Chris," Eisen said, "no can do. Given what I know, and what I've found out, I'd never make it to trial. I bet Paulson ordered you to bring me in 'dead or alive,' didn't he?"

Blair winced, embarrassed to reply.

"What I figured. I jumped because I had to if I want the truth known. I stand as much chance of making it to trial as a Cat jailer showing up at a convention of former POWs. This is the only way."

Blair looked at his diminishing weapons ranges. Eisen's shuttle was within extreme laser shot. His duty, his orders, were to kill his friend. He knew, even as he checked his weapons configuration, that he couldn't do it.

"Colonel," Maniac said, "I've got bogies inbound from the jump point up ahead. I'd say from their speed that they're light jobs, maybe Arrows or Ferrets. What do we do?"

Blair heard his scanner click to the fighters' frequency. "Cobra Four to Cobra leader, I picked up *Lex*'s traffic control authorizing launches from the *starboard* bay, where the spookies are." His voice sounded worried to Blair. "I got two, four, six . . . ten Hellcats . . . all heading towards us."

Another voice, cold as an arctic wind, broke into the channel. "Banshee Leader to Cobra Leader. I am assuming control of your flight. Complete your orders. Engage the shuttle."

"Well," Maniac said, using the channel he shared with Eisen and Blair, "that tears it. What do I do, Colonel?"

"You obey orders," Blair replied, "*my* orders." He switched back to the main tactical frequency. "Tiger to Cobra Leader. Form your element on my wing and wait for instructions. Disregard Banshee Leader." He glanced around him at the other three Hellcats as they shuffled positions.

"Ah, Colonel Blair," the cold voice said in his earpiece, "what a pleasant surprise. Execute your orders."

"*I* command this wing," Blair snapped, "and I don't appreciate having my people co-opted. Who the hell are you?"

"Your command is . . . suspended," the cold voice replied, "by order of the *Lexington*'s commanding officer."

The casual arrogance in the voice annoyed Blair as much as the words. "Wrong," he replied tightly, "I don't accept your authority." He paused. "And get the hell off my channel."

"You will regret this, Colonel," the cold voice said.

Blair looked at his tactical plot. The shuttle was in plain view, centered and locked in his sights. He hastily switched to his navigation plot. The intercepting fighters and Banshee Hellcats converged on the shuttle, with

Maniac's small ready group directly between them.

Blair saw the drive plumes of the first rebel light fighter in the distance. His scanner clicked as Eisen keyed his microphone. "Todd, Chris," he said, "this is the moment of truth. Believe me, I did not enter into this lightly. There are terrible things happening, things I couldn't be a part of—things I know you would not want to be a part of. Join me . . . help me put a stop to it."

"Help you put a stop to *what*?" Blair demanded. "Tell me!"

"I can't," Eisen said, "not here, not without compromising too much."

"I can't do this," Blair said, deeply torn. He couldn't accept that Eisen, who had been his friend, mentor, and superior, would commit treason—not even when the evidence stared him in the face. Had Eisen discovered a secret so vile that his conscience compelled him to defect? His own doubts about the mission and the conversation Maniac had played for him nagged at him. Could Eisen be right?

Duty won over doubt, but not by much. "I can't just walk out," he said, his voice firming as he made his decision, "not like this, not without something tangible. I gave my oath."

"I understand, Chris," Eisen said in a disappointed voice. "You have your duty . . . and I have mine."

Blair closed the channel and checked the nav plot. He would not, could not destroy the shuttle. His friendship with Eisen was too strong for him to even consider that as a possibility. There was therefore no reason to engage his fighters against the interceptors and risk his wingmates. It was time to get them out from between the converging fighters and the impending battle.

He switched back to the ready group's main tactical frequency. "Tiger to Cobra elements. Stand by to come about. We're going home. Assume course zero-three-two for the *Lexington*, Z plus thirty until we get past the Banshees."

Blair brought his Hellcat around, closely followed by the section. He didn't realize at first that Maniac and his wingmate maintained their old course, boring in on the shuttle. "NO, Maniac!" Blair yelled as Maniac set up his attack run. "Colonel," Maniac said, his voice calm and cool, "you made your decision. Now I'll make mine."

The Hellcat accelerated towards the shuttle, picking up speed as it bored in on the defenseless ship. Blair looked on in horror as Maniac's Hellcat swept in, lining up for a belly shot that would gut the little ship and erase its pilot. "Damn you, Maniac," Blair swore into his throat mike, "abort your attack!"

Blair nearly turned his own ship to pursue Maniac, but held off as the interceptors closed on the Hellcat. Blair saw they were still too far from Eisen to be any help to him. He felt sick as he watched Maniac close on Eisen, who made no effort to evade.

Maniac veered away at the last second to take up station on Eisen's port side. Blair stared in shock as the realization sank in that Maniac had intended defection, rather than attack. He watched as the two Hellcats flew close escort over the shuttle. The approaching fighters swarmed protectively around them. Blair's disquiet at Maniac's unexpected defection was balanced by his quiet relief that Marshall would be there to defend Eisen from the Banshees.

"Sorry, Colonel," Maniac said, "but after Tyr, I'm betting the Cap'n's right."

"Damn you, Blair," Banshee Leader said as Maniac signed off, "you had your orders. You were to stop that shuttle. You'll pay for this."

Blair felt his temper heat at the Banshee leader's arrogant tone. He managed to restrain himself from making an obscene remark on the open channel. "I told you once to get off my channel," he growled, "whoever the hell you are."

Blair and his wingmate angled towards the rest of the ready group. The Banshee ships flashed past, hitting full afterburners as they blazed after the shuttle and its protectors. Blair hoped the shuttle, and escort, had enough of a head start to get away, if only to spite Banshee Leader.

The leading Hellcats closed enough to take the trailing edges of the fleeing group under fire. Blair watched from far astern as the Hellcat leader singled out one Ferret for attention, then methodically picked it apart. He was relieved to see a yellow blip appear on his tactical screen as the Ferret's pilot ejected. "Now we'll have some answers," he mumbled.

The rebel fighters began to vanish through a jump point ahead. Blair felt his eyebrows hike up into his head. How the hell did they accomplish that? The only fighter he knew of that had been jump capable had been the Excalibur he'd used to bomb Kilrah. Regular deck fighters shouldn't be able to manage the trick. He watched, stunned, as fighter after fighter vanished in a blue-white flash through the jump point.

"Damn! Damn! DAMN!" Banshee Leader swore. Blair could sense underlying tones of frustration and fury in the man's voice. Good, he thought to himself, you can be touched.

The black Hellcats swirled around the jump point, checking to make sure their quarry had truly escaped.

"Banshee Leader to Banshees, stand by to return home." Blair thought he'd recovered very quickly from his fit of pique. "Form on my wing." The black Hellcats quickly assembled and turned about. The leader dodged out of formation long enough to lock onto the pilot's escape pod with a tractor beam.

Blair led the glum and diminished Cobra flight back towards the *Lexington*, all the while keeping a careful eye on the Banshees, who had assumed a parallel course. Blair found his attention drawn to the thin blue streamer that reeled the captured pilot in towards the Banshee's wing. Blair watched as the Banshee pilot made the delicate corrections necessary to attach the lifepod to an unused underwing hardpoint.

Blair relaxed slightly as the pilot made the trap. The ability to perform an SAR function had been a design afterthought. Only a few of the latest model Hellcats had the equipment, and the system had never worked well in the field. Blair considered the trap a success more as a result of the pilot's skill rather than through any particular virtue of the hardware.

He grinned as he glanced at the pod nesting beneath the wing. It was the first live prisoner they'd captured. Blair hoped the pilot would be able to shed some light on what the hell was going on.

He frowned, thinking over this encounter with the Border Worlds forces and his comrades' defections. The whole situation seemed to be spinning out of control. Human killing human had been a daily event for thousands of years, and not worth comment. Somehow, the cooperation needed by humans to survive the Kilrathi had changed that. The idea of human fratricide seemed obscene to him. He thought of the chaos the Kilrathi civilization had fallen into. Their Clans were locked into a five-way civil war and torn by interfactional warfare. Was that the direction in which humanity was heading?

The thought of Maniac reminded him of one other loose end he had to tie up. He reached under the instrument console and removed the flight recorder. He used the metal clip on his pen to short out the poles and wipe the volatile memory core, zapping any record of his conversations with Eisen. He was safe, thanks to Maniac, unless they'd bugged his cockpit. He stiffened, alarmed at the possibility until he remembered that his decision to join the patrol had been a spur of the moment thing. He shook his head, annoyed with himself. He wondered, as he replaced the flight recorder, if he was getting paranoid.

He remembered an old adage, "even paranoids have enemies," which was enough to keep him on pins and needles until the carrier hove into sight. He normally felt the relief of being home, but the realization that he was not among friends made his stomach tense.

He entered the landing cycle, and was somewhat surprised to see the Banshee Leader's Hellcat enter the same pattern, rather than landing on the starboard side with the others.

He watched as the Banshee pilot delicately maneuvered his ship alongside the *Lexington*'s drive plume, all the while being careful not to expose the captured pilot to the exhaust. The black ship's pilot carefully rotated the ship in space and gently nosed his ship into the crossing fields of the *Lex*'s tractors. The operator controlling the tractor turrets had an especially soft touch. He brought the fighter through the force curtain and into the landing bay with little more than a bump.

Blair followed the black Hellcat into the port landing bay. The gravity and air had been restored, roughening what otherwise would have been a smooth touchdown. He popped his canopy even before the fuel regulators and drive turbines cycled down, placed the helmet on the control yoke, and removed his restraining harness. The recovery crew looked up, startled, as he slid his legs over the side of the cockpit and dropped to the ground.

He unhooked the throat catch to his flight suit as he stormed towards the black ship. The Banshee pilot, still wearing his helmet, crossed to where two Marines held the slumping prisoner between them. Medtechs clustered around, pointing diagnostics equipment at the unfortunate young man who stirred briefly in the Marines' tight grip.

Banshee Leader stepped up to the captured pilot and removed his helmet. Somehow, Blair was not surprised to see Seether had been Banshee Leader, and that he had led the reaction from the starboard bay. The black Hellcats were very well armed for a research team, he noticed.

Seether tossed his helmet to the Marine on the prisoner's left. "What ship are you from?"

The young pilot, shaking with fear, answered in a quavering voice. "P-provisional L-l-lieutenant K-Kyle Lee, sir," the man stammered, "o-of the B-border Worlds Union. S-serial number 284H5237." He tried to straighten and come to attention. "According t-to the Geneva C-convention, that's all I h-have to tell you." He stared at the floor, shivering and silent.

Blair crossed behind a small tractor that was backing up to the nose wheel of one of the wing's Hellcats, and wormed his way through the crewpeople who clustered around the edge of the scene. Several growled protests until they saw the colonel's pips embossed on his flight suit.

He ignored them. The pilot's name and face looked familiar. He dimly recalled that Kyle had been one of the rookies on board the *Victory* during the last days of the war. He stepped forward, thinking he might be able to use that half-remembered contact to glean some information.

Seether continued his own interrogation, a half smile on his face. "The Geneva Convention only applies to real soldiers," he said calmly, "and real countries. Not pirates." He tipped his head to one side, studying the pilot. "And I don't recall this Border Worlds Union of yours as being a country." His smile faded. "You are a traitor—a rebel taken in arms against your government. You have no rights except those *I* choose to give you. Tell me what I want to know and I'll make it easy for you."

The pilot trembled visibly. "L-l-lee, K-kyle. Buh-border W-worlds. 284H5237."

"Not good enough," Seether replied. The pilot looked up and met Blair's eye. His eyes widened in recognition. Hope shined on his face, along with a silent plea for Blair to intervene.

Seether followed his gaze and saw Blair standing in the front of the crowd. Blair's sense of time slowed as Seether glanced first at him, then at the prisoner. The Border Worlds pilot grinned and opened his mouth to speak.

All sound faded as Blair took a step forward. Seether glanced again at him, then at the pilot. He drew a laser pistol from his survival vest, pressed it against the side of the pilot's head, and pulled the trigger. Blair halted in shock as hot blood and bits of brain matter spattered him. The pilot collapsed in a heap, limbs thrashing.

Blair froze, stunned by the sudden malice of the killing. He looked down at the body, then back up at Seether. The black-clad pilot met his eye, his expression one of utter contempt. Blair felt the crowd give way, stunned by the unexpected violence. The right-hand Marine dropped Seether's helmet and wiped the side of his head. He stared at his bloodied hand.

Time snapped back. The sounds of the bay flooded Blair's ears as a pool of blood poured out of the dead man's head.

"You *son of a bitch!*" Blair growled, his shock turning to rage as the pilot's heels drummed against the deck. He heard boot heels pounding the deck as someone on the far side of the crowd broke and ran for the maintenance bay doors. "You didn't have to *kill* him!"

Seether snorted and shrugged, unconcerned. "Traitors get what they deserve."

Seether's bland face and contemptuous smile infuriated him. "That man was a prisoner!" Blair yelled. He saw out of the corner of his eye that he had drawn the attention of everyone on the deck. Good. The more witnesses the better. "He had rights!"

The pilot smiled again. "He was scum, Colonel. Rebel scum." He looked at the corpse a moment, then deliberately spat on it.

Blair felt his world go red. Rage swept over him. He ground out an obscenity between clenched teeth and lunged for Seether with his fists. He knew he couldn't beat the smirking pilot, but was bound to try and smash the smile off the bastard's face. Seether raised his steaming laser to his shoulder, cocking his arm at the elbow and readying it for use.

Blair's Hellcat crew chief and the bloody Marine threw themselves between the two officers, grabbing and holding Blair back. The crowd faded back, alarmed both by the possibility of gunplay and by the sight of senior officers attacking each other on the flight deck.

"Come on, you gutless wonder," Seether snapped, "you want me. Here I am. All you got to do is get to me." He seemed more amused by Blair's struggles than concerned.

Blair, his arms pinned, fought to get free.

"Come on, coward," taunted Seether, "can't handle a little dying? How'd you kill all those Cats, then?" Blair realized through his haze of rage that Seether was actually *enjoying* the confrontation.

Seether's voice turned nasty. "Maybe I was interrogating the wrong traitor. You let Eisen go—didn't even fire a shot. Then you let that psycho follow him. What kind of wing are you running—Colonel?" He made Blair's rank sound like an insult.

Chris struggled against the men restraining him. "I don't kill prisoners," he said savagely.

"I do," Seether said. He raised the pistol and pointed it at Blair's head.

"You better shoot straight, you son of a bitch," Blair snarled. "You won't get a second chance."

Seether smiled. "Don't worry about that, Colonel Heart of the Tiger." He sighted in. Blair heard a flurry of movement and running footfalls on the flight deck.

The men holding Blair's arms scattered as Seether began to squeeze the trigger. Blair, still straining against them, stumbled forward. He brought his arms up in a futile attempt to ward off the laser when Gunderson stepped between him and Seether. Blair saw only the back of the man's gray head and a growing bald spot.

"You want him," the master chief growled, "you gotta shoot me first."

"No problem," Seether replied, "just one more traitor."

". . . An' if you kill me, I can assure you my crews'll drag you down," Gunderson said, his voice as calm as Seether's.

The pilot glanced around, seeing a dozen puffing maintenance techs, each carrying a heavy wrench or other blunt instrument. Seether appeared to be calculating the odds when Gunderson turned to face Blair.

"What the hell were you thinking of?" he said, jabbing his finger into Blair's chest and pushing him backward into the safety of the crowd. "Going up against a man wit' a gun like that?" Blair, still off balance, reeled backward. Thad stalked him, still bawling him out and putting more distance between Blair and Seether. Blair managed a quick glance over Thad's shoulder and saw a line of maintenance techs separating them.

Blair clenched his fist. Gunderson leaned close, his voice softening as he hissed in Blair's ear. "Don't do it. He wants you to go for him. Then he can say it was self-defense." He shook his head. "Dammit, Blair, don't give him what he wants!"

Blair paused, then took a deep breath as he tried to get control over his emotions. Seether's smile slipped slightly as he saw Blair relax his fighting stance.

"Coward," he called.

Captain Paulson appeared, surrounded by a detachment of his Marines. He took in the whole scene: the dead pilot, Seether with the drawn pistol, the armed and grim-faced maintenance crews, and Blair, whose tempered fury was rising again. Paulson, his expression unreadable, pointed to Seether. "You," he said, "report to your quarters." His voice had more iron in it than Blair would have expected.

The black-clad pilot stood a few moments, his eyebrows raised in sardonic surprise. He holstered his pistol without comment and walked away.

Paulson rounded on Blair and Gunderson. "Master Chief," he said, "disperse this crowd and get medical up here." He turned his attention to Blair. "Colonel, come to my day cabin. We need to talk."

Blair sat, his back rigid as he fought to keep his composure. Paulson puttered around the wet bar. "Captain Eisen left an impressive collection of liquors," he said, a trifle disapprovingly. "*I* don't drink, of course." He gestured towards the racked bottles. "Would you care for something?"

Blair shook his head. "No." He didn't tell Paulson that accepting Eisen's liquor from his hand felt vaguely obscene.

Paulson sat across from him, his handsome face unreadable. "I heard about the, umm . . . event in the landing bay," he said; his textured voice was full of tones of concern. "It was a terrible, unnecessary tragedy."

Blair raised his hand to his head, trying to ward off an impending headache. "A tragedy?" he said in a disbelieving voice. "The bastard shot him down—murdered him in cold blood."

Paulson looked uncomfortable. "Well," he said, "what Seether did was wrong, perhaps . . ."

"Perhaps?" Blair challenged. "That kid was scared to death. He was no threat to anyone."

Paulson pursed his lips a moment, thinking. "Sure," he said, "what Seether did was wrong." His voice grew warmer, more persuasive. "But that pilot wasn't technically an enemy. He wasn't entitled to the protections of a prisoner of war."

"He had *rights*," Blair said, his voice rising as his carefully maintained control slipped a notch. ". . . if not as a prisoner of war, then as an accused criminal. He deserved due process, the right to trial, that sort of thing."

Paulson raised one eyebrow. "Colonel," he said, as though he were a father admonishing a cherished, yet erring, son, "I will not be yelled at. Not on my own ship." He smiled. "Please, let's try to be civilized." He sighed, as though attempting a difficult task. "That pilot was, as the law-tapes say, 'taken in arms,' serving a terrorist rebel organization." He shrugged. "He was a traitor. He deserved to be summarily executed."

"Since when?" Blair retorted. "Article Nine of the Confederation Charter prohibits punishment without due process. Every kid learns that in school—it's part of the primary curriculum. Damn it, sir, we showed more compassion to Kilrathi POWs taken in battle than that bastard did to that poor kid. The Kilrathi weren't covered by any article but their pilots were warriors worthy of respect."

Paulson smiled. "The Admiralty Court has ruled that the rebels have rejected the Confederation's authority. Therefore, they are not entitled to the privileges of citizenship."

Blair was certain he looked as appalled as he felt. "Since when does a court have the power to suspend the Articles of Confederation?"

"Emergency Decree 242, the so-called Martial Law declaration, grants military authorities 'extraordinary powers.'" Paulson said in a lecturing tone. "The Assembly never rescinded it after the war."

"I didn't know that."

"Well," Paulson said, "a lot of civilian authority broke down towards the end, especially on the frontier. The military *had* to step in, you know, to keep the peace." He smiled thinly. "The problem is that the warlords and pirates who sprang up in the interim now have to be suppressed." He shook his head, his expression sad. "So we're caught in an undeclared war against our brethren—and all because of a few criminals and opportunists." He leaned forward, towards Blair, his palms open and spread in a gesture of supplication. "You *must* understand that the credibility, and ultimately the survival of the Confederation, depends on suppressing this rebellion and restoring responsible government."

Blair understood that he was beginning to get tired of Paulson's "why we fight" lecture. So far the man had done everything except wave the flag and play bugles. He had expected Paulson to play on his sense of duty, but the rehearsed delivery of the pitch caught him off balance. He was beginning to understand how Paulson had survived as a non-combatant in a war-economy Fleet, and how he'd cozened himself command of the *Lexington*.

"I'm rather confused on one point," Blair said. He smiled to himself, realizing just how true the statement was. "I didn't think that the Outer Worlds had signed the Articles of Confederation. So don't they have a right to be free?"

"That's the argument the terrorists use," Paulson replied, "but it's simplistic in the extreme." He smiled. "If I build a new house within an existing community, do I have to formally join?" He shook his head. "Of course not. My simple presence within the community is enough to give me membership. In our house analogy, it would be the same thing as if I decided I was immune to taxes because I never was formally enrolled as a member of the community." He shrugged his shoulders. "This, of course, would be after I'd used the constabulary, the medics, and the other city services."

He looked at Blair. "The Border Worlds never needed to sign the Articles of Confederation because they *already* were members. They were offshoots of existing Confederated worlds, and so carried their citizenship with them."

Paulson's expression became one of determination, perfectly matched to his shifting tone of voice. Blair wondered if the captain had ever been an actor. "The Confederation must stay united if it is to survive. We must end this chaos on the frontier and we must restore order." He spread his palms. "And unfortunately that may call for harsher measures than we would all prefer. These are, after all, harsh times."

Paulson took a deep breath. "So, you see," he said, concluding his speech, "what Mr. Seether did was all very legal, though his methods left something to be desired—"

"Mister," Blair said interrupting, "he's a warrant officer? Warrant officers are titled 'Mister.' "

"Umm . . . no, he's not," Paulson answered, after the slightest hesitation.

"Then what rank is he?" Blair pressed.

Paulson steepled his fingers in his lap. "That's, umm, classified. Need to know only."

Blair shook his head in disbelief. He could not, in the

course of his entire career, recall hearing an odder statement. "His rank is classified?"

"Yes," Paulson replied, "his duties require his rank be kept secret."

Blair leaned back in his chair. Who the hell is Seether? he thought to himself. Even the man's name made him nervous, like a snake. He thought back to the event in the bar, when Seether had slammed him into the wall. Blair knew his own reflexes and thinking speed were fast, fast enough to survive two decades of often hellish combat. The farm work had kept his upper body strong, though he had grown a paunch. He should have been able to hold his own against the pilot, yet the man had tossed him around as though he was a kitten.

Blair decided there was something odd about Seether's look. His features were plain, almost too plain, like an unfinished canvas. His agility was almost superhuman— it had to be to beat Blair's reflexes. That, combined with his great strength and intelligence, made him seem an almost superior being.

That made him pause. Was he looking at the future of humanity? That would explain the almost primal fear the pilot struck in him. Blair couldn't help wondering if he was feeling what the Cro-Magnons felt when faced with Homo sapiens.

His thoughts drifted to the pilots who'd come on board with Seether. He recalled their cold, emotionless faces and similar features. How many Seethers were there? And *what* were they?

Blair looked at Paulson, who appeared content to let him sit and think. "Who are the pilots who came on board with Seether?" he asked. "Scuttlebutt says they're part of a research project. Yet I don't know any of them." He smiled. "They looked pretty grim to be researchers."

Paulson stared at him, looking as though he'd swallowed a live toad. Blair realized he'd made a serious tactical error. The guard who'd seen him on the flight deck apparently hadn't reported the contact. It was obvious that the only

way Blair could have seen the pilots was for him to have
been on the flight deck. That would have required him
to have both disobeyed orders and concealed himself from
the security teams. He watched the changes in Paulson's
expression as the captain worked through the implications
of Blair's remark.

Paulson looked him, his face stony. All warmth vanished
from his voice. "The presence of those officers on board
this ship is none of your business. You will forget you saw
them. End of story."

He walked over to the desk Eisen had never used, and
sat. Blair followed him, grimly aware of the change in
tenor. He noted that Paulson did not offer him the facing
chair. So that's how it's going to be, he thought. He assumed
the position of parade rest in anticipation of an ass-chewing.

"Colonel," Paulson said grimly, "you must understand
that I hold you in the highest regard. Your record and
your reputation describe you as proficient and professional."
He glanced downward a moment, then up. "So far, I haven't
seen much evidence of either."

Blair kept his expression neutral.

"In my brief time on board," Paulson said, "you have
disobeyed orders twice, once in combat when you allowed
your affection for your friend to overcome your sense of
duty. You have also been lax in not monitoring your pilots
for signs of disaffection. That lapse cost this ship a valuable
squadron commander and a top-of-the-line Hellcat V."
He looked up at Blair. "Do you have anything to say?"

Blair focused on a spot on the wall over Paulson's head.
He'd learned early in his career to keep his mouth shut
when being called on the carpet. Still, Paulson seemed
to expect some response. "No, sir," he said.

Paulson looked at him a long moment, then rubbed his
lip with his index finger. Blair noticed the nail appeared
to have been manicured. He waved Blair towards the chair.
"Please sit."

Blair understood the offer was not a request. He obeyed,
then used the opportunity to study Paulson.

The captain tented his hands in front of his face, giving him a studious, professorial air. "We have just fought a tragic thirty-year war," Paulson said, his hard edges softening as he tried to make peace. "Yet some good came out of it." He raised one finger for emphasis, before Blair could comment. "The war did serve to focus our energy as a species, to direct all of our efforts against a single objective. The Kilrathi were a catalyst. They gave us something to focus on—an enemy we could test ourselves against."

He opened his hands, in a gesture Blair thought calculated to draw him in. "Now that the war is over, Colonel, we're beginning to drift." He shrugged. "This is a dangerous time, both socially and politically. We need . . . to maintain our focus, and that requires something to focus on." He tipped his head to one side. "Another catalyst. Do you understand?"

"No," Blair said, "I'm not sure I do.

Paulson took a deep breath. "The Border Worlders are barbarians, Colonel, they're criminals and iconoclasts. They even trade with the Kilrathi, for God's sake. They've no discipline, no drive—they're a blight on humanity. Most of them aren't even from good stock, good families."

"Good stock," Blair said, amused. "It sounds like you're talking about cattle, not people."

Paulson made a wry face. "Sorry. It was a poor choice of words. It's just that we've gone soft since the war. We need something to keep our edge."

Blair sat, thunderstruck. He realized with cold clarity that Paulson was talking about engineering an enemy, of creating a threat that the Confederation would need to defend against.

The Border Worlds were the perfect bogeymen. The Colonials were notoriously touchy and half paranoid about the Confederation anyway. Their navy was strong enough to be a threat, but lacked the force projection necessary to prosecute a war on the Confederation's scale. It wouldn't take much provocation to nudge the prickly Border

Worlders into open warfare. Then the Confederation would have its war and could still claim to be the injured party.

The whole scenario felt totally, deeply wrong, yet he wasn't certain how to refute Paulson's arguments. Paulson, Blair decided, might not know how to shoot straight, but he had definitely seen lots of political action. Blair mulled through who would benefit from a simmering little war. His quick list of winners was as short as it was significant.

The Admiralty Court was once a joke, but now, with its ever broadening mandate and growing power—it could stay in business forever if the emergency decrees were never lifted.

Chris supposed elements within the civilian government benefited as well. The emergency decrees had suspended civil liberties, suppressed political opposition, delayed elections, and restricted public oversight—all deemed necessary to keep the Confederation in the war after the Kilrathi pasted Earth. Some senators doubtless enjoyed their freedom from public scrutiny and Earth's rambunctious press establishment. They might not be overly enthusiastic about unmuzzling an often raucous press.

Many of those same legislators sat on the appropriations committees that allocated funds to the Fleet. Peace meant fewer credits for ships and troops and less largesse to distribute to member planets.

It was no secret that the sharp reductions in defense spending had created havoc in an economy that had become geared for war. He'd seen that for himself hundreds of times, the latest in Nephele's bar. Cancelled orders for military hardware closed factories and caused suppliers to slash work forces. The sharp spike in unemployment, coupled with the influx of hundreds of thousands of released troops, had spiralled a dozen planets, including Earth, into depression. Even Blair could see that some politicians would go for a quick fix by reinflating the economy through defense purchases.

He doubted that a conspiracy would involve all of the

circles that would benefit from war, but a few key officers backed by the right powers and deep enough coffers might be enough to start the process. Then, like a rolling stone that triggers an avalanche, events could be expected to cascade out of control. They would have their war, their full employment, their fleets of shiny new ships, even their fresh cadres of newly minted combat veterans.

At what cost? he asked himself. The images of the dozens of friends killed and maimed in battle against the Kilrathi flashed through his mind. They were the bill paid for a similar focus against the Cats. The war against the Border Worlds would kill more. The image of Seether and the captured pilot loomed in his mind. The sight of the kid's twitching corpse would be repeated thousands of times if the war progressed.

"So," Paulson said, after leaving Blair to think, "has our little chat helped clear things up?"

Blair nodded, "Yes, sir," he replied with complete honesty.

"Well," Paulson said, rising to his feet, "I knew we could count on you." He looked at the wall clock Eisen had left behind. "We begin the next phase of our operations tomorrow, Colonel, so why don't you go get some shut-eye."

Blair stood and took Paulson's proffered hand. Blair noticed that while the captain's expression was friendly and open, his eyes were cool and calculating. Keep it cool, Chris, he said to himself.

Paulson nodded fractionally, apparently satisfied he'd found what he was looking for. "I'm sure things'll seem clearer to you in the morning. We're supposed to step up operations against the carrier that launched those fighters. It must be nearby. Fleet HQ has signalled us that we are to eliminate the rebels' presence from the Masa system and to secure the jump point. I'm counting on you to lead your wing against the rebels." He clapped Blair's shoulder.

Blair, his mind and spirit in turmoil, said nothing.

• CHAPTER SIX

Blair lay in bed that evening, dreaming. He and Jeannette were dressed for a party. She stood a few meters away, beautiful in her teal dress. The body-hugging sheath had been slashed where Prince Thrakhath had disemboweled her, but her skin underneath was intact.

They were celebrating. She laughed at his joke, the silver wires she'd woven into her hair glinting as she tipped her head back. He'd always loved her laugh. It was uninhibited, a mature woman's enjoyment of life, not a giggle.

She raised her glass. Their eyes met, hers full of love and laughter. "To old friends, comrades," his Angel said, smiling, "and friends future and unmet."

He raised his glass to return the Fleet toast. "And to comrades gone," he replied, smiling at her. In that moment, all was well with the universe.

She looked at him, puzzled. "Chris, *mon ami*, why are you pointing that gun at me?"

He looked down at his hand. His glass had become a laser. "You were born in the Colonies," he said, his voice sounding muffled in his ears, "that makes you the enemy. I'm sorry, my love." He raised his pistol, sighted carefully, and . . .

. . . awoke, trembling and soaked with sweat. He untangled the twisted and rumpled bedclothes, wrinkling his nose at the acrid smell of perspiration. He looked at his clock. Two-thirty. He'd been asleep a little more than an hour. He took a deep breath, trying to slow his beating heart. The dream had been *that* vivid, in full color and with such detail he thought he could smell her perfume. He turned the lights up. These quarters, so like hers, only added to the eerie feeling. He killed the lights and lay back down.

He tried to compose himself to go back to sleep. His mind, whirling from the dream and Paulson's lecture, refused to cooperate. His thoughts were drawn like iron to a magnet by Paulson's claim that Earth needed a focus, an enemy, to keep itself going.

He thought back across his two decades of service, remembering all of the tests and tribulations of holding a commission in the Fleet during the war. He remembered botched missions, incompetent officers (mercifully few—extended battle imposes its own brand of Darwinism), and stupid lies told to salvage pointless mistakes and paper over the needlessly dead.

Blair knew that in spite of everything he'd seen, his loyalty had never been tested. He thought back to the dark times, after he'd been relegated to flying Ferrets on leg patrols. In those days he'd been suspected of being either a turncoat, a coward or, worse yet, incompetent. Yet he'd remained loyal, and eventually had been given the opportunity to rehabilitate himself on the *Concordia*.

In his experience, the Fleet took care of its own, both good and bad. The service had done what it could to salvage the worst of the mistakes and warriors were too precious to squander to salvage egos. The Fleet tried to do right by its people, even if it stumbled and was occasionally heavy-handed.

The warrior caste within the military did its part by accepting into its ranks anyone who shared its goal of taking the war to the Kilrathi. The only credential needed for acceptance into the club was the desire to make the furballs pay in blood for their desire to conquer humanity. The tests of war did the rest to mold them into a unified force.

The peacetime Fleet lacked that warm camaraderie. Majors competed for precious few colonel postings. Officers of every grade were forced to look at their peers as competition. Failure meant discharge, leaving men and women who had commanded ships and squadrons on the beach and without prospects.

He'd sensed the first wisps of change at the end of the

war. He recalled that what many officers considered reality, that the Kilrathi were winning, was labelled as defeatism by Fleet Headquarters. Captains were admonished to keep an eye on their wardrooms and report "defeatist" officers. Few skippers had bothered, but the regulation had remained in force to remind the pilots they were being watched and to watch their mouths.

The pilots, for their part, had strapped into cockpits day after day, fighting numbers that never seemed to shrink even as their own forces dwindled and the prospect of winning faded. He, like most pilots, had been so focused on taking as many of the furry bastards with them as possible that they'd long since abandoned wondering what fruits victory might bring. Looking back, he realized they'd had a taste of that surprisingly bitter harvest during the disruptions that followed the Kilrathi's false truce.

Paulson's view of the war, that it had been a unifying force that brought humanity together, overlooked history and reality. Paulson, Blair thought scornfully, had never been closer to a real battle than a newsfax, the assault on Earth not withstanding. How could he know that in the end, the war had become a series of desperate hopes, each more forlorn than the last? Operation Behemoth and the Temblor Bomb had both depended far too much on luck. He couldn't help recalling that, in spite of his own participation in both operations, he'd been skeptical of success.

No, Paulson had it wrong. And he was part of the group that wanted to take Blair and all humanity back into that hell.

Paulson's war wouldn't be about defending humanity. Instead, it would cement into permanence structures created in the desperate times after the Earth was bombed and the civilian government fell into chaos. Martial law had been declared only to keep things running until freedom and democracy could be restored.

He had always thought the roots of their democracy ran deep and would weather any storm short of Kilrathi victory. Now he wasn't so sure. What was freedom? What did he know about democracy? He had been a child when the war began, and fought almost all of his adult life in a most undemocratic Fleet.

Younger officers had even less experience with representative government than he did. Many of them had grown up after the war began and civilian freedoms had already been suspended. Many considered the Senate self-righteous and out of touch, and blamed the politicos for accepting the Kilrathi olive branch and the horrible consequences that stemmed from that foolishness. How many Fleet officers, if offered a choice between the chance to pursue their careers in Paulson's ordered society, and an amorphous, chaotic democracy, might choose order?

Blair winced at the possibility that elements within the Fleet might be undermining the freedoms they had fought so hard to secure, and in doing so, were turning their backs on the dead who had died for those freedoms. It hurt him to think that the Fleet, once the bulwark of the Confederation, now seemingly led the charge to disable what so many had died to protect.

He wondered what sort of government the conspirators had in mind. The emergency decrees, martial law, the trend towards centralizing power, the suspension of civil liberties, the forming of secret cabals within the military with even more secret agendas: all had some of the trappings of the Kilrathi Imperial system. He wondered if the old adage about war was true—that in the end one becomes like one's enemy. Was that to be the price of victory, that they become like their enemies?

That thought worried him as few others had. He rolled away, physically rejecting the idea. He didn't know what was right, but he sure as hell knew what was wrong. And Paulson's plan was dead wrong. But what to do about it?

He considered Eisen's offer to leave the Confederation and join the rebels, then discarded it. He couldn't abandon his comrades by turning his coat any more than he could abandon the sense of duty that had sustained him in the horrible times after he'd realized he'd destroyed an entire planet with the Temblor Bomb. It had been his shield then. He couldn't abandon it now.

He tossed and turned, trying to decide what to do. He considered and discarded the possibility of resigning his commission. He'd seen officers resign in protest before. He had thought them quitters and had no desire to be tarred with the same brush. They also became obscure martyrs, fading quickly once they had left. He had gotten a chip in the big game and had no desire to cash it in yet and go back to the farm.

He had no real alternative than to blow the whistle on Paulson and company while performing his duties. He pursed his lips, trying to decide whom to contact first. Tolwyn seemed the best bet. The admiral had placed him on the *Lexington*, and while he and Blair had little affection for each other, Blair could get access to him. Tolwyn also detested rear echelon officers and would be less than thrilled that someone had put an armchair commando like Paulson in charge of one of his precious fleet carriers. Blair smiled. The admiral could be counted on to fix *that* travesty, at least.

His troubles seemed more manageable once he'd found a course of action that didn't require treason. He relaxed. Fatigue washed over him like a tide.

Sleep had just claimed him when the ship's klaxon sounded, summoning all crew members to action stations. His eyes snapped open as he heard shouts and running footsteps in the corridor. He sprang out of bed, his heart racing with excitement, and flipped on a light. The comm-station's screen came to life.

"What's going on?" he demanded as he climbed into his flight suit and hit its closure tab.

"A leg patrol from the cruiser *Dominion* blundered into a rebel squadron," the lieutenant replied. "They've called for reinforcements. The commander, Third Fleet, has ordered us to react."

"What're Paulson's orders?" Blair snapped as he reached for his boots.

"Magnum launch," Naismith replied. "A full deck strike." He paused. "I'm getting the ready group in the tubes now. It's shaping up as a meeting engagement. Long range telemetry suggests the rebels are vectoring in reinforcements."

"Damn," Blair said, "log me as the officer-in-charge of the ready group."

"Sir," Naismith protested, "Lieutenant Colonel Fan's listed on the flight roster as the OIC."

"Negative," Blair retorted. "I'll need her to muster the main deck strike." Naismith looked as though he might protest again. "Do it!" He closed the contact, cutting Naismith off before he could retort. Blair pulled on his boots and sprinted for the hanger bay.

He arrived at a dead run and scanned the bay for his Hellcat. He saw a welter of scrambling ground crews, the controlled chaos of sequencing the launch cradles into the chute, and the last minute adjustments as pilots called for orders, but no Hellcat with wing commander's markings. He grew worried. His fighter was not in its usual maintenance slot and a quick check at the wall-sized ready board showed it was not already spotted.

He turned, ready to grab the first tech he saw, when Gunderson grabbed his sleeve. "This way, sir."

"What the hell's going on?" Blair demanded. He heard the distant roar and felt the vibration as the first fighters catapulted down the launch bays and into space. Operating an entire wing from a single bay would slow reaction time, requiring the fighters to orbit while the squadrons formed up. That would necessitate deploying in waves, a tactic Blair thought was fine—as long as he was in the first wave.

The master chief pointed towards one dark corner of the bay. Blair saw his Hellcat, its guts torn out and crash carts arranged around it. The ship looked to be rigged to a half-dozen diagnostic machines. He whirled Gunderson, his temper dangerously close to exploding. "What the *hell*?"

"Paulson's ordered a Class Three diagnostic," Gunderson said. "Apparently, you had a spontaneous power flux that cooked your flight recorder. That's the second unexplained surge in two days, so Paulson ordered it torn apart." He pointed towards the lift. "I've got you spotted in a Thunderbolt. It's in the cycle for twelfth spot. You'd better hurry."

Blair, confused by the quick turn of events, nodded. They arrived on the launch deck just as the last of the ready group's eight Hellcats launched. A Thunderbolt stood waiting to one side of the ready lift, its cockpit open, and its launch cradle oriented on the magnetic tracks that led to the launch tube. He sprinted for the heavy fighter, scrambled up the retractable ladder and jumped in. Gunderson helped snap him into his harness and plug him into his comm-panel.

Blair glanced around at the cockpit and saw that everything had already been pre-flighted for him. He looked up at the master chief, uncertain how to express his thanks. Gunderson cut him off. "It's okay, sir, just be careful out there." He looked quickly around. "Watch your back, sir. There wasn't time to scrounge up a tail gunner, so'll you'll have make due with automatics."

He reached into the cockpit and keyed the canopy lever before Blair could speak. The thick canopy closed around the cockpit just as the *hrr-thrrruuum* of the first Thunderbolt launching drowned out all sound in the bay. Blair's fighter bumped forward into the launch tube as two more Thunderbolts rocketed into space.

Then it was his turn. The push-slam of the engines and catapult pressed him into his seat as the heavy fighter hurtled forward and out the tube. The launch proved rough and his clearing turn slow, the results of having been away from the big ships for two years.

He tested the Thunderbolt's control yoke, easing it back and forth as he got the feel of the craft. He found himself over-controlling as he tried to handle it the way he would his Arrow or Hellcat. He had to remember that the process went "stick over, pause, then sluggish turn."

He worked a pair of slalom turns, slewing the Thunderbolt up and out, then pulling it back onto its base course. He lost his heading on his first couple of attempts, then managed to keep it on course, through tighter and tighter sequences as old reflexes and conditioning quickly reasserted themselves.

"Naismith to Ready Group Three," the comm officer said, his voice sounding tinny in Blair's headset. "Engage enemy fighters on course three-three-zero, Z minus zero. Colonel Blair, callsign Tiger, will assume control. Strike group Gamma, under Colonel Fan, will begin launch cycle as loadout is complete."

Blair switched to the tactical frequency and passed his flight instructions to the sixteen ships that formed the ready group. He placed the four Thunderbolts in the middle of the diamond formation, with one section of Hellcats above and below. The four Arrows darted ahead, scouting to give him a more accurate picture of the battle that was shaping up on his scanners.

It appeared at first that the *Dominion's* half-squadron was heavily engaged against a slightly larger force of Border Worlds craft. The cruiser's fighters seemed to be holding their own, however, in spite of the enemy's edge in numbers. They remained locked in a swirling defensive formation while the rebel fighters swarmed around outside. There didn't seem to be whole lot of shooting going on. Blair guessed the rebels were more interested in keeping the Confed pilots tied up than they were in pressing the attack.

"Strike King to Tiger," the lead Arrow transmitted. "Tallyho, I got visual contact."

"What do you see?" Blair asked while starting the voice recorder attached to his knee board. He would need the Arrow's initial sighting for his after-action report.

"Approximately twelve bogies," Strike King said. "It looks like a motley mix of Ferrets and Rapiers, with a couple of Sabers. There's a second group inbound. Probably about the same numbers. Stand by telemetry."

The scout fighter transmitted his tactical scan. Blair's

mission called for him to extract the *Dominion*'s fighters, likely killing pilots who were not his enemies. "I have good copy, Strike King," he said. "Loiter and wait for the ready group. We'll take 'em with one punch." He hoped, in spite of his tough words, that keeping the Arrows out of the fight would keep the lid on the fight long enough for him to get the balance of his strike on the scene for a show of force that might make the rebels withdraw.

The last few minutes were the most difficult. Colonel Fan delegated the second strike to the next lower-ranking squadron commander in order to get some ships behind him. Up ahead, red and white streaks marked the distant battle. They redoubled as the *Dominion*'s ships, emboldened by the relief force, broke out of their hedgehog to attack. Blair felt his guts knot with worry that the Arrows had disobeyed orders. "Strike King," he said, switching channels, "what's going on?"

The Arrow pilot's face appeared in his comm-panel. "Somebody jumped 'em," Strike King said, his young features excited. "Four Hellcats came out of nowhere and just pitched in! They're tearing the hell out of the rebels!"

He saw twin red and yellow blooms, explosions marking the end of two Border Worlds fighters. The balance of the rebel flotilla started to fall back, ending their harassment of the *Dominion*'s patrol.

Blair kicked his throttles to maximum. The roar of the powerful engines was an impressive thunder next to his beloved Arrow's higher pitched murmur. The T-bolt, for all its noise, lacked the speed of the lighter ships. It made up for its lack of maneuverability with its up-front ordnance: twin plasma and photon guns. A T-bolt's Sunday punch could kill even small capital ships.

The *Lexington*'s relief force closed the gap quickly enough for Blair to identify the individual ships engaged. The rebels, caught between the mystery force and Blair's ships, scattered and ran for home. A Hellcat with a matte-black paint scheme appeared on his right side, performed a snap-roll and took out another rebel ship with a high deflection shot. Blair whistled in admiration.

Strike King's face appeared on his comm-panel. "Shall we pursue, sir?"

"Negative," Blair replied. "We'll trail 'em and make certain they stay out of trouble."

A badly damaged rebel Rapier, trailing debris and unable to keep station, appeared in his sights. He fired across its bows, signalling it to surrender. It cold-dumped its missiles and slowed, indicating its willingness to give in.

A pair of black Hellcats flashed into Blair's view from his lower right. The lead ship, afterburners glowing, lined up on the crippled rebel ship and fired. The Rapier vanished, engulfed in an expanding ball of exploding gas.

A white box appeared around the Hellcat as Blair's AI registered a radio transmission. Seether's face appeared in the comm-box. "Disregard that last order. All forces break and attack." Seether paused, then smiled. "By order of Admiral Petranova herself."

Blair, already furious over the death of the surrendered fighter, stabbed his control yoke's comm-button. "Do that again, you son of a bitch," he growled, "and I'll kill you."

Seether's ship turned in space and slashed after the retreating forces. His three Hellcats and the *Dominion*'s fighters followed. "Sir," asked a flight leader, "aren't we going to engage?"

Blair closed his eyes, pained. There it was. He'd thought he'd get off easy, by calling Tolwyn and letting the old man take care of it. Now he saw he'd have to take a stand himself. Petranova had given the order to engage. He was just about to cue his comm-button when he caught the tail end of a transmission. ". . . and Colonel Fan, if Blair refuses, then take command and carry out his orders."

That tears it, Blair said. He keyed his all-call. "Tiger to Ready Group. Break and attack in echelon. Maintain section integrity." The need to keep the fighters in groups of four would slow the attack down enough to give the Border Worlders a chance to escape.

He punched his own fighter forward, keeping pace with the Hellcats that blazed on ahead. His wingmates followed suit, loosening up the section's tight diamond and dropping into a shallow, trailing "V."

The Border Worlds forces began to turn and reengage. They hit the *Dominion's* fighters using massed fire to flare two. The black Hellcats tore into the rebels a moment later, avenging one of the cruiser's destroyed ships. Blair watched, heartsick, as his own Arrows attacked, killing a Ferret and firing missiles at a Rapier. The Rapier fired back, hitting one Arrow amidships before the first of several missiles struck it. The rebel ship turned into a fireball and an expanding cloud of junk.

Blair's Hellcats tore in, followed by his own Thunderbolts. The fast approach of three rebel Rapiers and a Saber pushed his worries aside. He slammed his throttles forward, bracing for the usual punch as the afterburners kicked in. He heard the roar as the Thunderbolt's engines spooled up, but the response was sluggish compared to a Hellcat's. The first Rapier homed in and fired while the other two broke and turned, one heading for each of his flanks. Blair kicked out a pair of signal decoys in anticipation of a missile strike, then put the T-bolt into a lazy right-hand turn. The lead Rapier's hits registered on the heavy fighter's screens, flaring the phase shields but accomplishing little else. The Saber bored in after it. He checked his tail-gunner, and was pleased to see that Gunderson's computer control was engaging the trailing Rapiers as they came around astern. The tailstinger wouldn't accomplish much, but it would keep the rebels honest.

The Saber cut to its right, then left, trying to avoid Blair's front arc. He waited until the rebel committed itself, keyed an infrared missile, and fired. The missile launched after its target. The Saber jinked hard, kicking out a string of decoys. The evasion attempt slowed its own maneuver enough for Blair to bring it into his gun line. He fired two short bursts with his plasma guns, then poured on the coal with all weapons as he saw its phase shields flare. The salvo of doubled plasma and photon guns plowed into its spine, ripping it in two. There was no secondary explosion, giving the pilot a good chance of escaping.

The lead Rapier came into his line of sight almost at once, firing its afterburners in its attempt to cut him off while the two other ships swung around and angled for his flanks. Blair, having seen this maneuver a dozen times in the Kilrathi War, turned head-on to the lead Rapier, and cued an IFF missile.

The rebel ship grew in his sights, then foreshortened as it tried to maneuver out of his front arc. The Rapier was smaller, had weaker shields and lighter weapons, and could take less damage. There was no shame in running, not under those circumstances.

The IFF's crosshairs crossed his targeting reticule, the red box flashing as the missile's seekerhead locked on target. He fired the warhead, pulling sharply away as the second Rapier opened fire. His shields absorbed several hits before he evaded. They'd been knocked down about three-quarters, but the armor belt remained intact.

Blair looked straight up through his cockpit canopy as he came over the top of his loop and saw the lead Rapier directly overhead. The IFF missile hit the Rapier. Its intake bloomed fire. The ship survived the hit and swerved away, trailing debris from a small secondary explosion.

Blair tightened his loop, coming in over the top of the Rapier as the pilot struggled to control the ship. He toggled his weapon selector switch to his plasma cannon, then kicked a line of bolts along the damaged fighter's foresection. The ship staggered under the abuse, then flew apart—disintegrating from front to back as the cannon shots lost coherency and dissipated their energy charges into the Rapier's frame.

Blair's heart thumped in his chest as he watched the fighter die. The fighter's frame broke up before the pilot could eject. He felt dirty and sickened by what he had done, even though he'd had no choice. Blair had rarely fired on Confed-built ships, and the memories of each time he had done so plagued his dreams.

A barrage of laser bolts from his back right drew his eye upward. The last Rapier flashed overhead, scoring a line of hits that weakened Blair's phase shields but still didn't penetrate.

He pulled hard right, allowing his badly depleted capacitors to recharge while he maneuvered against the last Rapier. A *Lexington* Hellcat appeared in the Rapier's hind quarter, fired a volley from its ion cannon and released a missile. The Rapier, caught between Blair's turret and the Hellcat, tried to turn away. The missile took it amidships, destroying it. A gout of flame shot through the cockpit, finishing the pilot.

He kicked the Thunderbolt ahead, passing through the last of the defending fighters. The sky ahead was clear, except for the drive plumes and navigation lights of a pair of small frigates. He plotted an attack course for the small warships, then dove. Defensive fire from their turrets began to flash past his canopy.

He checked his scanner, unamused to see the Border Worlds ships falling back to protect the frigates. The much faster Ferrets and Arrows were already past him, vectoring towards the frigates before turning. The *Lex*'s Arrows raged after them in hot pursuit. One Arrow caught a frigate's defensive bolt in its teeth and vanished. The rest, undaunted, fired as they passed him, their pilots clogging the radio channels as they tried to coordinate their attack. He caught a quick signal burst as Colonel Fan's wave plowed into the far side of the battle, catching those Border Worlds ships that couldn't disengage in a pincer.

The Border Worlds forces, overmatched by both Confed numbers and technology, gave way. Blair, his blood up, slipped between the retreating ships and went for the frigates. The cap ships jinked and dodged, trying to avoid him as he pressed home his attack.

A *Lexington* Hellcat closed on his port side.

"Colonel Blair," Maniac called, matching his course to Blair's, "abort your attack!"

"I don't listen to traitors," he snarled as he fired on the frigate. The little ship's phase shields flared, absorbing the punch. The trick would be to whittle its defenses down, then hit it with his Sunday punch. A second point-blank barrage cut through the forward screen, knocking it down. He aimed in again, intent on slagging the small ship.

"Colonel!" Maniac said, desperation coloring his voice, "please listen. The frigates're carrying refugees from a Confed raid. They're just tryin' to get out of harm's way! I swear it!"

Blair looked from his comm-panel to the frigate. The ship's guns and missiles might have been sufficient reinforcement to salvage the situation for the Border Worlds forces, if they had committed to the battle. The fact they hadn't suggested Maniac was telling the truth. "On your oath?" he demanded. "For whatever it's worth."

"Colonel, I swear it's true," Maniac said. "Both ships are loaded with non-combatants. They even removed their torpedoes to make more room for refugees."

"Tell 'em to run full ID's and shut off their turrets, and I'll call off the dogs," Blair said tiredly. "If you've lied to me, I'll hunt you down."

"I haven't lied," Maniac said dryly, "though I appreciate the vote of confidence."

Blair considered smoking him, just on general principles. He confined himself to cuing his tactical circuit. "Tiger to Wing. The primary target running ID's are non-belligerents. You will consider them non-valid targets."

He knew with grim certainty that the black ships would disobey, and wasn't the least bit surprised when one turned towards the damaged frigate. The Hellcat didn't have the ordnance to take down a shielded frigate by itself, but it had plenty of juice to deal with an unshielded one. The black ship made a tight snap turn and fired, its ion cannon picking holes in the frigate's hull. Maniac saw-bucked his fighter, kicking it around and firing first one missile, then another at the black ship. The fighter looped in a complicated roll and corkscrew maneuver, dodging the missiles as smoothly as a matador evading a bull.

Maniac swept up after it, firing as it came out of its tight spiral. The black ship nimbly dodged Maniac's beams, then slashed across his course. Maniac tried to follow it into another complicated roll-and-tuck corkscrew. The Hellcat pulled away from him as easily as a veteran leading a novice, then flipped over on its back. Maniac tried to evade without success.

Ion and laser cannon fire bloomed from its wings. The point-blank beams raked Maniac's belly, punching through the phase shields and armor to score the hull beneath. Maniac jerked his fighter to the side, trying to avoid the killing beams, but to no avail. Blair saw white hot pieces fly from Maniac's ship.

Blair watched the fighter close on Maniac, whose crippled bird spewed fuel and hydraulic fluid. The fighter slowed, lining up a killing shot on Maniac's cockpit. Maniac, his controls nearly shot away, still attempted to evade. The black fighter toyed with him, firing close along one side, then hulling the ship again.

That final piece of cruelty was the last straw for Blair. His fury rose like a red haze. He bucked the nose of his Thunderbolt around and aimed it at the black ship. The black Hellcat began to turn, readying the final shot for Maniac.

Blair switched to his full bank of frontal weapons and hit his trigger. Beams lanced out from his ship, crossing space to strike the aft portion of the Hellcat. The Hellcat pulled hard to the right, banking and slewing as it tried to evade. The maneuver presented Blair with a shallow deflection shot against the black Hellcat as he crossed its "T."

He goosed his stick back and left, crossing the smaller ship's steeper bank, then hit his firing trigger as he straightened out his course. The beams cut directly in front of the Hellcat, which tried to snap-roll away. A single beam licked through its armor. Blair saw a flare, then a small explosion.

The damaged ship pulled ahead, using a burst of afterburners to escape the heavy fighter. Blair made a minute course adjustment, then hit his own burners. The Hellcat, slowed by battle damage, walked into the curtain of fire.

Blair held his trigger down, watching his capacitors dip deep into the yellow as he poured shot after shot into the Hellcat, chewing through the shields, armor, and finally the ship itself. Pieces spalled away under the abuse and one engine flared and caught fire. Blair keyed his weapons again. Nothing happened. He looked down and swore as he saw he'd run his capacitors deep into the red.

The fighter, badly damaged, turned back towards the battle and into the shelter of two more black Hellcats. The comm-panel cleared. Blair found himself looking at an infuriated Seether. "Well, Colonel," he snarled, "I guess honors are even. Enjoy your victory. You aren't going to be around to enjoy it long."

Blair glanced quickly at his tactical. Marshall's damaged Hellcat had taken up station with the frigates, escorting them on the final leg towards the jump point. Blair watched the first refugee ship enter the jump point, a flare of brilliant blue energy exploding from the point as the ship activated its jump engines and passed through. The second frigate followed a second later, trailed by a trickle of Border Worlds fighters.

Maniac's damaged fighter hovered near the gate. "Colonel," Maniac said, his face jumping and fuzzing in the jump point's electronic interference, "you'd better come with us. You can't go back."

Blair saw that was true. No one would believe his story of protecting helpless civilians, especially after the frigates had fired on his ships. It was also undeniable that he had fired on another Confed ship. He guessed that even if he were to escape punishment for letting the frigates go, he'd exposed himself as an enemy of the conspiracy.

He had no choice, not if he wanted to live. "Where are we going?"

Marshall's face frizzed out as his camera failed. "Home," he said, "such as it is."

Blair reluctantly turned and followed Maniac through the jump point.

• CHAPTER SEVEN

Blair brought his Thunderbolt through the jump point, closing his eyes and gritting his teeth against the inevitable jump shock. Somehow, the shock seemed worse in a small fighter than it did in a cap ship. He breathed shallowly while the nausea passed. Only then did he examine his surroundings.

A huge red giant star hung in space like a baleful bloodshot eye. Prominences boiled off its surface, throwing planet-sized tendrils far out into space, only to fall back into the star's mass. His earpieces picked up the electronic interference as static intense enough to break the transmitter's squelch. The nav plot jumped and skipped as the sensitive pickups adjusted themselves to accommodate the white noise.

A small flotilla emerged over the star's horizon. The fleeing frigates matched courses, sliding smoothly into orbit behind and below the main body. They joined an ancient light cruiser, a fistful of corvettes and a half-dozen old revenue cutters. A pair of fast transports with flared ore-shuttle decks hovered protectively over a single carrier.

The CV looked to have begun life as one of the old destroyers the Confederation had discarded and sold off. The Border Worlds had slung a single launch bay beneath its belly, reconfiguring it as a light carrier.

"What ship is that?" he asked, indicating the carrier.

"That's the *Intrepid*," Marshall replied, "the flagship of the Outer Worlds Fleet." He laughed. "It used to be the TCS *Delphi*, one of the old Durango-class heavy destroyers."

"The Durangos were obsolete ten years ago!" Blair interjected.

Maniac laughed at the disbelief in his voice. "Welcome to the Border Worlds, where everything's seen better days."

An obsolete corvette with a large parabolic antenna that looked to have been salvaged from an obsolete orbiting microwave power station separated itself from the main body. The huge dish oriented towards the jump point, looking like a massive sail on top of the small ship.

Two Border Worlds fighters, a damaged Rapier and an early model Arrow, emerged from the jump point and oriented towards the carrier. Feedback discharged from point to point across the dish, matching the jump point's characteristic blue flare.

He had heard rumors that secret experiments had been under way towards the end of the war that would allow cap ships to open small rifts in the jump points, rifts just large enough for fighters to pass through as a means of cross-system raiding. He was gratified that, for a change, the rumors had turned out to be true. The generators were one of the few improvements the last couple of years had seen. Most everything else seemed to have gone downhill.

Four Rapiers, the *Intrepid*'s Combat Area Patrol, broke from the vicinity of the carrier and angled towards them. The CAP would be very sensitive about strange fighters without proper IFF ID's operating in the vicinity of their mothership. The Rapiers' drive plumes brightened as the four ships touched their afterburners and angled towards them. "Unidentified Thunderbolt," the flight leader said, "drop your screens!"

"I'd do it if I were you," Marshall warned him. "You're still running Fleet IFF transponder codes. The locals don't know you're friendly." Blair hurried to obey as Marshall contacted the carrier below.

"Maniac to *Intrepid* control. I'm bringing in a recruit. Don't fire."

"Roger," Blair heard a woman's voice respond in a throaty contralto that made him think of warm nights and inviting arms. She probably weighs a hundred-twenty kilos, he thought, but she's got a voice that could launch a thousand ships.

"Fleet Thunderbolt Two-Seven-One," she said. "Identify yourself."

Blair keyed his comm-panel. "Blair, Christopher, Colonel Space Forces Reserve." He paused, unable to resist adding a touch of sarcastic humor. "Or, at least I was, until about two minutes ago."

There was a long pause on the other end.

"Callsign?"

He normally disliked his Kilrathi hero-name. It was too pretentious for his taste. There were times, though, when its fame came in handy. "Callsign Heart of the Tiger," he said.

He took a certain malicious pleasure in hearing her sharp intake of breath. "Can anyone vouch for you?" she said.

"Yeah," Maniac said, "me. He saved the frigates from his buddies. The frigate masters'll vouch for him, too."

"Roger, umm . . . Colonel Tiger," she said, sounding a bit flustered. Her voice steadied as she reverted to duty. "Assume a standard reverse-course let-down approach," she said. "Our instrument-tractor system is down, so you'll have to do it on manual. *Intrepid* out."

Blair smiled, wondering what she looked like. She must be pretty young, he thought, to get so tossed by his presence. He switched back to his main tactical channel, then cut to his short-range laser transmitter. "Who was that?"

"That," Maniac said archly, "was Lieutenant Sosa, also known as Admiral Richards' girl Friday. She's filling in as the comm officer." He laughed. "She's a looker."

"Oh, yeah?" Blair replied, playing the role of the randy pilot. "I think I'm going to like being a traitor."

"Let's go back to the barn, Casanova," Maniac said dryly. He peeled his limping fighter away, leaving behind bits of burned armor and debris.

Blair tucked in behind him. The four escorting Rapiers held station, close enough to react if Blair tried an attack, but not so close as to spook him. Maniac led the little group into the *Intrepid*'s holding pattern, using broad turns that gave them a wide berth from the other fighters orbiting the carrier.

Blair used the delay to study the flotilla. Most of the ships had a slightly moth-eaten look about them, together with the patchwork appearance of battle damage hastily repaired in space.

Two fighters, a Rapier and a Saber, angled in and joined the queue over the carrier. Blair looked around at the firefly glows of the little ships as they swirled around, waiting their turns to land. Another cluster of fighters, this time Ferrets and what looked like a single Arrow, filtered through the jump point and aimed for the two fast transports.

"What the hell are those?" he said.

"What the hell are what?" Maniac replied.

"The transports," Blair said. "It looks like they're taking on fighters."

"They are," Maniac answered. "We're staging smaller ships, Ferrets mostly, and a few Rapiers, off them."

"Those're too small to have launch tubes!"

"They don't," Maniac confirmed, "they just kind of push their birds out the back and let them fend for themselves. They lose one occasionally." He clucked his tongue. "They do shuttle runs, picking up fresh birds and pilots when we get low, and transfer 'em over here to fill in our losses. They'll eventually empty out. Then they'll go back to the boneyards and pick up more rehabbed ships and the latest graduates of what they call flight school." He frowned. "Most of the rookies don't last long, or so I'm told."

Blair stared at the transports, appalled at the waste. "Half-baked pilots in obsolete craft—that's crazy."

"Welcome to the lunatic fringe," Maniac replied dryly. "The Border Worlds don't have the numbers the Fleet does, so they have to get more creative more quickly to keep going. A lot of what they're doing gets pilots killed, but it does allow a magnum launch of more than six birds."

Blair winced at the acid in Maniac's voice.

The *Intrepid* loomed close. The ship had been badly damaged. The entire top level of its superstructure, containing the bridge, control systems, and crew berths, looked to have been totally demolished. Several sections of the hull had been opened and peeled away, revealing blackened frames that jutted like clawing fingers into space.

One of the three drive cones was dark, its only emission a white plume that trailed from below one side. Several weapons emplacements on the stern quarter had been damaged, as had the main communications array. A cluster of pressure-suited figures with cutting torches worked at cutting away piece of fallen machinery that had collapsed across one point-defense turret.

"What the hell happened?" Blair asked.

"I'm told," Maniac said, "that the *Intrepid* had a run-in with a pod of Confed fighters backed by a pair of cruisers, the TCS *Achilles* and the *Dornier*. They fought a running battle through three systems. The *Achilles* is no more."

The *Achilles*, sister ship of the *Agamemnon*, was one of the Fleet's most powerful heavy cruisers. Three hundred and fifty good people dead on the Fleet side alone, and God only knew how many more Border Worlders. The Border Worlds must have paid a heavy price for killing the cruiser.

The communications officer hailed them, her honeyed voice clear in spite of the interference. "*Intrepid* to Thunderbolt Two-Seven-One. You are authorized to begin visual landing sequence. Be advised, the beam tracking system and tractor traps are down. Good luck."

Blair cleared his throat. He hadn't done a real eyes-only landing in a decade, and that had been in a fighter a lot more maneuverable than the Thunderbolt. He wasn't terribly fond of the T-Bolt, derisively known as the "lead sled," in the first place.

His fuel gauge read less than half-full and returning to the *Lexington* wasn't an option. He took a deep breath, held it a moment, then blew it out in a long whistle.

The situation felt like one of the old training simulator scenarios involving bizarre, unrealistic situations like the complete failure of failsafe systems like carrier deck landing systems or communications arrays.

Blair held to what he thought was the proper approach angle, a little steeper than he would have used in an Arrow or Hellcat, but also much slower. He kept his rate of descent steady, and repeatedly checked his range to target. It reeled off numbers with impressive speed. He slowed the ship again and dropped his landing gear. The tell-tale indicated that it had locked down. Well, Chris, he said to himself, here goes nothing. The deck grew rapidly, rushing up to meet him.

He chopped his throttles all the way back, cutting his drives and depending on momentum to carry him through the force curtain that kept the ship's atmosphere inside. The deck came up quickly, too quickly. He flared his approach out at the last second, easing his control yoke back to raise the nose. He swore softly as the back wheels hit and bounced. The fighter's characteristics had changed the moment he'd hit the atmosphere and the ship's artificial gravity. He'd forgotten to compensate for the lift his wings provided when in atmosphere.

He hit his navigation thrusters, trying to bleed off speed before he plowed into an obstacle. Open space beckoned at the far end of the open bay, the stars twinkling in the force curtain's haze. If worse came to worst, he could boost his speed and touch-and-go, passing completely through the bay and launching out the other side to try the landing again. He'd catch hell for it, perhaps even get shot at, but it was a better option than slapping twenty plus metric tons into the flight deck or bay walls.

He reached for the throttle control, ready to ram it to the stops. The first of the trap cables, designed to protect fighters in the front part of the launch deck, caught the Thunderbolt's nose gear.

The fighter slid sideways along the angled cable, showering sparks on the deck, before it shuddered to a halt and finally tipped over onto one wing. Blair winced at the crunch noise the stabilizer and outer weapon's hardpoint made as the fighter's weight settled.

He popped his canopy, whipped his helmet off, and swore sulphurously as he shut down the engines and internal power. The fuel-feed turbines whined down, exchanging their high-pitched whir for a lower pitched whuffing sound. He dropped his helmet on the yoke and looked around, checking for signs of fire.

Old, cool smoke hazed the inside of the bay. About half the illumination strips were out, either dead or shattered, and the launch deck showed definite signs of battle damage. A cacophony of loudhailers, shouts, and noises of the crowded deck washed over him. A motley-looking ground crew sprinted for the fallen Thunderbolt.

"Clear that piece of junk!" the loudhailer boomed. "We got more fighters inbound!"

Small lift cranes and tractors scuttled from sockets along the bay's walls to the stranded Thunderbolt. One ground crew frantically wrapped a cable around the crumpled wing while another released the arrestor line and recoiled it for later use. The crane operator lowered her hook to the wing crew, snagged the cable, and hauled the fighter upright. Blair heard the squeak and creak as the T-bolt came upright then tipped back onto its gear. It rocked back and forth, squeaking as the hydraulic cylinders in the gear took the changing loads.

He saw fuel spilling from the ruptured wing tank and pointed. One crew member, a little quicker than the others, grabbed a bag of absorbent material from the back of the lift and liberally spread it over the spill. The tractor hooked up to the Thunderbolt's bent front gear and tugged it out of the landing area. The area was barely clear before a Rapier with an engine fire came in on a steep approach.

The pilot held the damaged fighter together long enough to execute a wobbly three-point landing, then slewed sideways in a shower of sparks.

Blair heard something burst under the sidewards strain.

The canopy popped open as the pilot cut her one working drive to keep from playing the exhaust stream over the ground crews huddled behind crash barriers on either side of the deck. She taxied off the landing targets and into the recovery area, leaving behind a trail of synthetic rubber. Flames burst out over the Rapier's upper hull. Fire crews swarmed over the ship, plying the engine with slurried foam while the pilot slid to the ground.

Blair had the impression of a young woman with one side of her face covered in blood. She walked away from the burning Rapier, her head down, ignoring the corpsman who tried to staunch the blood flowing down her face and neck.

Blair coughed a little as Maniac walked up to him, his helmet hanging from his flight suit. "What the hell's wrong with the air in here?" he said, waving his hands in front of his face. "If it were any thicker, you could serve it on toast."

"The soot and smoke from the fires overwhelmed the scrubbers and air filtration units," Maniac answered. "They're trying to rig some electrostatics to clean it, but they're shorthanded and it ain't a priority. The damage control chief told me they're too busy trying to keep the carbon monoxide and toxins down to manageable levels to have to worry about how they're gonna clean a hundred thousand cubic meters of air." He looked meaningfully around. "I'm told it would be simpler just to do a whole air exchange, but that would require a refit. Which would require taking us off-line, which they can't afford to do." Maniac laughed without humor and gestured around him at the smoky air. "Don't worry. This stuff's going to thin out on its own. We're leaking atmosphere like a sieve."

Blair, aware of the fatigue that gnawed at him, glanced around the darkened bay. "Where do I bunk in?"

Marshall led him over to a table where a rating poured coffee and issued blankets. Maniac picked up two cups and gestured for Blair to get a blanket. He pointed with his chin towards a curtained-off area in one particularly dark corner of the bay. "There you go," he said, "pilots' quarters."

"That's it?" Blair asked, dumbfounded.

"Yeah," Maniac answered. "The *Achilles'* fighters took out the living quarters topside, along with everything else above Deck Three." He shrugged. "At least we've got plenty of room."

"How's that?" Blair asked.

"A third of the crew was in quarters when they got hit." Blair closed his eyes.

"Most of the crew just drop in place when they need sleep," Maniac said. Blair followed his gesture and saw several filthy crew members asleep on a tractor. Their ability to sleep in the middle of the bay's din spoke volumes about their fatigue. "This old girl's being held together with baling wire and prayer," Marshall continued. "Most of the crew are pulling eighteen-hour-plus days to keep her from coming apart."

They walked over to the pilots' "quarters." Blair dropped his blanket on an unused patch of deck. He saw several unoccupied cots, but declined to take one. They looked to have been soaked in something he guessed was dried blood.

"Now what?" he asked Maniac.

"We go up to Operations," Maniac said. "They'll be thrilled to know you're aboard."

Blair looked at Maniac, uncertain if he was being sarcastic. He said nothing as the major led him towards the stairs.

"The lifts are down," Maniac supplied. "Most other luxuries, too. Only one APU is working, so the lights fade a lot. The rest of the reactors went off line when the portside engine room got hit." He smiled. "You've also had your last shower for a while."

Maniac led Blair to a metal access tube and started climbing the steep stairway. "I'm impressed," Blair said to Maniac's back, "that you've managed to find your way around so quickly. You only defected yesterday."

"It's a small ship," Marshall replied, his voice muffled by his body, "smaller now that a third's been blown to hell. I managed to find all the important places: the chowhall, the bar, the head." He laughed. "Still haven't found the tail, though."

Maniac led Blair up two more levels, each time passing through open dogging hatches. The hatches were held open with electromagnets and were designed to seal if atmospheric pressure dropped or changed radically. The obsolete system had never had the bugs fully ironed out. The hatches, each weighing half a metric ton, closed at odd moments, very occasionally crushing personnel underneath. He looked at each warily as they climbed.

Maniac stopped at the third deck and opened the access door for Blair to step through. The air on this deck made the air below seem sweet by comparison. It reeked of burned conduit, plastics, bedding, and other, less wholesome smells. He felt its bite on the back of his throat as he inhaled. He coughed lightly as he tried to rid himself of the irritation.

"You'll get used to it," Marshall said, his voice flat.

They ducked back against the bulkhead as two sweaty and sooty crews scurried past. Some carried portable fire extinguishers, breathing apparatus, and tools. One grim-faced team carried stretchers, each with a single, savagely burned body. Blair turned away, gagging on the reek of scorched, decomposing flesh.

He swallowed hard, grateful that he hadn't eaten breakfast.

"They're just now getting some of the bodies out," Maniac said, "but there're still fires burning for'ard." Marshall glanced down at one shrouded form, without expression. "Dust in the air handlers ignited when the top decks got hit. A fireball flashed downward, into the workshops and crew spaces, igniting everything that would burn. They've been fighting fires for the last couple of days."

Blair furrowed his brow, trying to recall his damage control procedures. "Why don't they just suck the air out, or vent the areas into space?"

"Can't," said a voice from behind him. He turned and saw a short woman wearing a shiny lieutenant colonel's insignia and bronzed pilot's wings. She looked to be in her late twenties, and seemed very attractive, even though she was layered with soot and grease. She tipped her head back, meeting Blair's stare. One lock of black hair strayed from her tightly bound hair and into her eyes. She pulled it back with an impatient gesture.

"The flash fire may have warped the sectional control valves," she said, her voice tough and frank. "We can't be certain we wouldn't lose what atmosphere we've got left." She gave him a thin-lipped, wintery grin. "Although that would take care of the fires."

She extended her hand to him. "Tamara Farnsworth," she said, "*Colonel* Tamara Farnsworth." He shook her hand, surprised both by her grip and her forthrightness. He guessed she could hold her own with anyone, male or female, and look good doing it.

"My callsign's Panther. I'm the acting Damage Control officer." The way she said "acting" made it plain to him that she was not doing the job out of love.

A second officer joined them. He looked to be even younger than Farnsworth, closer to his mid-twenties. Blair stuck out his hand. "Chris Blair," he said, introducing himself. "Reserve Colonel . . . or at least I was until this morning." The officer's face tickled Blair's memory. They had met before.

"Blair?" the second officer asked. "Colonel Blair—the Heart of the Tiger? That Blair?"

Blair nodded carefully.

"I monitored your radio traffic," the man said. He smiled, realizing he was being remiss. "I'm Colonel Jacob Manley." Blair saw the smile didn't extend beyond his thin, fleshless lips. "I'm filling in as logistics officer."

Blair looked at him. The memory locked into place. "I've heard of you. You were stationed in the Astoria System, weren't you?"

"We both were," Farnsworth said, interrupting.

Blair opened his mouth to ask another question. Manley cut him off with a single raised hand. "Look, Blair," he said, "we'd really like to chat, but we've got work to do. Let's do this some other time, okay?" He turned away, drawing Farnsworth after him. "Now, Tamara, about that foam . . ." They walked off, leaving Blair and Maniac standing awkwardly.

"He's friendly," Blair said dryly.

"Manley's got a rep for having brass balls," Maniac said, "and for not caring too much about how he wins, as long as he does." He glanced around. "He got cashiered from the Fleet for reckless endangerment of lives and property."

"What'd he do?" Blair asked.

Marshall shrugged. "After the war, he landed a billet as an advanced flight instructor at the Academy, while waiting for a squadron command to become available. He hid a squadron of trainees in an asteroid field during an exercise. One of his students got hit by a 'roid and killed. He justified it to the review board on the grounds that the ruse allowed them to get to and 'kill' their target, and increased training realism.

"The review board let him take an early retirement rather than recommend a court-martial. The Border Worlds was hiring pilots and was more concerned with combat experience than politeness. It was a natural fit." He laughed. "Manley's as Terran as they come, but his loyalty's to his paymaster. He wraps himself in his payslip now, rather than the flag."

Blair looked at him, startled by the acid in Maniac's voice. "I thought he'd be someone you'd like, you know, a kindred soul."

Maniac smiled, then looked sidelong at Blair. "Sorry," he said, "but I learned long ago to never fly with anyone crazier than myself." Blair, who had similar reservations about Maniac, maintained a discreet silence. Marshall tipped his chin towards Manley's retreating back. "Hawk isn't happy that the hero roster's filling up."

"How's that?" Blair asked.

Maniac made a rude face. "He usually starts a conversation with the fact that he's got ninety-six confirmed kills. I think he resents you for ending the war before he got his century award. That's the kind of thing he'd take seriously." Maniac rubbed the triangular badge inked over his left breast pocket. "He liked being this ship's designated hero. He ain't happy sharing that with me, much less you."

Farnsworth's voice echoed down the hall, "Dammit, Carlson, we need more retarding foam forward of frame eleven. Get a move on it! Do you want to burn to death?"

Blair and Maniac looked at each other. Marshall made a gesture to Blair with his hand. "This way to the bridge," Maniac said. Blair furrowed his brows at Marshall's odd tone of voice.

They moved down the central corridor, stepping around a corpsman and several prostrate crew members. One crewman sucked from an oxygen bottle while the corpsman placed wet cloths on the others' foreheads.

Maniac turned a corner, leading Blair to a heavily armored door embossed with the words AUXILIARY CONTROL ROOM. A sign taped below that said OPERATIONS/COMBAT INFORMATION CENTER. A second, even more hastily lettered sign read CHAOS CENTRAL.

Maniac opened the heavy durasteel hatch. The makeshift bridge's most noticeable characteristics were the relative brightness of the room and the cleanliness of the air.

The smoke-free bridge indicated the room had its own self-contained atmosphere. The air smelled faintly of lubricating oil and the slight staleness from being in the tank too long, but it was pure ambrosia compared to what the crew breathed.

The carrier's CIC looked to be a scrimped together copy of a Fleet CV's combat center. He took in the cramped bridge stations, smaller twins of the ones destroyed topside, and the central holographic tank. Flat screens had been bolted in place between exposed pipes to accommodate several additional fighter control stations. Even with better lighting and air, the CIC was small and cramped, and inadequate for either the mission or the staff it had to support.

An officer broke away from the small knot clustered around the holo-tank. It took Blair a moment for his watering eyes to adjust to the bright lights. "Captain?" he asked, his voice rising in pleased surprise.

Eisen grinned, taking Blair's proffered hand and pumping it enthusiastically. "Damn, Chris," he said, "you have no idea how glad I am to see you." Blair frowned. Eisen looked careworn and thin, as though he had aged a decade since his defection.

Blair glanced around the cramped control room. "Well," he said, "this sure ain't the *Lex*."

Eisen made a face. "Yeah," he agreed, "it's a fixer-upper all right."

"How bad is it?" Blair asked him.

Eisen nodded, his voice grim. "They tell me Captain Dominguez was on the bridge when the *Achilles* attacked them with two torpedoes. He died, along with most of the bridge crew, and anyone who was in the crew spaces. They lost a third of the crew." He looked around. "We're still picking up the pieces."

"I'm sorry," Blair said. "Did you know Captain Dominguez?"

"Yeah," Eisen replied, "he was two classes ahead of me at the Academy. We served together during the Venice Offensive. That was three decades ago." Eisen smiled. "Admiral Richards knew we'd worked together. So he asked Raul to handle my, um, change of heart." Eisen's smile faded. "Now he's dead . . . along with a lot of others, and for what?" He lowered his head to sip from his cup. "What a waste."

The officers by the 'tank quietly filed into a small briefing room attached to the bridge. Manley stood at the door, looking impatient.

"Well," Eisen said, "it's showtime."

"What's up?" Blair asked.

"C'mon," Maniac said, "you might as well see for yourself."

Blair looked at Eisen, who made a "go ahead" gesture. The three shipmates crossed to the briefing room and entered, squeezing past a rack of data cores to stand in the back.

Colonel Manley moved past them to the front of the room. "Now that we're all here," he said glancing without warmth at Blair, "let's get started. It was agreed that I'd preside here as I'm the senior-most officer with a Colonial commission. I thought we'd start with a review of our situation, move onto our damage control status, and then discuss what we're going to do about a commanding officer."

Blair looked a question at Maniac, who pressed a finger to his lips.

Manley cued a hastily installed projection map. Blair saw the *Intrepid's* small task group had moved back away from the jump point and appeared to be retreating across the system to the far point. The *Lexington's* task force and a second smaller group, labelled CLOSE ACTION GROUP-III FLEET? were shown as being somewhere within an ellipse based on elapsed time and movement probabilities.

"We're down to thirty-one front line strike craft, with seventeen obsolete models—Sabers, Scimitars, and Ferrets—still in storage belowdecks. The flight deck is operational and we've got nine fighters, mostly obsolete, that we can fix, more or less. They're mostly older jobs," he looked at Blair, "with some notable exceptions.

"The *Lexington* is holding steady on the other side of the jump point, though with our array down, the telemetry we're getting is spotty. Lieutenant Sosa," he said, tipping his head to the raven-haired woman, "maintains, based on traffic patterns and intercepted communications, that the *Lex's* command group is in disarray. She doesn't expect them to move for some time.

"On other subjects, we've pulled far enough back from the jump point to give us some breathing room if she's wrong. We're still running at reduced speed. With the fuel residue we're leaking from the number one engine, we'll leave a trail wherever we go." He gave Farnsworth a wintery smile. "But now I'm stepping on Panther's thunder."

He gestured towards her. "Tamara, would you care to report?"

"Well," she said, "the fires have been contained up to frame nine, but are still pretty much out of control forward from there. We'll get it out eventually, but I can't tell you when."

"What's the problem?" Manley asked.

"Residual heat," she answered. "The fires are heating the metal bulkheads. Also, once we clear a room, we have to fog it to cool it enough for the fire crews to move through, and that takes time. We've also had problems with flashback, fires crawling along insulation or conductibles, and heat exhaustion among the fire crews."

"I see," Manley said. "And what about the reactors?"

"Well," Tamara replied, "I'd best pass that off to Captain Eisen. He's been gracious enough to look into it for us."

"Captain?" Manley said, shifting his attention to Eisen.

Blair could tell from the slight stress that Manley placed on Eisen's rank that he considered it honorary.

"All right," Eisen said, pausing as if to gather his thoughts. He glanced at Tamara, who nodded. "Since I've been filling in down in engineering, I'll start there." He paused. "The number one reactor breached before it could be scrammed and dumped into space. The whole number one drive is contaminated and is leaking fuel. We won't be able to relight it without some serious drydock time." He looked around at the grim-faced officers. "I don't think any of the engineering staff is going to make it. Most took lethal doses when the core breached, the rest exceeded their lifetime curie limits almost immediately afterwards. We don't have enough radiation abatement medication in the dispensary to handle the number of cases we have. We're going to lose at least some of the patients.

"Also," he said, his expression sober, "we're down from three to one auxiliary power unit. The single APU is trying to do the job of all three: maintaining internal power, the fire suppression apparatus, the shields, and the floor field. It's pulling too much of a load as it is . . . that's why the lights keep browning out." He took a deep breath. "The unit's down to ninety percent as a result of overheating. If it drops too much more we might lose the gravity field."

Blair winced. A momentary flux in either the floor field or the inertial dampers would subject the crew to the full effects of the ship's acceleration. The ship's company would wind up as strawberry-colored smears on the rearward bulkheads. The expressions he saw on the other officers' faces told him they'd worked through to the same conclusions.

"What are our options?" Manley asked.

Eisen shrugged. "You have to take the strain off the unit. That's going to mean cutting all non-essentials. Jettison the frozen food, reset the thermostats to forty degrees celsius, and drop your phase shields. That should lower your output requirements enough to let the APU cool. We probably won't recover any efficiency, but at least we won't lose anymore."

"Tamara?" Manley asked, inviting her to comment.

"He's the line officer," she answered, "not me. I don't have any engineering time."

"Well," Manley said, "now that we have that out of the way, shall we move onto the next order of business?" He paused to glance at the assembly. "Our long range array is still out. Electronic interference from the gas giant is blocking our trans-light capability." He paused, taking a deep breath. "We need to figure out who's going to captain this rustbucket. We can't wait for a formal appointment from Richards."

No one spoke. Manley scratched his cheek. "I'd like to propose Lieutenant Garibaldi for the job. He's the senior line officer on board, and technically the next in the chain of command on the Fleet side." He pointed to a young man with flaming red hair, who looked totally overwhelmed at the prospect.

Sosa leaned forward in her chair, giving Blair his first

good look at her. Her black hair tumbled around her face, framing her porcelain face. Blair was struck both by her beauty and the ready intelligence in her face. "Isn't Captain Eisen senior?" she asked.

Blair looked at Maniac, who mimed an hourglass with his hands and mouthed "Sosa." He raised his fingertips to his lips and kissed them. Eisen looked at them and glared, silently ordering them to behave.

Manley frowned. "Captain Eisen's rank's Confederation, not Colonial. He's not part of our fleet."

"That's nonsense," Sosa snapped. "Captain Dominguez arranged Captain Eisen's defection. He was promised a full conversion. Full rank, seniority, and pay."

"His arrangement was with Dominguez," Manley replied, "not us. We're not bound to honor that."

"Don't you think we ought to ask him?" Sosa asked.

"All right," Manley said. He looked at Eisen. "Do you have anything you want to say?"

Eisen looked pained, as though recalling a difficult memory. "It's only fair that you know why I'm here, and given that I owe certain friends an explanation," he said with a side look at Blair, "I can kill two birds with one stone."

He took a deep breath. "I was given the *Lex* when she came out of drydock," he said. "I received her commissioning pennant from Tolwyn himself." He frowned at the *Intrepid* officers' reaction to the SRA chief's name.

"I began to have some concerns when a special ops man and his lot came on board. Their orders said they were supposed to be doing assessments of pieces of captured Kilrathi hardware. This guy, Seether, had authorization from Tolwyn himself to take whatever he needed for his 'project.' No questions asked." Blair saw Eisen's face cloud at the remembered outrage. "They evicted my crew from my launch bay and set up shop. *I* wasn't even allowed in, and it was *my* damn ship. It was the most highhanded thing I'd ever seen."

Eisen took another sip from his coffee cup. He made a

face at the taste. "Seether's people then set up their own communications array and began transmitting and receiving trans-light messages. There was also evidence that they were tapping into the *Lexington*'s array, monitoring the ship's traffic."

"And?" Manley said, prompting Eisen to continue.

"I make it a point to review and initial the communications logs every day," Eisen said. "I noticed a lot of message traffic originating from Earth and going directly to Seether and his crew. I used my command override to check the message numbers. Within twelve hours I received a personal message from Tolwyn himself telling me to mind my own business."

"Wait a second," Sosa said, "I thought it was the commander's prerogative to inspect the logs."

"So I understand," Eisen replied acidly. "Three days later I got a conference call from Admirals Harnett and Petranova. They gave me the 'we're all in this together for humanity' speech. It took me a while to realize they were trying to recruit me for something. I passed on what they were selling, and within two hours my command override had been suspended."

"That was fast work," Blair injected.

Eisen shrugged. "You could probably tell I was having grave doubts about the missions we were flying. We were being fed information that didn't fit what I was seeing. I'd been a little skeptical of the Holy Writ that said you Border Worlders were behind the crisis on the frontier."

"Thanks," Manley said dryly, "we appreciate the vote of confidence."

Blair noticed Farnsworth kick him in the ankle. Eisen appeared to ignore the by-play.

He set his coffee cup on the lectern behind him. "I took advantage of a lull to send Admiral Richards a private message."

Blair nodded, recalling Richards' wartime reputation as the Confederation's preeminent code breaker and signals intelligence specialist. The man had first detected the Kilrathi super carriers via SIGINT and had tipped off the authorities in time to mount some kind of defense. Blair hadn't heard that Richards had returned to the Border Worlds. In a way, he was glad. No computer was safe and no network was secure with Richards and his band of electronic pirates on the loose.

"Anyway," Eisen said, "Richards sent me a set of files and some rudimentary code-breaking programs. They weren't terribly sophisticated, just enough to crack the *Lexington*'s protections and read the externals and address groups. We ran three hundred sequenced messages from Earth, Fleet Headquarters, and four coded systems. Seether's people were using code systems years ahead of the Fleet's. Mind you, this was supposed to be a research group, and they were receiving tactical signals.

"I ended up playing detective for Richards; copying coded transmissions, collecting mission data, and comparing those to Fleet movements. We found an early correlation when traffic would increase *before* a 'crisis' happened. I really began to worry when I saw that."

Eisen rubbed his hand across his brow. "I was just getting ready to package up the whole thing for Richards when I got relieved." He shook his head, his expression rueful. "Paulson's first act was to shut off my access codes, leaving me with no way to transmit my data. I had to carry it here by hand—and that meant defecting.

"Richards arranged it with Dominguez, who knew me by sight." He tipped his head towards Sosa. "He also sent the lieutenant here to meet me here with a porta-comp stuffed with cryptography programs." He glanced upwards. "I guess it was her bad luck that this ship got hit and lost its entire comm-section. She's been working on getting the ship back on-line."

Sosa raised her hand. "I have had some time to look at it," she said. She sounded slightly defensive to Blair. "It's all heavily coded, with lots of polyheuristics, but it *is* breakable. I think I can crack it—if given time. In the meantime we know very little about what's going on."

"What's to know?" a pilot interjected from the seats.

"All we need to know is that we're under attack while being blamed for raids we haven't done."

"The details are in the radio traffic," Eisen insisted. "All we have to do is find it. If we can prove what's going on, we might be able to stop a war."

"Or start one," someone mumbled.

Blair saw that Eisen looked less than confident. "We're still missing a lot of the evidence. But I do know the Border Worlds and the Confed are being manipulated, pushed into a war we'd both lose." He pointed to Sosa. "Those tapes hopefully will identify who they are." He looked at Manley. "Are you satisfied I'm on the level, Colonel?"

Manley looked around, polling the room for support, and not getting much back. "You're doubtless the most qualified, Captain," he said, smoothly changing sides, "I hope you'll fill in until Admiral Richards posts a replacement."

Eisen gave him a long look. "Thank you, Colonel." He took a deep breath. "I think the first order of business is going to be to pull the *Intrepid* back long enough for a refit."

"We're running away?" a voice asked from the crowd.

Blair felt Maniac bristle next to him. Marshall might be an iconoclast, but he apparently didn't appreciate seeing insubordination in others.

"No," Eisen replied, choosing to take the questions head-on, rather than withdrawing behind his rank. Blair realized that the rough-and-tumble nature of the Border Worlds fleet allowed for tougher questioning than the Confed permitted. Eisen seemed to understand the same thing. He chose to answer questions he'd have shrugged off if he had still been on the *Lex*. "We won't remain combat operational for long on one-third power. We need to relight at least one more APU and flush the residual radiation out the number one drive bay. That'll keep us marginal until we get to a drydock. Any other questions?"

He waited a moment, while the officers glanced back and forth. "Also," he said, "we're getting short on torpedoes and missiles—not to mention first-line fighters and pilots. We're in no shape to go toe-to-toe with the *Lexington* as we are." He flipped through the maps on the flat screen behind him until he found a sector chart. He tapped the jump point on the far side of the system with his fingertip, then traced a parabolic arc around the gas giant. "We'll slingshot around to the jump point, picking up some speed due to orbital mechanics. That'll let us cut our drives. Once we get to the jump point, we'll go through the Silenos Nebula to cover our tracks, then withdraw to the Orestes system. We'll do a combat resupply there as well as a hasty refit."

Blair watched the *Intrepid*'s surviving officers glance back and forth. No one ventured a comment.

"Now," Eisen said, "it's time for the dreaded personnel shuffle. I'm going to appoint Major Marshall to fill in provisionally for Colonel Shima. Her squadron'll need a senior officer, at least until we can get a permanent replacement." He tapped his finger on the lectern. "Lieutenant Garibaldi'll serve as my exec." He looked at the sober-faced, red-headed officer. "Your first order is to cut yourself an order for promoting yourself to lieutenant-commander. I don't like my executive officers to be *too* junior."

"Sir!" Garibaldi piped. "Can you do that?"

"I don't know," Eisen answered, "but I know it's easier to beg forgiveness than ask permission."

A Colonial officer sitting in front of Blair turned to her fellow. "I think he's gonna work out," she whispered.

"Let's see," Eisen continued, "that leaves a hole at Ops. Colonel Blair will fill in as the operations officer." He looked up. "Chris—what was your degree in?"

"Electronic engineering," Blair answered, "but that was thirty years ago!"

Eisen smiled. "You'll also take over communications from Lieutenant Sosa. That'll free her to work on her code breaking." He shifted his gaze to Sosa. "Lieutenant, you'll drop back to deputy CommO and OpsO. That'll keep Blair on the flight roster. Get him up to speed and get to work on that cryptography.

"Other than that, there're no changes. Colonel Farnsworth'll stay on as Damage Control, and Colonel Manley—you'll retain the wing, as well as your logistics and squadron commander's hats."

He took in the whole group. "Are there any questions?" Blair noticed he waited about two seconds before wrapping up the briefing. "All right then, people, get to work. We're burning daylight."

Blair noticed it was a tribute to his skills that the officers jumped up and responded as though Eisen had been in command for months, rather than minutes. Even Manley.

Maniac turned to Blair, then grinned. "Well, hero," he said, "I'd better shove off." Blair followed his gaze and saw Sosa working her way across the briefing room towards them. "Lucky bastard," Blair heard him mumble as he left.

Blair watched her approach. He guessed she was in her middle-to-late twenties. He noticed her shoulder-length black hair and china-blue eyes, then chided himself for noticing. Don't get interested, Chris, he told himself, or it'll be like Rachel all over again.

He wasn't listening.

"Colonel Blair?" she said as she stepped up to him. She smiled, a little nervously. "I'm First Lieutenant Velina Sosa—I run the 'switchboard' here. I guess you're taking over?"

"Not really," he answered. She had an engaging personality and an open, friendly smile. "I'll just be running blocker for you, Lieutenant, so you can finish breaking those files."

She smiled again and extended her hand. "Fair enough, I guess. Shall I show you what passes for a comm center here?"

They shook hands. The warmth of her skin surprised him. Of course her skin's hot, the voice inside him said, the whole damn ship's hot. "Uhh . . . lead on, Lieutenant," he said, feeling a little silly.

She led him out of the briefing room, giving him a view of her trim figure. He sighed, suddenly feeling his age.

She took him from station to station, explaining the purpose of each and answering his questions. Blair was heartily grateful for her in-depth knowledge of the system. He'd served as the officer of the deck on innumerable occasions in his career, and worked as an operations and flight deck officer repeatedly, but the hodge-podge equipment was new to his experience.

"How often does this stuff break down?" he asked her.

"Daily," she replied.

"What do you do then?"

She smiled. The male in him noticed she was just tall enough to see over his shoulder, the perfect height for a dancing partner. He swallowed, telling himself to behave.

"We fix it," she said. She laughed at his pained expression. "You *do* have an engineering degree, don't you?"

"Barely," he replied. "What I wanted to do was fly. I learned just enough to get my basic degree and get into flight school." He looked at her. "What'd you do your degree work in?"

"Dual Masters in theoretical mathematics and linguistics from Oxford. I was doing my doctoral work on theoretical numbers and phase-shift inducers when Admiral Richards recruited me."

Blair nodded politely, aware he was out of his depth. "Anyway," she laughed, "I've been on the admiral's staff—one of the 'Black Gang'—for about the last two years."

They shared another smile. Sosa seemed suddenly nervous. She looked away. "Let's go over to the light table. I'd better bring you up to speed on the system diagrams. The fires have been melting the fiber optics systems, so I'd better show you where the bridges are."

Blair followed her to the damage control station and watched as she cued the ship's schematics. The ship was much more badly damaged than it first appeared. Almost a third of the internal sections glowed either amber or red, indicating partial or full damage. The core fighting systems appeared to be intact, and, except for the power shortage, appeared battle-ready. Either the *Achilles* had been especially good at hitting non-essential systems or the damage control parties were exceptionally good.

She took him through the major communications and electronic countermeasures sub-systems, pointing out where her crews had cobbled things together. He caught a whiff of her perfume as she idly tucked one bang back behind her ear. He found himself wondering how she managed to smell clean, with just a hint of spiciness, on a ship with no showers.

A chirping noise from her pocket interrupted her briefing. She pulled it out and opened it. "Sosa," she said.

Blair heard a tinny voice coming from the unit's tiny speaker. "Velina, it's Pliers. Is Colonel Blair with you?"

"Yes," she replied, "do you need him?"

"Have him come down to the flight deck. We got his bird fixed, and I need him to sign off on the repairs."

"Okay," she said. "Sosa out." She closed the comm-unit.

Blair looked at his watch. "That was fast." He laughed. "You really have a maintenance tech named Pliers?"

She smiled, showing dimples. "He was a master chief for the Confed Fleet who retired out this way after the war." She shrugged. "He treats me like I'm his daughter."

"I see," Blair said, grinning, "I guess I ought to head down there."

She dipped her head. "If there's anything else I can help you with, Colonel, please don't hesitate to call."

He nodded and returned to the flight deck. He found his thoughts turning to her as he walked. She'd seemed just a little friendlier and more open than her duties required. Was she interested in him, or was his imagination working overtime? He laughed at himself. You old goat, he thought. What would she want with your old carcass?

He descended the ladder, coughing a little in the noxious air. Rachel Corialis' face sprang, unbidden, into his mind. He felt the pain of her departure as sharply as if she had just left him. He wasn't ready to go through that again, he told himself firmly. His thoughts, betraying him again, turned to Sosa's clean, spicy scent.

He stepped onto the flight deck, swearing at himself for his folly.

An older man, his coveralls spotted with grease and other, less identifiable fluids, walked up to him. "You Blair?" he asked in a gravelly voice. Blair took a long look at the leather-faced old coot with his fringe of snow white hair.

"I'm Colonel Blair," Chris corrected, putting the slightest stress on his rank.

The maintenance tech looked at Blair skeptically, tipping his head to one side. "So," he said sourly, "if it ain't the new kid, here to save us from the Feds."

Blair felt his eyebrows rise. He could not recall the last time he'd been called "kid," certainly not since he had turned forty. "I don't know about that," he said, feeling the tension between them.

The tech looked at him, the corners of his eyes crinkling into crow's-feet as he looked at Blair. He grinned and burst out laughing. "Pleased ta know you, kid." He tapped his chest. "Chief Tech Bob Sykes. Most folks call me Pliers."

"Most folks don't call me 'kid,' " Blair said dryly.

"Most folks ain't as old as I am," Pliers retorted, "so everybody's a kid to me." He crooked a finger at Blair. "You'd better come see what I did with the crate you brought in."

He led Blair towards the flight deck. Chris saw lines of the *Intrepid*'s fighters lined up, facing forward.

"This is your ready group?" he asked.

"Yup," Pliers answered, "ready group, strike group, and magnum launch, all rolled into one." He stopped and pointed at the painted marks. "We don't have a catapult, so we got to run them here on the deck—get them going under full afterburners, push them out, and pray. We can only use a third of the deck for spotting, so that cuts down on how many we can launch at a time." Pliers walked away, heading around the last rank of spotted fighters. "I'm told being in the back's better, 'cause it gives you a little extra distance for getting up to speed." Blair frowned at the tech's malicious grin.

He followed Pliers around the last fighter, to where his Thunderbolt stood, ready for launch. He wasn't certain what surprised him more, that it had been repaired, or that it had a Mark IV torpedo slung from its belly.

"Is that a torpedo?" Blair asked.

Pliers looked at him, long and hard. "You're observant, kid," he said sarcastically. "We ain't got but six ships that'll carry torps, and yours is one of them." He pointed to the back rank of fighters. He saw, in addition to his own Thunderbolt, a pair of tired-looking Broadswords and three old Saber conversions.

Pliers smiled. Blair saw a gleam in his eyes as he looked at the T-bolt. "Ain't worked on one of those birds in a while. Not since the war."

"How'd you fix her so fast?" Blair asked. "I thought the bent wing would have to be pulled and replaced."

"Naw," Pliers said, "the T-bolt uses the same strut and bow assembly as the Rapier, and we've got four of those we're using for parts. All we had to do was match panels and cut them to fit." He shrugged. "Your wing tank's a write-off, so your fuel'll be low, but I did get the thrusters fixed and aligned."

"I'm impressed," Blair replied.

Pliers took a packet out of his pocket and removed a black-looking clump that he stuffed into his mouth.

Blair winced. "Is that tobacco?" he said, trying to keep the disgust out of his voice.

"Yeah," Pliers replied, holding the pouch out to Blair. "You want some?"

Blair kept his expression still as Pliers bit down and chewed at the lump in his cheek. "Thanks, no."

"Suit yourself," the old man said as he rolled the pouch up and put it back into his pocket. He leaned over and spat a long, brown stream onto the deck. Blair winced again.

"Yup," Pliers said, "when you kids bend 'em, I fix 'em.

That's a later model than I've seen before, though." He looked at the fighter again, his expression wistful. "Yep, I could do a few things with that baby—touch up the engines, tweak the specs a little." He looked at Blair. "Give me a couple of days, and I could give you one hot ship."

Blair thought about all of the times he'd been outrun or outmaneuvered in a Thunderbolt. The idea of matching the heavy fighter's firepower with a lighter ship's speed or maneuverability appealed to him. Especially with Seether lurking out there somewhere. "This I'd like to see."

Pliers spat another jet onto the deck and smiled. "You just wait and you will see."

Blair opened his mouth to respond when red lights began to flash around the perimeter of the bay. An old fashioned loudspeaker began to bray the ship's alarm code.

"It's a scramble!" Pliers yelled. Blair sprinted for his ship, grateful he still wore his dirty flight suit.

"Attention!" a voice said. Blair recognized Sosa's voice through the loudhailer's crackle and distortion. "All hands to action stations. Fighters inbound. All pilots to launch deck. Attention! This is not a drill."

Blair dashed across the last few meters of the flight deck, dodging crew members who emerged from nowhere, springing up from crash carts or tiny niches from which they could steal some shut-eye.

Deck hands rolled a ladder up to the Thunderbolt. Blair scrambled up as the canopy whirred open. He slid into the acceleration chair, grabbed the helmet from its place on the control yoke, and popped it on. Willing hands grabbed the straps, snapping him into place, and plugging in his intercom wires. All around him he saw other ships readying, their crews prepping the pilots. Engines fired, filling the cavernous bay with sound and smoke. Loose scraps of paper and blanket material swirled in the dark, cluttered bay.

Pliers heaved himself up the ladder. Blair had to lean towards him to hear what he was saying. ". . . and you don't have enough rolling room to clear the deck!" the old man yelled.

"What!?" Blair yelled back, convinced he was hearing about one word in three.

"We rigged you with a pair of JATO bottles," Pliers yelled.

"What's a JATO?" Blair yelled back.

"Jet Assisted Take-Off," Pliers said, his lips against Blair's helmet. "Booster rockets. We think it'll be enough."

"You *think*?"

"Well," Pliers said, "the computer says it'll work . . . but it's an old computer."

Blair stared at him, dumbfounded. Pliers clapped him on the shoulder and retreated, pulling the ladder away with him. Blair, shaking his head in disbelief, matched his bearing and started his fuel-feed system. The turbines span up smoothly, ready to feed steady fuel to the thirsty main engines. His fuel reading flicked down a notch, then steadied out at seventy-five percent. He looked down at the ground crewman stationed on each wing. They each raised one thumb, indicating the area behind the ship was clear. He raised his own thumb, making eye contact with each in turn, then hit his main drives.

The ship shuddered as the twin engines spun up and ignited. He felt the fighter jerk forward.

"Flight control to wing," Sosa said, her warm voice taut with excitement. "The TCS *Lexington* followed us through the jump point. We've got thirty-plus fighters inbound."

"Roger," Hawk said, answering for the wing. "Panther, you and I'll have to keep them from getting to the carrier. Blair . . . Tiger, you take the bomber group and Maniac. Try to take out the carrier. Your callsign'll be Thor." He paused, the static crackling in Blair's ears as the local stars added their voices to the frequency. "If we blow this, it'll be a long float home."

"Stand by for launch," Sosa said. Blair felt his stomach grow queasy at the thought of firing on the *Lex*. They were his friends, his comrades.

"Launch!" she ordered. The first Rapier hurled itself

forward, its afterburners on full thrust. It cut through the force curtain and into space. The fighters fired off the deck in five-second intervals. The Scimitar in front of Blair's Thunderbolt vanished in a cloud of smoke and a circular blue compression ring. Blair saw only the groundcrews scrambling for the safety of the dock edges.

He looked down at Pliers and raised his right hand. He used his left to spool up his afterburners. He felt the Thunderbolt shake and shudder as it strained to move forward. He waited for the engine thrust to edge into the red, then cut his arm down. The crewmen pulled the blocks.

The Thunderbolt blazed forward, pushing him back in his seat. The JATO bottles ignited a moment later, their thrust slamming him hard against his chair. He breathed deeply, trying to keep his breastbone from kissing his spine.

He raced through the force curtain and into space. The weight fell away from his chest as the fighter's inertial dampers took over from the ship's artificial gravity. He hauled his stick to the left, entering the recovery orbit and finishing his clearing turn. The JATO bottles failed, the last of their thrust bleeding away as they expended their fuel.

He jettisoned them. Telemetry began to roll in from Sosa's communications operators. Blair saw the *Lexington*, advancing alone on the battered *Intrepid* behind a wall of fighters. Where the hell were the escorts? A fleet carrier was simply too valuable to be allowed to go anywhere by itself, especially on an attack.

He scanned his tactical plot, then checked his map. The wall of *Lexington* fighters prevented him from approaching the flattop directly. Perhaps he could slip around one flank . . .

He cued his radio. "Thor Leader to Thor elements. Form on me, base course two-seven-zero, Z minus twenty-five." He angled down and away from the small task group, taking himself out of the ship's plane to make it easier for his scattered ships to assemble. The remainder of the *Intrepid*'s forces swirled and dove, seeking to form up into their respective squadrons. The delay in organizing allowed the Confed fighters to close on the rebels. This was the time, Blair thought, that the Border Worlders would feel the hurt of their primitive systems.

The leading edge of the *Lexington*'s forces were visibly nearer the rebel carrier as the first of Hawk's patrols engaged them. Blair switched to his targeting computer and saw the cluster of blue and red dots begin to swirl around each other as both sides fed forces into the fray.

Blair glanced outside the cockpit to check on his rump squadron. Both Broadswords were present, as were two of the three Sabers. His eye was drawn to the distant battle. Red, blue, and white beams arced across the night sky, appearing from Blair's perspective to connect star to star. It was weirdly beautiful, even the bright flashes that marked the end of one ship or another.

The carrier behind Blair opened up, the heavier weapons of her anti-boat batteries lancing out to engage the fighters that wandered into range. A trickle of light ships, Ferrets and an odd Arrow, still emerged from the *Intrepid*'s bay as ground crews brought them up from below and spotted them for launch. The latecomers were fed into the blazing fight in singles and pairs, adding their guns and missiles to the *Intrepid*'s weight. The frigates and smaller escorts began to creep closer to the dogfight, interposing themselves between the fighters and the battered, vulnerable ship behind.

Blair listened to the babble on the primary channels, the curses and shouts of victors, the screams and pleas of the dying, Hawk's and Panther's commands as they tried to hold the wolves away from the carrier, and Sosa's calm voice as she coordinated the disparate elements of the defense. Blair glanced at the fight, at his assembled charges, and then checked his nav map.

"Well, boss," Maniac said, "we don't stand a chance in that. What do we do?"

Maniac closed up on his right flank, flying a Rapier with markings from an old cruiser, the TCS *Caledonia*. Behind

him straggled three other early model Rapiers, the balance
of Marshall's "squadron." The fire behind Blair intensified
as several Confed fighters broke from the main group to
begin their attack run. The light escorts opened up in
earnest, attempting to swat them down before they could
begin their torpedo runs.

He looked at the map again, then out his cockpit at the
huge, red gas giant that dominated one quarter of the
view. He stared at it a moment, while the edges of a plan
took shape. "Thor Leader to Thors, assume course one-
nine-one, Z minus fifteen. Maximum burn."

Maniac appeared a moment later, as Blair knew he would.
"We're running away?"

"No," Blair replied, "remember what you told me about
Hawk?"

Maniac paused. "You mean the asteroids?"

"Yeah," Blair answered, "we're gonna do the same thing.
We'll dogleg around the fight, swing down behind the gas
giant, then come around and hit *Lex* as she passes."

"I like it," Maniac replied.

Blair used his short-range laser link to file his attack
plan with the *Intrepid*'s CIC, then led his force out and
away from the fight. Once free of the immediate vicinity
of the battle, he cut his Thunderbolt sharply over and dove
hard for the large gas giant that was the system's third
planet. He pulled his fighter into a tight orbit, settling
himself inside the planet's uppermost layer of atmosphere.
A close approach would mask his ships within the planet's
clutter, making him functionally invisible. His phase shields
began to register damage as the upper atmosphere lashed
at his ship.

The close presence of the planet masked almost all of
Blair's communications, though snippets of chatter did
get through. It was obvious even from a few brief sentences
that the *Intrepid* and her fighters were in trouble. The
carrier had been hit once again, though she still seemed
to be in the fight. Her fighters had broken and were falling
back while the *Lexington*'s howled after them in hot pursuit.

His tactical plot skipped and jumped as the *Lexington*'s drive plume came into sight. "All right," he said, "ease forward until you can start your lock-on sequence. Sabers, you stay under cover. If we botch this, then you'll take over as a second wave." He goosed his throttles, powering his Thunderbolt forward and out of its tight orbit. He switched his ordnance control to his torpedo, then began his countdown cycle.

The two Broadswords eased out from behind the planet's bulk and began their own targeting sequences. Maniac and company held to their flanks, ready to guard them during the vulnerable time it took for their AIs to defeat the *Lexington*'s phase shielding and transmit a firing solution to the torpedoes.

He watched the *Lex* power closer, sliding from a port quarter to three-quarter view as the torpedo's reticule crawled towards the center of his HUD. The *Lexington* reoriented and launched another small cluster of fighters. Blair saw both bays were in operation, a fact that both chilled and reassured him that his decision to defect had been the correct one.

The torpedo locked on—breaking his musing and forcing the moment of truth. The Broadswords tipped up, presenting their bellies to the carrier as they armed their active locks and readied to fire. He pushed his throttles forward, sliding out of the planet's shelter and pushing forward towards the ship. "Thor Leader to Thors," he said, "stand fast. I'll take the first shot. If I miss, or get blown away, then launch. Go for a fire-power kill, rather than a ship kill. It'll be enough if we knock her out of the battle."

He watched his range counter dropping. He waited for the carrier's defensive batteries to fire, the ship to begin evasive maneuvering, or interceptors to launch against him. Nothing. The *Lex* continued straight on, intent on its distant prey and seemingly oblivious to the threat that was literally under its nose. Blair's ships had achieved the rare situation of having complete surprise.

The carrier's vulnerability screamed of incompetence. She'd advanced without escort after a desperate opponent, apparently without even arming her defensive batteries.

Blair used Paulson's sloppiness to his advantage, angling to his left for a solid, bows-on shot. His range counter continued to drop, until it showed he was within twenty-five hundred kilometers of the target. He fired the Mark IV, noting the red-blue flare of its drive plume as it launched away. "Fox One," he reported, "bearings set and matched. Running hot and true." He held his course, tracking the weapon's approach. It bored in on the ship, ready to wreak havoc.

His gut twinged at the deaths that would be on his hands. Catscratch, Vagabond, and the others he'd met had done nothing to deserve what he was about to deliver. He suspected many in the *Lexington*'s crew would rebel if they knew what they were serving. He realized he didn't have it in him to destroy the carrier. He raised his eyebrows. Perhaps he didn't have to kill the carrier to make it go away.

He opened the torpedo's "auto-destruct" cover switch and depressed the arming button. The torpedo closed on the carrier, moving into terminal guidance mode as it entered the ship's electromagnetic field. Blair mashed the button again, detonating the warhead about a hundred meters from its target.

The fusion detonation enveloped the front of the ship, coruscating the phase shields in a shower of red, blue, and green. Plumes of static discharge spread around the bows and trailed back, like ripples in water. The shockwave hit the *Lexington* a second later, shaking the front of the ship like a terrier with a bone. Blair sighed with relief when he saw the ship's intact bows emerging from the near side of the blast. He hadn't hit it after all.

The fireball conformed itself to the chin under the bows that formed the ends of the launch tubes. The fading energy swept along and through the weaker force curtains that protected the tubes' mouths. Blair saw secondary explosions ripple along the leading edges of the launch bays.

A single Arrow launched into the middle of the maelstrom. It hit the swirling energy and tumbled out of control, swinging upward and slamming into the carrier's belly. The wreckage swept back into the starboard bay's mouth like a fly disappearing into a fish. Fires raged along the fronts of both bays, halting launch operations. The *Lexington* could recover fighters, but little else. She was effectively out of the battle.

Maniac's close-in communications laser painted Blair's array. "Funny how the torpedo blew up like that, all nice and premature," Maniac said, laughing. "I'll bet nobody got hurt, and it looks like you got those bays knocked out good and proper. This must be your lucky day."

"What do you mean?" Blair asked.

"My instruments say their hull integrity is intact. They got off lightly, other than being toasty-warm up front." He laughed again. "I have to give you credit for that. I didn't think you'd do it."

"And?" Blair said, expecting the worst.

"Don't worry," Maniac said. "I think you made the right decision."

"Thanks," Blair said.

"Besides," Maniac said, "you drove her off. The *Lady*'s turning away. Her fighters are withdrawing. Good job, hero." Blair thought that, for once, Maniac didn't sound sarcastic.

"Fine," he replied, a little shortly. "Let's go home. We've got to get out of this system."

Maniac chuckled again as he came alongside. "Right, boss," he said. "Anything you say."

Seether sat in Paulson's plush, jump-capable shuttle, reading the captain's report on the *Lexington*'s damage. The portside bay had lost the final alignment stage of the bays' firing coils. The pilots, their morale already battered by the defection of two of their senior officers and the

loss of five comrades' ejection pods to the rebels or to
space, had refused to essay the bay without the final stage
being repaired. Paulson had caved in to their deputation,
effectively ending offensive flight operations from the port
bay until it was fixed. It would figure that an alignment
coil required depot echelon maintenance. For want of a
nail . . .

He had to admit to himself that he would have done the
same thing if he had been in the pilots' boots. They needed
the alignment coil to ensure the launch cradles' accurate
retraction and the final positioning of the fighters as they
emerged from the tubes. Without it, each launch was
unpredictable, as was cradle retraction. The combination
could be fatal.

The starboard bay had suffered even more physical
damage. An Arrow had detonated and had lodged in the
bay's throat. Its ordnance had exploded, sending burning
fuel and pieces of payload into the launch area proper.
Six Project personnel had died.

The carrier would be out of action for a month, perhaps
six weeks. Admiral Petranova was throwing a ring-tailed
fit over the damage to her sole fleet carrier. More
importantly, The Project was losing its main portable
platform. Their remote base would have to pick up the
slack, lengthening mission times and increasing the risks
of detection until they could get another asset like the
Lexington under their control.

Those assets, like competent and loyal carrier skippers,
weren't exactly growing on trees. There would also be a
time delay in closing up shop on the Lex, sterilizing the
work area, and moving the test platforms elsewhere.
Seether was amazed at how much damage could be wrought
during one three-hour nap.

He looked slowly up at Paulson, the architect of this
mess. He found himself surprisingly in control of his
temper. His emotion control drills were paying off.

Paulson paced between the starboard portholes and the
airlock, his actor's face outwardly calm. Only the tic above

his right eye gave some indicator of the man's state of mind. "My God," he said quietly, over and over, "what a disaster."

He looked up from his pacing and saw Seether watching him. "You have to support me," he blurted. "You've got to back me with Petranova!"

"Stop your whining," Seether replied. He felt his temper heat a notch as Paulson tried to wriggle off the hook he'd sunk into himself. "You were given the *Lexington* with the understanding that you'd obey my orders." He ticked off the points on his fingers. "You chose to take off after the rebels on your own initiative, you left the escorts behind, you didn't sweep for ambushes, you committed your pilots to battle piecemeal, and at the first sight of trouble you abandoned the fight and any pilots who'd ejected. The choice to commit was yours . . . and so are the consequences."

"B-but you were in charge," Paulson said. His voice hardened. "I'll take you down, too, you son of a bitch, if you don't back my play. I'll expose the whole lot of you."

Seether felt his temper heat. How dare this man try and threaten him, threaten all they'd worked for, to save himself? Paulson was nothing more than a professional bureaucrat, a bottom feeding glad-hander whose principle skills were blaming others and shedding his mistakes the way a duck shed water.

"I think everyone will agree that even *I* have to sleep sometime," Seether replied. He had made just enough of a mistake in leaving Paulson unsupervised for the captain to cloud the issue. The man might yet wriggle out of this.

Not this time, Seether thought grimly. He stepped up to Paulson, who looked at him with mixed desperation and aggression. Paulson stopped pacing, unknowingly placing his back to the airlock. "You'd better back me up," he repeated, "or else."

"You're right," Seether said, dissembling, "I *am* somewhat responsible." He smiled. "But I think forgiveness is possible. You didn't know any better."

Paulson smiled nervously, not liking Seether's tone but grasping at the proffered straw. "You think so? What'll happen to me?"

"Oh," Seether replied, "I think you'll be reassigned. Probably a deep space command. A *very* deep space command."

He handed the sheaf of papers to Paulson with his left hand, who instinctively looked down and raised his hands to take them. Seether flicked his right wrist, flipping the laser knife from its concealed pouch up his sleeve. He snapped it open and hit the power button with one deft movement. Paulson had taken the papers when Seether slashed him across the throat.

Arterial blood sprayed inside the shuttle, spattering Seether, the richly appointed chairs, the bulkheads, floor, and overhead. Paulson, a stunned expression on his face, dropped the papers and raised his hand to his throat. A stream of bubbles blew from his opened airway as he tried to scream. Seether heard only a gassy noise as Paulson went to his knees. Seether stepped forward and hit the inner airlock door. Paulson's chest heaved as he tried to draw air into his lungs and inhaled only blood.

The shuttle's alarm chimed as Seether hit the override. The inner door slid open. Seether grabbed Paulson by the hair and flung him into the lock. He quickly closed it and hit the "Emergency Purge" control. The outer door blew, launching Paulson into space with the unrecovered atmosphere.

"See," Seether said, "I've forgiven you already." Paulson, his face frozen in a rictus of agonized horror, drifted alongside a moment, then began to fall back as the shuttle's autopilot made a small course correction.

Seether turned and looked at the inside of the shuttle. The place looked like an abattoir. He looked down at the blood on his hands, on the knife, and on his clothes. He considered advising Petranova that he'd dealt with Paulson, then changed his mind. Ludmilla Petranova, Third Fleet Commander, wasn't on his list of favorite people, not after the reaming she'd given him over Paulson's debacle. She'd learn about Paulson's fate through channels. It would remind her of her status within The Project.

He shrugged, returned the knife to its pouch, and went forward to program the shuttle for jump.

• CHAPTER EIGHT

Senator James Taggart leaned over the wet bar. His cloak of office lay casually thrown over a chair back, alongside the gavel that marked his position as the year's Master of the Assembly. The gavel conferred no special powers outside the Great Hall, but its presence in the small committee rooms lent him a certain weight and respect not usually accorded a freshman senator.

The day's Ways and Means Committee meeting had been reasonably successful, or at least no more rancorous and chaotic than usual. The committee decided what programs lived and died, which military bases closed, which planets received largesse, how much taxes increased, and who paid them. It was a key committee and a plum assignment. It was also a royal headache.

He sighed. He supposed it was inevitable that he and his colleagues would be called the "God Squad," but they simply didn't have the money to meet basic expenses, much less to fund all the projects that the senators begged them to consider. His esteemed colleagues often fought like dogs over scraps, with entrenched interests locked in mortal combat over sparse resources.

Unfortunately, many of the contenders were deserving. So many planets desperately needed help, and with tax receipts down, they had little to give. Their task was to reach above the squabbling and find projects whose impact would be out of proportion to their funding, rather than the other way around.

The funding issues and Ways and Means problems didn't cut much ice with politicians who had built their careers on larding up their home planets, or faced reelection and were desperate to take their restless, unemployed constituents at home some tangible proof of their efforts. Threats and bribes flowed freely as elections closed in on those whose heads were on the block.

Och, Paladin, me boy, don't take on like that, he chided himself, th' others're just tryin' tae do the best they can for th' folks back home.

He was lucky that, unlike the bottom feeders infesting the Assembly, he didn't have to whore himself to take care of the home folks. His own planet, Altair, was a soldiers' colony. Altairians appreciated soldier's talk, the blunter the better. He had promised his people only to try his best. He felt proud to serve them, proud they placed their trust in him.

He rubbed his finger along his jawline. "Now where hae' I put that wee bottle o' single malt?"

The door chimed, announcing a visitor.

"Come in."

Geoffrey Tolwyn entered, wearing an everyday uniform. Taggart took that in, along with his sober expression and stiff back. Tolwyn rarely came to the Senate in anything less than full dress, and then only to address full committees. The fact that he would deign to visit a single senator in his office suggested something was up.

Tolwyn looked around the small room. He nodded in approval. "You're doing well, Paladin, to rate an office this close to the Assembly Hall."

"I'm gettin' by, Admiral," he said, smiling. "To what do I owe this pleasant surprise?"

Had Tolwyn come to gloat? He had gotten his defense budget, or nearly all of it, in a tough fight against Taggart's faction, who had fought to expand the merchant marine and subsidize shipbuilding. His esoteric arguments for more commercial hulls to haul freight had failed against Tolwyn's visceral appeals that cutting the budget equalled emasculating the military.

Tolwyn looked uneasy. "I'm supposed to present my biennial report to the defense committee tomorrow," he said. "I figured I'd best give it to you first."

Taggart waved him towards a chair. "Och, is it about your wee super-carriers?"

"No," Tolwyn replied, "we've pushed up the production schedule. The *Vesuvius*'ll be ready for shakedowns in a week or so. The crew's looking forward to you christening the ship, Senator, it'll be an inspiration to them."

Taggart nodded, ignoring Tolwyn's glad-handing. "And the *St. Helens*?"

Tolwyn scratched his cheek. "Her engine and run-up tests are complete. She's taking on fuel and weapons. We're shifting to an accelerated construction schedule to finish the bays."

"Why the rush?" Taggart asked, mentally toting up the cost of speeding up the already ruinously expensive program.

"Bad news from the frontier, Paladin," Tolwyn answered. "We need those carriers in service as soon as possible."

"What kind of trouble?"

Tolwyn's face grew even longer. "Treason."

Taggart refused to let himself be drawn. "Will you join me for a glass, then? Bad news should ne'er pass a dry throat."

"No," Tolwyn replied. He took a deep breath. "Eisen, Blair, and Maniac Marshall all defected to the rebels. They went over three days back. According to our telemetry, either Blair or Marshall torpedoed the *Lexington*. She's out of action, and heading in for repairs."

Taggart nearly dropped the bottle he'd snagged from the bar. He looked down at it, trying to cover his confusion. At that moment, Tolwyn could have knocked him over with a feather. "My God," he choked out. "The lad was always strong-willed . . . but this is shocking. What happened?"

"We don't really know, Paladin. But they hurt the *Lex*."

Taggart felt he'd been pummelled. "How many dead?"

"Casualty figures have yet to come in," Tolwyn said, his voice flat and unreadable. "But we lost three-hundred thirty on the *Achilles* last week. We don't know if Eisen or Blair helped the rebels before they went over. Eisen had the *Lex's* command codes. He could have fed them telemetry on the *Achilles*."

"Why?" he asked, his accent failing him. "They're some of the best men we've got, all old and trusted comrades. What would make them go . . ." He paused, unable to bring himself to say the word "betray." ". . . over like that?"

"I don't know," Tolwyn answered. "I'm just as confused by this as you are." He spread his palms. "What intelligence we've managed to collect is . . . unreliable. Our networks are collapsing; the data we get from them is erratic. All we know is that the frontier is on the verge of war."

Taggart looked at him carefully, trying to see behind his eyes. "You still don't have any idea of who's behind all this?"

Tolwyn replied, "None, at least not specifically. One thing is clear, however. The Border Worlds forces are increasingly aggressive. Blair was flying off a Border Worlds carrier when he hit the *Lexington*. We think this ship destroyed the *Achilles*."

Taggart leaned against the bar. "Is that confirmed, Admiral? An active service Border Worlds ship?" He closed his eyes at Tolwyn's single confirming nod. "Then it'll be war," he said softly. "The Senate won't stand for that. Not a bit."

"No," Tolwyn said, shaking his head, "my aides tell me a resolution declaring war on the Border Worlds will be brought up for debate before the full Assembly within a week." He stopped himself. "Let's hope war isn't our only option. . . ."

Taggart had to struggle to keep his face still. Tolwyn wasn't giving his report until the following morning. So how could he possibly know what the Assembly might do in response?

"I still don't understand how this could happen," he said, hoping to draw him out.

Tolwyn looked away. "Who knows why anything happens anymore? The whole damned structure of society is collapsing around us. Debts are mounting, trade and trust are falling, and even Earth, the center of our culture, is blighted. The center is failing and the periphery is falling into chaos. Is it any wonder that insane things are happening?"

"I'm not sure I'm following you," Taggart replied, a little alarmed by Tolwyn's response. The admiral looked at him, his eyes alive with uncharacteristic intensity.

"Surely you can see it for yourself, Paladin, even from up there in your council rooms. Our Confederation is disintegrating. We're losing our frontier stars while the central government haggles over words and nuances of laws that will just be ignored. We're falling into anarchy, atrophying as our economies falter, our Fleet withers away, and our so-called leaders squabble. We're fraying, flying apart as we lose our common ground, our center." He fixed Taggart with a fierce stare. "People are starving and as they starve, they forget their civilization. Face it, our golden age is passing and all that awaits is ruination and conquest by whatever force decides it wants us."

Taggart studied Tolwyn's face as the admiral ranted. The Tolwyn he knew subscribed to bitter logic, never flinching from the hard choices or cold, calculated decisions that often cost lives. The Tolwyn of old never would have permitted himself this rambling discourse.

Had the strain on the admiral proven too much? Taggart knew he wasn't ready to essay that kind of judgement. Thinking of Tolwyn's gloomy take on the human condition, however, only added to his own worries. "I'm not sure that it's all that bad," he replied, trying to put the best face on the situation. "We've had worse problems before, and we've found ways out of them. I'm sure we will again."

"Then you're blind." Tolwyn turned away and opened the door. "If I hear anything new about Eisen or Blair, I'll keep you posted." He swept out of the room, less a man and more a force of nature. The door, sensing his departure, closed behind him.

Taggart looked down at the bottle, seeing the label for

the first time. "There you are," he said, as he poured himself a generous drink from the bottle of single malt.

He could not accept that Eisen and Blair could be disloyal. Something must have driven them to it, something serious. "What are ye into, Geoff me boy," he said to the closed door, "that'd make good men go bad like that?"

Perhaps it was time to dust off his cloak and dagger and do some discreet checking into Tolwyn's activities. But not just yet. It was senseless to pour good scotch and then not drink it.

He took a deep sip, letting the amber liquid roll around his tongue. "Och, that's good."

Blair lay on the deck, his stiff back separated from the hard durasteel floor plates by a single thin blanket. At least the air was clean and clear. The two-day refit at Orestes had accomplished other miracles as well. The fires were finally out, the air had been exchanged, the excess heat had been bled away, and the number two APU had been restarted. They had power and water for showers, if not quarters, and the freezers had been restocked. He hadn't realized how good a steak and vegetables would taste after a week of breathing smoke and eating condensed emergency rations.

The *Intrepid* was by no means operating at one hundred percent. The number one drive assembly was still out, but at least it wasn't pumping gamma radiation into Engineering or fuel into space. Several damaged fiber optic cables had been replaced, allowing the CIC to function without worrying about losing contact with the outside world at odd moments. The bridge, the top deck, and the fire-gutted bow had been abandoned. The ship should have been withdrawn from service, but that wasn't an option with the Confederation breathing down their necks.

At least, he thought, the ship wouldn't be quite as vulnerable. They had enough power now to maintain both phase shields and guns.

They had also managed to transfer the prisoners captured

in the dogfight to a hotel for transfer back to Earth. The pilots had been relieved to see him and Maniac, and didn't seem to bear too many grudges against them for changing sides. Maniac had speculated that several might be ripe for conversion, his euphemism for what Blair still considered treason. Blair had demurred. He didn't mind putting his own head in the noose, but he wasn't going to encourage others to do it. Instead, the prisoners would go home to Earth with stories of honorable treatment and greetings from friends and loved ones.

He cupped his hands behind his head and listened to the heavy snores from the pilots and crew sprawled around him.

Velina Sosa's image popped unbidden into his head, as it had been wont to do lately. They'd worked side by side the entire two days at Orestes and had been possibly the only two people other than Eisen who hadn't taken an eight-hour shore leave. He'd found her warm and engaging, and his reading of her body language suggested she found him at least the same.

He rolled onto his side, disgusted with himself. He was old enough to be her father, and besides, hadn't he gone down that road once with Rachel? Still, her attentions were flattering, and she had helped him feel younger than he had since he'd retired. The heat, exercise, and bad food he'd eaten onboard the *Intrepid* had helped him shed most of his extra weight, enough that he didn't feel like a paunchy old man standing next to her. Now, he thought dryly, he was a trim one.

He sat up. Sleep didn't seem to be an option. He might as well take advantage of the opportunity to get some work done. He fumbled for his flight suit in the semi-dark and wormed his way into it.

The lights and power came up. Sosa's voice sounded over the loudhailer. "Scramble! All pilots and crews to flight deck! Stand by for launching instructions." Blair closed the suit's front tab and stepped into his boots.

Pliers waited by the T-bolt's side as Blair navigated the

crews and pilots scrambling to ready their fighters. He followed Blair up the ladder and bent to check his rig. Blair wrinkled his nose at the old man's tobacco reek.

"Remember the mods I gave you," he said. "You can autoslide now, though you're going to move like a pregnant pig. Remember—"

"Yeah," Blair said, interrupting, "it's not that the pig sings well that's important, it's that it sings at all."

They laughed together before Pliers continued. "I've tweaked your max speed up to 420 KPS, so you can run with a Hellcat, at least for short distances. Watch your engine overheat lights and your fuel consumption. Your max afterburner hasn't changed, but I did install wider nozzles on your maneuvering thrusters, which should add to your turning speed."

"What am I giving up?" Blair asked, firmly aware that every design modification required trade-offs.

"You're losing some fine control, and a lot of range. All these mods're going to cost fuel, so try to conserve where you can."

"Got it," he looked down at the wing pods and the JATO bottles that replaced his outboard missile stations. "Any way we can get rid of those?"

"Not without a longer deck or a catapult."

Blair nodded, then finished his preflights. Telemetry began to roll onto his nav plot as the CIC finished its mission prep. Their flight plan would take them across the "border" and into what had been Kilrathi space. He whistled at that, then heard the babble on his circuit as other pilots read the same data.

Sosa's voice crackled across the circuit. "Hawk's and Panther's squadrons will assume tight orbit around the carrier as a CAP against attack. Colonel Blair, you will take Maniac and his squadron and assist a ship in distress. Assume course three-six-zero, zee plus fourteen, and cross the border. You will render customary aid and comfort as required by the Geneva Conventions."

Hawk cut into the circuit. "Are the ships Kilrathi?"

Sosa paused. "We're obligated, under interstellar law, to render aid to *any* ship in distress. These ships are under attack and are asking for help. We have to give it to them."

"So they're Kilrathi," Hawk said. "Why should we care?"

Eisen broke into the channel, his voice cold as ice. "You have your orders, pilot. Execute them."

Hawk snapped, "Why should we go out of our way for Cats?" Panther cut him off before he could protest again. "Dammit, you agreed he'd be captain," she said angrily, "so let him captain. File your complaint through channels."

"Why's Blair going?" Hawk pressed. "I'm the wing commander!"

Eisen's cold voice indicated he was losing patience. "Colonel Blair has a certain notoriety where the Cats are concerned. You don't. He goes. You stay. Enough said."

Hawk, grumbling, launched, leading the strike off the *Intrepid*'s deck. Blair, needing more room to get his T-bolt up to speed, launched last. He quickly found Maniac's formed squadron and led them towards the border. Maniac had acquired three additional Rapiers at Orleans, courtesy of Kruger's Landreich, as well as his repaired Hellcat. He had, of course, readopted the 'Cat. The squadron was still under strength, but eight craft at least made two full-strength flights.

He listened in on the pilots' chatter. They were *very* unhappy at being asked to rescue Kilrathi. He was a little surprised that he really didn't care much one way or another. They and the Kilrathi had been bitterest enemies, and he would have expected his reactions to be more like his pilots'. He hated those who'd killed Angel, but that was personal. Why didn't he extend that to the race as a whole?

His AI chimed when it picked up the signal from the border markers, then chimed again as they crossed into Kilrathi space. A number of red pips appeared on his target tracker at extreme range. He switched to the interstellar distress channel, wondering whether or not to use his hero-name. It was better that the Cats knew who they were dealing with. "Heart of the Tiger to distressed ships . . . what is your status?"

His comm-panel fuzzed and blurred. Blair couldn't make out the Kilrathi's face, but it seemed vaguely familiar.

"Shintahr Melek to Blair," the alien replied. "Have you come to gloat over our passing? Have you forgotten my personal surrender to you already?"

Blair felt his guts roil. Melek had been Prince Thrakhath's retainer and a formidable enemy in his own right, a senior commander whose ability to forgive and forget the destruction of his home world was likely to be zero. That made them even. Melek's master had killed his Angel.

"Negative," he replied tightly. "Under the Geneva Accords, we're obligated to help all ships in need. What can we do?"

Melek's face steadied in the tiny screen. He deflated before Blair's eyes. "We were thirteen ships out of what you call 89 Hydrae B, bound for the Pasqual system." He paused. "We are under attack by four to six attack craft. Our escorts have been driven off or destroyed. They seem to be able to cloak at will. Can you help us? Or, rather, will you help us?"

"Yes," Blair answered, then switched to his tactical channel. "Maniac, did you copy that?"

"Yeah, boss," he replied, "I got it, we're about two minutes out. I'm getting a range to target on the freighters and . . . TallyHO! I got one—two—four bogies inbound."

"Roger." His blood went cold. Enemy fighters flickered in and out of sight. They had cloaking devices.

Maniac keyed his mike, sending out a burst of static. "Maniac to Wolfpack. Break and attack."

The fighters peeled off the squadron's Vee formation, climbing and diving in groups of two as they sought advantage against the raiders. Blair was surprised to see Maniac sidle into his wing slot. "I figured you'd go haring in by yourself."

"Can't," Maniac replied, "I got me a squadron now. I can't act that way and expect them to listen when I tell them not to."

Blair, surprised to the core by Maniac's spurt of maturity, didn't answer. The raiding ships decloaked and closed on the fighters, using full afterburners to get inside missile range.

"Bandits!" Maniac yelled. "Here they come!" He broke away, accelerating away at an angle from Blair.

"So much for obeying orders," Blair mumbled.

He pulled the stick back into his lap and hit his afterburner, pulling hard into his Z-axis and changing plane and direction from Maniac. Marshall saw-bucked his Hellcat, rocking in short random changes that altered his course and speed without costing him inertia. One raider tried to stick in behind him, its heavy ordnance searching for Maniac's ship. Marshall flat-kicked his 'Cat around, cutting his drives and tumbling his fighter, then hitting his thrusters in a line perpendicular to his former direction. He side-slipped his Hellcat out of the raider's line of fire, and then cross-cut the other's path to fire a high deflection burst that scattered shots along and across the raider's spine. The Hellcat's ion cannon flared the ship's phase shields but did no appreciable damage.

The pirate spun past Maniac, frantically trying to rotate to follow its target. Maniac rotated his ship back into his direction of travel and reengaged his drives. It was, Blair had to admit, a smooth piece of flying. Maniac had been practicing since Seether had taken him down.

Blair turned his Thunderbolt towards the raider, its ponderous maneuverability helped considerably by Pliers' mods. The raider, beset by two enemies, easily evaded him. It flashed past, close enough for him to get a good, long look. The fighter was like nothing he had ever seen. He noted its chisel-pointed bow and chin-mounted weapons pods and a pair of large glowing Bussard intakes nested between two tail strakes. The damned thing looked big, at least as long as his T-bolt, and far too big to be as fast or as nimble as it seemed. He pulled his stick around, getting off a single barrage with his plasma guns before it passed. He missed badly.

He tried to follow it around for a second shot. His turn ratio, even with Pliers' mods, remained far too slow to give it much of a fight. Maniac, with his lighter and more nimble ship, was having difficulties keeping it away from his tail. The raider bored in close, fired a missile up his tail, then deftly rotated towards Blair and fired again. Blair, amazed by the feat, didn't react until his missile warning chimed.

He sawed his control yoke back and forth, steepening the angle of his cross-cuts to try and throw off the missile's tracking. Down-the-throat shots presented the missiles with the smallest target profiles and were the hardest to hit. He hoped that if he could throw its tracking off long enough, he'd slip past it, an effect much like a child's game of crack-the-whip.

He jinked and swerved. It flashed past. Blair looked frantically back out of his cockpit as he dodged and swerved, checking the missile's progress. It looped into the distinctive IFF-style search pattern, locked on, then roared after him. He dumped several decoys, hoping it would take off after one of them. It didn't.

"Damn," he said. "Maniac, I got an IFF. Can you help?"

"Negative," Maniac said tightly, "I got one, too. Who was that son of a bitch?"

Blair ignored him to concentrate on the missile. It bored in after him, corkscrewing as its seekerhead fought to keep the wildly gyrating T-bolt in its field of view. Blair flat-kicked his own ship around, watching his field of view sluggishly change by ninety degrees, pushed the flight stick all the way forward and right, and kicked in his afterburners. The T-bolt launched forward in a twisting outside loop, changing his vector and position in all three axis. He gave the ship a moment to reorient on its new course, then hauled the stick back and right, spinning the fighter into a sequence of tight corkscrews.

He felt the blood immediately rush into his head. His inertial dampers soaked up enough of his acceleration that he didn't black out or give himself an aneurism, but the tight spirals still put his head far enough from the ship's centerline for him to run the risk of blacking out. He clenched his neck muscles and gritted his teeth, trying to slow the blood flow, while breathing through his mouth.

The missile bored in, unimpressed with his gyrations. A black ship flickered out of cloak on his port side. He held his course as it closed on him, then reversed his corkscrew. The raider's front quarter glowed redly as it discharged its heavy weapons. The ordnance missed completely. Blair let out a single explosive laugh. The pirate would need to be a fancy deflection shooter to hit him under those circumstances.

He dumped the spiral, hauling the stick first back and to the right, then left, then pushing forward into a broad split "S" designed to bleed off forward motion without dumping inertia. The raider flashed past, so close overhead that Blair ducked.

The missile hooked in from the right. The T-bolt's missile alarm sounded, its Doppler tones warning him of its proximity. He armed and fired a chaff pod, then another, before he hauled the yoke back into his lap, breaking his Thunderbolt out of the pod's plane. The missile detonated against the second pod, close enough for Blair's shields to flare briefly.

He brought the fighter's nose down, seeking the black ship. The enemy banked hard away, trying to turn the tables. Blair had learned his lesson. Rather than trying to turn with the more nimble enemy, he held his acceleration and course steady. The raider cut upward and into a steep right-hand turn, seeking a deflection shot as Blair passed him.

Blair altered his course to cut across the raider's arc. He selected his full ordnance and locked his tracker on the raider. He would continue to track it, regardless of what other targets wandered into range. His AI projected a targeting pipper, showing him where to lead the raider in order to hit it.

The pilot, seeing that Blair had outfoxed him, activated

his cloaker. The black ship flickered out of his sight, killing his lock-on. He fired anyway, hosing blank space with his full battery.

Four energy beams lanced from the front of his Thunderbolt, flaring the raider's shields with pulse after pulse of energy. He poured on the coal, crossing the arc and firing into the cloaked ship, using its flashing shields and impacting beams as target references. His capacitors dipped deeply into the red. His fire volume slowed. A secondary explosion bloomed along the raider's wing. He missed with his next shot, giving the black fighter enough respite to turn and escape. He fired a few more random shots, then turned back to the main convoy.

Maniac's squadron appeared to have driven the rest of the raiding ships back. He did a quick count of friendly forces and came up with eight. Everyone was accounted for.

A single black ship flickered into view ahead of him, oriented towards a freighter. Blair checked his capacitors and swore as he saw they were back to little more than half-strength. He hit his afterburners, trying to close the distance.

The black ship grew quickly in his forward view. Blair toggled his ordnance to plasma guns and fired as soon as the reticule settled on the raider. The enemy ship jumped forward as though scalded. Blair's shots missed completely, falling behind the raider as it dove for the Kilrathi freighter.

He hauled his stick around to the left, trying to drag the sluggish T-bolt around by main force. He slopped into a pursuit angle and hit his afterburners. The raider rolled over and released a silvery colored object that impacted against the freighter's side. Blair saw no detonation as the black ship dove under the freighter's belly. Blair followed in hot pursuit. The black ship veered suddenly upward, slinging back around the topside of the transport. Blair, holding his stick against his belly, tried to hold to the raider's tight parabolic arc.

His maneuvers were clumsy in comparison to the raider's.

He got out of the turn and blazed after the raider as it crossed the freighter's plane. He fired his plasma guns, more for his benefit than for any hope of hitting the enemy ship.

A giant explosion flashed upward from the Kilrathi vessel as the delay blast mine detonated. The expanding shockwave and fireball engulfed the Thunderbolt. The raider, its rear phase shields flickering, rode the leading edge of the explosion outward, hitting its afterburners and boosting to an incredible speed. Blair sat, dumbstruck, as it vanished into the distance. The other raiders dropped out of cloak to boost after the pilot, abandoning the fight with Maniac's squadron and the Kilrathi ships.

His cockpit alarms sounded, warning him of the Thunderbolt's dire straits. The mine explosion had collapsed both the front and rear phase shields, chewed through his armor, and wreaked havoc on his internal systems, including his comm-panel, target tracker, and internal damage monitor. All of his starboard side thrusters appeared to be out, as was his afterburner and fuel reserve. He doubtless had other damage, but with that sub-system on the fritz, he couldn't trust his monitor to report it.

"Did . . . see that?" Maniac said, as he made a close pass by Blair. "You're . . . chewed up. Can . . . make . . . *Intrepid*?"

Blair looked at his system display, tapping it to see if he could coax some cooperation from it. "I don't know," he replied, trying to sound laconic in the face of his growing worry. His display cleared a moment, showing most systems glowing either red or yellow. "Maybe. I'm transmitting telemetry." He crossed his fingers and hoped his system display made it to Marshall's board.

Maniac was gone long enough for Blair to think his communications had gone out completely. When Marshall returned, his face had an odd expression. "Um . . . Melek offers you hospitality, for you to assess damage. He also wants to talk."

Blair made Maniac repeat himself twice to make certain

he understood the message correctly. He considered switching back to the distress channel to talk to the Shintahr himself, but wasn't sure he'd be able to lock onto it, or even to return to his own tactical frequency. It was better to let Maniac relay.

He shook his head. What the hell did Melek want? His ship was hurt badly enough for the Kilrathi lord to blow him away, if he was willing to risk the consequences from Maniac's squadron.

He checked his readouts. The damage from the raider's mine explosion really left him no choice but to accept. His return to the *Intrepid* was iffy and the Kilrathi vessel was directly under his lee. He couldn't afford to pass up the opportunity to check his damage before he committed himself to trying to get back.

"Tell him it's a deal. Get landing instructions and tell him we'll give him a CAP until he gets clear of the system."

Maniac relayed the message. Blair's communications fuzzed again as Maniac tried to relay landing instructions. It took Blair three tries before he understood that Maniac was to lead him to Melek's ship. Then a Kilrathi tractor beam would pull him inside. He hadn't the slightest idea of what would happen next.

The docking procedure went smoothly, with the Kilrathi beam operator catching him with only the slightest bump and depositing him inside a large, open cargo hold. He guessed from the shape of the clamshell doors that this ship served in a capacity similar to the packets that had been with the *Intrepid*. Almost all of the Kilrathi fleet had been destroyed over Kilrah in the aftereffects of the Temblor Bomb. Makeshifts like this one would have to serve until Kilrathi shipbuilding came back on-line.

Blair waited for the clamshell doors to close and the bay to repressurize before he removed his helmet and popped his canopy. There was a slight hiss as the pressures equalized. He sniffed the air. It smelled a little musty but seemed okay. He keyed the retractable handholds in the T-bolt's side and climbed down.

A delegation of Kilrathi led by a tall male wrapped in a cloak of rank entered the hold through a pressure door and walked towards Blair, who reflexively checked his sidearm. He always forgot how damned *big* the Kilrathi were. The leader and his guard of knife-wielding warriors were well past two meters tall and massed a hundred twenty-five kilos on the hoof. Any one of them could have taken him apart without batting an eye.

Blair waited for Melek to approach. The Kilrathi Shintahr had more gray in his fur than Blair remembered.

Melek stopped a few meters short of Blair, and to his great surprise, bowed deeply from the waist. "I place your claws to my throat," Melek said, his voice a deep bass rumble.

Blair fumbled to find the correct Kilrathi response. "I retract my claws and offer you . . ." He fumbled with his equipment, looking for something suitable to give his host. A flashlight seemed inadequate and emergency rations insulting. His hand touched his holster. He carefully removed his sidearm, so as not to alarm the guards, and offered it to Melek. The Kilrathi leader took it, making it disappear into the folds of his cloak. He produced a little packet of what looked like crackers. "I offer you bread and salt."

Blair tried not to smile. "Thank you," he said. The custom wasn't his, but he accepted the gift in the spirit intended. He tucked the pouch into his flight suit.

"I name you guest of my *hrai*," Melek said formally, then indicated Blair was to walk with him. He tried to remember his Kilrathi customs. Hobbes had told him much, but much of that had turned out to be useless misinformation planted by a deep-cover spy. He did know that warriors did not keep other warriors waiting. "Why did you invite me here?" he asked, getting to the point. "It certainly wasn't to trade food and guns."

"Yes," Melek answered, "we need to exchange information, and the radio was no way to do it. Only eye to eye will do." He turned towards the bay door and gestured for Blair to pass through. They stepped into a corridor carpeted in deep greens and russets. The walls and bulkheads were painted with murals of Kilrathi stalking, fighting, eating, and if Blair understood his Cat anatomy, making love. Melek gave him a moment to study the paintings, then ushered him forward.

"Ships of my *hrai* and those of the other clans are being attacked from your side of the border," he said. "Some of the attackers have markings of your Border Worlds. We have tapes."

"I don't care what you've got," Blair replied with some heat, "we didn't do it."

"I agree," Melek replied, "it is too obvious a ploy. If you really wanted to attack us, you would not be so stupid. You would cast your clues elsewhere to lead us off in different directions, not back to your own lairs."

"You invited me here to tell me *that*?" Blair said.

"Yes," Melek said. "Many on your side of the border would not believe a message from us, regardless of the reason. By bringing you here and giving to you the tape we have made, you can see for yourself that what we say is true."

Blair looked up at Melek. "It must be hard for you to work with me. I appreciate that you are being so forthcoming." I don't understand it, he thought to himself, but I'm glad this isn't just an excuse to rip my guts out personally.

"You have high status within my *hrai*," Melek said. "It is not often we get to meet a savior."

He stopped, stock-still, and stared at the Kilrathi. "A *what*?"

"A savior," Melek repeated. "Our savior."

Blair searched his face for something he could recognize as humor, or insanity, or anything that would provide him with a rational explanation for Melek's words. "I don't understand. I would have thought your people would want to disembowel me for what I did." The image of Jeannette, dying in agony from Thrakhath's slash, sprang into his mind.

"I would have," Melek replied, "until I understood your

purpose." His face assumed a sober air. "Our war with you corrupted us," he began. "As the war went on and as we continued to spend lives, we learned from you. Both good things like tactics, and bad things like treachery and asssa . . . ashashi . . ." He sighed, giving up on the tough word.

"Assassination?" Blair supplied.

Melek nodded. "Yes. We learned that from you, and we learned it well. When we offered you the false treaty, there were many, like me, who thought we were perverting ourselves, becoming lowly like humans."

Blair kept his face still.

"The attack on your planets should have been a sacrifice to Sivar, our victory dance on your graves. Yet Sivar denied us victory. Some of us realized that we had spoiled the sacrifice, by using duplicity. It was like using a tainted knife to draw blood, an abomination to Sivar."

He guided Blair up a set of broad stairs and forward. They passed several Kilrathi females, some clothed, others naked. They turned their faces from the males. They were the first enemy females he had seen that weren't on an autopsy table.

He looked up at Melek, uncertain how to phrase the questions that threatened to pour out of him in a torrent. Melek looked at him.

"Those of us who had doubts did nothing. I confess I felt little except rage against humans. Your taint had sunk deep within our leadership. An attempt was made to assas . . . to murder by stealth our Emperor. The plot failed, but the seed was planted." He shook his head sadly.

"So how do I fit into this?" Blair asked.

"Sivar raised you up, gave you many victories. You became the equal of any Kilrathi, enough that you were honored by our people as much as by yours. Your hero-name reflected that honor." They entered a small, dark room. Melek bent to remove his loose shoes. He gestured for Blair to do the same.

"The Heart of the People of Sivar became corrupt. You

became the blade that purified the People, that excised the corruption. You were our ritual of atonement, our *Pukcal*."

Blair reeled from the implications of what Melek said. "Let me get this straight. You think that operation over Kilrah was the fulfillment of a purpose set in motion by your own god?" He shook his head. "You think I was part of some massive bloodletting ritual?"

"Yes," Melek said. He looked again at Blair. "I *have* to believe the death of so many of my *hrai*, so many of my race, was for some purpose. This way they are redeemed by sacrifice and can rejoin us for the future hunts and fights we shall wage in the name of Sivar."

He opened the inner door and gestured. Blair entered, and stopped, at first startled by the lack of light. He smelled a thick, cloying scent that he thought at first was incense. It took him a moment to realize it was burned blood. He peered around, slowly taking in the details of the chapel. The paintings on the walls depicted sacrifices, hunts, battles, and victory. Towards the front of the room, above a smoking brazier were a number of figures holding their hands up to make offerings to the Kilrathi god. He looked at Melek.

"The prophets of Sivar," Melek replied. He gestured for Blair to move forward. He did, and gasped in involuntary shock. There, among the prophets offering sacrifices to the god, were his own face and hands offering up what looked suspiciously like a torpedo. He turned to Melek, unable to speak.

"You have helped my *hrai* find the true way, the honorable way. The taint at our core had to be cleansed in blood. Kilrah had to die for Kilrathi to live. Sivar smiles on us again."

Blair licked his lips. His throat felt dry and tight. "What will you do?" he asked. He stared at the mural.

"We will fight with the other *hrai*, the other Clans, until one is on top," Melek replied. "Then there will be a new Emperor, a new Empire."

Blair didn't like the sound of that. The very little he

had heard about the Kilrathi since his retirement said they were locked in a five-way civil war. It would be a long time, if ever, before one clan would rise from that mess to rule. If it had been anyone except the Kilrathi he would have laid odds that it wouldn't happen. But he knew the Kilrathi would someday be back, tempered by their suffering and stronger than ever.

Melek led him from the altar room. "Will you guest with us while we fix your ship so that you may return home?"

Blair looked at him a long moment, then glanced back towards the chapel. "I'd like that. Thank you."

Blair sniffled while Sosa played back his after-action report. He was allergic to something on Melek's ship, probably Cat fur. Hobbes had never given him any trouble, but Prince Ralgha had been one Cat among humans, and not the other way around. The concubine Melek had given him for honor's sake was probably to blame. She'd fancied him no more than he had her, but she'd insisted they respect proprieties and had *very* specific ideas about where she should sleep. Blair, not wanting to anger a female with three-centimeter-long claws who outmassed him by twenty kilos, had gone along. The morning after brought sniffles and itchy eyes, not to mention his host's amused glances.

Sosa snapped off the recorder in exasperation. "That's *it*? He warned you about the attacks, gave you the tapes, and invited you for dinner? Nothing else?"

Blair had decided on the flight back to the *Intrepid* that he would say nothing about the chapel or the mural. It struck him too deeply for him to want to share it. He'd had nightmares after using the Temblor Bomb and killing Kilrah. To have his enemy not only absolve him of the act, but to actually embrace it, tossed him into a tailspin. Melek seemed to think that his hero-name was literal— that he could in fact represent the heart of the Kilrathi nation. The idea frightened and confused him. The one thing he knew was that his time with Melek was terribly personal and he had no desire to share it with anyone.

"Ye-up," he replied, "that's pretty much it."

She looked up at him from the other side of the table, her expression unreadable. Her professional interrogator's demeanor dropped away. "I was worried about you," she said softly, so softly he might not have heard her.

He felt his pulse skip a beat. The statement might have been nothing more than a simple statement of concern for his safe return, or it might mean a lot more. He still wasn't certain what he wanted from her, or what he himself was prepared to give. "You needn't have been," he replied. He kept his tones friendly, not inviting closer intimacy, but not rejecting it either.

Velina shook her head softly and stood. "I've completed my debriefing," she said, while stuffing her equipment into her bag. She paused, then idly picked at a loose spot on the table with the edge of her painted nail. "Unless there's something you'd like to add." She looked up. The offer could have meant everything or nothing. He looked at her face. Her eyes appeared to be shining a bit. Or was it just a trick of the light?

"Yes," he said, unbending a bit. "Thank you for being worried. Not too many people are."

She smiled. His eyes met hers. The room grew warm. She turned away with an embarrassed cough, ending the moment.

"The captain's holding his last briefing in a few minutes."

"Last briefing?"

"Captain Eisen's been transferred," she said, "haven't you heard?" She swept out of the debriefing room, exercising her woman's prerogative to have the last word. Blair followed her, taking the last seat in the briefing room.

Eisen entered, waving them all to their seats when they stood at attention. He opened the conference without preamble. "As you should all know by now, I'm being transferred off this rust bucket." He nodded towards Hawk. "Some of you may be more distressed to hear that than others." Manley, unrepentant, stared back.

Eisen took a deep breath. "Lieutenant Sosa has cracked most of the files I brought from the *Lex*. Her analysis suggests a pattern of systematic Confederation involvement in the attacks. We have orders, date-time groups, and mission instructions linking a number of unusual movements of Confed resources to some of the raids. It isn't a smoking gun, but it's close.

"We can show that Confederation forces are doing this. We've got my files, Melek's tapes, and the depositions taken from Blair and Hawk. Together, it makes a pretty strong case. Unfortunately, we still don't know who's giving the orders or what the ultimate objective is."

He smiled. "My job will be to infiltrate back to Earth. I've got friends in low places there. I'll try to get our evidence to them. We're missing a few key pieces, but hopefully we've got enough to make our case." He looked at Chris. "That, basically, is that. Colonel Blair, are you ready to brief us on your Kilrathi encounter?"

He almost answered no. "Yes, sir." He gave an overview of his actions, sharply editing his story about what had transpired on board Melek's ship. The gun camera footage and Melek's tapes served to illustrate the battle. He finished his running commentary on the action and froze the tape with the scene of the fighter accelerating away, riding the mine's blast while his own Thunderbolt was engulfed.

"Anyway," he concluded, "the pirates got seven of the thirteen ships, including two with that weird new weapon. It went right through the ships' phase shields and ignited the air within. The crews and passengers, about five hundred on each ship, were dead within seconds."

Hawk leaned forward in his chair, his expression intense. "Could you run back that least sequence?" he asked. "The one leading up to the mine explosion."

Blair did as he was asked, running the scene three more times at Hawk's direction. "No," Hawk said, "it isn't possible."

"What isn't?" Blair asked.

"I went to flight school with a guy who was working on

that," Hawk said excitedly. "He had all the theoretical work done, and was practicing it in the simulator. He finally perfected it, just before we graduated." He furrowed his brow. "He got pulled right after that. The word was that he'd been booted out for performing dangerous and unauthorized maneuvers. I remember I didn't buy that. There was no way we'd give up on a hot pilot like that because he broke some rules."

Blair looked at Maniac, who had the good grace to look sheepish.

Hawk rubbed his hand across his jaw, still trying to recall details. "There was also a story that he'd gone to a secret unit . . . some kind of special ops thing."

"What was his name?" Blair pressed.

Hawk shook his head. "I dunno. Sanders, Seeker, Slither . . . something like that."

Blair looked at Eisen, whose eyebrows had climbed halfway to his scalp. "Seether?" they both asked at once.

Hawk considered, then nodded. "Yeah, I think so." He looked at Eisen and Blair. "Umm, why are you two staring at me?"

"Because, Colonel," Eisen replied, "you have given us the first direct link, our first solid name, in the conspiracy." He looked at Blair. "Now we have someplace to start."

Hawk looked confused. "We do?"

"Seether came aboard the *Lexington* armed with orders," Eisen said, "orders someone wrote. Someone in the conspiracy."

"We have Paulson, too," Blair added, "I saw them together on the *Lex*'s flight deck."

"Right," Eisen said, "someone cut Paulson's orders relieving me. Either they are involved, or the person above them is. Either way, we have a starting point." He looked at Hawk. "Lieutenant Colonel Manley, I'm relieving you of duty as of this moment." He raised his hand to forestall Hawk's protest. "You are our only living witness linking Seether to the conspiracy and the files. You are far too valuable to us to risk you in space."

Eisen looked at Maniac. "Lieutenant Colonel Marshall, I'm promoting you to wing commander in Hawk's place."

"Hey," Manley piped up angrily. "What about Farnsworth? Panther's got first crack at it!"

"Colonel Farnsworth is being transferred as well." Eisen turned to Panther. "You'll be running a specialized planning staff, in addition to your squadron. Admiral Wilford's taking over for Admiral Richards. He requested you by name as his staff operations officer."

Panther smiled and dipped her head in acknowledgement. "The admiral and I served together on the *Tarawa*, before it went to the Landreich. It'll be a pleasure to work for him again."

Maniac raised his hand. "You said 'Lieutenant Colonel Marshall,' didn't you? Did I hear that right?"

"Yeah," Eisen said, "Congrats. You've been promoted."

"Well, hot damn!" Maniac declared. His expression soured. "It'd figure I'd have to commit treason to move up."

Blair ignored him. "Who's taking over for you, Captain?"

Eisen raised an eyebrow. "You are."

Blair nearly choked. "Me!? I'm Space Forces, not Fleet. I don't know the first thing about commanding a carrier."

"No," Eisen said, "but we need someone of your rank to command the ship. You're the only one we have available." He laughed at Blair. "You don't have to look so stricken, Chris. Garibaldi'll be there. He'll stand at your right elbow and whisper sweet nothings in your ear."

"Why not him, then?" Blair asked, "Then we wouldn't need the charade."

"Sorry," Eisen said, "he's too junior. It's you, Chris."

Blair thought, from the twinkle in his eye, that Eisen wasn't sorry in the least.

He was still worried twelve hours later while he waited with Eisen and a few well-wishers and watched a jump-capable transfer shuttle make a glass-smooth landing on the *Intrepid*'s flight deck.

Eisen turned to him and extended his hand. "Take good

care of her, Chris. Hopefully, I'll get to Earth and back with a political solution before you have to do much fighting." He let out a long breath. "This is the kind of change of command I like. Short and sweet with no formations or bands." He turned to shake hands with the officers and ratings who came to see him off. Sosa was there, with Pliers and Panther. Blair met her eye as she waited her turn to say good-bye to Eisen. She smiled warmly at him, warmly enough for Maniac to elbow him in the ribs.

"Been doing docking maneuvers, eh?" he asked, leering.

"Mind your own business, Colonel," Blair snapped. Maniac grinned in response.

A single man descended from the shuttle the moment the side hatch opened. He was wearing mottled black-and-gray shipboard camouflage and carrying a pack and a map case. He was also carrying a short-barrelled laser rifle slung barrel down.

Eisen looked at him in surprise as the man came to attention, his boot heels clicking together as he assumed a parade ground brace. "You the captain?" he asked, his voice as casual as his body was stiff.

Eisen hiked a thumb towards Blair. The Marine looked nonplussed. "Oh," he said, "sorry." He stepped over to Blair. He looked momentarily confused as he saw Blair's Space Forces tab. "Are you the boss?" he asked in a surprisingly bass voice.

Blair had received similar treatment from Marines before. He'd long since chalked it up to bad breeding. "Something like that," he replied.

The grunt offered his hand. "Sir, I'm Lieutenant Colonel Dekker. Some call me Gash. Wilford's assigned me aboard as your ground contingent commander."

Blair sized him up. Gash Dekker was short, his head barely clearing Blair's chin. He looked to be in his middle thirties, except for his eyes. Blair hoped he'd never look like that.

"Gash Dekker," he said, trying to recall where he'd heard

the name. "Weren't you in a prisoner-of-war camp?"

Dekker didn't look amused. "Briefly," he replied. "Got captured after you lot bugged out and left us on Repleetah. They took a few years of my life." He grinned ferally. "Of course I took quite a few of theirs, too."

Blair nodded. Repleetah had been a space-borne assault on a Kilrathi world that had gone down twisted. The Space Forces commander had ordered a withdrawal, abandoning the better part of a Marine combat brigade on the planet's surface. Tolwyn had decorated the Space Forces commander for cool thinking, much to the Marines' fury.

He tried to put the best face on an awkward situation. "Welcome to the *Intrepid*. I'm Colonel Blair, the commander."

It was Dekker's turn to size him up. "The Cat-killer?"

Blair smiled thinly. "Once, maybe, but not anymore."

Dekker nodded. "Fair enough."

"How many troops will you be bringing aboard?" he asked, thinking about where to put them on the damaged ship.

Dekker's mobile features turned sober. "We're listed as a company, but we've been in pretty deep. I'm down to three squads, organized as a platoon. They'll be aboard in about an hour." He grinned. "They won't look like much, but each is an expert in hand-to-hand combat, weapons, explosives, you name it."

Blair's face remained still. "Colonel, I think we'll put your troops in the forward cargo bay. It'll be big enough for all your people and'll give you some room for training."

The Marine came to attention. "Yes, sir, and thank you, sir."

Blair laughed. "Don't thank me until you've seen it."

It was Dekker's turn to laugh. "I'm sure it'll be better than the last accommodations I had, courtesy of Space Forces."

Eisen interrupted, saving Blair the need to reply. "Well, gentlemen, it's time for me to go." He shook hands all around, then walked out to the shuttle Dekker had arrived in. The little ship wasted no time in departing.

Blair waited for the ship to depart before he made a beeline for the bridge, hoping to find Garibaldi before the man went off duty. He found him in the CIC, relaxing with a cup of coffee and surveying the cramped bridge stations. He looked up, saw Blair, and grinned. "Captain on the bridge!" he announced.

Blair said softly, "So you know already?"

"Yes, sir," Garibaldi answered. He lowered his voice. "Don't worry, Colonel," he said, "I'll walk you through it." He tipped his head to one side. "You have orders waiting for you in your cabin, sir. I took the liberty of using Captain Eisen's command codes to read them." He paused. "Admiral Wilford's ordered us to the Peleus system. I've got the course laid in, sir. All you have to do is give the word."

Blair looked at him. "Do it."

Garibaldi laughed. "Actually, sir, the correct command is to have the helm read back the plotted course, then you say 'Initiate course blah-blah' and 'Execute.' Then they 'do it.' "

Blair tried to glower and failed. Garibaldi was too affable for him to get angry. "I see, Lieutenant Commander, that as long as I have you, my humility will remain intact." He paused as something the exec had said sunk in. "I have quarters?"

Garibaldi laughed. "They used to be the Purser's Office, before things got taken down a notch or two. Two doors down, on the right. Everything you'll need is in there."

"Thanks," Blair said. "Anything else I should know?"

"I'll let you know, sir," Garibaldi said. "It's your first day on the job, sir. I don't want to give you too much at once."

"Thanks," Blair replied dryly.

He walked down to his cabin and entered. The small cabin was barely large enough for a narrow bed, a desk with a computer terminal, and a private shower. The place looked like a palace compared to the flight deck. He ached to try both the hot water and the bed, but duty called. He saw a message chip in the reader and the terminal's green light winking.

He cued the reader and was surprised to see Wilford's seamed face in the desktop holo-tank. The sixtyish admiral wore a shabby sweater with his rank pinned to his breast rather than a uniform.

"Colonel," Wilford's taped voice said. "We've been getting some strange, troubling reports out of the Peleus system. We've received a report of some kind of jamming weapon being used against our forces there. Peleus is absolutely vital to our efforts—it sits astride three major space lanes and is a major source of fuel. It is crucial that we hold it. I've enclosed a holo-recording we received from a pilot who managed to get a tight-beam burst transmission out."

Wilford's face vanished to be replaced by a grainy two-dee of a pilot. "Mayday . . ." the pilot said. Blair could hear the edge of panic in his voice. ". . . day, elec . . . ics are out, . . . all systems . . . scrambled. My . . . and three others affected . . . out, as are trackers . . . and weapons. We're . . . attack. Mayday. May—" The recording ended and Wilford's face reappeared.

"We have had two similar incidents in the last forty hours," he said. He smiled thinly. "Now that you've finished your vacation, your job is to jump into Peleus, find out what is going on, and stop it. I've encoded separate instructions for your helm. Good luck and good hunting. That is all." His face faded, leaving behind a moment's static.

Blair sat back in the chair, wondering why his world had become so complicated.

• CHAPTER NINE

Colonel Blair sat at the desk in what he still considered Eisen's quarters and fretted. The flight board displayed on the holo-terminal showed Maniac's squadron strength patrol as "Deployed," with no additional information. Maniac was damned close to exceeding the Hellcat's eight-hour endurance.

The holo-terminal buzzed. He willed himself to be calm and activated the screen. Velina's face appeared. "Has there been any word from Maniac?" he asked her.

"Negative, sir," she replied, her expression frustrated. "Nothing since he launched. I wish I knew what, or who, was causing this interference. My specialty is code breaking, not electronic warfare. I've got very little time in Electronic-Counter-Counter Measures. My people are doing their best, but ECCM's a pretty exotic field."

Blair rubbed his forehead. "With our comm systems and scanners still out we're effectively blind, deaf, and mute."

"We've fired a pair of proximity beacons along his outbound vector," Sosa replied. "Those might help them get home."

"Thank you, Velina," he said absently.

"You're welcome, sir," she answered, smiling. "I didn't know you knew my first name. That's the first time you've used it."

"My apologies, Lieutenant."

"Please don't apologize, sir," she answered, "I like it." Her face sobered. "We'll call you if we hear anything."

"Thank you." He closed the contact, then stood and paced the tiny room. He had never been good at waiting safely behind the lines while others took the risks. He worried for his pilots; knowing that there was nothing he

235

could do to help them only made the minutes drag longer. If he were in the cockpit, he'd be doing something important, rather than brooding and pacing.

A flight tech, one of Sosa's trainees, cleared his throat and spoke into the all-call. "All hands to general quarters," he said excitedly. "Prepare to recover fighters."

Blair nearly leapt to the holo-box. The "Deployed" boxes began to ripple and shift, changing to "Inbound" and "Pending." He cued his comm-circuit, contacting the flight officer. "Launch the ready group," he ordered, "but keep it in close-in CAP. We don't know what might have followed us home."

"Aye, sir," the woman answered.

Sosa called him a moment later. "We're getting short-ranged comms with Maniac. It looks like he managed a kill, even though he lost his trackers and communications. He's bringing a pilot home. I'll do the interrogation in the debriefing closet," she said, again smiling and showing her dimples.

"May I watch?" Blair said, "I've seen debriefs done before, but rarely prisoner interrogations. It might help if I get picked up again."

She hesitated. "Okay," she said after such a long delay that Blair wondered if she'd heard him, "but give me time to get started. These things usually take a while, and I'll want to wear them down a bit before I get spectators."

"Okay," he said, signing off.

He walked down to the pilot's ready room, arriving just as the first returnees trooped happily in from the flight line. They were grinning from ear to ear and chattering with the pent up energy that a long, dangerous mission left behind. Many would collapse into sleep the moment the nervous energy ebbed. He met Maniac trailing the group, his knee board and helmet in one hand.

"How'd it go?" he asked.

Marshall looked him in the eye. "We had no radios, no scanners, no trackers, and no solid weapons lock-ons. We shot dumbfires. How do you think it went?"

"Well," Blair said, trying to put the best face on it, "you brought everybody home."

"We were lucky. They jumped us, six of those damned black painted Hellcats. Their systems seemed to work fine." He sighed. "I got one on the first pass, a high-deflection shot that caught his fuel tanks. I think the rest thought we weren't affected by the jamming. They ran."

"What took so long?" Blair asked.

Maniac smiled, his expression turning feral. "We got lost. Couldn't find our way back." He turned towards Blair. "Colonel, sending us out there like that was a mistake. We got out alive because we were lucky. We should have been toast."

"All right," Blair said, "finish your debrief and come up to my quarters. Bring Hawk and Panther . . . we have to talk."

Maniac nodded. "Are you puttin' them back on flight status?"

"Yeah," Blair answered. "Those two are rattling around like pebbles in a can. Panther's in charge of a planning section that's got nothing to plan and Hawk's convinced this was all a plot to put you in charge of his wing. I won't buck Wilford by giving it back to him, but I'll put him back in rotation. I hope he doesn't go and get himself killed before he testifies."

Blair turned away and walked towards the debriefing room and the captured pilot. He chewed the inside of his lip, worried that he was becoming to the *Intrepid* what Paulson was to the *Lexington*. He, like Paulson, really didn't have the background needed to command the ship, and couldn't stand the notion of being merely a figurehead. Paulson's folly had almost cost him the *Lexington*. Had his almost cost Maniac's patrol?

He entered the interrogation room. The pilot sat, his back turned to Blair. The man seemed old to be a flier. He had short-cropped, grizzled gray hair. Sosa, her makeup scrubbed from her face, and dressed in a shapeless gray coverall, leaned across the brightly lit table. The room had no adornment, except for a small recorder and a pickup pointed at her subject. "I'm asking you again," she said harshly, "what ship did you launch from? How are you jamming us?"

Blair was startled at the change in her. She looked tough and intimidating as she stood over the shackled prisoner.

The pilot looked up at her, nonplussed. "Spare me the routine. I've got daughters your age, so I'm not impressed. I'm obligated to give you my name and rank. That's all."

Blair thought the voice sounded familiar. He stepped around to the side to look at the man Maniac had captured. The pilot looked familiar. "I know you!" Sosa looked up at him, her lips pursed with annoyance. He ignored her. "You're the vet I helped in the bar!"

The pilot slowly turned his head. He stared at Blair a long moment, then cracked what might have been a smile under other circumstances. "Nearly got you killed, too, helping me out."

"What'd you do to set him off?" Blair asked, thinking of his first encounter with Seether.

The vet shrugged. "Some folks're just sensitive about giving a handout." His eyes hooded, hiding his thoughts.

Blair shook his head. "What the hell are you doing here?"

"Well, Colonel, I reckon' I owe you." He rattled his shackles. "A favor for a favor?"

"I can't make any promises," Blair replied. He glanced over at Sosa, who nodded her head with approval. He saw her casually reangle the pickup to catch the vet's voice.

"I'll take what I can get," the pilot said, his face grim. "It ain't like I really got much choice." He shrugged, placing himself at Blair's mercy. "They came right after the fight, Confed recruiters looking for volunteers. You had to have ten years experience, minimum, and be able to relocate with no questions asked. They said it was ta fight rebels an' pirates. I signed up." He shrugged as well as his shackles would allow. "Hell, I didn't have anything better to do."

"And?" Blair prompted.

"It wasn't like the old days," the vet continued. "The show's being run by a bunch of dark looking characters. We used to stick together, back in the war, everybody looking out for everybody else. It ain't like that now."

"How's that?" Blair asked.

"Well," the vet said, "they don't have no honor. We been using these unmarked ships, Hellcats mostly, but uprated, to hit Kilrathi, Border Worlders, sometimes even what they said was renegade Confeds. It's all hit and run, you know? I seen them burn down escape pods, blast transports, and surrendering don't mean anything to them. They don't look out for each other, much less us. Somebody gets fragged, that's his own tough luck. It's watch your own ass, or tough shit." He looked at Sosa. "Begging your pardon, ma'am."

"No problem," she replied. She pursed her lips, looking at Blair. "Who are these 'dark' folks you mentioned?" she asked.

"Well," he said, "they ain't really 'dark.' Most of them in charge are blonds." He licked his lips. "I guess it's because of the black flight suits they wear, more than anything else." He paused. "Most of them are young looking, too young to have been in the war too long. They're damned hot pilots, though. They fly like naturals."

Blair thought back to the *Lexington*, and the black suited pilots he'd seen there. Alarms began to go off in his head. "Do you remember a fellow named Seether?"

"Yeah," the pilot replied. "I'll never forget him, not after the bar at Nephele. He showed up a couple of days back, with some more of his goons. They've been running the show since."

"Do you know how the jamming works?" Sosa asked.

"Yeah," he replied. "You're lookin' for an old cap ship. They reoutfitted it, you'd hardly know it was ever one of ours." He paused, gathering his thoughts. "It moves around a lot. I hear it's all reactors and jammers, and not much else. Supposed to be able to blank comms in an entire system. Frankly, I hope you take the bastard out. I want to fight straight-up for a change. This sneaking around is starting to wear thin."

"Why weren't you affected by the jamming?" Blair asked.

The pilot shrugged. "It's got a frequency agile system that leaves clear spaces for us to transmit. It changes a couple hundred times a second. The systems on our 'Cats're synchronized to it, so we can transmit and track in the holes. Our gear's also got special tempesting. I was told that it was something that special ops was workin' on when the war ended. Scuttlebutt said they were getting ready to use it for something else, but I don't know what."

"What's tempest?" he asked, looking at Sosa.

"It's an insulating procedure," she replied. "It blocks out spurious signals. It would have to be substantial to block this kind of interference, though."

Blair looked at the pilot. "Will you give us the coordinates for this jammer?"

"No," he replied, rattling his chains suggestively. "But I'll take you there."

"How's that?" Blair asked.

"I got nothing for them," the vet replied, "and I've seen more of the folks like I served with here than there. This seems more like home to me. I want to lash up."

Blair looked at Sosa, who shrugged, giving him no help at all. He scowled at her, then looked at the pilot. "All right," he said. "Report to Maj—Lieutenant Colonel Marshall for your flight assignment."

Sosa, her expression unreadable, stepped over and released the shackles. The pilot stood, his face split by a broad grin. "Thank you, Colonel!" he said, rubbing his wrists.

"What's your name, anyway?" Blair asked.

"Bean, Colonel, Evan Bean."

"Well, Bean," Blair said, extending his hand, "welcome aboard."

Four hours later Blair sat in his command chair, worrying a thumbnail and wondering if he had made a grave mistake in trusting Bean. Maniac had launched, backed by a full magnum launch. Only a few light fighters, mostly obsolete Ferrets were left to guard the ship. Maniac and the strike force had vanished into space, following Bean to god only knew where. Had they been duped by the old man?

Sosa stepped onto the CIC, her face still and sober. Blair looked at her, his eyes searching her face. She dipped her head fractionally, indicating she had received no word.

He had nearly given up when the ship's systems suddenly came up, lights winking on control boards as startled techs were jogged from their dozing. He watched as the holo-tank and external displays lit up and the tactical plot began to fill in details of the Peleus system. Sosa sprang to the communications station, nearly running over a startled tech carrying a clipboard. Garibaldi, a napkin around his neck and mustard on the corner of his mouth, came through the connecting door to the briefing room.

"What's up?" he asked.

"Maniac's taken out the jammer," Blair replied.

Maniac's voice sounded over the CIC's speakers. "Strike Alpha to Mother."

"Go ahead, Alpha," Sosa replied in her warm and honeyed voice.

"We got target designated Green," Maniac said. "We are 'feet wet' on inbound track two."

Blair nodded. "Feet wet" meant they were away from the target zone.

"The target was defended," Marshall continued, "by four Hellcat type fighters, painted black. No markings." Blair could hear the acid humor in Maniac's voice. "They weren't ready for a full deck strike."

"Roger, Alpha," Sosa said. "Losses?"

"Three," Maniac replied, "the new pilot, Bean, and two from Hawk's squadron . . . Gremlin and Scarab. One ejected. Gremlin—I think. One of the bastards nailed him before we could tractor him home." Maniac's voice was flat and expressionless, as though discussing crop reports.

Blair closed his eyes, thinking of the pilot who'd been

killed in a lifepod. Fighting an enemy was one thing, but going after helpless lifepods was something else entirely.

"Give me an active scan," he said grimly, opening his eyes and setting his jaw. A scan might give him a retaliatory target for Maniac to hit on the way home. He wouldn't stoop to lashing out at the defenseless, but any valid military targets were soon going to be junk.

Sosa looked at him, worried. Garibaldi was more direct. "Sir, an active scan will show them where we are!"

"Good. Maybe that'll bring them to us." Blair looked at him, his temper on edge. "No, don't worry. If they were going to come after us, they would have followed Marshall's strike."

Garibaldi looked at the sensor officer and twitched one finger. She ran her hands over her controls. Details began to fill into the screen as the ship's powerful radar and translight targeting and scanning beams played over the system. A single triangular graphic appeared, the words CONFED RESEARCH STATION flashing beneath.

A smaller pip appeared alongside and began to move away. The tech tweaked her controls. The pip grew into a computer enhanced view of a standard high-priority, jump-capable shuttle moving out of the system.

"Damn it all," Blair cursed. "Can Maniac intercept?"

"Negative," Sosa replied, "he's too far, and his ships' fuel reserves are too low for sustained afterburner."

Blair drummed his fingers on his arm of his command chair. "Garibaldi," he snapped, "take the con."

The lieutenant commander, quietly removing the napkin from around his neck, looked at Blair. "*What?*" He looked startled as Blair sprang up out of the seat and started for the CIC's blast door. "Where are you going, sir?"

Blair looked back at the shuttle's image in the holo-tank. "After that ship," he snapped, "before it gets away."

The junior officer met his eye and after a long pause, said "Yes, sir, what shall we do?"

"Follow me," Blair said. "I want that ship." He turned and stomped off the bridge.

Pliers was waiting for him on the launch deck, having apparently been warned by Garibaldi or Sosa. "What's in the 'chute? I want something with a tractor beam."

"Well," Pliers said, scratching his head, "your T-bolt ain't ready yet."

Blair held onto his temper. "I didn't ask you for the Thunderbolt. I asked you what you had."

Pliers looked at him, then turned towards the deck. "The only thing I've got is an old Broadsword. We've stripped it down, and made it into a light patrol bomber. It's only got one torpedo, two guns, no side turrets, and half armor."

"That'll do."

He strapped into the ship, clapped his helmet on his head, and launched, setting his course for the shuttle and adjusting as he received updated telemetry from the *Intrepid*. He stabbed the throttles forward, kicking in the afterburners.

"Heave to," Blair snapped, "or be hulled."

The shuttle ignored him and began evasive maneuvers. Blair dogged it with contemptuous ease, finally ducking out to one side to turn towards the shuttle and fire across its bows. The second shot nearly snipped off the shuttle's bows. It did a quick endover, almost reversing course as it attempted escape. Blair snagged it as it came out of its loop, then cued his tractor. The beam caught the shuttle. It thrashed like a fish caught on a hook, then shut down as its engines overheated. Blair dragged it back to the *Intrepid*, which had followed at the best speed it could manage on two engines.

He pulled it behind him onto the carrier's flight deck. Dekker appeared from behind a Ferret, leading a heavily armed half squad while he scrambled out of his fighter and sprinted for the shuttle's side hatch. Grunts hit on either side of the hatch, their weapons pointed toward the portal.

Blair drew his sidearm. "Stay back," he snarled at the Marines. He cued the access, wondering if his folly was about to get him killed.

No one shot him when the hatch opened, revealing a darkened interior. The smells of old blood, detergent and something else wafted out of the open airlock. The Marine on his left, a blonde corporal with pair of wound stripes, twitched her nostrils. "Did something die in there?"

The lock cycled, allowing Blair to step inside. She put her hand on his arm as he started to step inside. "Here," she said, handing him a handlight. "You've got ten minutes. Then we come in." By the way she hefted her evil-looking machine pistol, he knew she was serious.

He stepped inside, letting the airlock cycle behind him. The inner door opened, revealing a darkened interior, lit only by the cockpit's telltales glowing through the open door forward. Blair raised his pistol to his shoulder. "You might as well come out. I've got a light, and a gun."

A single reading lamp came on, revealing a white-haired figure sitting in one of the rearward facing seats. He puffed a cigar, the red embers lighting his brows in a red glow.

"Admiral Tolwyn," Blair said. Somehow, he had expected this.

"Hello, Chris," Tolwyn replied, his expression cool. He tapped the cigar against a dish. "How's the treason business?"

"I'm not in the mood for small talk," Blair replied harshly, "What are you doing here?"

Tolwyn smiled, his lips twitching upward. "The same thing you are. I'm trying to figure out what the hell's going on."

"I don't follow," Blair said, playing for time while he determined his best approach.

Tolwyn gestured outward. "The whole situation out here is fluid, chaotic. The reports we're getting back on Earth are as disturbing as they are incomplete. I came out personally to investigate." He laughed without humor. "I just didn't expect to get caught in that damned jammer. It took my comms, navigation, everything. I was lucky to find that research station." He frowned. "It's been abandoned, incidentally."

"Why did you decide to do this personally?" Blair asked.

Tolwyn tapped his cigar. "The Confederation is about to launch a full-scale war. From our side, it looks like your people are harassing our legitimate space operations, killing innocent people and destroying defenseless ships."

Blair replied, "I've been in this long enough to see it's not the Outer Worlds that's driving this."

"Yes," Tolwyn said, looking sad, "you have been in it, haven't you. You torpedoed the *Lexington*, Chris. Eighty people, all of them your shipmates, were killed or injured. There is also the little matter of the *Achilles*. Three hundred people died on that ship. We will have to retaliate, you know."

Blair collapsed in the chair across from Tolwyn. His voice sounded bleak in his own ears. "Can we head this off?"

"I hope so," Tolwyn replied.

Blair looked at him, a little surprised. "Somebody's trying to trigger an all-out war."

Tolwyn dusted the cigar against the dish. "Yes, I believe you're right." He smiled. "Don't look so stunned, Chris. I think your perception of things is, for the most part, on target."

Tolwyn puffed again, sending up another noxious cloud. "Paladin agreed that I should come out here and take a look, to try and get to the bottom of this. *Someone* is hell-bent on war. I'm here to find out who, and if it's Confed, to shut them down."

"Thank you, Admiral," Blair said, "for giving it a shot."

Tolwyn looked at him. "Chris, I have to know. Why did you betray us?"

Blair shook his head. "It wasn't a planned thing. Captain Paulson ordered a mission, where some of the ships got out of hand. They were attacking defenseless refugees. I shot the leader down. After that I couldn't go back."

"Because of Paulson?" Tolwyn asked.

"Yeah," Blair said simply. "And his goons."

Tolwyn shook his head. "Day-to-day personnel movement

is not my domain. I've asked for a full report on Paulson's assignment. I plan to know how a professional bureaucrat like that got a hold of one of my carriers."

He looked at Blair speculatively. "Technically, Chris, you are the enemy now . . . or you will be if the Senate has its way. That makes me your prisoner. What do you plan to do with me?"

Blair raised his hands, palms outward, the pistol lying in his open hand. "I haven't a clue."

"It would be best for you to let me go on my way," Tolwyn said. "Things are grim enough without word getting out that you've kidnapped Earth's senior commander. That'd spark a war for sure."

He leaned forward towards Blair, his elbows resting on his knees. "You know, of course, that we're still on the same side. We both want an end to this, a resolution that avoids war," Tolwyn said, his voice coaxing. "I understand now why you went over the wall." He smiled. "I can't say I'd have done it any differently if I were you." He drew his brows together, thinking hard. "Come back with me, Chris, come back into the fold. You'll have to go before a review board, maybe a court-martial. I'm certain they'll exonerate you. Show them you want to heal wounds." He met Blair's eyes. "Bring the carrier with you. That could be the thing, the first tug that pulls us back from the brink we all face."

"How's that?" Blair asked.

"Look," Tolwyn said persuasively, "this gesture would show both sides that humanity's bonds are stronger than our political differences. It could keep the Senate from declaring war, and it would help restore confidence. Circumstances forced you to turn traitor—I'm sure the same is true for the other good people who are with you. Take the first step, Chris, bring your people in."

Blair looked at him, recalling the turbulent years he'd known Tolwyn. The man could be a cold, calculating bastard. Blair had hated him once, before he'd learned how difficult a mistress duty could be. Tolwyn had the toughest burden of all, and while Blair couldn't say he liked the man, he did respect him. There was the other side of him as well that still seemed to shine somewhere below the surface . . . the hero who had saved Earth in the darkest moment of the war, the man who had risked his career to bring *Tarawa* out after the raid on Kilrah, motivated by loyalty to the brave men and women of that famous ship. Blair had even heard how Tolwyn had broken down and wept when his nephew Kevin, who had been reported missing during the Battle of Earth, was recovered and brought safely in.

There was that part of Tolwyn that confused him now, a man who in so many ways represented the highest ideals of the Fleet, and yet now was something else.

"What would happen to the *Intrepid*?" he asked.

"We'd put her on the front lines, right where you are now. We'd hunt down the real perpetrators. Together."

Blair sat back, sorely tempted by Tolwyn's offer. Could he really deliver on his promise? "The others, Maniac and Eisen, will they be granted amnesty, too?"

"Well," Tolwyn temporized, "I'm certain their years of honorable service would be factored in . . ."

Blair nodded. If Tolwyn had said anything else he would have known the Admiral lied.

He thought back to Paulson . . . and Seether.

"Sorry, Admiral, I can't," he said. "It's like Ben Franklin said, back when the Americans revolted. It was something like: 'Well, now we all need to hang together, for if we don't, we shall surely hang separately.' " He shook his head regretfully. "I've seen too many things that suggest that there are elements in the Confederation that are driving this. If I—we—came back, we wouldn't know who our allies were. I at least know what side I'm on out here."

Tolwyn's expression grew pained. "I'm sorry, son. I'm not sure I'll be able to help you after this, not if you keep to this course. The Senate intends war, and soon. I'd hoped to take something back with me that would forestall them, but so far I haven't found it."

Blair shook his head. "I'll make you a deal, Admiral.

I'll keep working on the problem from this end, while you tackle it from yours. Maybe we can meet somewhere in the middle?"

Tolwyn stood. "I'd like that, Chris. Am I free to go?"

"Yes, sir," Blair said, also standing. He holstered his pistol. "I've only got one name so far, one name that keeps cropping up. His name is Seether. I've got witnesses that place him with the raiders, and I saw him on the *Lexington*. He took over a project Paulson claimed was working directly for you."

Tolwyn's face might have been carved in stone for all the response he showed. "Seether?"

Blair looked at him. "Yes, do you know him?"

"Well," Tolwyn answered, "he was part of some secret experiments that were going on near the war's end. Special Ops had gotten pretty much out of control by that point. They kept cooking up wonder weapon after wonder weapon and soaking up more and more money. This thing Seether was involved with was more of the same, another whizbang that was supposed to save us from certain doom. We were desperate and grasping at straws." He face grew sour. "Sort of like the Behemoth. And to think I bought into that."

Blair nodded in sympathy, recalling its disastrous loss and the damage it had done to Tolwyn's reputation.

Tolwyn looked sharply at him. "But don't forget the Excaliburs and Paladin's little bomb also came out of that same special operations budget. So it wasn't all bad."

Blair nodded. "What kind of program was Seether in?"

Tolwyn glanced at him. "Those programs were tightly compartmented, very strictly need to know. I didn't get the full brief until after the war, when I took over SRA." He rubbed his jaw. "As I recall, it was a little number called GE, short for genetic enhancement. It was some kind of selective breeding program, or eugenics. I'm not certain on the details."

Blair told him about his encounters with Seether's pilots and Bean's descriptions. "Was there cloning?"

"No," Tolwyn answered, "at least not so far as I know. I'm told they never mastered the technology." He furrowed his brow, trying to recall the dusty memory. "I think they'd worked out what they called 'optimal templates.'" He looked troubled. "There shouldn't be that many GEs running around. I was told that the program had been pulled up by its roots."

Blair looked at him, perplexed. "You were told? How many more of these Special Ops projects are lurking out there that you haven't been told about?"

Tolwyn looked a little sheepish. "A lot of these things are buried deep. The problem is, how do you shut down programs hardly anyone even knows about? If you can tell me, I'd do it." Blair studied his face. Tolwyn looked sincere. Blair saw he had no other choice but to take Tolwyn at face value. He sure as hell wasn't going to take him prisoner. He held out his hand. "I'm sorry I shanghaied you, Admiral."

"Hell, son, I'm not," Tolwyn replied. "Now at least I've got some kind of handle on what's going on. That's more than I had before." He took Blair's hand, giving it a warm squeeze. "You take care of yourself, son, and try not to let your people do anything that makes things worse."

"I can't promise that, Admiral," Blair replied. "It looks to me like the folks driving this are on your side."

"If that's true," Tolwyn said grimly, as he guided Blair back to the airlock, "then there'll be hell to pay."

Blair stopped. "What is that smell?"

"Smell?" Tolwyn replied.

"Yeah, it smells like blood back here."

Tolwyn sniffed. "I don't smell anything. Perhaps it's something in the filters." He indicated the airlock.

Blair passed through, then stood on the deck as Tolwyn turned the shuttle and departed out the back of the flight deck.

"What the hell did you do that for?" Dekker said, as he stepped up beside Blair. He took a long look at Blair's thoughtful expression and added a belated "sir."

"It seemed the thing to do at the time," Blair answered. "It certainly was a better option than holding the chief of the SRA. Things're bad enough with Earth without adding that provocation."

Dekker shook his head. "Well, I think you'll live to regret this decision."

Blair turned towards him. "Probably."

He stood on the flight deck, thinking about Tolwyn's offer, until all of Marshall's strike ships landed. He greeted each pilot in turn, thanking them for a job well done. He stayed until the last fighter had either been stowed below for maintenance or was spotted forward for relaunch.

His comm-link buzzed. He unclipped it and spoke into it absently, "Yes?"

"Lieutenant Sosa's compliments, sir," the comm tech said, "but we've got new orders. She forwarded them to your quarters, sir."

"Thank you," he answered and signed off.

He made the long, slow climb back up to the CIC, then turned towards his quarters. He was a little surprised to see his door open. He peered in and saw Sosa leaning over his desk, loading a chip into the message reader. She had changed out of uniform and was wearing a loose white frock and rust-colored skirt. He could see a hint of cleavage from his vantage point. She absently tucked her loose, shoulder-length black hair behind her ear as she worked, seemingly unaware he watched her from the door.

She finally glanced up, did a double take, and slid off the desk. "Sorry, sir. I thought I'd load this for you while you were gone. I didn't expect you to be back."

"So I see," he said, entering his quarters. He left the door behind him open. She stood, looking young and lovely under the room's indirect lighting. Be careful, Chris, he told himself. There's danger that way.

She caught his eye. The silence stretched as he thought of how Jeannette had looked under similar lighting, and Rachel. He knew it wasn't fair to compare Sosa to either of them, yet he couldn't help himself. He wished he was just five years younger and she five older, then it would be all right. As it was they had too many years and too much rank separating them. Still . . .

Her hand went to her throat. "Is something wrong?" She looked down at herself. "Oh, I was just going off duty . . . down to the chowhall for dinner. I got tired of wearing my uniform. Captain Eisen permitted civvies for dining." She stopped herself. "I'm babbling. I'd better go." She started to slide past him.

"Please, wait," he said, then found himself casting about for a reason to ask her to stay. He glanced at his worktable and saw the stewards had left a salver on a heating pad, with a thermos of coffee. "I usually dine in my quarters," he said, "but that gets lonely. Would you like to eat with me?" He felt clumsy and oafish as he looked at her, aware that as opening lines went, he was asking to get shot down. "I'm sure there'll be enough for two," he added lamely.

Sosa smiled, showing dimples. "I'd love to, sir."

He stepped to the serving tray and opened it. Aromatic steam poured out. His mouth watered as he saw the slabs of roast beef, surrounded by carrots and potatoes. "Oh, look," he said, trying to be witty, "roast tire."

She laughed politely as she stepped beside him and took one of the small stack of plates that had collected. "And haunch of vacuum pump," she answered, joining the game. He took a deep breath, inhaling the wonderful scent of her perfume. It felt good for her to be there. He suddenly regretted leaving the door open. There would be no scandal if they were seen together, but it would keep him from really relaxing.

They collected their food. Blair sat behind his desk, after making room for her plate. There was only one chair. Velina perched on one corner of the desk, taking dainty bites of beef.

The silence stretched. He was at a loss for words. "Umm," he said, gesturing towards the chip reader with his fork, "have you seen the orders?"

She grinned. "That's a taboo question, Colonel, sir. I'm

the comm officer. I see *everything* that we send and receive. But it's not polite for me to tell the Colonel I know what his orders are before he does."

"Well," Blair replied, "*I'm* still curious, so if you don't mind . . ."

"Not at all," she said.

Blair turned the tank around to where she could see it, then hit the play button. The screen darkened to reveal Admiral Wilford's face. Blair noticed his cardigan had changed.

"Colonel Blair, I'd like to offer you my condolences on the loss of your pilots. I read your after-action report." Blair looked up at Sosa, who mouthed the word "Garibaldi." He pursed his lips. The *Intrepid's* exec was just a little *too* efficient. He understood now why Eisen insisted on initialing all outgoing reports. It might be a good practice for him to emulate.

He turned his attention back to Wilford. "We're sending you to Speradon system on a high-priority mission. The Confederation has established a forward base inside our territory. Admiral Richards believes this base includes a shipyard and is intended to be part of their mobilization against us. Our data suggests the base is vulnerable, if we act fast." He looked down at his notes. "Your mission will be in the Speradon system as part of a smash-and-grab operation on the shipyard. Our goals'll be two-fold. First, we'll go for proof that the Confed is operating inside Border Worlds' space. And second—we'll carry off as much equipment as we can. We need the hardware.

"I'm sending a separate package to Colonel Farnsworth so she can begin detailed planning for the operation. In the meantime, you'll link up with us here in the Lennox system. There'll be transports there, so you'll have a partial resupply, and tankers, so you can top off." He paused. "I'll be shifting my flag to your ship, so make sure Panther and her staff are ready with at least a preliminary plan by the time I get there. Godspeed, Blair. I'm looking forward to meeting you."

He cued the 'tank off, before it broke to static. He looked at Sosa. "Did Panther get her stuff?"

"Yes, sir," she replied. "About an hour ago, in fact."

He rolled his eyes. "Am I the last to know everything on this ship?"

Sosa smiled, but maintained a discreet silence. Blair decided he liked her smile. It transformed her face, making her look radiant. He found himself making excuses to extend their evening by asking questions about the ship, the crew, and her time on Admiral Richards' staff. And because turnabout was fair play, he answered a few of hers. It wasn't until much later in the evening, as he was pouring his heart out to her about his losing Rachel, that he realized how dangerous it was to start a personal conversation with an interrogator.

• CHAPTER TEN

Blair, along with Admiral Wilford's staff and the task force's command officers, sat waiting for the admiral to arrive. It was Wilford's prerogative to be late and the briefing couldn't start till he showed. In the meantime, they sat, cooling their heels. That was how the military food chain worked.

The arrival of the admiral and his staff had started another round of musical chairs. The extra officers stressed the *Intrepid's* limited amenities past the breaking point. Wilford had started the game by displacing him from the quarters he'd inherited from Eisen. He had, in turn, bumped Garibaldi from his even smaller cubicle. The exec had bunked in with the senior engineer, pushing her deputy out.

He had no doubt that at least one officer would be sleeping with the pilots or the ratings on the flight deck, or, worse yet, with the grunts in the forward hold. Dekker's troops were an earthy bunch, whose senses of humor were likely to be a bit rough-hewn. He could only imagine the torments they'd inflict on a Fleetie assigned to bunk in with them. He hoped the unknown unfortunate had a thick hide.

The room came to attention. Wilford swept in and took his seat. Panther, taking her cue from the admiral, stood and began. Tamara, he had learned, liked things done right, on time, and with no nonsense, and she was doubtless displeased she'd been kept waiting, even by a senior. Wilford was a special case, though. He had a reputation for adopting and nurturing promising young officers, and Tamara Farnsworth wanted to go far. This briefing was her big chance.

"Vice Admiral Wilford," she said without preamble, nodding to the man seated in the chair, "will command the fleet against the covert Confederation shipyard located here, in the Speradon system." The graphic behind her changed, showing a large, egg-shaped gas and dust cloud. Several protostars illuminated it from the inside, giving it a reddish-yellow glow. "The base," she continued, "is concealed within the nebula's electronic interference zone. The interference is due to the passage of the stars' charged particles through the nebular dust."

She paused while the screen behind her split into three images. "There are actually three distinct targets within the shipyard. These are the shipyard itself, a shake-down area for new fighters, and a weapons factory. Our intention is to raid all three targets, plunder what we can, and destroy what's left. We'll do this as close to simultaneously as we can manage."

She smiled, waiting for the explosion that had to come. "All three!" Maniac's bray rose above the others'. "At once?"

"At once," she repeated. "We looked at hitting the targets in sequence, but it just wasn't practicable. We'll lose the element of surprise once we hit the first objective. By the time we hit the second they'll have withdrawn the juicy parts, and stacked the defenses." She turned towards the screen. "Frankly, these targets are so lucrative that it's worth the risk.

"The timing won't have to be that fine, not if we can hit all three within an hour or so. Also, none of the missions are time dependent on the others. When you're done, you go home."

She smiled. "Here's where it gets complicated." She tapped the lectern, which appeared to Blair to be the signal to change the graphic. "The first target will be flown by Colonel Marshall's squadron. It's a staging area for fighters awaiting shakedown. They mass here, then begin their test runs. This is an ideal time to grab their newest birds, fresh off the line.

"Maniac, you'll also be escorting the BWS *Tango*. She's

a fast transport with four tractor beams rigged behind her main cargo bay. Once you've cleaned out the defenses, you'll go after the fighters. Your ships will be equipped with a new weapon, what the eggheads are calling a 'leech gun.' Basically, it drains their power, scrambles their systems, and leaves them dead for a time. You'll use the guns to sweep the area and zap any fighters you can. The *Tango*'ll then make a passthrough and rake in everything she can carry. Once she's loaded, or things get too hot, you'll smoke whatever's left and bug out."

The wall screen behind her changed, showing what appeared to an orbital factory. "Hawk, your mission is the simplest. Your squadron'll escort the Longbow and Broadsword bombers from Admiral Wilford's two escort carriers and destroy the factory. No subtlety. Just kill it. You can expect there to be substantial local defenses. We're told that most of the system's reserve forces are stationed there."

She tapped the third objective. "And this, Colonel Blair, is your target, the TCS *Princeton*." The wall screen shifted again, showing a new Concordia-class fleet carrier surrounded by a spidery-looking space dock. "It's the centerpiece of the raid."

"Me?" Blair said.

Admiral Wilford turned in his seat to look at him. "You, Colonel Blair. I'm sure Commander Garibaldi and I can somehow manage to keep this old girl in space while you're gone. We need our best where they can do their best."

"I'm to kill her?" Blair asked, making notes on his pad.

"No," Farnsworth replied, "you're to capture her."

The silence in the room was deafening. "You must be joking," Blair said after a long moment.

"No," Panther replied, "her reactors are on line. She's poorly guarded, most of her crew's on shore leave. All of her stores are intact, and as far as we know, she's carrying a full load of ordnance and fighters. She's ripe for picking. We expect you to have light resistance."

Blair glanced at Maniac, who rolled his eyes. They had

both heard that promise far too many times for either to believe it.

Farnsworth quickly shifted graphics again, before Blair could protest. "You'll hit her with light weapons, just enough to skin her turrets. Once you've done that, Colonel Dekker's Marines will do an assault landing and secure a landing bay. Sosa's been working on descrambling the phase shield codes. Dekker, you should be able to punch the code and waltz right in."

"Yeah," Gash replied, "I'll bet." He peered at her. "Three squads against a whole carrier?"

She smiled. Blair noticed it wasn't friendly. "Well, Colonel, you're always telling us how tough your Marines are, compared to us Fleeties. Now's your chance to prove it."

She turned back to her map. He and Gash shared a look.

"Once our fearless Marines have the ship under control," she continued, "the *Johns Hopkins* will close and transfer her teams, who'll get the *Princeton* under way and out of the system. Colonel Blair will remain on board as the ranking officer until relieved."

She switched graphics again, this time to a larger overview of the space dock complex. "After you've pulled the carrier free, or, in the event you fail, Admiral Wilford will attack the installations with the fleet. Once the base has been destroyed, we'll retrograde the hell out." She slapped her right fist into her left palm. "That's basically it."

She gestured to a thick stack of color-coded envelopes stacked on a table in front of her. "These are your briefing packets. Manic's forces are red, Hawk's green, and Blair's gold. Study them. If you have any questions, see me. Otherwise, we go in twelve hours." She gestured towards the two ratings assigned to the audio-visual console who began to distribute the packets.

Blair retired to his cramped little room to study the packet. It contained a packet of crisp recon photos of the target, the deck plans of a Concordia-class carrier, written directions to a Concordia's critical areas, a detailed timeline of the operation, and a memory chip loaded with computer simulations of the target area. He studied materials in turn, memorizing everything except the deck plans. He'd spent enough time on the *Concordia* and the *Lexington* to know his way around.

He checked the segment Farnsworth had included on Dekker's instructions. He whistled, dismayed at the tight schedule Panther expected the grunts to keep. She planned for the Marines to seize one landing bay within a few minutes, then to fan out and suppress local defenses. She hoped to have the first *Hopkins* team on board and on its way to the bridge within twenty minutes of the Marines' touchdown. The grunts, already stretched thin, were also expected to maintain ready teams to provide security for the *Hopkins'* people and to defend against an auto-destruct sequence or a counterattack from the main shipyard.

Dekker would read his orders, keep his mouth shut regardless of his reservations, and give the mission his formidable best. But if anyone could pull off Farnsworth's audacious timetable, it would be him.

Blair had his own worries. Panther's squadron had twelve birds, a third of which might charitably be considered front line. The rest were either obsolete or old, and certainly couldn't be considered adequate for the mission. None of the forces involved, for that matter, had the resources needed to guarantee success. Farnsworth's plan counted on luck and surprise to carry them through, both of which were notoriously fickle.

He shifted to his single chair, memorizing callsigns and frequencies, timelines, operations details, call words, recall signals, and the other minutiae of a complex operation. He started his sixth repetition when Pliers rapped on his open door. "Come!" he yelled.

The crew chief entered, grinning. "Well, sir, I've got good news and bad. Which do you want first?"

Blair didn't hesitate. "Good."

"I got your T-bolt back on line," he said, "and then some. I opened the thrusters a little more, giving you better manuvering, and recored the main drives. You should get 40-50 KPS more on both standard and afterburner." He grinned. "Hell, that's enough to get you off the deck without JATO's. I figured you could use an ace-in-the-hole."

"Great!" Blair said, smiling. "Now, what's the bad news?"

"I got her patched up, Colonel, but she ain't gonna hold together long. This will probably be her last flight."

"Why?" Blair asked, sobering from his earlier elation.

"Well," Pliers replied, "I scanned the insides. That mine explosion did a lot of structural damage. You got fatigue cracks all along the main supports and two struts have failed completely. I patched them, but they won't stand up to the kind of abuse you dish out. Also, my mods'll cost you combat radius and engine life." He scratched his head. "You won't have any catastrophic failures, but you're not going to *want* to fly this bird again, not after this mission."

"Well," Blair replied, "let's just get through this one, shall we?"

"You got it!" He grinned again. "What time do you want me to send someone to wake you, son?"

Blair took this as a subtle hint for him to get some sleep. "What time is pilot's brief?"

Pliers didn't even look at his watch. "About four hours. I'll send someone for you." He snapped out the overhead light.

"Thanks," Blair said. He expected to have trouble sleeping, and was pleasantly surprised to have an orderly shaking him after what seemed only moments. It took him only a minute to pull his boots on and to make his way down to the flight deck.

He stepped out of the passageway darkened for ship's night and into the brightly lit bay. Ground crews were hard at work, prepping and fueling the strike wing for launch. Most of the first wave had already been spotted on the painted marks and were ready for takeoff. Blair conducted his preflight inspection on his T-bolt, then walked around a couple of other fighters picked at random. All appeared to be in order, but his Thunderbolt wasn't the only refugee from the boneyard.

He assembled his squadron and conducted his flight briefing from the wing of his battered fighter. Maniac did the same thing across the deck, while Panther filled in for Hawk. Colonel Manley had already departed for the escort carriers to brief their flight crews on their roles.

The launch went well. He watched as the ground crews crossed their fingers while several tattered-looking fighters roared off the deck. Then his turn came. The launch officer pointed to Blair, then out into space. He saluted the deck officer, hit his afterburners, and prayed. Armed with extra missiles and modified engines, he made the launch, but not by much. He suspected he left paint and sponge armor on the front lip of the *Intrepid*'s launch deck.

He switched his comm-panel to the force's combined local traffic frequency. Panther had assigned Sosa to traffic control. The strike wings kept her busy sorting them out. Her warm voice sounded unusually brisk as she assigned orbiting slots to the fighters, aligned the frigates for their raids, and generally coordinated the communications.

A corvette and the *Tango* did picket duty, giving Hawk and Maniac objects for their squadrons to orbit while they assembled. Blair joined Panther's squadron and the Marines' three assault shuttles in orbiting the *Johns Hopkins*. Assembling a single raid was enough of a stone bitch—coordinating three at once through the *Intrepid*'s damaged array multiplied the chaos. His elapsed time counter showed they were already late and getting later. That didn't bode well for the operation.

He repeatedly checked his squadron, making certain his fighters remained on station and in their correct order while Sosa and Farnsworth scrambled to sort out the mess. Panther had insisted he not brief his pilots until the last minute as a security precaution and ordered strict radio silence. Blair understood her reasoning, but the result was chaos. Pilots, uncertain of their rally points, wandered from ship to ship, looking for their squadrons. Several of the Rapiers were already reporting fuel loads in the low seventy-percent range when they finally formed.

Eventually, Sosa managed to get the strike wings sorted out. "Group Alpha, *go!*" she said, sounding jubilant. Maniac's ships peeled off, each winging over and blazing into the nebular dust in a long, loose column. The *Tango*, her drive stream glowing blue, followed. She would lose ground behind the faster fighters, but would still be relatively close when they hit the staging point.

"Group Beta, *go!*" Hawk's forces, the fighters arranged in neat vees over and under the bombers, hit their afterburners as a group and vanished. They had the furthest distance to go, and anticipated the most resistance.

"Group Gamma, *go!*" Blair waggled his wings, signalling his squadron to form on him. He checked the course programmed into his autopilot, then selected it from his menu of pre-set nav points. He glanced back, saw that his squadron remained correctly aligned, and turned onto his approach course. The squadron followed smoothly.

Blair kept a sharp watch as they passed through the nebula. The gas and dust were pretty thin stuff, at least when viewed from the inside. Its real asset was its EM activity which both hid the base from prying outsiders and concealed the strike force. Of course, Confed fighters might also be hiding in the nebula. He scanned the space around him, glancing from quadrant to quadrant in search of enemy telltales. He glanced back to check his rear and was dismayed to see the fighters' phase shields and drive trails glowing as they reacted with the charged dust particles. The trails were a glittering, silvery sign pointing to his fighters. He gritted his teeth. It couldn't be helped.

By some trick of the nebula, his radio scanner locked onto faint signals from Maniac's forces as they attacked. The battle had begun. There would be no turning back now. He checked his nav plot and saw they were minutes from their objective.

"Mother Goose to goslings," he said, "assume attack formation. Sections one and three will hit the carrier's turrets, sections two and four will provide top cover."

He listened as each section leader acknowledged the order. The squadron drifted apart as the sub-leaders took control of their elements. Blair's two wingmen tucked in tight behind him, one Rapier hugging each wing. "Remember," he said, "light weapons only. We don't want to hull the ship."

The last shreds of the nebula cleared. The recon photos and simulations hadn't done justice to the sheer *size* of the damned complex. Huge factories orbited a spider web-shaped space dock. The carrier, a full-sized fleet CV, occupied one quadrant of the dock. A pair of sleek new destroyers nested within a second quadrant with room to spare.

He swore. The destroyers were new, and hadn't appeared on yesterday's recon tapes. They could be counted upon to mount a spirited anti-fighter defense once they got organized. The factories appeared to be dotted with flak towers, which would also mean a hot time for anyone foolish enough to stray into their effective range. A flight of Confed Arrows crossed towards the carrier, further complicating the picture.

He shook his head. Their odds had just gotten a lot longer. He heard his pilots' murmurs as they saw the size of their objective. He knew it wasn't possible to abort the attack, not with Maniac having already engaged. They had to go.

He keyed his microphone. "Mother Goose to goslings, break and attack assigned targets. Good luck."

He punched his afterburner, feeling an unexpected pressure against his back as the T-bolt launched forward. The fighter felt rough and sloppy to him, but Pliers' promised mods were working. He angled for the carrier with his wingmen in tow.

His supporting flights jumped the Confed fighters, surprising them and smoking two out in the first seconds with a volley of missiles. The surviving Arrows, rather than breaking and running as Blair expected, turned towards the raiders and attacked. One Ferret, then another, exploded and died as the Confed ships pitched into the *Intrepid*'s strike.

Blair heard his AI's proximity alarm chime. He looked up and saw the space dock fast approaching. He sloped into the gap between the latticework and the carrier, then angled to begin his attack run. His wingmen broke away to engage their own sectors.

The carrier's bows flashed past. His targeting reticule centered on the first turret. He stabbed his firing key. Twin plasma beams lanced out, piercing the turret and killing it. A second turret flashed into view. The AI projected his correct "windage." He fired, exploding the laser turret.

He hugged the carrier's smooth outer hull, raking its defensive turrets as they appeared, and taking out hardpoint after hardpoint. The *Princeton* reacted first, firing along the hull at him. He laughed as he saw their panicky first shots plowing into the space dock's superstructure, sowing damage in the work pods that clustered over the ship. He blazed over the rear of the ship, then down to begin his outbound leg. The CV's drive plumes brightened, nearly cooking him as he desperately fought to maintain control of his ship in the drives' buffeting.

He maintained control of his Thunderbolt, firing his outboard thrusters to compensate for the stream's side pressure. He cleared the drives, sweeping underneath the carrier. The carrier's laser nets grew more intense as more undamaged turrets came on-line. Beams criss-crossed in front of the T-bolt, the misses tearing gaping holes in the superstructure overhead.

Not all the laser bolts missed. Hits from surviving turrets scored against his phase shields, chipping away at his defenses while he raked the carrier's underbelly. He powered through an especially nasty cross fire, shifting his course from left to right as he destroyed first one, then another of his tormenters.

A bright ball of fire glowed beneath the carrier, then slammed into it, briefly spreading a pool of flame across its surface before vacuum snuffed it. Pieces of a shattered Rapier drifted alongside the ship. A second Rapier, also burning, flashed across his front. It was on fire, but still hammered the carrier's point defenses. Then, it too slammed into the cap ship's hull, taking out one final hardpoint as it died.

He held his course steady, aware that evasive maneuvers only made his task of hitting the surviving hardpoints more difficult. His capacitors dipped into yellow, and then into red as he scattered shots across the hull. The defenders' fire seemed to slacken as he recrossed the ship's bows and fled for open space.

Open space proved no safer than the tight confines of the space dock. His Ferrets were either dead or fled, leaving the Arrows to struggle with an equal number of newer Confed models. Three of his Rapiers were dead as well. He frowned. His squadron wouldn't last long under punishment that intense.

The flak towers on the orbital factories opened up, criss-crossing the sky with clusters of lasers. They fired with more enthusiasm than accuracy, though that might change once their operators calmed down. The attackers' only break had been that so far neither destroyer had shown much reaction.

A Hellcat dropped onto his stern. His automatic rear guns fired even as his missile alarm chimed: He banked hard right, using Plier's boosted roll rate to slip the heatseeker that tried to crawl up his back. He brought his big ship around, turning the tables on the Hellcat. The Confed ship fired a second missile off into deep space, then tried to turn away. Blair, watching his capacitors creep back up out of the red, switched his ordnance to missiles and toggled off one of his own heatseekers. He felt the bump as the explosive bolts cold-fired the warhead, then watched it arc ahead. The infrared warhead caught the 'Cat as it slung around, trying to bring its guns to bear.

The missile impacted at a high deflection angle, piercing its phase shields and shattering one drive. The Hellcat did a quarter-turn under the blow, then steadied out. The pilot regained control, then again tried to bring the ship around to attack.

Blair, surprised by the Hellcat pilot's suicidal nerve, held his course a moment too long. The Hellcat raked him with its sole surviving ion cannon. His phase shields flared and he felt the impacts as dull thuds against the base of his spine. The missile targeting reticule centered on the Hellcat. He switched ordnance and pounded the 'Cat with his plasma cannon. The Hellcat vanished, its structure engulfed in a fireball as the shots ripped it open. He silently cursed the suicidal bravery of the pilot, hoping that it wasn't someone he had once called comrade.

He sheered away from the expanding explosion and turned back towards the carrier. A burning ship, either a Rapier or a Hellcat, tumbled across his line of sight and exploded. The pilot never had a chance to escape.

He scanned the babble on the tactical channels to ensure that all three of the mission's elements were engaged. They were. Panther's plan had succeeded in bringing them to grips with three enemy forces at the same time. His quick sense of the other two attacks was that they had encountered much stiffer resistance than they had anticipated. He smiled bitterly. Underestimating the enemy was one of the few constants of war.

The *Princeton* emerged from the dock and into space like a butterfly from a chrysalis. Fires from burning hardpoints and turret sockets glowed and winked along its length. A single fighter launched from the carrier's portside bay. It arced upward and exploded as a missile struck it amidships, splitting it in half.

Blair checked his capacitors, pleased to see they had recovered their full charge. He turned the Thunderbolt back towards the carrier. He swept down on the carrier, lining up his sighting reticule on a dual laser turret that sprayed the area around him with deadly red beams. He fired his plasma guns. The turret slewed around, then froze as the plasma beams opened it to the hard vacuum of space.

He scanned the top of the carrier, looking for more turrets to hit. Whole sections of the CV's upper and lower hulls were dark, except for winking fires. A few scattered turrets maintained their fire, but were quickly silenced by the two surviving Rapiers. He assigned them to fly CAP over the carrier, scouring the carrier's hull for targets of opportunity.

He glanced up at the fight in open space. The last of the Confed Arrows broke and ran for the flak towers. The support group howled after them.

Much to his surprise, they had accomplished the first part of the mission. The carrier's defenses had been cut down and the space around it had been cleared of fighters. The CV had fully emerged from the dock and turned towards open space, a move that made it more vulnerable, not less.

He switched channels. "Blair to Dekker, shall we dance?"

"Roger," the Marine replied. "I'll lead."

Blair saw the drive plumes of Dekker's three shuttles against the nebular backdrop. They swept in towards the carrier, using boost packs to close on the vulnerable ship. Dekker kept the *Princeton*'s bulk between them and the flak towers on the nearest orbital factory.

Blair stayed close by, matching their course and speed to better protect them from unexpected threats. A single turret on the *Princeton*'s upper hull tracked the lead shuttle. He targeted it and fired. Twin plasma beams reduced it to junk.

"Thanks, Tiger," Dekker replied. "Stand by for Code-Key." The shuttles, their speeds now reduced to match the carrier's, angled in towards the landing deck. The seconds stretched as Dekker tried to disable the phase shields in order to board. He tried sequence after sequence. "Got it!"

Dekker's shuttle, trailed by its fellows, dove for the landing deck and pierced the force curtain that held in the atmosphere. Blair saw the three ships through the curtain, sliding to a halt in the midst of showers of sparks. Ramps fell and the Marines ripped into the defenders. Refraction from the energy weapons against the force curtain blocked any further sight.

"Dancer to Blair," Dekker shouted. Blair could barely hear him over the recorded sound of blaring bugles and hammering weapons. "We're in!"

He monitored the Marine's helmet radios, listening in as they bounded into a firestorm. Several Marines went down at once, ambushed by a surprisingly spirited defense. He heard Dekker and his subordinate leaders calling up fire, concentrating ordnance against strongpoints in the bay, and finally, desperately, opening up with the shuttles' defensive turrets. The roar of the firefight grew even more intense, as the Marines' crew served weapons and heavier ordnance joined the laser rifles.

The fire eventually slackened, then trailed off. "Dekker to Blair," he said, sounding exhausted. "We've got the deck mostly secured." Blair wanted to ask what "mostly" meant to a combat Marine, but Dekker didn't give him a chance. "You can come in."

Blair lined his ship up on the final approach to the deck, hit the threshold, then fired his maneuvering thrusters to stop the Thunderbolt. The larger thrusters accomplished the job more quickly than he had expected, but the rattling of their gimbals told him they were on their last legs. He'd make it home, as Pliers had predicted, but not much further.

He popped the canopy as soon as the T-bolt came to a halt, then immediately ducked beneath the sill. Laser rifle fire spattered off the T-bolt's frontal armor and glanced off the heavy canopy. A fléchette gun roared from underneath one shuttle, pouring fire into and around a flaming pile of canisters where several defenders hid. The heavy penetrators shredded the plastic and metal containers like cardboard, spreading their volatile cargoes and providing fresh fuel for the fire. Greasy black smoke roiled though the bay. Two black-clad crewmen armed with laser rifles were driven into the open by the heat and smoke. The Marines' fléchette gun caught them and literally tore them apart.

Blair looked around, frantically seeking cover. He saw Dekker, a laser rifle in one hand, waving to him. He sprinted towards the Marine commander. A line of laser hits pitted the floor around his legs. He flopped to the ground behind Dekker as the Marine hosed off a dozen quick shots.

"I thought you said the bay was secured!" Blair yelled as he fumbled for his sidearm.

Dekker hooked a foot around a laser rifle clutched in a dead Marine's hands. He tugged it towards Blair, who looked in horror at the blood that soaked the weapon. "I said 'mostly,' " he replied with a grin. "Watch out for the ones in black suits."

A ricocheting round ripped his cheek, drawing a long jagged cut in the flesh. Dekker absently dabbed the blood with his fingers, then fired off another salvo at the entrenched enemy. "I got my demo teams in. They're working on cutting off the blacksuits before they can blow the ship. Some of the *Princeton*'s crew're helping them."

"What?" Blair said, uncertain whether to ask first about the self-destruct or the crew's help.

Dekker pointed with his chin. Blair looked over to where most of the bay's crew lay face down and with their hands over their heads. Their nominal guard, his back to his charges, crouched behind a partially slagged barrel and cranked off shots at the concealed enemy. Two of the *Princeton*'s crew, armed with lasers taken from fallen Marines, knelt shoulder to shoulder with him and fired on the blacksuits.

Another barrage from the shuttle's turret fragged the last of the blacksuits' shelter. They burst into the open, firing wildly as they scrambled for cover. Two were cut down in midstride by Marines' fire. One, his arm blown off, lay on his side, still firing at Dekker's troops. He caught one of the *Princeton* men as he leaned over his barricade to fire. Blair flinched away as blood and brains exploded out of the back of the man's scalp. The wounded defender was hit again, his body nearly shredded by the fléchette machine gun. The rest of the blacksuits made it to cover, firing into the bay from the shelter of the connecting passage.

Blair raised his rifle. Dekker placed his hand over Blair's weapon, pushing it down. Blair looked at him. Dekker pointed.

Three Marines, armed with machine pistols and knives, crept along the dead ground on either side of the open hatch. The defenders pumped burst after burst into the bay, growing bolder as the Marines' fire slacked off. The assault party crouched behind the hatch. Blair saw a flurry of movement.

A flash-bang grenade went off in the middle of the defenders. The Marines, machine pistols chattering, exploded around the door and into the confined space. Miraculously, most of the black-suited crewmen were still on their feet, in spite of the powerful stunning charge.

One Marine rammed his pistol into a blacksuit's gut and fired, spraying rounds and a sheet of blood onto the bulkhead. A second defender, blood pouring from his nose and ears, grabbed a Marine, turned him, and snapped his neck. The blacksuit fell a moment later as the third snap-kicked him in the head, pivoted, and rammed her trench knife into his gut. Dying, he still reached out for her. She casually rammed the heel of her hand into his neck.

The Marine stepped among the fallen blacksuits. Her knife flicked out twice. Blair looked at Dekker, horrified. "Stop her! She's killing the wounded!"

Dekker nodded. "The bastards don't give up. We lost a corpsman to one. She was trying to stabilize one of those blacksuits who'd lost a leg. He armed a grenade and took them both out. Now, I can't take any chances with our people."

Dekker moved to secure the bay, sending one squad to assist the demolition team while the other took up defensive positions around the exits. Dekker limped to the back of one shuttle, followed by Blair. The Marine leaned against the ramp and opened a medkit. Blair saw that he had been wounded at least two other times, in addition to the gash on his cheek. Blood soaked the right shoulder of his fatigues and he held his arm stiffly.

"Damn," Dekker said as he flexed his fingers. "I never thought they'd put up that fanatical a defense. We gave them every chance to surrender. They wouldn't take it—just kept fighting." He shook his head. "They fought like freakin' *Marines*, for crissakes. These were supposed to be support crews!" He glanced down at the nearest of the fallen blacksuits, an expression akin to respect on his face. "I sure as hell don't want to meet any of their grunts." He looked up at Blair. "Who the hell were those guys, anyway?"

"I don't know," Blair replied, then saw the first of the *Princeton*'s crew emerge from cover looking dazed and shocked. "But I know who does." Dekker turned to follow his gaze, and nodded. "Good idea," he said.

The carrier's crewpeople filtered towards the parked shuttles. A female warrant officer looked vaguely familiar to him. She smiled in relief as he approached. "Damn, Colonel Blair, are you a sight for sore eyes."

"Who the hell *are* those guys?" he asked, pointing with his thumb to the small pile of dead blacksuits the Marines were collecting. He had to look away as he saw one sergeant moving among them, rifling their pockets and collecting identification and personal effects. He knew body triage was an important part of intelligence gathering, but seeing it made him queasy. Its effect on the crewwoman wasn't much different.

She looked green as she met his eye. "They're a bunch of hot-shot pilots and ground crew that came aboard while we were doing shakedowns. Ran a bunch of missions off the starboard deck while we were officially still on training cycles." She looked at the dead again. "I can't say I'm sorry to see them gone."

"How's that?" Blair asked.

"They mostly pushed us aside when they came aboard—greenies, twenty-year vets, we didn't matter to them. It got worse after they took over. They treated us like we were scum."

Blair heard a flurry of shots from deep within the ship, followed by a series of muffled explosions. He looked worriedly at Dekker, who grinned and raised one thumb.

The warrant officer met his eye. "A lot of us think we might stand a better chance with you. That's why Thomsen and Hing took your Marines down the shortcut to the magazine. The blacksuits had self-destruct charges rigged. It was part of the threat they used to keep us in line." She looked bitter. "It's too bad you couldn't have been here yesterday."

"Why?" he asked.

"Their commander was here, inspecting the ship. They don't seem to have ranks, but I knew this guy was the boss from the way the others acted. They treated him with respect."

"Do you remember anything about him?" Blair asked.

"Only his eyes," she replied. "They were the coldest, most inhuman eyes I've ever seen."

"Seether." Blair said.

She nodded. "Yeah, that's what they called him."

"Thanks," Blair said. "If you or the crew wants to lash up with us, we can use you. It's voluntary. Otherwise, we'll figure out a way to get you all back to Earth when this is over."

She smiled. "I can only speak for myself, sir, but if it's all the same to you, I'd like to join."

Blair returned her smile. "We got a tough row to hoe, Ms.—?"

"Ellison," she replied, "Caroline Ellison. I knew Rachel Corialis from tech school. She used to talk about you."

Blair expected to feel the familiar jolt of hurt. He was surprised when it didn't happen. "Okay, get everyone together who wants to enlist, then consider them enlisted. There's going to be a power-up team coming aboard to bring this baby out. Your people can turn to and help them."

He saw the first of the *Hopkins'* shuttles swarming in even as he turned away from the warrant officer. Crews loaded down with sidearms and equipment fanned out from the shuttle and sprinted for their duty stations.

A full commander, with a Technical Services tab on his flight suit, stepped up and saluted Blair. "You did it, sir. Looks like we've got us another carrier."

A Marine ran up to him. "Colonel, come quick! You gotta see this!"

He followed the Marine forward and down into the maintenance bay. The automatic lights came up to reveal rows of black ships, all nested in their launch cradles. They were the same style he fought against over Melek's convoy, and the same as the ones in the Kilrathi tapes. The fighters were sleek and otherworldly, with spare lines and a honed, finished appearance. They made even the Hellcats look chunky and rough-hewn by comparison.

The first of the *Intrepid*'s boarding contingent wandered in, each stopping to stare.

He turned and saw Pliers, a tool kit slung over his shoulder, standing in the door. "They're beautiful," the old man whispered, "absolutely beautiful." He made as if to spit tobacco juice on the deck, then stopped himself. He glanced around and picked up a discarded plastic can. He spat into that, then walked over to the nearest bird and ran his fingers over the spongy armor. "Hello, beauty," he murmured.

Blair watched in amusement as the crew chief dropped his shoulder bag, dug out a spanner, and went to work on an access plate. "Let's see what secrets you're hiding, little lady," he crooned. Blair turned away as the *Intrepid*'s techs, looking like kids at Christmas, swarmed over their new toys. He left them alone to poke and prod the fighters. The black fighter impressed him as much as it did them, but he'd never managed to get excited over cunningly designed wire harnesses.

He emerged from the launch bay in time to see Sosa

crossing the recovery area for the personnel lift. She pulled a handcart behind her that had been piled high with decrypting equipment.

He felt the deck heel slightly, then realized he felt an increased vibration in the floor.

The loudspeaker crackled. "Colonel Blair to Auxiliary Control." He walked quickly back to the landing deck and saw a few remaining Marines lounging by their shuttles. Dekker sat against a landing strut, armed with a shaving mirror and a can of wound sealer. He was busy spraying the pinkish artificial skin over the cut in his face, while a corpsman stood by with an amused expression. Dekker looked tired and very, very happy.

He looked up as Blair approached.

"How'd we do?" Blair asked.

Dekker raised a thumb. "The *Tango* snagged about a dozen ships and pilots. The other group took some heavy hits. They got the weapons factory, though."

Blair nodded soberly, pleased at the success while being saddened by the losses. "And Wilford's raid?"

Dekker tapped his ear. "Reports are sketchy. The *Intrepid* took some hits. A couple of the frigates bought it, too, when those destroyers finally got their act together." He paused. "The word in the trenches, though, is that the mission was a complete success. It looks like we got away clean."

Blair smiled tiredly. "Good," he answered. He turned to go to Auxiliary Control, crossing the deck and taking the personnel lift up one deck. The lift was a luxury after having to climb everywhere on the *Intrepid*.

Commander Toliver, the recovery teams leader, met him outside the control room as he stepped off the lift.

"Yes," Blair said, "what can I do for you?"

Toliver smiled. "Well, sir, you are the nominal captain of this ship, or at least the ranking officer. I thought it best that I give you my report."

Blair nodded. "Go ahead."

Toliver looked forward, then back along the corridor.

"We've got the engines and navigation systems on-line and we're moving at about half speed. We don't dare do more, considering how thin we are. We are getting a lot of help from the *Princeton*'s crew. About forty crossed over." He paused. "There are rumors that some of those special troops are holed up somewhere aft. Dekker says he'll put search teams out." He looked at Blair. "Frankly, it's a damned big ship for his people to search. So stay forward and don't lose your sidearm."

"Got it," Blair said. "Is there anything I can do?"

"Yes, sir," Toliver replied. "Only a few of us have service time on a Concordia. Studying a map doesn't help much when you're stuck in a wiring trunk."

Blair laughed. "Okay, I'll direct traffic." Unlike on the *Intrepid*, there was plenty here for him to do. The *Princeton*, designed to be operated by several hundred, seemed infested by gremlins when staffed by only ninety. Blair quickly found himself dispatching increasingly harried work crews to crisis spot after crisis spot. He hadn't realized how much time had passed until a young woman in civilian coveralls tapped him on the shoulder. "Sir," she said, "I'm your relief."

He was at first surprised at how much time had passed. The ache in his neck from peering over schematics told him that while he might not have noticed, his body had. "Thank you, miss."

He stood, waved a cheery goodnight to the crew in Auxiliary Control and went to his quarters. He was fatigued enough to simply let his feet carry him where they would. It wasn't until he keyed the doors to the wing commander's quarters that he remembered he was on the *Princeton*, not the *Lexington*. Still, he was there and the quarters had a bed. He entered.

He saw the connecting door to the washroom was open and heard the sound of the shower running. He remembered Toliver's warning about possible surviving blacksuits. He drew his sidearm, crept to the door, and burst in.

Sosa, wearing only a towel, was bent forward, rubbing

another towel through her luxuriant black hair. She squeaked as he crashed through the door and she went for her own sidearm. She pointed it at him, then realized who he was and grabbed for her forgotten towel. They stood a few meters apart, laughing nervously as the tension ebbed away.

"What are you doing in here?" he asked.

"I was searching the senior officers' quarters," she replied, "looking for a databank, a notebook, something I could use as a starting point for the decryption process. I came in here and saw the shower. I couldn't resist." She smiled at him. He noticed, not for the first time, how it transformed her features. "You have no idea what a luxury it is to take a private, hot shower. Well, sort of private."

He looked away, embarrassed.

"Umm, could you excuse me, please?" she asked. Blair gave the air near her a slight bow, then backed out of the room.

He turned his attention to the quarters. They were stark, even compared to his on the *Lexington*. They contained only a rack, neatly made with precise hospital corners and a folded blanket, a single lamp, a desk with a monitor, a bureau, and a couch. There were no individual mementos, no awards, no pictures on the wall. There was absolutely nothing to distinguish the occupant.

He crossed to the closet and opened it. Inside were a dozen black flight suits, each precisely hung. He pulled one out. The name "DuMont" had been stencilled in red on each. He saw no rank, no badges, and no awards.

"It's like the Spartans," Sosa said from behind him.

He turned. She had scrambled back into her uniform. "Oh?"

"Sparta was the city-state that finally defeated Athens in the Peloponnesian Wars," she said. "Their culture was based on the warrior, and their whole society was dedicated to the enhancement of discipline and military virtue."

"I'm not sure I'm following you."

She rubbed her still-damp hair vigorously. "The core

of Spartan society was the mess, as in mess hall, or a group of young men who lived communally. Each Spartan was expected to contribute heavily to his mess. Individuality was suppressed in favor of the group. Spartans might marry, might even have children, but the mess—his comrades, and his duty to the state—came first."

"Is that what you see happening here?" Blair said.

It was her turn to nod. "Yes. The irony is that while the Spartans won the war with the Athenians, they couldn't win the peace. Their power was shattered within a generation by a new coalition that rose up against them."

She laughed.

"What's funny?" he asked.

"Me," she replied, her eyes dancing with mirth. "I had every schoolgirl's fantasy, to be alone, almost naked, with the most famous man in the Confederation, and here I am, talking about dead cultures."

The shift in topic threw Blair for a loop. "Oh?" he said, the expression a time filler while he tried to think of something more intelligent to say.

She gazed at him directly. "I first heard of you after the raid on Kilrah when you and your pilots took out the shipyards there. I followed the press and propaganda stories—I never missed an episode of *Heros of the Confederation.* I knew it was all fluff, of course, but I had a terrible crush on you."

He thought over his own interest in her, the age differences, and his past with Rachel, who hadn't been much older than she was, even if he had been younger then.

She smiled. "Then, there *you* were, on the *Intrepid.* I couldn't believe it. I'd always wanted to meet you, then I did. And it was wonderful." She looked up at him, her blue eyes framed by her slightly disheveled hair. He thought she looked compellingly lovely. "I still have that crush on you, you know."

He felt his own desire for her as a physical ache. He wanted to take her in his arms, to pull her close. Her shining eyes were an open invitation to him. Her lips were slightly parted, as though waiting to be kissed.

He saw, in that moment, two courses open to him—to them. It would be so easy for him to take the first step towards her. They were alone together, the door was even closed. The crew was too busy and the ship too big for anyone to remark on their absence together. There would be no scandal. No one would know.

The second road was harsher. He saw himself, an aging pilot, using her youth and beauty to try and reclaim some of his own spent years. It would be a classic midlife crisis. He'd tried a May-December romance with Rachel, and while he knew he'd driven her away with his drinking and bitterness, the hurt was still there when it failed. He didn't want to go through that again.

He realized that he couldn't trust his own motives where Velina Sosa was concerned, and because of that, he didn't move, didn't take the first step. "Velina," he said. "I . . ." He broke off, uncertain how to continue.

Her eyes searched his face. He watched her drawing her conclusion from his stance and his tone of voice. Her expression shifted as she tried not to look hurt. "I'm sorry," she said, looking down, "I've embarrassed myself terribly. I should go." She seemed to draw in on herself as she turned to collect the things she'd left in the bathroom.

"It's not what you think," he said, trying to salvage the situation.

"Oh?" she said, her face closed and still.

"Look," he said, aware he was foundering, "I'm forty, you're twenty-five. I'm almost old enough to be your father."

She shook her head. "Well," she replied, "you'd have had to start young." She set her jaw and looked up. Her eyes searched his as he fought to keep his face expressionless. "I see," she said after nearly a full minute, "so that's how it is."

"I'm looking out for you as much as I am me," he said. He realized too late how badly that came out, making him sound both self-righteous and condescending.

Her expression hardened. "In case you haven't noticed, *Colonel*, I'm all grown up. I'm a big girl. I can take my own risks. I don't need you to do me any favors." She grabbed her small bag and stormed out, leaving him staring after her.

Then she was gone, the door closing automatically behind her. He sat on the edge of the bunk and held his head in his hands.

• CHAPTER ELEVEN

Blair rubbed his gritty eyes as he stepped into the *Princeton*'s Auxiliary Control room. He had revisited his last conversation with Velina over and over as he'd tried to sleep. He'd eventually given up tossing and turning, to walk the darkened halls of the *Princeton*. The carrier, so like the *Concordia*, had roused the ghosts of his memory. Sleep wasn't an option after that.

He sipped from the coffee mug he'd liberated from the Marines. Dekker brewed his coffee black and heavy. The caffeine jolt brought him to some semblance of alertness.

Toliver looked up from the *Princeton*'s command chair. "Good morning, Colonel. I got a priority message from Admiral Wilford. He wants you back on the *Evil I*."

Blair nodded, as aware of anyone in the fleet, over the bad luck ships named *Intrepid* seemed to share. "How soon?"

"Yesterday," Toliver replied. He held the flimsy out to Blair. "There's trouble."

Blair took the scrap and began reading it. "What's up?"

"I don't know," Toliver said, "but it must be bad—real bad."

Blair considered stopping to shave, then decided that if Wilford wanted him that badly he could put up with a little five o'clock shadow. "Tell the admiral that I'm on my way."

He made his way down to the launch deck without seeing Velina, which both troubled and relieved him. He was still chewing on the implications of that when the lift arrived at the flight deck. Pliers met him as he stepped out.

"Toliver gave me the word, kid," he said. "We've got

279

you all spotted on 'Cat One. Your pre-flights are finished and she's ready to go."

Blair followed him, already anticipating the flight back to the *Intrepid*, and hopefully a long nap soon after that. They stepped into the launch bay. Blair looked around for his Thunderbolt. "Where's my bird?"

Pliers pointed him towards the black fighter mounted on the launch cradle. "Black Lance Five-Four, at your service. Son." He grinned smugly at Blair's stunned look.

"Black Lance?"

"We cracked open a box of technical tapes," Pliers said, "that's what they call 'em. Black Lances. Callsign's usually Dragon." He spat a long dark stream into a can. He was apparently still unwilling to defile the *Princeton*'s deck with tobacco juice. "They're easy to maintain, almost do it themselves, in fact." He grinned. "You should see the wiring harnesses on this baby. Brilliant. Absolutely brilliant."

Pliers grinned happily. "These're show pieces, works of art. Every detail's perfect. Hell, they don't even have to fly. Just put 'em in galleries, where people can admire 'em."

Blair smiled. "I don't think we want these to be museum pieces just yet."

"Ha," Pliers laughed. "Just like a pilot. Ain't happy unless he's jockin' around at 800 per. Still, there ain't nothin' in space like these babies. And they all have a real, live, functioning cloaking devices. Definitely Kilrathi derivative, and definitely functional." He pointed up at the large intakes mounted behind the pilot and along the leading edges of the wings. "See those Bussard intakes? They scoop in everything, hydrogen, dust, anything their magnetic fields catch. The matter feeds a whole new power plant—matter/antimatter. Do you know what that means?"

Blair nodded his head. He'd first encountered the antimatter engines on the experimental Excalibur fighters he'd used for the attack on Kilrah that ended the war. Those engines, the first successful attempt at miniaturizing the cap ships' drives, allowed virtually unlimited range.

He peered at the fighter, scrutinizing its lines. Shave here, add there, change the camber of the wing and reposition the intakes. He could see the family resemblance once he knew what to look for. The Excaliburs had been prototypes for the Black Lances.

"Yeah," he said at last, "a jump capability and no need to stop and refuel. You can run on afterburner forever, as long as you can find hydrogen."

Pliers nodded enthusiastically. "Your guns and shields'll be some drain on the system, but there isn't anything in space that'll touch you."

Blair thought of Seether. "Except another Black Lance."

Pliers bobbed his head, unwilling to take his eyes off the ship. "Yeah, but imagine the speed!" He spat a lump of something black and disgusting into the can, then fished his pouch from his pocket and reloaded his cheek.

"Son, you got one hot rocket prepped and ready on Number One. Are you gonna sit here all day, or are you gonna cruise?"

Blair turned towards him. "Don't you think this'll make our people a touch nervous?"

Pliers laughed. "Who cares? You can outrun 'em, outturn 'em, and if that doesn't work, you can just cloak." He jerked his thumb at the fighter. "Besides, I loaded the IFF codes for the *Intrepid*. You'll be fine."

Blair looked up. His palms itched to try the ship out. "Where's my helmet?"

Pliers slapped his back. "That's the spirit. It's sitting on your control yoke."

Blair climbed into the cockpit. Pliers helped him strap in, then went over the various flight controls with him. He could really see the Excalibur family resemblance in the cockpit layout. He ran his hands over the controls, refamiliarizing himself, while Pliers checked his equipment. The only odd item was a line of covered switches. Several were crudely marked by Pliers, and were for arming and firing mines. The rest were unlabeled. He knew better than to toy with them.

The launch proved an anticlimax. The Lance had power enough to get it off the deck without assistance, and Pliers' knowledge of the launch board made the shot uneventful.

The Black Lance flew more smoothly than Blair believed possible. Every ship, including Excaliburs, had some roughness, some point on the power scale where the engines vibrated or the controls were sluggish. The Lance had none of that. He brought it up to maximum standard cruise, then put it through its paces. The maneuverability and precision were better than the Hellcat's and nearly on a par with the Arrow's. The Black Lance was a pilot's dream. It had the ordnance and staying power of a heavy fighter, and the nimble speed and quickness of a light ship.

The *Intrepid's* CAP, made up of pilots from Maniac's badly depleted squadron, reacted poorly. It took him a fair amount of fast talk and IFF interrogations before they left him alone while he swooped and dove, jinked and weaved, and put the frame through as much stress as he could. He heard none of the creaks and squeaks that indicated lurking trouble, and the Lance performed like a champ. He decided, as he entered the *Intrepid's* landing cycle, that he was in love.

He was still suffused in the warm afterglow when he stepped onto the *Intrepid's* cramped little CIC. The odor of burned circuitry permeated the air, making him sneeze. He noted that a quarter of the CIC's displays were out and heavy portable conduits connected the data cores to a pair of rollaways that had been set up to take the place of the navigation station. The main-viewscreen and holo-tank were down as well. The *Intrepid*, he realized, had taken yet another pounding.

Wilford turned in the command chair to face Blair. "It took you long enough," he said without preamble.

"I got delayed," Blair replied.

"I saw your little joyride," Wilford said. He waved his hand around his face. "Had time to go for a flight, but not enough to shave, huh?"

Blair shrugged. He looked at Wilford, noting the bags

under the admiral's eyes and his glum face. Wilford should have been ecstatic. "What's up?" he asked, trying to change the subject.

Wilford gestured to a small holo-tank set above a damaged console. "We received an SOS message last night," he said. "It's pretty grim." He stood and gestured for Blair to precede him to the terminal. "This came in from the Telamon system." He tipped his head towards the communications tech, who placed a chip into the reader and cued the screen.

The image in the reader was female. Snow almost blotted the picture out, and the audio faded into static. "It gets better later, sir," the tech said. "A lot of it's getting washed out by the nebula. Telamon's also got a lot of sunspot activity."

". . . under attack from some kind of virus," the woman said, ". . . canisters were found . . . bio-weapon of some sort. We are issuing . . . general plea for help. We need medicines, trained medical personnel, anyone you can send. We have thousands lying in the streets, dying. We need your help." The image cleared and the static faded. The picture jumped and fuzzed, then froze as the tape came to an end.

The Telamon woman, wearing a doctor's lab coat, stood in front of what was obviously a hospital ward. Hundreds of people were crowded into an area meant for a few dozen. Beds were occupied two and three deep. Other victims lined every inch of floor and lay in pools of their own vomit, blood, and excrement. The victims all had terrible, bleeding lesions on their exposed skin, and their bodies appeared to sag as the flesh drooped. The image embodied the worst human nightmares of the plague, like a scene from a Bosch painting.

Blair turned away, sickened. "Oh, my god. This was an attack?"

Wilford looked at the frozen image. "It looks that way." He leaned towards the viewer and snapped the horrific image off. "I dispatched a bio-hazard team to Telamon as soon as we got the message." He glanced at his watch. "They should be reporting anytime. I'm putting out a call for volunteers, medical personnel. We don't know what the possibility of infection is, so this will be a one-way trip for those who go." He rubbed his face, aging several decade before Blair's eyes. "I've had a dozen takers, so far. Bless their hearts."

He turned away. The comm tech, his voice carefully controlled, spoke into the silence. "Sirs, I've got a message coming in from Telamon. It's on the bio-team's trans-light freq."

Wilford set his jaw. "Run it." The screen snowed, then settled as the transmitters matched. A man in his early thirties appeared. His wild eyes gave Blair some indication of the nightmares he'd seen firsthand.

"Admiral, this is Dr. Clivers. We made landfall about five hours ago. This is a preliminary report, based mostly on data the Telamon inhabitants gave us." He took a deep breath.

"It's bad down here, worse than I've ever seen, and worse than the distress beacon indicated. This stuff is virulent, it's everywhere, and, until we can get a handle on its toxicity, we're considering it unstoppable by conventional medical means.

"Admiral, you have no choice except to impose an ironclad quarantine of the planet." He looked away from the viewer a moment and murmured to a person off-camera. "You better make the quarantine shoot to kill. This can't get out."

"What is it?" Wilford asked. "How bad is it?"

Clivers chose to take the second question first. "Do you remember those old death camp two-dees, from Auschwitz and Bergen-Belsen? The Nazi stuff? This is worse. A thousand times worse. We've got bodies lying in the streets, for a lack of anyone to collect them. Most of the population's dying, so there's fewer people every day to keep things running. Thank God, temperatures have been cool. That's slowed the decomposition somewhat, but the whole planet reeks like a charnel house. The rotting bodies will add another round of epidemics to the crisis, cholera and secondary transmissions could carry off those who make it through this."

He ran one hand through his hair. "And as for what it is . . . there is no hell hot enough or deep enough for the bastard that cooked this up."

"So it *is* a weapon?" Wilford asked.

"Oh, it's a weapon all right," the doctor responded. "There are small canisters all over the place. The locals say they were dropped by some kind of black fighter plane. The details were sketchy, but the birds didn't sound like anything in our inventory." He took a deep breath.

"The cans were covered with a residue of these sonsabitches." The image faded to be replaced by a photo of what looked at first like a tiny, hard-edged spider. The image changed again, showing other views and scenes of the same organism. It looked to Blair like a virus, with tiny prongs and probes. Something that looked like a set of pincers extended from one end. The usual contours had a precise, machined look.

The doctor's voice continued as a voiceover as the images shifted. "You're looking at a bio-engineered microcomputer."

"A what?" Blair asked.

The last of the graphics faded to be replaced by Clivers' face. "Think of them as microscopic computers. It looks like an airborne vector. They seem to get into the body best as an airborne viral infection, but there's no reason they can't also be transmitted by water, food or even sex." He laughed harshly. "Especially sex. They really seem to like the gametes.

"They get into the body, get picked up by the blood, then begin to reproduce by heisting the cell's DNA and using it to replicate themselves."

"Just like a virus?" Wilford asked.

"Worse," Clivers replied. "They do a genome comparison of your DNA helix. If they don't like what they find, they start attacking your RNA, converting it into malignant cancers, pathological hemocytes, and a dozen forms of what looks superficially like organ rejection. Your cells stop replicating and begin killing each other. Your connective tissue fails, giving the distinctive slack-faced look reminiscent of stroke.

"That's the last stage. By then, your organs are all but destroyed. Then you die. It takes from sixty to ninety hours to run its course. The locals are calling it DRT."

"DRT?" Blair and Wilford asked together.

Clivers smiled without humor. "Dead Right There— it's first cousin to being DOA—Dead On Arrival." He gestured at the room behind him. "You contract this, you're DRT." Blair saw body bags stacked from floor to ceiling. "We've cut open a dozen, so far," Clivers continued, "and we're seeing the same thing over and over again."

"Why aren't you dead then?" Blair blurted.

"I will be, in a couple of days. About half my team seems to be okay. The little bastards seem to like their DNA."

"How's that?" Blair asked, trying to come to grips with the fact he was talking to a dead man.

"This isn't random," Clivers said. "The microcomputers seem to leave about one in ten alone."

"Why them?" Wilford asked. "Is it immunity?"

Clivers shrugged. "We don't know what it is. The stuff seems to invade their genetic material as well, and it does take over enough cells to replicate, but it doesn't attack the host. Our very preliminary guess is that it's making tiny alterations in the victim's genetic code, but we don't know. We've been more interested in the dying than we are in doing much research on those who seem to be immune. That'll change, of course, but right now we're just trying to assess and contain the damage."

Clivers mopped his brow. Blair could see runnels of sweat running down his face, even as his breath smoked in the slightly chilly air. "As I said," the doctor continued, "we don't know what the causal factors are. It could be any single genetic characteristic or a combination. Hair color, body fat percentages, skin color, we just don't know.

The sample of the dead is so broad and their DNA is so disrupted that we often can't even place what the genome looked like originally."

He looked bitter. "You can program anything. Don't like fat people? Zap." He cocked one finger like a gun as he spoke. "Myopia? Pow. Sickle cell trait? Zowie. Just tweak the program and kill off the defectives of your choice."

Blair looked at Wilford. The Nazi analogy seemed closer than ever. "Do you think the Kilrathi are involved? They used some pretty noxious bio-weaps on us the last years of the war."

Clivers, overhearing Blair's question, shook his head. "I don't think so. Those Cat plagues were all designed to depopulate. No subtlety at all. This seems slightly different. More advanced technology. More malevolent, if that's possible."

Blair looked at Wilford. "What do we do?"

Wilford looked tired and much older as he wrestled with the implications of the attack. "We'll jump into Telamon, and do what we can for the victims. We'll also try to find out who did this." His shoulders sagged. "This takes precedence over everything, including the war. If one shuttle should escape, carrying this . . . thing, it could spread throughout the human worlds, including the Confederation. We have to stop it. Now."

Clivers' head in the viewscreen nodded emphatically. "The local defense forces have been enforcing a blockade up till now. They've shot down about thirty ships, all infected. Most of the pilots are subject to the disease as well, and there aren't enough ground crew to service the fighters they have left. They're fading fast."

"Got it," Wilford replied. He looked at his aide de camp, whose face was pale as a sheet. "Order all personnel back to their ships, and make ready to move the fleet to Telamon." He paused. "Transfer as many of those new Hellcats over from the *Princeton* as we can fit. Then move whatever Rapiers and Ferrets we can to the escort carriers. Their groups suffered pretty heavily in yesterday's attack."

Wilford looked at the doctor. "We're sending teams of volunteers to help."

Clivers laughed harshly. "Don't bother, Admiral, unless you want them to die too. Just keep this from going anywhere else."

Wilford nodded heavily, the weight of the universe literally on his shoulders. "Then, son," he said, "there really isn't much I can do for you. Have you any family, anyone you want us to contact?"

Clivers smiled sadly, "Once. Remember, I'm from Sirius."

Blair looked at the image of the volunteer doctor and understood now why he had volunteered for all but certain death. The Sirius colonies had been annihilated during the Kilrathi offensive against Earth. When everything is gone. . . . Blair understood the death wish; Death had flirted with him all too often.

"No, Admiral, there's no one now," Clivers said, "but thank you." He closed the contact, ending the message.

They stood a long time in a gloomy circle. The aide was the first to break the silence. "Admiral, what about the *Princeton?*"

Blair thought it took Wilford an unusually long time to answer. "Send her and two escorts to Orestes system," he said. "I'll contact Richards and get a top priority for her repair. We'll also try to fit out a crew there. She won't be much good to us for a while, but she'll get in the fight eventually."

Blair saw the old admiral was mouthing the words, but that his heart wasn't in it. Wilford turned away, his shoulders sagging, and walked out of the CIC. Blair assumed his place in the command chair. It wasn't until the shuttles bringing the *Intrepid's* crew were in the landing cycle that it occurred to Blair that he had no handler. He was, for the first time, truly in command of the *Intrepid*. He wondered how long it would take for one to show up.

Blair looked down on the blue and green cloud-covered world of Telamon. It looks so beautiful and so peaceful from up here, he mused, it's hard to believe the world's dying.

The huge losses to DRT had, as predicted, triggered secondary epidemics. Virulent influenza proliferated as water treatment facilities failed and insects swarmed on the millions of uncovered, uncollected dead. The secondary epidemics, bred in the mutated cells of the dying, spread like wildfire among the weakened population.

The *Intrepid*'s CAP had been focused inward, shooting down any craft that sought to escape from Telamon. It was heartbreaking work, both for the pilots who did the killing and for the commanders who knew what the inhabitants faced. Rescue shuttles and relief ships entered the planet's atmosphere to land supplies and relief workers. The fighters destroyed the ships as soon as they unloaded, preventing them from being used to attempt an escape that might spread the infection to other systems. *Intrepid*'s pilots and crew grew quickly demoralized.

Maniac had risen to the crisis, proving himself to be a better wing commander than Blair believed possible. He had worked hard to keep the flight rotation fair, making certain all the senior officers had their turn in the box. Blair himself had flown several missions, each time gritting his teeth and hating what he was doing. Maniac's flight status reports were beginning to show sick-call referrals to the ship's mental health professionals. Fights between crew mates broke out and the booze consumption tripled.

Maniac, in an attempt to bolster morale, had ordered the dozen black Dragons to be repainted in Border Worlds colors and distributed among the remaining three squadrons. Blair and Maniac agreed that it would have been better to keep the fighters in a single compact group, but Maniac appreciated the more compelling need to distribute them fairly to boost morale.

The new birds had immediately triggered a good-natured competition amongst the pilots about who would get to fly them. That had lasted until they killed four shuttles of begging pleading refugees. Then morale sagged again.

Blair found he missed Velina badly. She had chosen to remain on the *Princeton*, ostensibly to continue her decryption of the carrier's comm files. The one time he'd spoken to her she'd been cool and correct to him. He'd tried to be philosophical about it, telling himself that it was for the best. He hadn't realized how much he enjoyed her company until she was gone. The hurt, combined with their nasty mission, made him more miserable than he had been at any time since Rachel had left. Well, Chris, he told himself, it is your fault.

In the days that followed the *Intrepid*'s move to Telamon, she had been busy earning her keep. She'd finally cracked the Fleet's newest code, with the help of files she'd downloaded from the *Princeton* and a notebook she'd found in the captain's desk. Blair had been dismayed to learn that a code was considered "broken" when it was fifteen to twenty percent readable. That had confirmed in his mind why so many intelligence estimates were either dead wrong or partially wrong.

He had monitored the heavy volume of messages labelled "most secret" that had passed between Sosa and Wilford, hoping she might have one for him. Whatever she had found out had necessitated volumes of message traffic that took up most of the *Intrepid*'s meager resources.

He was reviewing the comm logs when his chair intercom buzzed. "Blair," he said.

"Colonel," Wilford asked, his voice tired and dry, "would you come to my cabin? I've something to discuss with you."

Blair found the request odd. "Of course, sir." He flicked a thumb at Garibaldi, then stood. The *Intrepid*'s exec smoothly shifted seats, assuming the con as Blair left the CIC.

Blair knocked on the door that had so recently been his, and before that, Eisen's. The thought of his former captain drew him up short. What had become of Eisen? The man had vanished in order to attempt to infiltrate the Confederation. Nothing more had been heard from him.

Blair doubted he'd been captured. The Confederation's propaganda people would have trumpeted the capture of so famous a traitor from one end of human controlled space to the other.

"Come in," Wilford said, his voice barely audible through the heavy metal door. Blair opened it to see Wilford, dressed in his trademark cardigan sweater, sitting at the desk that Velina had perched on such a short time ago.

"Yes, sir?" he said, making the routine response into a question. He heard Sosa's voice coming from the holo-screen. Wilford gestured Blair to the facing chair, then turned the screen around so they could both see it. Blair noted the small "playback" graphic in the corner.

". . . so you see, Admiral," she was saying, "I can't prove to you that the location we've identified as Base X is in the Axius system, but it does make sense.

"We first came across repeated references to stopping at X, and while we don't have as much of the code as we'd like, we do see the same polynumeric grouping in the same places. We believe they are navigation coordinates, based on where they are located in relation to the groups we have broken."

She brushed her hand along her ear, pulling back one stray lock. "We've run triangulations of the various known Confed activities, and compared those to date-time groups we recovered from Eisen's files. Axius is well within range of all of the target locations, based upon commonly accepted intersystem travel times and fuel consumption rates. We can also show a loose correlation between certain messages sent by Confed ships and attacks that took place."

"Do you have anything else?" Blair heard Wilford's voice ask. She looked nervous, as though she'd presented a case that seemed airtight, then failed to make her point.

"Yes," she replied, "maybe. I did some research on Axius. I'm sending you everything we have. The primary is a main sequence red giant, very hot right now but cooling rapidly. The planets there are deserts, barren and lifeless, cooked by the star's heat. It's unpopulated and virtually uninhabitable—just the perfect place to build an out-of-the-way base."

She brushed the tips of her fingers together. "Also, two of the *Princeton's* scanner entries make open mention of capitol ships entering the system. Why? There shouldn't be anything there. Axius is a logical guess, Admiral. It's close, it fits, and it feels right, at least to me." She dipped her head. "I'll be the first to admit this isn't definitive—I can't prove it, at least not yet. But it feels right to me."

"Thank you, Lieutenant," Wilford's disembodied voice said on the tape, "you've made a compelling argument. Let me talk to some people at this end. Keep up the good work. Wilford out." The tape ended with a Border Worlds logo and the words "Most Secret" flashing in red.

Wilford looked at Blair. "What do you think?"

Blair paused, gathering his thoughts before speaking. "I'd be inclined to trust her hunches, Admiral. It seems to me that it might be worth launching a long range reconnaissance probe to take a look-see." He leaned over Wilford's desk and keyed the star map. "I'd use a frigate, sir, and I'd launch it from Callimachus. That system's barren, too, so the odds of detection are low. It's close to Axius, close enough for a tight-beam laser link, yet far enough to have a good head start if the probe sets off a hornet's nest."

"All right," Wilford said, "do it." He sounded even more depressed than before.

"What's wrong, Admiral?" Blair asked.

"I know what you're going to find," Wilford replied, his voice thin and tired. "Axius was one of our—the Confed's, rather—centers for 'black budget research' during the war. Sosa's right. The system is barren, no biosphere whatsoever. It's the ideal place to test weapons, especially bio-weapons."

"How do you know about it?" Blair asked.

"I was briefed on it when I took over the sector command just before the war ended." He took a deep breath. "It was supposed to be shut down after the Kilrathi War.

Apparently it wasn't. If the bio-weapons came from there, then it's possible they were developed there. Either that, or there will be some record, some hard evidence, of their transfer."

"If we could get that," Blair replied, trying to lift Wilford's spirits, "we could blow the lid off this whole thing. That'd be the smoking gun! That kind of proof would be enough to bring down the conspiracy, maybe even the whole government."

Wilford laughed dryly. "Those 'black projects' bases're as close as you can get to invulnerable. We certainly don't have the firepower for that sort of thing."

He seemed to age before Blair's eyes. "Besides," he said, "these hit and run raids are getting us nowhere. We hit the Speradon system with the same goal in mind, to expose the conspiracy and gather hard evidence. We accomplished our mission. We captured examples of the raiding ships. We found the proof that the Confed's been raiding us. We even captured a fleet carrier and enough resources to prosecute the war. And what did we achieve? Nothing."

"How's that?" Blair asked. "It was a great success!"

"Pyrrhus won battles, too," Wilford countered, "and look what it got him. We killed thousands of defense workers when we took out that orbital factory—civilians, not military personnel. I've been following the news feeds out of the Confederation. That fact has completely obscured everything else and alienated the moderates in the Confederation. Even the people who support us, or at least oppose the Confed's aggressive policy, won't dare speak out against those who want war." He shook his head sadly. "We've played right into our enemies' hands, made ourselves pariahs." He laughed bitterly. "And to think the plan was my idea."

Blair frowned, considering the implications. "So, what do we do?"

Wilford looked grim. "We've given the Confederation the provocation they need for a full-scale war. They'll mobilize as soon as they get their declaration of war. The Border Worlds will get crushed when that happens."

"We have to keep that from happening, sir," Blair replied. "We have to derail this war before it can start." He shook his head. "Hell, that's why I came over in the first place— to keep this thing from getting out of hand."

"How can we stop this?" Wilford said. "That base is impregnable. And even if we were to succeed, it would only add more fuel to the fire."

Blair looked at the deck, then back at Wilford. "Sir, we'll launch the probe and get a readout on the defenses. Then, someone will have to use the Black Lance we captured to fly the defenses, infiltrate the base, get the evidence, and get out."

Wilford gave him a long look. "Who're we going to find who knows those planes well enough to fake it?"

Blair stood up. "I trained on the Excalibur—the prototype for the Black Lances. If you'll order the probe launched, sir, I'll start getting ready."

Wilford studied his face. "You know what wartime protocol is when it comes to captured spies."

Blair nodded. "Yes, sir."

Wilford furrowed his brow. He studied Blair a long time.

"Admiral, you know there's nothing for me to do here. I belong in a fighter plane. I'm not a ship's commander type. And even if I was, they wouldn't trust me on my own, without a Border Worlder keeper. This kind of mission is what I'm made for. If civilians like Dr. Clivers can make their sacrifices, let me do what I can."

"All right, Blair. Do what you have to."

Blair came to attention, then walked to the door.

"And Blair?" He turned to look back at Wilford. "Good luck, son."

"Thank you, Admiral."

• CHAPTER TWELVE

Pliers stood to one side of the ordnance handling crew, carefully supervising the weapons loadout on Blair's Black Lance. He worked the tobacco packed into his right cheek, milking the nicotine-laden juice and spitting it out on the *Intrepid*'s deck.

A loadout crew member let the side of the largish silvery metallic plate slip on the cart. It hit the side with a loud thump. The crew froze. "Damn it," Pliers cursed, "what do you think that is—a crate of bananas? That's a fusion weapon, for crissakes. Be careful with it."

"Be careful with what?" Blair asked, stepping up next to the crew chief. Pliers turned. Whatever comment he had in mind died when he saw Blair. "What the hell kind of getup is that?"

Blair looked down at the black flight suit he wore with "DuMont" stencilled on his right breast pocket.

Blair cracked a thin smile. "Hell, Pliers, you don't expect me to sneak in wearing a 'Hi, I'm a spy' name tag, do you?"

Pliers looked dubious. "You know what'll happen if you're captured in that—costume?"

Blair dipped his head. He hadn't told anyone he had spent the night before tidying up his affairs and writing a short letter to Velina. "Yeah," he said bleakly, "summary execution." He changed the subject, before Pliers could reply. "You're putting everything back like it was?"

The crew carefully loaded a second silvery, convex-shaped disk into the central bay. "That's right," Pliers replied. "Everything we took out, we're putting back in, minus two IFFs. That's part of your alibi."

The crew worked a second silvery dish underneath the centerline bay.

"What the hell is it?" Blair asked.

Pliers smiled. "Well, kid, the tech manual calls it a flash-pak." He stepped forward and rubbed his hand along its side. "Apparently, it was a Kilrathi idea—the 'Cats were trying to build a weapon light enough for their Strakha stealth fighters that would let then take out cap ships. They came up with the basic idea and someone on the Confed side refined it."

"How does it work?" Blair asked.

Pliers shrugged. "The tech manual don't say. It looks like a variation of the old strip-fusion bomb. Those ignited water by stripping the hydrogen, then recombining them explosively. All these books say, though, is that the detonators are stored separately within the fighters, due to the hazard. Waldos screw them in just before launch."

Blair looked at the dish, recalling Melek's recording of the attack on his convey, and the ships whose atmospheres had burned, destroying them from the inside out.

His blood ran cold. *This* was the conspiracy's secret weapon—the Black Lance mated to the flash-paks and bio-weapons. The Lance, with its matter/antimatter engine and cloaking device, had unlimited range and complete stealth, enough to penetrate planetary and system defense grids in order to launch canisters. The flash-paks gave the fighter an unparalleled destructive capability—one shot, one kill, something that even the Longbow couldn't match.

Pliers looked at his watch. "Son, Maniac's patrol is leaving in ten minutes. If you want their launch to cover yours, you'd best get ready."

Blair bobbed his head in acknowledgement. "Yes, Dad," he replied, trying to see if he could get under the crew chief's skin. Pliers grinned broadly. He reached into his pocket, pulled out a pouch, and loaded more of the black, noxious smelling stuff into his cheek. "That's more like it, son," he mumbled, spitting a long stream onto the deck.

Blair grunted, then began his inspection walk around the fighter. He pulled and tugged at the recessed ordnance, making certain the pins were tight and the safety tags had been pulled. Once he was satisfied the Lance had been correctly prepared he ascended the ladder to the cockpit and slipped inside. Pliers plugged him into his console and handed him a clipboard which he signed, certifying that the load-out teams had done their jobs.

Pliers hunkered down beside him as Blair did his internal pre-flights. "You got the IFF codes Lieutenant Sosa uploaded?"

"Check."

"Flight recorder with updated telemetry?"

"Check."

"Got your cover story memorized?"

"Go to hell, Pliers."

"No bullet holes or laser burns in the flight suit?"

"Not anymore."

"Okay, son, you're ready."

Pliers started to back down the ladder. He reached out and gave Blair a squeeze on the shoulder. "Good luck, Colonel."

"Thanks, Pliers," he said. "What're the bets running?"

"Twenty-one to one against," the grizzled crew chief replied, grinning.

"Great," he answered. "Put me in for twenty, would you?"

"Just come back to collect it." Pliers gave him a final smile, then backed down the ladder. Blair ran the rest of his pre-flights as Maniac's Rapier and Hellcat patrol spun up their fuel compressors and fired their engines. Drives ignited all around him, rumbling through the bay. The star field ahead whirled as the *Intrepid* turned away from the Border Worlds fleet to launch fighters. Blair was grateful to Wilford for that small gesture. He might have been the hottest fighter on this side of the war, but he still had no desire to pass through a destroyer's drive plume.

"Stand by for launch," the flight officer said, his voice young and nervous. Blair winced. He'd gotten used to Velina's honeyed tones.

"Launch!" Maniac's afterburners glowed. The brand-new, up-rated fighter nearly stood on its tail as it rocketed off the deck. The squadron roared after him in close intervals, shaking the inside of the bay with their thunder and vibration. Blair waited until Maniac's last patrol fighter cleared the flight deck before he goosed his throttle controls.

The Lance responded, boosting down the deck and off into space with a smoothness that was almost disconcerting. The fighter damned near flew itself. He hit his cloaking device the moment he cleared the *Intrepid* and executed his clearing turn. He cued the worm program that began to creep through his computer core, destroying his Border Worlds' IFF codes. He set his course for the system's jump point and the first of two diversionary jumps from Telamon before he proceeded to Axius.

He took one final look at Telamon and the glittering blue-white diamonds that marked Maniac's distant fighters. The patrol squadron moved towards its assigned positions and its grim task of enforcing the quarantine over the stricken world.

He set his ship to autopilot, opened his Bussard intakes, and accelerated towards the first jump point.

The Black Lance performed flawlessly in navigating the second sphere of mines surrounding Axius. The safe path had been pieced together from Sosa's analysis and data recovered from the flight recorder. He reasoned that if the path through the meandering field was big enough for a cap ship to pass, his little fighter had nothing to fear. The mines' real intent was to channel and delay an enemy while the locals arranged a welcoming committee.

His AI chirped, indicating he'd passed the second field. He checked his knee board for his estimated safe distances. The inner mine belt had to extend far enough away from the planet for the base to orbit safely. He glanced out of the cockpit and saw no sign of the base. He cursed to himself. It would be just his luck that he'd come through the passage while the base was on the far side of the planet.

"Dragon Five-Four to Axius Control, request landing instructions." He swallowed, feeling the tension build in his gut. Sosa had sent him a chip via messenger drone that would hopefully overlay DuMont's voice print over Blair's radioed voice, making him sound like the dead pilot. He knew the ruse wouldn't fool a sophisticated VP analysis, but it should work for routine communications. He hoped that Axius didn't voiceprint every communication, or he was a dead man.

Time stretched while Axius control kept him on ice. Nervous sweat soaked his armpits.

"Verr-ry good, umm, Five-Four, is it?" a man's voice said.

Blair closed his eyes. "Yes, Dragon Five-Four out of Speradon. Lucas DuMont."

"Where have you been . . . DuMont?"

Blair could hear the skepticism in his voice.

"We got hit, bad," Blair said, running out the cover story they'd worked out. DuMont had been killed on the Princeton's flight deck, in the opening moments of the Marine assault. Later inspection of his flight recorder determined his patrol route and Blair's alibi.

He just hoped the base didn't have the Speradon flight roster, or he was screwed. "I was on a leg patrol and didn't get back until it was too late. I shadowed the renegade carrier to Orestes," he said.

Time lagged again. "Five-Four, stand by for authentication." Blair was ready. He slid the recorder out of his pocket. "Authenticate."

Blair hit the button on the recorder. "DuMont, Lucas DuMont. I count one . . . two . . . three . . ." He waited nervously while they puzzled through what to do.

"Thank you, DuMont, assume course one-two-three standard approach for inbound. You are first in the chute. Welcome home."

"Thanks," Blair replied.

He slid his fighter onto the proper course, then goosed his throttles. The fighter smoothly entered orbit and closed on the black, weapon-encrusted fortress hovering above the planet's horizon. The orbital base looked evil to him, a repository of malice capable of spawning Telamon's misery all by itself.

He heard a soft hiss in his comm-panel. A computer voice, its tones distantly female, scratched in his ears. He wondered why they would deliberately select such an overtly mechanical response when a natural voice was just as easy to program in.

"Key identification for landing instructions," it said. "Supply identification for clearance."

Blair hit his IFF sequencer and prayed Sosa knew her job.

The machine chewed on the IFF signal. "Landing clearance granted. Conduct single orbit letdown to main bay. Align with strobes and stand by for tractor beam insertion."

Blair sighed with relief, then began to loop around the base to the flashing strobes that marked the landing bay. A second cigar-shaped body appeared on the horizon. It, like the base, had been hidden from his view by the planet's bulk. He thought at first it might be a tanker, but the size was completely out of scale to the surroundings. He swiveled his head to follow its passage. "The *Vesuvius?*" he whispered, shocked. "What's *that* doing *here?*" He thought that ship would be under construction for some time to come.

His stomach roiled with worry. The huge ship's presence at Axius suggested the conspiracy within the Confederation was much more powerful than they had suspected. Eisen believed the number of conspirators to be relatively small and that they were key people who pulled strings and manipulated events like a band of modern-day real-life Illuminati. If the conspirators had the power to crew the ship and send it to Axius, then the cabal might be far larger and more powerful than anyone had dreamed.

He controlled his racing thoughts to close on the hulking base and enter the landing cycle. The tractor beams caught him in the first try, pulling him across the bay's threshold and through the outer force curtain. The net of electromagnetic "grab" plates caught him and pulled him gently through the inner force curtain, gently depositing him on the pressurized, positive gravity fighter bay.

The bay hummed with activity. Ground crews scurried back and forth, servicing a line of shuttles and Marine transports distinguished by a logo of an exploding volcano superimposed on a large "V." Neat pyramids of duffels stood beside the first row of shuttles. Black Hellcats lined the walls and stood three deep in a red-painted arming area. Further away, under guard, stood a small cluster of Black Lances.

A harried-looking ground crewman in black coveralls stepped in front of Blair's fighter. He raised his light batons directly over his head, guiding the fighter towards the corner of the cavernous bay that held the Lances. He pulled into the indicated space and shut down his engines.

The Lances parked on either side were plugged into standard issue crash carts. The flickering monitors indicated the status of their routine post-mission data dump. Blair cued his AI, keyed it to "purge," and crossed his fingers. The "worm" program, another gift from Velina, would root out and destroy the DuMont voice pattern program and any other stray bits of Border Worlds programming or data that might have accidentally been left behind by earlier erasures. The worm would then destroy itself, hopefully leaving the Black Lance clean of incriminating data.

A ground crewman slammed a ladder against the Lance's side and climbed up beside the cockpit. Blair unsealed the cockpit. The crewman, his breath smelling of garlic, leaned in to help him remove his helmet and straps.

After a moment's hesitation, he gave him the helmet. The team planning his raid had reluctantly discarded the idea of wearing the helmet inside the ship. He knew his face had been famous, but he was older now, and his looks seemed similar enough to many of the others on board

that he might pass for one of them, at least for a time.
Wearing the helmet would cover his face, but might attract
more attention than he might otherwise. Instead, they
bandaged half his head.

"Do you need to see the docs? You'd better hurry," the
crewman said conversationally.

"How's that?" Blair asked.

The crewman gave him an odd look. "The old man
himself's come in to check things out. He's supposed to
give a briefing for you Dragons."

Blair scrambled to cover himself. "That's today?" The
crewman furrowed his brow. "I just came in from following
the ships that hit Speradon," Blair said, launching into
his cover story. "I was out of the net long enough to lose
track of time."

The crewman nodded. "That's rough." He offered his
arm to Blair, who used it to lever himself up and out of
the cockpit. "I need a fast turnaround," Blair said, "I'm
supposed to re-launch as soon as this is over."

"No problem," the tech replied.

Blair scrambled down the ladder, leaving the tech to
close out the ship's flight log and higher order systems. A
cluster of pilots, all in black, swept past him. "What are
you waiting on?" one called out. "You're gonna be late
for the show."

Blair fell in behind them, mumbling his thanks. The
group walked past a caged area festooned with bio-hazard
symbols. Blair saw, behind the heavy wire, a cluster of
Black Lances, and beside those, a pallet of canisters
identical to those Clivers had reported seeing on Telamon.

He struggled to maintain control of his facial features.
Here was the proof they needed, the positive link between
Seether, Paulson, the black ships, and the plague on
Telamon. Now all you have to is live long enough to tell
someone, he thought grimly.

The pilots, oblivious to his turmoil, laughed and joked
amongst themselves. They walked past the cage. He heard
one pilot start a joke, "How many Telamonders does it

take to . . ." Fortunately, the rest was drowned out by the pilots' cross-talk.

The group walked through an access way. Blair hoped the base followed the standard practice of locating the briefing rooms near the flight deck. Otherwise, he stood a better-than-even chance of getting lost trying to find his way back to the bay.

They made a right turn, then a left. Blair worried until they passed through an open door and into an auditorium-sized briefing room. He slipped away from the laughing pilots to slide among the black-clad personnel lining the back wall.

He found a good vantage just as an electronic voice boomed, "Attention!" The seated rows stood, blocking his view. He had caught a glimpse of a white-haired, black-clad man who marched purposefully across the stage and stood behind the lectern.

"At ease." The Dragons sat, revealing Admiral Geoffrey Tolwyn, dressed in a pilot's black uniform. Although Blair wasn't aware of it until he saw Tolwyn, a tiny piece of him wasn't surprised to see the admiral. The conspiracy needed someone in the highest echelons of the military. He was, he finally admitted to himself, more saddened than surprised.

He shook his head fractionally. Why, Admiral? he wanted to shout. After all that you did for preserving the Confederation, why this? A guard, walking along the aisle to Blair's right, stopped and stared. Blair glanced over, realizing that no matter what shock and anger he was feeling, it mustn't show. Their eyes met a moment. Blair broke the exchange, shifting his attention back to the podium, and adjusting his bandage casually.

Tolwyn rocked on his heels, smiling down on the crowd. "You, the select few," he said, beaming, "are on the brink of successfully completing the first phase of The Plan. Our goal, the salvation of humanity—from itself, and from outside enemies—comes tangibly closer as a consequence of your efforts and your sacrifice." Tolwyn stepped closer.

Apparently his remarks would be more of a pep talk than a military briefing. He saw Tolwyn as he never had, a true believer, preaching to the faithful. That image, so unlike the cool and distant Tolwyn he knew, disturbed him. He cursed silently, furious with himself that he hadn't thought to record the briefing. To have Tolwyn's words recorded would be the incontrovertible proof they needed to expose the conspiracy.

Tolwyn clasped his hands behind his back and stepped away from the lectern. "Twenty years ago," he said conversationally, "we ran an exhaustive computer analysis of the Kilrathi War. We used the best data we had to cover every possibility, no matter how remote. We programmed hundreds of variables and thousands of scenarios. Hundreds of millions of credits were spent to simply build the hardware we'd need to do the study."

He faced the crowd, his hands open, as though trying to embrace it. "The machine's results confirmed what we had secretly come to believe: that the war, as we fought it, wasn't winnable without a miracle. The Kilrathi, with their superior genetic structure and focused society, would bring to bear greater and greater resources and withstand the tribulations of protracted war better than our spoiled race. The fittest species would survive, and it wouldn't be us."

He assumed a professorial air as he turned and paced the stage. "The Black Projects division, the search for a miracle that would save us, was begun. Hand in glove with the short term goal of surviving the war came the realization that we needed to restructure society and even the race itself, if we were to have long-term viability. And so was born The Plan.

"It so shocked the higher-ups that they buried it—buried you. We were able to divert a small amount of money here. Those funds kept the research going, and provided the genetic templates for the future.

"We achieved our short-term goal." He tossed his head and raised his voice. "We won the war by a fluke! A lucky rabbit punch against a superior opponent delivered by an exceptional man."

His voice dropped again. "That short-term success did nothing to resolve the long-term issue. Fortune is notoriously fickle, and it is dangerous to expect every crisis to be resolved through benevolent interdiction, or luck."

Polite laughter rippled through the room.

"Humanity," he continued, "can't depend on miracles. Our long-term need remains imperative. We need a plan for survival, one that programs our development for a thousand years and a thousand years beyond that." He frowned. "As our current economic situation demonstrates, our race has proven incapable of planning from year to year, much less for the generations and centuries ahead. We must begin planning for the next war, for the next conflict that tests our race, even though we may not see it for a millennium."

He pointed his finger at them. "The Kilrathi will be back, eventually. While we wallow in misery at a little economic upheaval, they are testing their genetics in fratricidal wars. They fight, warrior against warrior, for the glory of their houses and themselves. They grow stronger, year by year, as the best prevail. In a generation or two, they will be back—rearmed, reorganized, and even stronger."

Blair felt the movement in the crowd. The pilots on either side of him were grinning and nodding, relishing the idea of renewed conflict.

Tolwyn gave them a moment to savor the possibility. "The Kilrathi aren't the only threat, however. Records we've decoded show that beyond them, closer to the galactic core, are races the Cats believe to be even more fearsome, ruthless, and technologically advanced than they are." He grinned ferally. "If the Kilrathi are afraid of them, then they must be truly awesome."

More laughter. Tolwyn stood still, waiting until he had their full attention again. "The Kilrathi were desperately preparing themselves for war with their core-ward enemies.

We were a sideshow, never rating their full strength." He paused, letting the moment build. "We'll be doomed if we, in our current sad condition, ever face those races."

He stopped and turned towards the audience. "There is only one way for us to be ready for the day they come. We must create a united, focused species joined in lockstep behind you, our vanguard. We have to be united towards the speeding of our evolution and producing a higher order of intellect and physique capable of waging and winning wars against the galaxy's best. If we don't, we'll be as extinct as the Neanderthal.

"Survival is our goal. We must accomplish it—without dissipating ourselves in divisive strife or internal conflict."

He walked to the front of the stage. "The answer, The Plan, shows us the way. Bio-convergence, the idea that we might program physiological changes in the species, allows us to begin the process of sifting and discarding the chaff of humanity while keeping you, the seeds of our future. You are the embodiment of The Plan, and Black Projects' finest miracle."

He smiled at the crowd. "You, my friends, the ground crews, and the infantry battalion, are the Second Generation. You are the first to gestate, and the first to come of age. Each of you is faster, better, and stronger than the best 'common' man has to offer. Your children born in The Plan's third generation, and augmented by bio-convergence, will outstrip your formidable talents. And so forth. In fifteen generations, your descendents will be like gods to us—and we, the foresighted, will be their ancestors."

The crowd burst into cheers, clapping and hailing Tolwyn.

The admiral raised his hands, urging them to silence. His voice grew, impassioned. "It is unfortunate that, for our program to succeed, we must take certain unpleasant steps." He frowned slightly. "I have heard that some of you have had qualms about delivering the bio-convergence canisters or have expressed concerns about the Telamon operation."

Blair nodded his head fractionally, finally understanding why the admiral was preaching to the choir. There had been grumbling in the ranks, and he would need to stamp that out before it blossomed into disaffection.

"Please understand," Tolwyn continued, "I did not order that from any desire to inflict suffering on the people of Telamon. It was, and is, necessary to neutralize the genetic pools that do not directly contribute to the species' survivability. We shall need the precious resources they consume for the coming struggles. It is sad that we must excise the surplus population, but we must if humanity is to survive.

"The Plan *is* harsh and it *is* cruel, but it *IS* necessary." He steepled his fingers under his nose a moment, as though thinking. "You may cry for the ones who must be neutralized, just as I do, but you must deliver the canisters. Otherwise, The Plan will fail and humanity will die."

He returned to his lectern. "To that end, I have engineered a war between the Border Worlds and the Confederation. The virus will be borne on the winds of war throughout the human hegemony, sowing change into worlds on both sides of the conflict. Each planet they touch will be rebuilt in our image, the image of the race that will defend humanity's place in the galaxy and, eventually, some day long in the future, will accomplish the conquest of that galaxy."

He grinned again. "Besides, we also need to practice. The conflict provides us with the live-fire training we need to hone our edge. The Border Worlds, ingenious and blessed with a mongrel frontier spirit, have been an excellent laboratory for us. They've given us an ideal situation to test weapons, refine tactics, and build our readiness." He sighed. "We owe them a debt of gratitude. You must not forget that they are serving our species by dying, just as surely as you serve it by living."

He opened his arms wide again, calling them to him. "My fellow warriors . . . your duty to your species, your fellows, and to me, lies before you. I know you won't disappoint me."

Tolwyn turned and left the podium as the warriors began clapping rhythmically. Blair joined them, trying to blend in. He was appalled, horrified to his core that what Tolwyn so casually discussed, if Telamon was any indication, involved the murdering of ninety percent of the human population, all in favor of his personal *Lebensborn*. He felt physically ill as he thought back to Dekker's warning that he would live to regret letting the admiral go free.

A motion on the stage drew Blair's eye. Seether stood and joined Tolwyn. The admiral took his hand warmly. They spoke. Blair gritted his teeth.

Seether stepped to the microphone. "You've heard the admiral's words. Now it's time for your orders. Phoenix wing will embark on the *Vesuvius* at zero-three hundred hours. Eagle's Claw wing will embark at zero-seven, together with the Marine battalion. We'll transfer other wings as they become available. You will have two notices before our departure to finalize any last-minute details. That is all."

Seether touched his finger to his ear, as though receiving a message from an earpiece. He frowned slightly and scanned the room. Blair looked to his right and saw the guard staring intently at him. Well, Chris, he thought, it's time to get the hell out.

He turned and began to work his way through the crowd that had begun to filter towards the exits. He wormed his way quickly through the pilots and walked quickly back to the flight bay. He fought the urge to break and run.

He arrived at the flight bay and sauntered casually towards his Lance, passing the security cage with the bio-hazard signs. He made it halfway to the fighter when an alarm sounded. "Intruder alert. Intruder alert. Main docking bay. Detain subject DuMont for questioning."

Although every nerve screamed for him to run, Blair continued his nonchalant walk and made it to his bird.

Blair scrambled up the ladder, and jumped inside. The contact light glowed green, indicating the canopy had sealed correctly.

He glanced up. The deck was thick with black forms, most armed. He ripped off the fake bandages, slammed his helmet on his head and fired up his engines. He waited a scant second for the drives to stabilize, then rolled his fighter towards the force curtain. He touched his afterburners, and heard the screams of the seared men and women behind him as he blasted down the ramp, through the portal, and out into space.

The fortress' smaller guns were already registering as he oriented his fighter towards the lane through the minefield. A single laser bolt hit his aft phase shield. He cloaked, jinked, and ran like hell for the *Intrepid*.

Tolwyn stood, looking out the porthole and watching the last of the search teams straggle in. He turned as the door opened. Seether entered, his expression tightly controlled, except for a single nerve jumping in his temple. Tolwyn turned to look back out into space.

"No luck?"

"None," Seether replied. "He was in a stolen Black Lance. He cloaked as soon as he was clear of the station."

Tolwyn counted to ten, slowly and silently, to ensure that when he spoke, he would be calm. "Is the guard certain it was Blair? His DNA was one of the templates we used. Twenty years back, those on the project were already watching him. Could it have been one of ours, gone renegade?"

"No," Seether replied, "it was Blair. The guard had served on the old *Concordia* and often spoke to him."

Tolwyn tugged at his tunic, straightening it. "I have to return to Earth to make certain the declaration of war goes as it should. Once we're at war, seed the first five Confed worlds on the target list with canisters. War hysteria will make it easy to blame the Border Worlds."

He looked back out the porthole. "You are to assume command of the *Vesuvius*. Hunt down the *Intrepid* and my 'prodigal son' and kill them. Then proceed to Point Luck and begin preparations for the drop. I'll notify you when we have a war." He took a deep breath and let it out slowly, still trying to control his temper. "I'm sorry I can only give you two wings. The *Princeton* was ferrying Serpent, and Griffin was destroyed at the Speradon factory complex."

"We'll make do, Admiral," Seether replied. "We always do."

• CHAPTER THIRTEEN

Admiral Wilford glanced at Maniac and the *Intrepid's* senior officers. "Do any of you have any questions for Colonel Blair?"

No one moved.

"Do you have anything to add, Colonel?"

"That's basically it, Admiral," Blair said. "Then I ran back to my ship and got the hell out of there."

Wilford, his skin gray and ashen, sighed heavily. "Tolwyn—of all people." He looked up Blair. "Has he gone insane?"

Blair shrugged. "I don't know, sir."

"What do we do, Admiral?" Hawk asked.

Wilford pondered the question. "What can we do? Tolwyn's gone to Earth, to get his declaration of war. He'll only drag all of humanity . . . Border Worlder and Confed, into the abyss with him." He frowned, making his decision. "We have to stop him. We have to take what information we have and go to Earth. Eisen should already be there. We can perhaps join forces with him."

Garibaldi raised his hand to speak. "Sir, the *Evil I* only has two working drives. She was never that fast to begin with. Our flank speed's going to be pretty pathetic."

Wilford exhaled heavily. Blair thought he looked more frail each day. It pained him to see the old admiral's body failing. His eyes were bright and alert, however, as was his mind.

"We'll make for Orestes," Wilford announced. "There we'll either transfer to the *Princeton*, continue on as we are, or use one of the fast frigates. If we get to Earth, we have a chance to stop the war. Anything else just prolongs the agony."

Blair was about to reply when the briefing room door opened. "Sir!" the scanner tech cried. "We have something. A big mother, coming out of the jump point. I've never seen anything this big!"

Blair felt ice run down his spine. "The *Vesuvius*."

"Hellfire!" Wilford swore, then pivoted towards the *Intrepid*'s second-in-command. "Garibaldi, get us out of here! Flank speed for the far jump point!" Years seemed to fall away as he rapped out orders. He looked at the pilots. "I'll need you three to slow them down and buy us some time. Use everything that'll fly." Maniac, Hawk, and Panther ran from the room, leaving Blair and Wilford alone.

"I'm going too," Blair said.

"No, Colonel, you're not. You're too important."

"Right now you need every pilot you've got," Blair argued. "I'm the only one rated on the Lance, and you're the one who said that we need all the firepower you can get." He thought a moment. "If we don't get out of this system, then my evidence doesn't mean a thing."

Wilford looked at him. "All right, Colonel. But be careful and if it looks like we're going down, then your orders are to abandon us, jump out of the system, and warn Orestes." He stared at Blair. "Those are direct orders. Do you understand?"

"Yes, sir," Blair replied.

"Sorry, Colonel, that wasn't the answer I was looking for."

"Aye, aye, sir."

"Thank you, Colonel, and good hunting."

He hit the flight deck and sprinted for his Black Lance. Fighters had been crowded past the flight deck's midpoint, and well past the safe run-up distance for even the smallest birds. He wasn't certain how Maniac planned to get that many fighters off the deck and into battle.

The loudhailer crackled and boomed, "Two minutes to shutdown!" He could feel the vibration in the deck as the *Intrepid* accelerated to flank speed.

He scrambled into his fighter. Pliers had already prepped

the ship. The safety tags had been removed and the displays had been put on-line. He took his helmet from the crewchief and plugged in. Maniac's face appeared in his comm-panel. "Colonel, what are you doing here?"

"I think that's obvious," he snapped. "What's the plan?"

Maniac smirked. "I never thought I'd see this day. Here I am, giving you orders." He paused. "We're going to ambush them. We're going to cold launch—just roll off the back of the deck like they do on those packets. That'll lower our emissions enough that they might not detect us. Then we lie in wait. Hopefully, when that bastard gets in range we can jump any CAP he has out, bomb-run him with our 'Swords and 'Bows, and run.

"Colonel, you're to bat cleanup. Hit them any way you can, confuse them as much as possible. But be careful, though, because you still look exactly like them. No one else can cloak, so you won't have a wingmate."

"Got it," Blair replied. "Any other good news?"

"Nope, that's it."

The loudhailer boomed again. "One minute to shutdown!" The last of the fighters' canopies closed. The ground crews sprinted for the exits. The last door had barely closed before Blair heard Maniac counting. "Three-two-one-SHUTDOWN!"

Blair gritted his teeth as his stomach felt the ship's artificial gravity deactivate. Several of the fighters began to float as the ship's vibrations rattled them off the deck. Blair glanced back and saw the rear force curtain shimmer and vanish.

Explosive decompression surrounded the ships in a howl of debris, tools, blankets, and lightweight gear. Several of the lighter birds, caught in the howling wind, drifted towards the exit or into one another. The fighters nearest the rear deck fired their maneuvering thrusters, giving them enough rearward movement to drift them off the deck and into space. Blair hit his own thrusters when he saw the deck behind him had cleared.

He kept a close eye around him as the ships drifted

into open space. Fighters and bombers fired their maneuvering jets to orient themselves towards the *Vesuvius*. Blair realized the *Intrepid* must have changed its course, crossing the huge ship's bows long enough to string the fighters out like a fence.

"We can still read you," Wilford said from the *Intrepid*. "Reduce your electronic emissions. Shut down IFF and trackers."

The ambush group shut its active emitters. The blue pips on his tracker turned red as the Lance detected their presence, but not their IFF codes. Blair cloaked to await developments.

A bright star burned in the distance, likely the *Vesuvius*, boring in towards the task force at flank speed. His tracker picked up a wave of about fifty fighters advancing ahead of the mother ship.

"Steady . . . steady," Wilford's voice said in his ears, urging coolness, "hold your positions. Don't jump the gun." The Confed ships continued to close. Blair saw the drive plumes of the leading edge of the Confed wedge. His target tracker settled on a Hellcat. The range counter spool ticked rapidly downward as the Confed fighters boosted into range.

"Steady," Wilford said, drawing the word out. "NOW!"

Thirty-eight ships, Maniac's entire wing, exploded from their masked positions and accelerated towards the startled Confed fighters. Blair heard a quick "Tallyho!" Volleys of missiles fired by the Border Worlds' ships lanced outward, each seeking its own target. He keyed an IFF missile on the Hellcat he'd targeted and fired. The Hellcat dodged another missile. Blair's IFF warhead impacted just aft of the cockpit. The damaged 'Cat reeled out of the battle and into deep space, its dead pilot trapped in the ruined cockpit, its drives still firing.

Several black ships flared as the warheads burst against their shields. He saw a few detonations as Confed fighters died, but not nearly enough to turn the tide of battle.

The Confed pilots reacted quickly, spinning their ships, trying to get in close to their ambushers—close enough to abate the missile hazard. Both sides traded shots and missiles at point-blank range. Explosions marked the passage of both Border Worlds and Confederation craft.

He brought the Lance around in a tight arc and recloaked to secretly close on a black Hellcat pursuing a Border Worlds Rapier. The Rapier pilot wrung everything he could out of his old bird as he tried to escape. The black 'Cat stayed right behind him. Blair got the Confed ship in his sights, dropped his cloak, and fired. His tachyon cannon flared the Confed ship's shields a brief moment before they penetrated, destroying the fighter in a red and yellow fireball. The Rapier pilot reacted to his salvation by pulling hard up into a half-loop and reversing course in a classic Immelman turn, scattering fire at Blair as it passed.

"Hey, it's Blair—Tiger," he yelled. "I'm on your side!"

"Sorry, Colonel." The Rapier waggled its wings in apology and returned to the fight.

Blair, feeling both relieved and silly, leaned over to check his IFF switch. It was active, showing him a blue pipper to his own side. He realized how little use it was likely to be. His coal black ship, indistinguishable from those the Confed flew, invited attack. He grinned, wondering how best to put that to his advantage.

The first of the Border Worlds' few Longbows blazed past him, hitting its throttles and blasting towards the distant carrier. Blair pulled up behind it, using it as bait for the Confed point-defense squadron that was bound to be about.

He had a short wait. Two Confed Hellcats vectored in, targeting the bomber and swinging around to attack from the rear hemisphere. The Longbow's rear turret engaged them, its particle gun bravely plinking away at them as they closed.

Blair waited for the first 'Cat to begin its attack run, then decloaked. He hit it hard, angling in on a high deflection shot and rippling shots down its spine as it flew through his stream of fire. It shuddered as its shields failed, then broke up as the tachyon beams punched deep holes into its structure.

The second Hellcat veered away. Blair toggled off an IFF missile that looped after the 'Cat, striking it amidships. It limped away, trailing debris.

Bluish white energy balls flashed past his cockpit. His phase shields flared as they recorded hits. He looked to his right and saw the Longbow's tail gunner firing at him.

He opened his mouth to yell at the bomber when the *Vesuvius* hove into view, surrounded by a literal curtain of laser fire as its defensive batteries engaged the attacking bombers. The Longbow ignored the heavy batteries as it blazed in towards the *Vesuvius'* bow. Blair saw it one second, pressing home its attack. The next instant it was gone, marked only by an expanding ball of gas.

He recloaked and swung the Lance back around and towards the main battle. The *Vesuvius'* fighters had been stalled by the ambush, preventing a torpedo strike on the Border Worlds ship.

The huge carrier cut through the wolfpacks of small ships that probed and tore at each other. Two torpedoes bloomed along the *Vesuvius'* flanks. Blair scanned the huge ship, looking in vain for damage.

He couldn't help but compare the chunky, awkward *Intrepid* with the smooth, sleek *Vesuvius*. The *Evil I* looked like what it was, a destroyer whose appearance had been hopelessly marred by the landing bay that had been cobbled onto it. The *Vesuvius*, by contrast, had two huge, cigar-shaped bays perfectly proportioned to the ship's central core.

The Confed fighters, apparently reacting to the torpedo strikes, broke to defend the ship. Blair saw a Broadsword, burning from multiple fighter hits and dogged by a pair of Hellcats, tip over and angle in towards the *Vesuvius*. It impacted against the carrier's side, a kamikaze. Its armed torpedoes detonated a moment later, raising a brilliant red and white explosion centered on the carrier's main hull. The expanding fireball illuminated the scores of small caliber barbettes dotting its hull and the dozen or so massive double turrets that housed its main armament. The explosion faded to leave a single winking secondary fire on the *Vesuvius'* hull.

The Confed fighters, distracted by the bombers and the kamikaze strike, fell back. Blair heard Maniac order his fighters to withdraw to the *Intrepid*, then counted a bare two-dozen fighters moving in retrograde. They had lost a third of their active strength on the first skirmish.

He trailed the retreating Border Worlds ships, attacking the few Confed ships who preyed on the damaged and lagging ships. He bagged one Hellcat and then a second that moved in to finish a damaged Ferret.

Pieces of the fighter spalled away from its hull as it tried to hold station. The frame couldn't take the abuse and broke up. The pilot ejected a moment later. With the rebels withdrawing from the system, he knew the pilot would have to be very lucky for anyone to pick him up.

The *Vesuvius* continued to pursue the *Intrepid*, using its superior maneuverability and acceleration to overtake the smaller and clumsier ship. Blair gauged the distance the *Evil I* needed to make the jump point safely against the speed and range of the *Vesuvius'* main battery. The *Intrepid* would come under ranging fire several minutes before she made the jump.

Wilford apparently drew the same conclusion. *Intrepid's* four surviving escort frigates turned and boosted towards the huge ship. They closed the range quickly, looking to Blair like brave terriers attacking a bull elephant. He heard the captains sounding off as they began the countdown for their torpedo runs. The *Vesuvius*, presented with a target for its primary batteries, commenced firing.

One frigate detonated as a single beam pierced its phase shields, hull armor, and the hull itself. The other three light ships scattered, counting on their speed to get them through the *Vesuvius'* fire. The *Vesuvius* turned, exposing its long side to the frigates as it brought its stern-mounted weaponry to bear. The carrier began to engage with its full primary battery, savaging the frigates as they completed their countdown times.

The *Intrepid*, given a reprieve, changed course slightly to better align itself for the jump. The carrier's recall warbled in his headsets. He knew that any non-jump capable fighter that didn't hit the flight deck before the *Intrepid* went through the point would be lost.

A second frigate staggered under a direct hit. Its drives failed and it drifted out of formation. A second weapon, a mass driver round, hit the stricken ship a moment later, destroying it in a spectacular explosion.

The remaining two frigates started their attack runs, hurtling towards their target. The defensive fire intensified as they came into the secondary batteries' range. Stream after stream of turret lasers and other heavy weapons probed space for the nimble little ships.

They held their courses long enough to fire their torpedo spreads and turn away to begin their run home. The *Vesuvius'* defensive batteries maintained continuous fire as the huge carrier attempted to evade the homing torpedoes. The frigates, job done, fled for the jump point.

Blair watched as a single Black Lance popped out of cloak above the trailing frigate. It fired something that attached itself to the frigate's hull. The frigate slewed to one side. The rear torpedo storage blew, ripping off most of the drive bays. The frigate, quickly dying, began to tumble. The Lance settled on the second, fired and recloaked.

The second frigate also slowed. Portholes and hatches on both ships blew outward as their atmospheres detonated. Blair hunted in vain a few moments more for the hidden enemy, then turned for home. He fired his afterburners, boosting himself up to maximum speed and away from the battle zone. Blue flares marked the *Intrepid's* and the surviving escorts' passage through the jump point in a single panicky mass.

Blair angled his own fighter through the jump point, then gritted his teeth against the inevitable feeling of jump shock. Passage through the jump point made every cell in his body feel as though it had been shredded.

He swerved as he emerged from the jump, dodging

the wrecked remains of a pair of corvettes. The *Intrepid*, her complement of escorts sadly depleted by the emergency passage through the jump point, had already set her course for the next point.

Blair dropped his cloak and sent his IFF signal. The officer standing in for Sosa replied in tones that conveyed both panic and relief. He received quick authority to land and blazed into the crowded, confused deck.

New ships brought up from below were being spotted for conventional launch. Pilots ran from their damaged or expended fighters to assist the ground crews while their grim-faced replacements climbed into their cockpits and readied for launch.

He saw Maniac run from his Hellcat to a Rapier and climb in. Obsolete Sabers and Scimitars, early model Rapiers, and even scratch-built bastards were being sent to face the Confederation's very best machines and pilots. They were scraping the bottom of the barrel.

Blair shook his head. The main complement of fighters needed time to refuel and rearm. That reality was inescapable. He knew, without a doubt, that most of the pilots launching from the *Intrepid*'s deck would die. That reality was also inescapable, and bitterly necessary.

He turned away, his heart heavy. An orderly sprinted up to him. "Sir!" he said. "The admiral wants you on the bridge!" He took off without waiting for Blair's acknowledgement. Pliers appeared from behind the Lance. "You'd better go, son," he said. "She'll be ready when you are."

Blair nodded, then began the long scramble to the bridge. When he arrived, Wilford waved him to a chair. "Colonel, the *Vesuvius* has just emerged from the warp point. We are seven minutes ahead of her, traveling at flank speed. We saw a hit by torpedoes, maybe more than one. Will that slow her?"

"No, sir," Blair answered, "the damage wasn't significant."

"And our frigates?"

"All gone." Blair shifted in his seat. "Sir, shouldn't I be getting ready to launch?"

"No, Colonel Blair. You have the uncanny ability to place yourself in harm's way, and the Border Worlds can't afford your famous luck to desert you. I made a mistake in letting you go the first time, and I won't make it again."

Blair looked up at the partially restored main screen. The graphic showed the *Intrepid*'s fighters launching. Lines of red dots began to emerge from the front end of the *Vesuvius*.

"Launches are coming from the starboard bay," the sensor officer reported. "It's a fresh wing. The last batch came from the port bay."

"Thank you," Wilford replied. "Come right to course two-seven-zero. We'll take an outward leg towards the Aleph Six jump point, then try for the Aleph Three in four minutes."

"Sir," the sensor officer cried, "that'll take us through the Ella system's asteroid field!"

"That's correct. That big so-and-so's going to have one fun time running that field at its max speed. It'll have to slow, or risk impact damage. We might make some time. Certainly we'll get a chance to test her captain's mettle." He paused, thinking. "Release the escort. They won't take much abuse in that asteroid field and there's no sense subjecting them to that. Loop one back around to the last system and see if you can recover the pilots who ejected or didn't make jump." He leaned back, trying to straighten stiffened muscles. "Also, send one ahead of us, around the belt and into the next system. Let's give them as much warning as we can."

Blair chafed in his seat as the drama played itself out. The fighters launched by the *Intrepid* approached the *Vesuvius*' craft. The monitor showed a swarm of red enemy dots engulfing their weak CAP. Blue dot after blue dot winked out, each representing a life and a fighter. In less than a minute the survivors broke and ran for the carrier. Blair counted a half dozen remaining of the eighteen that had launched.

The *Vesuvius*' wing slowed to reorganize. Blair didn't

see any perceptible difference in their numbers. It did, however, take them longer then he would have thought to reform. He realized, in a flash of insight, that while the blacksuits were all natural pilots and superbly trained, few had any real combat experience. It was easy to forget the enemy was, in many ways, green. He hoped he'd be able to figure out a way to use that to their advantage.

"Admiral, we're at the navigation point," Garibaldi said from his plotting board. Blair, unable to sit still, got up and joined him, plugging into the tactical officer's station.

"Very good," Wilford replied. "Come left to course one-nine-five, zee minus ten.

"One-nine-five minus ten, aye, Admiral," Garibaldi echoed. "Asteroid belt in two minutes. Aleph Three in six minutes."

"Thank you, steady as she goes. Activate phase shields and charge guns. Are the fighters aboard yet?"

"They're coming in now," the comm officer replied. "What there is of them anyway."

Wilford nodded. "As soon as they've recovered, start spotting the rearmed fighters. We'll need to have some kind of a defense if they catch us."

Blair checked the carrier's tactical board. Hawk's squadron was listed as ready for launch, while Panther's and Maniac's were rearming. The *Intrepid* had three of its six defensive turrets on-line, as well as the forward torpedo room. The carrier, much to his surprise, maintained her old destroyer's centerline armament. The *Vesuvius'* relentless pursuit had closed much of the gap when the *Intrepid* abruptly heeled over and entered the asteroid field. The ship's phase shields started to take damage at once, flaring under the asteroids' impacts. The ship's defensive turrets engaged what rocks they could, the debris arriving as a hail rather than a single, deadly mass. The shields dropped to seventy percent at once, and continued to bleed away as impacts weakened them.

The *Vesuvius* hit the field's edge. Blair saw the big ship's phase shields glow as it bulled its way through the stone sleet. Its defensive turrets opened up, outlining the ship in red laser beams as they tried to protect the ship, with imperfect success.

The old admiral had given the *Vesuvius* a Hobson's choice that used the Confed ship's speed against it. The *Vesuvius* would pay for each meter it gained on the *Intrepid* in additional damage. The other option, slowing, allowed the *Intrepid* to either maintain or extend its lead.

The *Vesuvius* thundered after them, its bow and forward sections flickering red as its phase shields were depleted by asteroid hits. Blair checked its velocity and saw no change in its acceleration. How much punishment could the big ship take?

The bridge crew cheered when its shields flared and died. The carrier slowed when the asteroids began to impact against its bow and portside bay.

He glanced down at his own tactical board in time to see their own shields fail. He heard the first thump a moment later as they rammed an asteroid. He winced as a second hit followed hard upon the first. "The one good thing," Wilford said to no one in particular, "about the bow and topside being already destroyed is that it gives us another layer of cushion." Wilford looked at him and shrugged as a third impact shuddered the ship. "Also, we have a smaller cross-section," he said casually, as though discussing the weather. "Less to hit."

They emerged from the belt with the *Vesuvius* lagging behind. She had visible damage. Several of her side turrets appeared to be out of action and a fire glowed where the port bay mated with the ship's main hull. A similar amount of damage on the *Intrepid* would have finished her.

"Steady on for Aleph Three," Wilford ordered, his voice calm and steady. "All ahead flank."

"Where will this jump take us, Admiral?" Blair asked.

"Orestes," Wilford replied. "The *Princeton* is there, with a nearly full complement of first-line fighters. I made Toliver the *Princeton*'s captain. He's had orders to fill out the carrier's crew and wing, even if he had to resort to press gangs." Blair swallowed, uncertain if Wilford was joking. The admiral's grim face suggested he was in deadly earnest.

Garibaldi cleared his throat and leaned towards the microphone. "Stand by for jump in three-two-one . . ." Blair gritted his teeth. The carrier hit the transition point at full speed. The wrenching nausea struck him like a wall, wringing his guts with jump shock. He hyperventilated, trying to get the surging pains under control. Around him, crewmembers and techs cried out, their bodies rebelling against the repeated jump shock.

Orestes floated in the sky ahead, a pristine world that was about to be in the center of a pitched battle.

"Advise *Princeton* of our situation," Wilford ordered, "and let Orestes' sector command know what's coming. They're going to be thrilled we brought *Vesuvius* with us, but that's something we can hash out later."

"Incoming signal from the *Princeton*, sir," the comm officer said. "Putting it on screen now."

"Toliver to Wilford: What can we do for you?"

"Have you been informed of our situation?"

"Yes, Admiral, your scout gave us the word. Our reactors are on-line and we've got about sixty-three birds ready for launch. I only have thirty pilots standing by, however."

"Okay, Commander," Wilford said, "I'm sending you enough pilots to fill out your wing. We'll shuttle them over to you."

Blair nodded. The *Princeton* had more fighters than pilots, while the *Intrepid* carried combat veterans flying craft older than they were. Wilford planned to use what little time he had in getting the vets into front-line craft. They would still be outnumbered, but not as badly outgunned.

Wilford looked at the navigation plot a moment, absentmindedly chewing his lip. "Here's the plan. I'll continue at flank speed into Orestes orbit and launch my shuttles. We'll then slingshot back out towards the *Vesuvius*. This ship was a destroyer, and she's still got her torps.

Launch your strike as we come about. We'll hit her with your birds, ours, and maybe torpedoes as well. Got it?"

"Got it, Admiral," Toliver replied. "Who'll lead the combined strike?"

"Maniac," Wilford said, causing Blair to stand in protest.

"Admiral," Toliver said, "Blair's the best we've got. His luck's famous. Our pilots might not be so quick to go into harm's way if they see you're holding back our best."

Wilford looked from Blair to the screen. "You flyboys are ganging up on me," he snapped angrily. He looked up at Blair, his eyes beetling under his heavy brows. "Get out of my sight."

Blair got. He sprinted down to the flight deck, sliding down the ladders without regard for his own safety. He heard the frames strain and groan as the ship went into its slingshot maneuver. He ran onto the depleted deck and towards his ship. Pliers met him, slapping a helmet into his hands and holding the ladder steady as he climbed.

"The *Vesuvius* appeared a couple of minutes ago," Pliers yelled. "All the pilots except you an' the 'Cats have gone over!"

Blair raised one thumb, indicating he'd heard. He checked his stores and saw that they'd only had time to reload one of his expended missiles, and that with a heatseeker.

He barely had time to hook the last of his straps before the amber light flashed over the launch end of the flight deck. "Stand by for magnum launch," Maniac ordered. "Remember people, this is going to be a two-wing strike. We'll be takin' orders from Heart o' the Tiger himself as the combined force commander once we get linked up. Do what he says and you'll make it back."

Blair knew Maniac's speech was intended as a morale booster only, and wasn't meant to be taken at face value. Nonetheless, it was a far cry from his attitude towards Blair on Nephele.

He brought his engines on-line and checked his fuel levels. The ground crews had refueled the fighter's tanks, saving him the bother and risk of leaving the intakes open to scoop free hydrogen during the battle.

He felt the deck heel again slightly. Orestes prime vanished from the view outside the launch bay. The star field twisted to the right as the carrier reoriented itself. "Magnum launch!" the comm officer screamed, losing control of himself in his excitement. "Go! *Go!* GO!"

Maniac led the Hellcats off the deck. Blair followed. He made his clearing turn. His tactical plot indicated the Confed forces would be on them before they could form up. He had no choice but to commit his forces piecemeal, in waves, and hope for the best. "Tiger to all units. Break and attack by squadrons. Attack at will."

The *Vesuvius* spat out her own fighters, launching them from both port and starboard bays. Neat lines of Confed ships aligned themselves into squadron Vees, only to have a section of Hellcats they'd captured from the *Princeton* slash through the formation. The ships ripple-fired their missiles, causing destruction out of proportion to their numbers. Five or so Confed fighters gang-fired in a string of yellow-red explosions. A flight of Black Lances in Border Worlds mufti flashed past him, headed for the enemy wings.

Squadrons on both sides angled in, wheeled over and hit afterburners, heading for the melee. Fighters engaged in the center ground between the carriers, with missiles and ordnance flashing and flaring as the dogfight grew more intense. Blair, followed by Maniac and the *Intrepid* contingent, tipped over one by one and dove into the battle.

He glanced up to see a blue flare from the jump point *behind* the *Vesuvius*. A second huge carrier emerged behind the first. His spirits flagged. The Confed had not one, but *two* of the massive ships. There was no way Wilford's forces could defeat that kind of power. They could only sell themselves as dearly as they could.

His scanner locked on the ship-to-ship channel. The comm-panel showed a dark, static-filled face that rapidly cleared. "Eisen to Wilford," the admiral said. "Can we be of assistance?"

"*Eisen?*" Wilford yelled. "What are you doing here?"

"I didn't make it to Earth, Admiral," Eisen replied. "I got 'detained' at Sirius. It seems the conspiracy's made quite a few enemies, enough to crew this ship at least. Some friends in low places gave us enough advance warning to mount a raid on the ship as she came out of an engine test run. They also sent enough technicians to keep us going." He paused. "The ship I'm in is the twin to the *Vesuvius*. Even these things have a few soft spots. I'm going to dump a whole lot of data on your comm officer—blueprints, IFF codes, the works."

"What's your combat status?" Wilford snapped.

"I don't have any torpedoes," Eisen replied. "The bays are still unfinished, and the shields and half the main guns have buggy software."

"Admiral!" Blair heard in the background. "Telemetry indicates the *Vesuvius* is turning."

"Well, Bill," Wilford said, "it looks like you're going to get first blood."

"Great," Eisen replied, "lucky me." He recited the hoary line used by every crew who'd ever faced a broadside. "For what we are about to receive, may we be truly grateful. Eisen out."

His face vanished from the comm-panel just as the *St. Helens'* main guns opened up, followed a second later by the *Vesuvius'*. The two huge ships lashed and tore at each other at diminishing ranges. Eisen turned his ship first, capping the "T" and bringing his full weight to bear on the *Vesuvius*. The Confed ship turned a moment later, staying on a converging course, slowly closing the range. The *Vesuvius'* secondary batteries fired in unison, then continued to hammer the other ship. Both carriers' phase shields glowed a solid red as each attempted to fend off the energy cast at it. Portions of the main guns' energies penetrated to strike the armor and probe the soft portions of the ships. The *St. Helens* took greater punishment from shots hitting its unfinished sections and punching deep inside. Blair guessed the *Vesuvius* had not had time to fully recover its shields after its run-in with the asteroid belt. Gout after gout of energy snapped between the two ships as they hammered each other.

The clash of the titans completely overshadowed the fighter duels in front of it. The small craft slashed and attacked, mirroring the vast combat in the background. Torpedo bombers from the *Intrepid* began their runs against the huge carrier, drawing the defenders back towards their own ship. Border Worlds Hellcats followed, doing their best to fend off the Confed birds.

Blair stayed under cloak, hunting Confed Black Lances that pounced on Border Worlds fighters. Confed Lances returned the favor, giving the emphasis to hit-and-run, flicker-in-shoot-fade-out tactics. Blair found cloaked combat bizarre, even as he smoked his second Lance.

He glanced down to check his ordnance and saw the flash-pak and mines glowing green in his centerline bay. He looked up at the *Vesuvius*, still trading hammerblows' with the *St. Helens*. He grinned, seeing the damaged areas of the *Vesuvius* where the *St. Helens* had taken out her secondary turrets. He armed a flash-pak and turned to begin his attack run.

"Tiger to Base," he said. "I'm going to try and ring their bells with one of their secret weapons."

"Be careful," Wilford replied. "Our analysis suggests that you probably won't be able to penetrate the hull. These two ships carry improved shielding to protect against what you're trying to do." Wilford paused. "You're going to have to get inside for the thing to work."

"Damn," Blair replied. "All right, I'm breaking off."

He swept back around in time to see a Black Lance drop out of cloak, rip a Hellcat, and turn away. A second Hellcat slashed in and fired, flaring the Lance's shields.

Maniac's face appeared in Blair's comm-screen. "Yee-Haw, take that, you son of a bitch!" He fired again, hitting the Lance as it turned to engage. Blair took advantage of the moment to drop his own cloak, and fire his fusion guns. The Confed Lance, caught in a pincer, tried to cloak.

Maniac let it, painting it with his lasers to give Blair a solid target. He pounded it with his guns, until it decloaked and slowed. Maniac fired again, his shots piercing its upper hull. The fighter detonated a moment after Blair saw its pod eject.

His comm-screen crackled and steadied. He glanced down, expecting it to be Maniac. His heart leapt into his throat as he saw the cold, cold eyes and expressionless face behind the helmet. "Hello, Colonel," Seether said, "I know you're out here. Close by, in fact. I've come for you, Colonel. You personally. Are you ready to die?"

Blair felt his heart hammer in his chest. He thought back to the moment in the bar, when Seether had held him helpless and begun to squeeze his throat. He realized he was afraid of the black-suited pilot. He swallowed. He would never be rid of that fear unless he confronted it. A piece of him *wanted* the confrontation, to resolve the issue . . . one way or the other.

"All right," he snapped. "Where are you?"

Seether smiled coldly. "Just off the *Vesuvius'* stern. Come and get me."

Maniac cut into his screen. "Who was that?"

"Seether," Blair replied tightly. "You put a gun in his ear back on Nephele."

"Him?!" Maniac replied, *"That's* Seether?"

"Yeah," Blair grunted. He rotated his Lance and dove on Seether's ship, hovering astern of the Confed carrier. Seether dodged to the right, inviting Blair to take the first shot.

Blair was more than willing to accommodate him. He punched his Lance forward, slashing his stick to the right and standing the fighter on its tail as he slewed it around and fired. Seether broke hard left. Blair's first salvo glanced off of his phase shield. He pulled his yoke back, autoslid, fired again, and missed again as Seether snap-rolled his ship out of trouble.

"Not bad, Colonel," Seether said, "but not good enough."

Blair gritted his teeth. He pulled his stick back, bringing

the Lance's nose up sharply into an inside loop. Midway through the loop, he eased the fighter into a half-roll, executing a classic Immelman turn that placed him level with Seether, who promptly broke away into his own corkscrewing dive. Blair dove after him, trying to align his fighter for a missile shot.

Seether easily outmaneuvered him, widening his spiral into an outside loop that cut across Blair's course. Blair, surprised by the sudden move, jerked his stick to the right, and blundered into Seether's fire. Rattled, he pulled back to the left. His phase shields flared again as Seether fired. Seether stayed one step ahead of him, breaking down his shields and taunting him.

Blair returned fire repeatedly, and hit nothing.

Seether laughed chillingly. "No, Colonel, like this." His Lance slashed in, its tachyon beams hitting Blair's shields, making them flare and coruscate under the abuse. Blair saw-bucked his ship to escape the probing beams, then cut right and plunged into a steep left-hand spiral. Seether stayed hard on his tail, peppering him with shots. Blair's rear shield flared again and again, weakening under the pounding. Seether pressed his attack.

Blair saw his chance. He feinted left, then point-turned his Lance, cutting his drives and pivoting it backwards along its axis. He switched his weapons toggle to tachyon and fusion guns and fired, catching Seether's Lance on the chin as the pilot swept in for another burst at Blair's vulnerable stern.

The big fighter lurched upward, then angled sharply away.

"You're almost out of time, Colonel," Seether taunted. "Any last thoughts?"

Blair saw a bright flash to his right. Maniac came up from below Seether's Lance, firing his twinned ion cannon and particle guns from a classic no-deflection, rear-hemisphere position. The salvos punched through Seether's weakened shield and chewed into his armor, but appeared to do no internal damage. Seether rolled tightly away, hitting

Blair's damaged fighter again in the tail section as he passed. Blair heard the warning as his right engine failed, effectively crippling him.

Seether rolled hard around, firing at an impossible deflection angle towards Maniac. Hits rippled along Maniac's front shield. Maniac cut away and fled for the shelter of the *Vesuvius'* nearby bulk. Seether tore after him in hot pursuit. Blair punched his afterburner, hoping to coax enough speed out of his remaining engine to stay in the fight.

Maniac gave Seether a run for his money, using the destroyed hulk of a Confed fighter as an obstacle. Maniac then cut down along the *Vesuvius'* hull, where Eisen's ship had skinned away the defensive turrets. Seether, close behind, poured a long volley into Maniac's stern. Blair switched to tachyon cannon and plinked from long range to distract Seether from Maniac. Seether ignored him and fired at the Hellcat, punching through the ship's rear shield and causing a small explosion.

Maniac slowed and turned. Blair continued firing, using single shots and short bursts to preserve his rapidly diminishing capacitors. Seether fired at Maniac, this time with fusion guns. Maniac's crippled fighter couldn't take much more.

"And here comes the other one," Seether said casually. "Come to watch your friend die?"

Blair fired. Seether rolled up and over, using his superior speed to clear Blair's front arc. Blair, swearing sulphurously, kicked out a missile that arced helplessly into space. Before Blair could turn and evade, Seether had cut through his rear shield. His remaining afterburner failed, as did his capacitor and inertial dampers.

He drifted close to the *Vesuvius*, again grateful that Eisen had obliterated the carrier's side turrets. He fired his maneuvering thrusters to keep him from bouncing against the carrier's side. Seether made one playful pass, then another. With his capacitor damaged, Blair knew the only weapons energy he had was what little remained in his banks.

"Colonel, you get to watch while I kill your friend, then I'm going to kill you." Seether's voice grew colder. "And you, Major, have you anything to say before you die?"

"Yeah," Maniac replied, "kiss my . . ." Static fuzzed out the rest of his epithet as his comm system failed. Blair watched Seether lining up on Maniac's fighter. He looked at his graphic and saw he still had four missiles, the flash-pak and the twelve mines. Mines. He looked at them, then back up at Seether. It just might work.

He toggled his ordnance to mines, then used his maneuvering jets to orient himself away from the massive carrier's hull. Seether made a slow pass past Maniac's fighter, now dead and tumbling in space. He accelerated towards Blair, then pivoted to begin his attack run on Maniac. "You're next, Colonel." Blair saw his drives flare.

Blair rotated his fighter so that the stern pointed at the nearby *Vesuvius*, then launched a mine at the carrier. A red graphic appeared on the lower corner of his heads-up display, counting down from five. He quickly toggled his missiles to volley fire. The mine counted down to zero, then detonated. Blair heard himself yelling as the explosion picked his fighter up and hurled it forward, towards Seether's Black Lance. He fired what weapons he had left as he closed, then toggled off his remaining missiles at once. Seether's Black Lance never deviated course. It flew straight towards Maniac until it was hit once, twice, three times. The last pierced the rear shield, clearing the stern for Blair's last shot, a dumb-fire missile. The heavy rocket pierced the hull, then detonated, shredding the stern. An expanding globe of fuel detonated, immolating the front half. Blair executed a victory roll as the shattered fighter hit the *Vesuvius'* side and rolled along it, breaking up.

"Got him!" Maniac shouted.

Blair looked up as the stern of the *Vesuvius* passed into view. The *St. Helens* had sheared away, badly damaged by its exchange with the *Vesuvius*. Fires raged along the entire length of the rebel ship. The *Vesuvius* had been damaged as well, but not as badly. Eisen's ship was clearly out of action, while the Confed still had fight in her. He pulled his own limping fighter around, intent on hauling back to the *Intrepid* for another ship. A nagging memory tugged at him. He looked down at his stores board and saw the flash-pak still winking green. He looked up, saw the *Vesuvius'* landing bays ahead, and smiled.

He armed the weapon, giving the waldos time to screw in the detonating mechanism and arm the device. He then angled towards the *Vesuvius* using his IFF to signal that he was in distress with a shot-out radio. The landing bay flicked its lights twice, indicating it understood. He let it vector him in, using the tractor beams to guide him across the threshold. He fired the flash-pak before the electromagnets could grab his landing gear, then hit his full reverse. Flames shot out of his damaged engine as super-hot fuel mixed with the air and an electrical short. He barely got the damaged ship back into space, tumbling almost sideways through the rear force curtain. The *Vesuvius'* tractor beams tried to catch him again and missed.

He watched the carrier slowly ease away from him, then saw a gigantic blue-white ball of fire spread through the launch bay.

• CHAPTER FOURTEEN •

Eisen looked at Blair. "Are you ready?"

Blair adjusted his dress uniform collar. "I don't know."

Taggart, resplendent in his senatorial robes, put one hand on his shoulder. "It'll be okay, son. The worst is over."

"Is it?" Blair asked. "Can we really stop this?"

"Well," Taggart replied, "we are'na gonna' know till we try, nae are we?" He stepped forward and hit the doors to the Assembly Hall with the heel of one hand. They swung silently open, revealing Admiral Tolwyn standing behind the lectern.

". . . and as my fact-finding mission has shown," he said, concluding his remarks, "the Border Worlds *are* to blame. My forces have recovered evidence of a concerted plan to raid Confederation shipping. It is a matter of public record that they have attacked and destroyed Confederation fighter craft, a Fleet cruiser, and even a factory base. They have killed Confederation military personnel by the hundreds and civilians by the thousand. This is public record and . . ." He paused dramatically. ". . . more than sufficient provocation for war." He raised his voice. "I have gained painful evidence that they seek to offset their weak military forces by using biological weapons to weaken our population. We have evidence that one such bio-agent got loose on one of their planets and killed ninety percent of the population." He lowered his head in humility. "Please, ladies and gentlemen of the Assembly, give me the tools I need to stop this perversion. Give me a declaration of war."

He looked up as a ripple of noise ran through the packed chamber. Paladin, Blair and Eisen stepped forward, entering the gallery. The hiss of noise as they were recognized worked its way around the chamber.

"I am Master of the Assembly," Taggart said, his voice electronically enhanced, "and am so empowered by this body to conduct fact-finding missions on my own authority. The facts I have learned are at odds with the admiral's."

"They're traitors!" a senator shouted. Others picked up the theme, until Taggart's raised fist silenced them. "Yes, they are," he snapped, "and that makes their tale doubly interesting." He gestured for Blair and Eisen to move towards the dais. The noise in the room grew louder and more chaotic as Senators stood and yelled for or against Taggart. Taggart might have been strolling in a park for all the reaction he showed to the hisses and catcalls. Tolwyn stood at the lectern, his hands gripping the wood possessively.

"Admiral, if you please?"

Tolwyn looked defiant a moment, then gave way. Taggart took his place on the dais and signalled Blair to the podium.

Blair looked up at the galleries, gone silent in anticipation of the spectacle. He wondered if this was how a gladiator felt just before going to face his death. He tried to speak, cursing his nervous and halting voice.

"It's true," he said, "that I fought on the side of the Border Worlds, and against my former comrades. I had to do this as a result of provocations and illegal activities I witnessed being committed by then Fleet Captain Paulson of the TCS *Lexington* and his right-hand man, a pilot named Seether.

"Captain William Eisen and Major Todd Marshall also found it necessary to take the same route I did, and for different reasons. All three of us were men regarded as highly loyal to the Confederation. For us to turn our coats, doesn't it follow that we'd have to have good reason?"

A few Senators hissed and catcalled. One stood and shouted "Money'll do it!" Many in the galleries seemed willing to listen, judging by their focused, intent expressions.

Tolwyn looked up at the Assembly. "Who is to say why corruption festers in their hearts?" he said, using the acoustics of the hall to project his voice unaided. "Did they try to work within the system? Did they bring their concerns to higher authorities? No, they turned traitor without so much as a by-your-leave. Now that treason and murder have been done, *now* they want you to listen when they tell you they served a higher cause?"

Blair ignored the taunt and tried to recapture the Senate's attention. "The Border Worlds have fallen victim to a plot which—if allowed to proceed—will victimize all of humanity. Captain Eisen has recovered files which show that Confederation forces, operating from the *Lexington*, as well as the base on Axius, engaged in acts of terrorism against both Confederation and Border Worlds forces. I myself infiltrated the secret base on Axius. There, I saw both the bio-weapon canisters and heard Admiral Tolwyn give a speech to the raiders." He paused to fish a memory chip out of his pocket. "Captain Eisen's data is ready for your inspection. I will submit to a psych-scan to prove that what I'm saying is true and that I'm not suffering from a personality overlay."

"This is outrageous!" Tolwyn snapped. "That these . . . traitors come here, wearing Confederation uniforms and mouthing this filth!"

"Our first desire," Blair said, trying to appeal to reason and logic, "was to take this up with lawful Confed authorities. I even spoke to Admiral Tolwyn on that point." He sighed. "The problem is that with the Emergency Decrees and the Admiralty Court still in place, there was no authority outside the military that could be trusted. And if we were right, they would never let our information get to you."

"This is preposterous," Tolwyn snapped. "Those mechanisms keep order in the human sectors. Without the Decrees and the Courts, central authority would fail."

Blair looked over at him. "What about the concepts of law and justice? Aren't they important, too?"

"What about them?" Tolwyn snapped. "What does an arbitrary standard of justice have to do with an orderly society? Given a choice between justice and food, Colonel, what do most people choose? The Decrees have ensured the populace survives."

"The entire populace, Admiral, or just the worthy few?"

"I don't know what you're talking about," Tolwyn snapped.

"Don't you, Admiral?" Blair pressed, feeling more tired than angry. He could recall the man Tolwyn had been, the man who grieved for their losses after the Battle of Earth yet spent his crews like water to preserve the Mother Planet, and who had cried for the thousands of frail civilian craft that sacrificed themselves to give Duke's Marines some cover for their assault.

He looked closely at Tolwyn, and saw only the fire of duty and the drive. He saw none of the humanity that had been there, often hidden, but usually present. The change nearly broke Blair's heart. "What happened, Admiral?" he asked. "Why did you do this?"

"I don't know what you mean," Tolwyn replied.

Taggart glanced down at Blair. "You'd better get on with it, Tiger, you're losing 'em."

"What about the Black Lances, Admiral?"

Tolwyn smiled. "If I may remind the Assembly, as Commander of the Strategic Readiness Agency, I am empowered to marshal whatever forces necessary to protect our galactic interests. The Lances are a new type of fighter craft. Unfortunately, Colonel Blair and his cohorts raided their base and stole several prototypes."

Blair nodded. "I have thirty-one depositions from Telamon survivors saying that the plague came from your Black Lances."

"They might have come from a Black Lance," Tolwyn said coolly. "I just admitted that several were stolen. The toxin you mentioned might even have been manufactured there, before it escaped. Any one of a dozen possibilities, none of which require the Confederation."

Blair shook his head. "What could the Border Worlds possibly gain from attacking the Confederation, Admiral?"

"How am I to know what goes on in a criminal's mind?" Tolwyn replied. "Perhaps they thought they could slice off some of our systems while we were weak. Perhaps they thought their bio-convergence weapon would turn the tide."

Blair pounced. "Bio-convergence, Admiral? How did you know the plague bombs dropped on Telamon were bio-convergence?"

Tolwyn's eyes narrowed. "Don't badger me, Colonel. I'm not on trial, here. I've read the reports, of course."

"What reports, Admiral?" Taggart interjected. "If you have data relevant to this attack, it is your duty to turn it over to the oversight committee. This is something that affects the whole Confederation."

"Et tu, Paladin," Tolwyn whispered. He straightened his collar, then stood defiant. "Whatever data I have gleaned is so superficial that I didn't deem disclosure necessary."

"I see," Blair replied. "What about the Black Lance pilots? Did you deem disclosure about them unnecessary, too? Or did the fact that they were products of your genetic enhancement program seem unnecessary to report?"

Tolwyn shrugged. "The GE program was stopped long ago."

"Was it?" Blair challenged. "What about that loose cannon, Seether?"

Tolwyn met his eye, his own expression tight with anger and something more. He whispered. "He is more of a warrior than you will ever be, Colonel. He is excellence personified—"

Blair smiled. "He's dead excellence, then, Admiral. I killed him."

Tolwyn blanched and rocked back on his heels.

Blair turned back to the Assembly. "At his speech to his troops—his Black Lance troops—Admiral Tolwyn stated his belief that our victory was a fluke, a lucky break. He is worried the Kilrathi, or worse, will be back—and that we won't be ready. He proposes to fix that by 'fixing' us, by tinkering with our genes."

Blair leaned forward, half-turning towards Tolwyn. "The bio-convergence plagues start the process by clearing out the dead-weight DNA, leaving behind the acceptable samples. It doesn't matter to him how many billions die along the way—well, they weren't worthy anyway. He wants us to be more like the Kilrathi, bred to conflict and war."

"And why not?" Tolwyn snapped. "One on one, a Kilrathi can break a human. We're pathetic and weak, hardly the stuff to rule even our pathetic corner of the galaxy. There are things beyond the Kilrathi, things that make them look like school yard bullies!" His face mottled with rage and he slammed one fist on the podium. "And after our fluke win, we sit back on our heels, getting fat and lazy, while the next enemy marches toward us!"

He sneered up at the gallery. "Look at us. We're falling apart, crumbling now that we have nothing to measure ourselves against. We were at our best when fighting the Kilrathi. Then we had goals, we had focus. Now, we've grown whiny and complacent and confused."

He looked up at the ranks, stabbing his finger at individual Senators, slipping into the familiar lines of his speeches to his troops. "Who'll protect your planet from the next race that wishes to dominate us? Who can tell where this threat will come from? Or when? We must be ready. We must continue to upgrade our capabilities, our weapons, even ourselves."

Blair frowned, hating himself even as he opened his mouth to speak. "Does that include tinkering with our DNA?"

"Yes! A few must always be sacrificed to make way for the future . . ." He stopped and stared at Blair, his angry face becoming horrified as he realized Blair had goaded him into a lapse.

Tolwyn looked up into the silent, stunned galleries. "Understand," he said, "it was necessary. Sacrifices had to be made. We must be ready . . ."

Blair, heartsick, looked at his feet. "I think we've heard enough."

Taggart gestured to a pair of guards who stepped up

behind Tolwyn. The admiral, his head high, looked first at Taggart, then at Blair. Blair met his eye, and saw only sorrow. "I had to," Tolwyn said quietly. "We were so close to losing the last one. And the next will be worse. I grieved for every one of them, but it had to be done."

His features seemed to be on the point of dissolving as he scanned his audience who sat silent, enraptured by the fall.

"You don't know what I had to do," he sighed. "How many of you looked into the eyes of green kids, twenty and straight out of fleet school, and sent them to their death and knew that tomorrow, and tomorrow, and tomorrow after that you'll send more of them out to die, while bastards like you," and he pointed up at the gallery, "grow fat and rich on the dead. I watched them die so you could live. I was there at the beginning of the war and remember the warnings, and you didn't listen, and billions died. I begged you not to sign the truce agreement, and billions died."

He lowered his head. "And billions died," he whispered. Eyes shining he looked back up.

"Next time we will all be dead." He looked back at the guards, who stood ready with their hands on their sidearms. He made a tiny half-bow and walked out between them, his head held high.

Taggart looked up into the silent, packed ranks of the gallery. "Now," he said, clearing his throat, "we will take a single binding vote. The Assembly Master moves that we resolve to end this undeclared war against the Border Worlds, that we stand down Confed forces in the Border Worlds area and remove them to Confed bases, and to establish a Joint Commission with the Border Worlders to resolve disputes. I also move that we close down any remaining Black Projects and launch an investigation." He rapped his gavel on his podium.

"Senators, you have ten minutes to lock in your decision. The tote board will record your votes. I will cast the deciding vote if it is a tie."

Blair turned away, feeling only sadness.

He looked up, realizing that Paladin was talking to him. "Colonel Blair," he said, softly. "You must clear the rostrum during the vote."

Blair nodded and walked towards the cloakroom door, where the guards had escorted Tolwyn.

He stood in the back of the room, awaiting the decision. The tally, when it finally came, was one-hundred thirty for and twenty-two against.

He looked at Eisen. The captain took his hand. "We did it, Colonel." His smile faded as they both looked to where Tolwyn had been led away.

"But at what cost?" Blair asked. "But at what cost?"

• CHAPTER FIFTEEN

Blair sat, ignoring the courtroom buzz, as Tolwyn entered through the prisoner's door. Flanked by armed Marines and resplendent in his full-dress uniform, he marched forward to stand in the dock and hear his fate. Five stern-faced judges looked down from their high seats. Admiral Harnett's seat was filled by a newcomer to the court. Harnett had suicided rather than face arrest.

The presiding judge cleared his voice. Blair felt a heavy sense of expectation permeate the room. The trial had been long and sensational, and had generated much embarrassment for the Fleet. Taggart had insisted the military clean its laundry in public, paving the way for full freedom of the press. The room stilled as the presiding judge unfolded a printout.

"Fleet Admiral Geoffrey Tolywn, this court regrets to inform you that it finds you guilty on the principle charges of conspiracy to commit genocide against Telamon, the ordering of same, and fifteen lesser felonies.

"As punishment for your heinous acts you shall be taken from this place and stripped of your rank, and thence to a cell where you shall spend the rest of your natural life without hope or opportunity for parole. Have you anything to say?"

Tolwyn shook his head once, a firm "no" that matched his grim expression. A guard took him by the arm and led him towards the small door.

Blair looked up at him as he passed. Tolwyn stopped and faced him. Blair stood. Their gazes met. Blair searched Tolwyn's eyes.

"The end has to justify the means," Tolwyn said. "I gave you the means to an end, to survival, and you rejected it. You have condemned all humanity."

Blair felt his throat close when he tried to speak. Tolwyn

341

nodded to his guards and led them away, proud and unbowed.

Marshall put his hand on Blair's shoulder. "Ready, Colonel? Admiral Eisen and Paladin want to see us."

Blair, still saddened by Tolwyn's fall, dipped his head once. They turned away and left the courtroom.

The admiral waited for them with drinks on the sideboard. "I thought you could use these," he said as Blair and Maniac entered. Maniac gratefully accepted a drink. Blair demurred, then went to stare out the window. Titan's terraforming had progressed well. They now had a real atmosphere and real flowering plants. He picked at one of the blooms, inhaling its deep, rich scent.

"How do you feel?" Eisen asked.

"Whatever he might have fallen to," Blair said, "he was a great man. He saw so much, understood so much, that I can't understand how he could be led astray."

"I don't think he was, Chris," Eisen replied. "In a sense, it was vintage Tolwyn—to look beyond the moment and seize the main chance. He forgot that those were people."

They turned back towards the main group.

Eisen made a noise in his throat, commanding the officers' attention. He removed an envelope from his tunic. "Colonel, this is for you."

Blair took the envelope and opened it. "To all who see these . . ." He looked up at Taggart, eyebrows raised, and continued reading. "Know ye that reposing special Trust and Confidence in Christopher Blair, we do appoint him to the grade of Brigadier General. . . ." He shook his head. "You must be kidding."

"Hell no, son," Paladin replied, "we hae already gi'en ye all th' medals we hae. There isna' else we caen do for ye, except tae promote ye."

"Oh, this is just great!" Maniac stormed.

"Major," Taggart replied, "there's an envelope for yae too." He held it out to Marshall, who ripped it open and scanned the pages. "Colonel," he said wonderingly, "full colonel?"

"They confirmed your treasonous rank," Taggart said, grinning, "yae auld sod, though heavens knows yae don't deserve it. Read on, there's more."

Maniac scanned the sheets. "Command school . . . The *Kiev* . . ." He looked up. "I'm getting a carrier?"

"A light carrier, actually," Taggart replied. "You'll have the task of policing the border."

Blair grinned knowingly at Maniac's beatific smile. Marshall had finally gotten his coveted independent command.

"Ye'll best read on yaerself, General Blair," Taggart said.

Blair flipped the page and read. "I'm supposed to take over the Confed fleet in the Border Worlds?"

"Yes," Paladin replied. "Your commission's to work with the locals in tracking down the real privateers in the region, as well as any of Tolwyn's blackguards that might have slipped off. It's a way of mending some fences with our neighbors."

Blair felt his good mood drain away at the mention of Tolwyn. Paladin caught the change in his expression. "Yes, it's a shame what Geoff fell to. Regardless of the provocation, nothing justifies what he was about."

Blair shook his head. "Genetic engineering to breed super soldiers. Destroying the population of a whole world. I still can't believe that happened and that Tolwyn was a part of it."

"Yes," Paladin agreed, "the worst of it is that path's been trod before. Forced genetics, death camps, all that Geoff was willin' to accept. And for what? That which makes us human, he'd have sacrificed first."

Blair closed his eyes as Marshall chimed in. The newly minted colonel sounded almost diffident. "There are darker things out there than the Kilrathi. Admi . . . Tolwyn showed us that. There will be war again, and maybe we won't win this one. Does that mean that we'll go the way so many other races did, crushed after taking their first steps into space?"

He looked at Blair and Eisen. "What if 'Crazy Geoff'

was right? What if we do need something like what he wanted to survive? Can we, as humanity, survive and still be human?"

Blair thought a long moment. "Yes," he said, pausing to choose his words carefully. "It is in our very humanity, our ability to adapt and overcome . . . and our 'killer angel' instincts, in the way we can hold a sword in one hand while reaching out with the other, that our true strength lies. Tolwyn would have made us individually more powerful, while weakening our compassion. I believe that his way offered more harm than good."

Eisen looked at his watch. "General Blair, I think you had best get going. You'll be taking the *Intrepid* out to the frontier area, courtesy of Captain Garibaldi." He laughed. "We've agreed to fix his plumbing and enough of the quarters to give you your own VIP berth. You'd best get going though, there isn't much time to waste." Blair set his drink down and shook both their hands. "Until next time," he said, and departed.

Geoffrey Tolwyn stood on the chair in his cell, contemplating his failure. He had pushed The Plan too quickly, he saw that now. He should have waited, bided his time. He hadn't realized until it was too late that the entire race need not be brought up to genetic standard. Steel spears had wooden shafts and were they not still lethal? The populace as a whole could remain the dregs so long as the fighting elite came from GE stock. It wasn't an ideal solution, of course, but it was workable.

He shook his head fractionally. Some GE elements remained at large, hidden away where no one could interfere. Nonetheless, through his haste, he had brought the project down. He could abide defeat, he could even abide failure when he had done his best, but he could not abide knowing his own mistakes had led to his removal before The Plan was self-sustaining.

He could abide anything, except knowing that he'd killed his race. He deserved the same punishment his miscalculation would visit on them. He stepped off the edge of the chair. The knotted and braided bed sheet closed about his throat, snapping his neck. As death released his grip, the Senatorial Medal of Honor which he had won for the defense of Earth, and the pips he had once worn as a newly commissioned ensign, fell from his hand.

Blair stepped into his newly refurbished cabin. The smells of fresh sealant and paint permeated the room. He cued the lightbar and saw a neat bed, a desk with a workstation, and a sofa and chair group.

He swung around as the inner door opened. Velina Sosa, her hair down and her uniform collar unbuttoned, stepped into the main room of the cabin. She carried a bottle and a pair of glasses. He noticed distractedly that she had captain's bars on her shoulders.

"Admiral Richards says that you'll need a Border Worlds liaison officer," she said, as she set the glasses down on the table. "He thought I might stand in."

Blair took a long look at her, and saw her smile. He felt himself smiling in return. "I'd like that," he replied. "I'd like that a lot." She smiled, her dimples showing.

He had a feeling this tour was starting out well, very well indeed.